THE NIGHT
(ALONE)

Also by Richard Meltzer:

THE NIGHT
(ALONE)

A NOVEL BY
RICHARD MELTZER

LITTLE, BROWN AND COMPANY

BOSTON   NEW YORK   TORONTO   LONDON

Library of Congress Cataloging-in-Publication Data

Meltzer, R. (Richard)
    The night (alone) : a novel by Richard Meltzer. — 1st ed.
        p.   cm.
    ISBN 0-316-56652-7
    I. Title.
PS3563.E452N5   1995
813'.54 — dc20   95-13822

10 9 8 7 6 5 4 3 2 1

MV-NY

*Published simultaneously in Canada
by Little, Brown & Company (Canada) Limited*

Printed in the United States of America

TO ME
(and I don't mean you)

Nothing in this book is true
(or good) (or beautiful).

CONTENTS

THE NIGHT (ALONE)

OKAY WITH YOU?

If you wanna kill me, and I know you do, stick my head in a cube of concrete four-foot square with two tiny airholes, just enough to breathe, and dump me out a chartered 707 seven miles above Lake Huron: sploosh! Or slice me with a guillotine the long way, from the scalp down, just in front of the ears, alongside the eyes, so I bleed 360 degrees with my face intact on sidewalk, lips kissing cement — I *love* cement (love it!) almost as much as asphalt. But if you can't find a professional model imported from France, try this: cold kiss of concrete scraping *fuck* out of my nose, eyes, cheeks, teeth, and don't forget the chin. Drag me with an anvil on my head as skin, cartilage and stubble from my beard become food for roaches, y'know the *large* kind, or here's an idea: drown me in Elmer's Glue. Elmer's in my nostrils, eye sockets, throat, or just shoot me in the face, whole face, close range, couple feet at most. A shotgun — make sure it's loaded — would be fine, okay. Okay with me if it's okay with you.

WOEFUL BLIND SAP

A tuned piano: it's not every jazz club that has one. In this airless town, where jazz clubs are scarcer than zazz clubs, it's a rare Thursday night you will find one fulfilling a jass role. Rarer still: tuned keyboard with an ashtray inside: klango PLANGO! Ashtray on the strings — this is no 'prepared' piano. (The pianist didn't prepare it.) Is anybody listening?

Dowagers at a far table, one pale as flour, the other pink as pigmeat, let's see . . . no. Breezeblown prettyperson, eyes like mice, with Leslie Howardish yuppie (a terrible word you should *never* use): also no. Six German industrialists — Germans love jazz, right? — not *these* Germs. (Nein times sechs.) Middleaged funcouple from Protestantport, Iowa (pop. 980): not listening. Bartender, waitress: not, not. Fourteen nots. And me, listening. Intently. A listening fool.

Solemn at the Steinway, the pianist espies neither clothing nor cleavage of they who ain't listening, nor of he who is. Nor do they, the ain'ts, seem aware the man cannot see them — he has not tipped it off by wearing shades. Blind but hardly deaf, he sees not their pores nor their teeth nor neuroses, but he can hear and does hear their humph pumph jawohl above whirrings and purrings of the multispeed blender preparing their frosty wet fizzes, slings, punches (hold the straw). Hotel fun, they're havin' it; but applause, no, no claps till *I* raise the issue: the loner claps first. Before the final note has even died of "Old Folks," "Giant Steps" and ostensive (not unquirky) originals. Another, sometimes two tables pick up the cue, renuancing the sonic pastiche like three crickets in a hailstorm.

My chore and welcome to it: to monitor and register quasiaudible approval of the shadeless one's licks & such, to sit in stanch wait for him to spill (if poss.) his guts with a touch never hamfisted, no, nor especially heavyhanded, a line neither turgid nor glib, a demeanor not a jot cloyingly ebullient (or insouciant) (or morose) — an unflaggingly not unwinsome ivory persona I would like to like, and don't dislike, but neither do I 'specially truly like . . . so why am I here?

I'm here because there is *no cover charge.* I am here 'cause in this dunzo town where few warmbodies play, and fewer come to play, you take your playing where you find it (if playfinding's your meat). If you don't take it, I've learned the hardway, they'll be dead before you get another crack. They came, they played (then left forev): Zoot Sims, Al Cohn, Philly Joe. Assaying the night for evermarginal uhyuh, I've made it my policy to go see any visiting warmblood over 50, anyone I ain't seen previous who if not among the top 22 of All Time, they being

1. Charlie Parker
2. Thelonious Monk
3. Duke Ellington
   Louis Armstrong
5. Lester Young
   Eric Dolphy
   Bud Powell
   Ornette Coleman
   Cecil Taylor
   Albert Ayler
11. Coleman Hawkins
    John Coltrane
    Fletcher Henderson
    Count Basie
    Billie Holiday
16. Charles Mingus
    Roy Eldridge
    Benny Carter
    Dizzy Gillespie
    Miles Davis
    Sidney Bechet
    Jelly Roll Morton,

is/was/has been at least nominally competent and on occasion more than: Lou Donaldson, y'know, Mal Waldron, Clifford Jordan. I'm here in the groundfloor lounge of a midrange inn on the Strip and not Catalina's for Johnny Griffin, 58, 'cause the latter venue told me *scram* for contesting a double cover charge assessed as I sat for a second set of Milt Jackson, 63; they said *never come back* and though never's a longtime tonight still seems too soon to try. I am here, thus, to take in a mildly touted newcomer to this squalid town (though he is closer to 38 than 58, and closer still, one suspects, to 28), to see/hear him and be done with it, both sets if nec.

Tryin' hard to like the guy (part 1-B), I decide he's 'eclectic' — will that do? Idiosyncratic? Like, alright, try this on for size: like Ran Blake or Jaki Byard. A tunesworth of trial, an original in 5/4 . . . no, not nearly, not as *distinct* as Ran Blake — distinct*ive*. His A just doesn't equal A, or the A it does equal isn't . . . nor distinct as Jaki Byard. Not enough surrender to his own, um . . . insufficient walk on the personal side. More *anonymous* than most eclecs and idios, too little revealed depth of I dunno, there's just not enough private mess (or something) to hang even a small hat on, well, a kid-size maybe but not, hey . . . at least he's not Oscar Peterson. Low filigree count, check . . . an unclunky dynamic with occasional odd chordings . . . peppy use of . . . Then suddenly: CLANG. 'S not one of *his* chords. PLANGblang . . . won't somebody save him?

Our semiharried waitress, all tables hers, serves a green drink and a brown drink to mouse eyes and her yuppie, then in midhop to her post she spots an object missing. Drinks, candles, ashtrays — details of the gig — and she keen-eyes the absence, yippee yay, got it, but ears not the related nearby presence. No tray on pianotop: replace that tray! (Scratch one savior.) For a half minute the clangblang continues, with no funchange in anyone's manner to suggest auditory cognition; is it down to me? So I get up, rush over, and before I'm there

4

he's already reaching down/around with his left hand, riffing in the bottom octave with his right. I stand silent, he gets it, I ask him: "You got it?" Am I friend, foe, he don' know, just sighs: "Good old Hyatt House."

At solo's end, Harry, that's him, dabs his unflinching sunglassless face with a hanky, unfolds a thin metal staff, makes his way to the bar, orders "Hot tea with lemon" — great idea. When the waitress comes 'round I order a not-tea, my third, and stare mawkishly at mouse eyes, no lipstick or makeup (ohboy: a *person*), her hair like unmade straw. I would horizont w/ her in straw ANYTIME, would I?, I probably would not. Her consort I would (wouldn't) smash in the nose with a cast-iron skillet.

New arrivals. Aussies or something in rugby shirts. Fortified by the orange pekoe, Harry plunges into a snaky New Orleans R&B-type thing, *snappy*. A broadstriped Australian bobs, bops his head . . . could it be? Hallelu — wait, no, he's wearing a walkman! Ah, but at least that tackles the problem of pegging the Music (the better to "access" it) — why even bother? Nonmusical vectors have been outvecting musical long enough anyway, so how 'bout we call it official, terminal f'r tonight, and get down to reeling in some bucknaked poignancy . . . not-fun . . . estrangement . . . and *oh*boy, dignity under fire?

To salute th' dignity, I try clapping louder than last set, I can't clap much sooner, or much louder either — it hurts — so I throw in a "Yeah!" with the clapclap. To pre-cue the throngs I try telepathic commands ("Clap or die . . . clap or die"), but the handclaps if anything decrease (without fatality). Slowly, steadily, my enthusiasm wanes, and by the fourth or fifth tune, a midtempo "Days of Wine and Roses," I can't shake a notion that the playing — back t' music — has become increasingly less valid, less cogent, an accompaniment (though *it* hasn't changed, not a mote, and maybe that *says it*) (what does "glib" mean anyway?) for either the player's burgeoning not-fun or mine: he *does* sound glib, sounds turgid (whatever that is); sounds as if he has quite possibly so sounded right from the start.

I realize, nay, confess I don't *care* for his goddam music (haven't all night) and now barely even his blindass dignity, and then mouse eyes returns from the bathroom or somewhere with lipstick that glows almost *orange*, and the Krauts're suddenly *very* intense, and I think of that line from the penultimate (I believe) Flying Wallenda crackup: *ich kann nicht mehr halten*. One Wallenda tells the others he can't hold it no more — just prior to dropping 'em — and I don't handle pressure too well either. Can't keep cheerleading this ballgame (in the name of bleeding everbloodiable humanity), can't hack shilling for a sap whose ongoing soundspew reveals not a soupçon of who- or whatever he may in fact be, who has prob'ly come to this clangdang town (it seems fair to infer) to *become* Oscar Peterson, or to receive his mantra and become McCoy Tyner, a pair of prospects that brings shivers to the bones of my face, and I can't stand the shabby sadnessofallthis, and I don't want another beer, so I pocket a souvenir ashtray and split in the rain to discover my car has been stolen.

PIXTURES, PLEASE!

Dear Mr. Metzgler,

Perhaps you can help me. That you can and may is my sincerest, deepest hope, as otherhap no stone remains unturned. For more than a year, both day and night, I have searched for a photographic pixture of you on LSD at your sister's wedding of spring '70. High and low; high and wide; in vain. I've tried the County Museum, the Arboretum, numerous branches of the Public Library, the *L.A. Times*, not to mention more swap meets and garage sales than I care to count — to no avail. Fortunately, I just to-day ran into close, dear friend-o-mine Mike Ventura, whose pixture request you recently filled with a beaut of yourself and Lester Bangs, 1973, weeing on the fence outside Graceland — and recommended you highly. I say "fortunate" advisedly, however, as my pixture requirements are as needy as they are specific, and I will take an 80 mg. valium if not utterly, totally satisfied.

For openers, you must be posed (standing) beneath flowers and ferns, nonartificial, next to sister Betsy, dressed in traditional bridal white, signifying virginity, she herself upright and smiling between you and husband-designate Bernie, upright and mustached. There is — or had better be — a flower, preferably a carnation, in the lapel of your mangy, ill-fitting borrowed tails, worn solely for vile-mannered "comic" intent — seeing as how you did not wish to be present *nohow* — borrowed from Hal Blump of 1-2-3 Black Light, who did not get them back. You should additionally be wearing an (a) pale green Indian shirt, the exact same which made it to '80 before being shredded, in a fit of drunken pique, for writing letters on; (b) too-tight Oakland A's cap, worn in honor of Reggie Jackson; (c) purple corduroy bell-bottoms, purchased three weeks earlier in Philly, where you'd been hoping to hole up till after the nuptials had passed, held up with a knotted cloth guitar strap; (d) either of the two pairs boots/ cowboy which you owned that season.

While acid and the Queens (N.Y.) marriage-factory ambience combine to "bring you down," it is essential that a bitter frown or snarl contort your lips, framing a short, wide flawless rectangle of gruesome tooth-anguish, the fingers of your right hand forming a fist as — if at all possible — Shari Keller, clad only in oversized home-knit "hippie dress" (cotton panties; no bra) and unbroke-in Dr. Scholl's, her hair at the baroque, stringy height of its "Meredith Brody" phase, stands opp. side you from sis, her thin, nearly authentic smile the mirror image of Bernie's, but without the mustache.

All of the above ought of course be contained within the borders of a *single bonafide pixture* — no collage, airbrush trickery, double (triple) exposure, or otherlike form of reconstructural sham — with the further stipulation that all action thus captured be the nonsimulative visual record of a fully posed awkward moment occurring *before* the marital ceremony (i.e., prior to your longest, loudest outburst of hideous acid-laughter, which is known to have caused distant relatives and close to wince and in some instances shudder). Likewise, do not try and humor me with *substitute* pixtures from after, as for e.g. when champagne arrived at your table, long-forgotten cousins and uncs, you took bottle from waiter — "Allow me" — and poured full, entire contents on tablecloth, cousins too slow (or aghast) to salvage a drop. A behavior I must admit I have always found amusing, but behavior is not a pixture — and I pray you do not try and sub me. I HAVE GOT THE VALIUM *AND KNOW HOW TO USE IT.*

Wally Brug
Canoga Park

Dear Wally: Have I got a pixture-4-U! Premarital, posed to the gills, and a *lovely* purple those cords are too — too bad we don't have color. Baseball cap, howev, was worn exclusively during the reception. As my sister spit looeys in the face of our people's atheist/apathist tradition by getting hitched nonsecular, I was forced, at many stages of the mirage proceedings, to don the prescriptive *yarmulke*, as shown. (Sorry if I've put you on a "bummer.")

Dear Rolf —

My husband and I have enjoyed your pixtures for years now, since virtually their inception, and are thus at times peeved at greedy, demanding pixture buffs who insist on having it *their way* — at your expense. I assure you we ain't that way, and far as is humanly possible, x-tra care will be took to put you over *no such barrels*.

Since soon we shall be welcoming as houseguests in our home a darling Japanasian family from overseas, it is only proper that we exhibit above the mantel a pixture of you and the semi-attractive Japanasian grad student whom you frequently sexed during late winter, spring, summer and early autumn of '72. Yoshiko, a.k.a. Kazuki. But 'cuz you lived with Shari Keller at the time, you could only intercourse her (Jap.) on Tuesdays in the aft . . . possibly you know all this as well as we.

In any event, it is one of these Tuesdays in which we have a *strong* pixture interest. While no exact date is available, I am speaking of the Tuesday you and her boatrode, counterclockwise, around Manhattan. You had by all accounts grown weary of your usual Tues. routine of fucking and sucking (w/ passion), a quick run to McDonald's (fish filet, large fries, root beer or cola), then over to the Japanasian film fest she recommended youse two attend to broaden your yankee horizons . . . again you may already know this, and I only bring it up on the chance that it stimulate a clear and brighter pixture I.D. Anyway you were fed up by then with *moving pixtures* (*Summer Soldier, Double Suicide, The Face of Another,* that 3-hr. epic on Japanasian organized labor whose name excapes me, etc., etc.), so to broaden *both* horizons a-boating you did go.

And a pixture was snapped, correct me if I'm wrong, by a male Japanasian businessman (total stranger). And you learned about bridges: Brooklyn, Manhattan, Williamsburg, 59th Street, Triboro, George Washington, Washington w/out the George (that old brick thing — remember? — way up the Upper East Side), Spyten Duyvil if I'm spelling it right, Henry Huds — Whoops, gosh, 3rd time sorry for carried away! Accept my apol. (please! please!) for boring you with data from a life you bye-byed *long ago.* I and my husband would feel *awful* if you too bored to locate a pixture — please say you ain't and we'll call it o.k!

THE PIXTURE WE SEEK: Snapped by unidentified Jap. tourist as the Circle Line cruiser on which you boated safely rounded Manhattan, Lower, facing east. Dress: Hawaiian-style shirt, tropical fish pattern, 2nd such garment you owned in your life, white jeans which later shrunk so bad you throwed them out, denim skirt on milady which on this occasion and at least once other you did not stick your face up, olive green "top" shrouding pendulous breasts, the type my poor vulgar spouse would call melonlike bazoomers, firmer, it's been said, than met the eye, underwear (both parties) *unknown.* PLEASE black out eyes so's to cause this bygone paramour no undue embarrassment, thankyou and keep up the goodwork — pixturewise!

Mrs. John Marsh
San Dimas

Dear Mrs. John: Eye-edited pixture, per yer request. Don't worry about boring me — it is done all the time. But Tuesday?

No, it was *Wednesday* we normally carnaled on the mattress or floor of Kazuko's paint-peeling Upper West Side hovel. Occasionally pixture fans commit errors concerning my life, hey it happens, so please don't feel foolish — it is simply my duty to correct yo' ass. You meantime omitted, *glaringly* I might add, one scarcely insignificant fact: Kazumi, though of another era entirely, is presently ranked as my NUMBER SIX OR SEVEN former gal of all time!

Dear "Metz":

Just finished reading *Afterbirth Crap*, volume one of *The Unillustrated AutoBio of Rolf Metzgler*, and think c'est fantastique. No I'm not French, but I must admit surprise that a man of pixtures could write so good. For technical qual and interestingness alone your pixtures have always been hard to beat, and now it is with great pleasure to say likewise for your lit. Where have you been hiding it all these years?

What impresses me most about *Afterbirth* is the way you were actually able, *without* pixtures except the cover, to communicate (by means of words) the traumas and garbage of living (ages 0-6) as we know it. I believe every American, expecially parents, should read it to their teens and tots — and teachers too. The world would be a worthwhile place, & happy as well, if more of us had the voice and expression to express their true feelings about mom and dad, expecially with the economy, style and grace of your opening sentence: "My father was shit, my mother was . . . shit."

Still, words can go only so far, and the absence of pixtures, due (as explained in the intro) to postal mishandlement en route to your publisher in Fresno, must be a source of grownup trauma as big and as bad as the kidstuff. It is truly a crying shame that someone whose life has always been *in* pixtures, whose livelihood has been associated *with* pixtures, and whose fantastic book was originally crammed full *of* pixtures, should now have to manage *without* pixtures. Although on second thought, maybe it's the challenge of obstacles that can sometimes make writing so good: writing without pixtures — what an amazing (& courageous) idea!

Even so, I would love to see a pixture or pixtures even *similar* to those lost by mailmen which might otherwise have occupied pixture space on the pages of your book had they not been sadly, forever lost and missing. I leave it to you to select the pix. It may be any one (or more) of your choosing, provided you specify the page and paragraph it relates to, and a little bit of background as to similarness.

To change the subject a moment, I am plenty p.o.'ed that I had to miss your live and in-person "reading" which accompanied the local release of *Afterbirth Crap*, but as I was slated for minor scrotum surgery the following a.m., docs decreed all the rest I could get. Completely recovered, I'm raring to go-go-go come August 14, the date of your Al's Bar reading from *Hotcold Bad Soup*, volume two of *The Unillustrated AutoBio of Rolf Metzgler.*

Dean Paterno
Agoura Hills

Dear Dean: Thanx about the writing. It's a little something I *do* sometimes. The pixture I have chosen, a rare and deliteful trauma-*free* pixture, relates to page 9 of *Crap*, paragraph 3, the part where "me, the ol' pud-head and Betsy observed Thanksgiving the old fashioned dipshit way." The similarness is me and my sis. The differentness is Teddy McCanley, cross-the-street neighbor and childhood friend, in place of Mr. Metzgler, senior. As pixtures need no explaining, *enjoy.* Sorry about your scrotum, Deano, but fret not: *The Afterbirth Crap Reading*, a Top Plop cassette, is available right now at a record and/or tape store near YOU, specially if you live on the 1700 block of Westwood Blvd., home of Rhino Records, 474-8685.

As tapes go I am hardly a judge to speak, but no less a critic than Chris Morris of the *L.A. Weasel* assures me it is worth the price. I look forward to meeting you — and the rest of my many, many pixture pals! — at Al's Bar, 305 S. Hewitt, 8:30 o'clock, Monday evening the 14th of August, summer-means-funtime U.S.A.

ANTERIOR METAPHYSICS

February 21

Dear _____,

Excuse the form letter, or don't excuse it, but you are one of a semi-handful of 'friends' I've elected to give my latest unlisted number. Unlike in previous fiascos, no slipups will be tolerated. It is yours to memorize and swallow, or memorize and flush, and NO ONE ELSE GETS IT. No third parties. I've had enough of mystery anuses calling at 3 AM to tell me "Write your will, shorty" — click — or "Tomorrow you're worm food." I've had plenty as well of marginal acquaintances I know *I* never shared my numerals with, fine folks and true I could live without speaking to for the next ninety winters, coaxing them from the less marginal and insinuating themselves, with sickening efficiency, in the fabric of my goddam et cetera.

Yes, I am one grimly somber RECLUSE-AND-A-HALF these days. A cheesy 'orientation' perhaps, one I may well live to regret and abandon, but such indeed is my current policy (and lot), and I'm requesting, hell I'm *imploring* you not to mess with it.

No exceptions! If my own mother, beat and bludgeoned by clubwielding scumbags without name or number, should crawl battered to your door, begging with her dying breath for her sonnybody's *numero d'Ameche*, I am asking that you tell her, as deadpan as possible: "Gee I'm sorry, Mrs. M, but I don't have it." Or: "Funny you should ask. I was about to ask *you*. The little prick never gave it to me."

Should some wiseass inquire as to how you in fact get in touch with me, you can tell him/her: "By mail, of course." Or: "He calls me." Or: "I'm rather disappointed, as the fuckhead has made no gesture of cordial mammal contact in, hmm, it must be 18 months."

ONCE AGAIN: Entreaties by the fundamentally fair of heart should be treated *no differently* than those by scuzzbos dripping pus and covered with flies real or metaphoric, but for your own soundness of mind let me assure you I will — following appropriate notification re a "show of interest" — give all due *consideration* to the phone-access needs of the former. But let *me* wrestle with the 'guilt,' the 'issue,' of who gets what — and let me be the one who does any and all possible dispensing.

MOREOVER, should the time come when someone you know (or believe) to have once legitimately possessed the number I now give you make claim of having somehow LOST IT, tell 'em sorry but you are no more their means of quick and easy *re*attainment than you were their initial source of same. "Yowie!" — sample rejoinder — "you must surely recall the old bastard's guidelines! He would have our hide if he even caught *wind* of this conversation. Let us hope he is not clairvoyant."

To put it simply: I am, in myriad ways, fighting for (for starters) my life. I'm running scared, I'm falling apart, I'm . . . who fucking cares, just PLEASE the fuck bear with me.

A final plea: Keep this number *out* of your rolodex, your address book, anywhere others could conceivably cop peeks while you're gone to the rest rm. If you wanna list it, code it. Code my name. Write the digits backwards, inside out, whatever. Thank you very much.

(Oh yes, the number: 213-272-6376. You are a pal and a saint.)

Yours,
Rico B. Mezzner

P.S. Almost forgot. Failure to comply with all terms above, either stated and implied, will likely result in your never having my number — any *subsequent* number — ever again.

Feb. 21

Dear acquaintance,

I hate to do this, but unendurable sickshit has forced my hand, compelling me to accept the necessity of a FINAL PHONE SOLUTION.

In the last few months, despite the luxury of an unlisted number, phonings by loathsome, heinous a-holes (I.D. unknown) have steadily increased in both frequency and heinousness. 10 calls a day . . . 20 . . . "You die Friday" . . . "Fire — soon — you burn". . . till this morning, when a nameless (by now familiar) voice intoned "Start your Toyota — *kaboom*," I decided *enough*. Sounds tame you say, 'playful'? In merry goddam CONTEXT, however . . . well that's *my* biz. While I don't (do not) in fact fear for my life, I've had quite my fill of flinching on other people's dotted lines.

Since unlisted has never, unfortunately, been sufficient guarantee of my privacy — someone or other, wittingly or whatnot, has always managed to leak each number out to the a-holes — I've resolved this time to simply disconnect the fucker, terminate home service, the end for now, the foreseeable future — rooty toot. Looks like I'll be saving all my change for the pay phone.

Fortunately from your end, I've lucked into a dandy, seemingly adequate 24-hour service. As you (I'm assuming, or you wouldn't be reading this) have not been the leak, I hereby provide you with its #: 213-651-2030. Though it could hardly afford anyone direct verbal access to my digs, you are *not* authorized to show it or speak it to another living soul. It's my little secret, your secret, *ours*. Let's keep it that way, OK?

(As backlogs are to be expected, please allow one full week, make that two, for return of call.)

Yours truly,
Rico Mezzner

CALLING ALL CUBISTS

"I'd like to stroke your cock." Well okay, good. She'd rejected the offer of congress in a shaded patch of brush not fifty yards distant, refusing to even let me carry her. "It's too *hot*," and so it was, one of those days where you hope it's 100 'cause if 90 is this bad you must be losing it, but we hadn't lain together in over a week. Nor would she roll with me in the air-conditioned back of her ex-husband's van. "Dog hairs, I'm allergic." She had excellent alibis.

And a lousy taste in slam films. "I finally rented *Body Heat*," she'd confided, "and all it gave me was an overwhelming urge to take a bath."

"It didn't remind you of . . ."

"*No*." It hadn't reminded her of the first through third of the eight-nine times we'd slammed organs, swum in sweat; had not, in any event, triggered *ardent* recollections of those Channel swimmings. The rapture, evidently, had escaped our fling. (Did he say rupture?)

"Do you think of me all the time?" she then asked. A funny question.

"*Much* of the time."

"Much of the day and much of the night?"

"Well" — I cannot tell a lie — "there are discontinuities. I'm a cubist."

"A what?"

"As opposed to, say, a surrealist. Cubist discontinuity is a lot more . . ." — wait, do I really feel like lecturing? "You've been to the museum, right? Didn't you go to, what show'd you go to?"

"I went, I forget what it was called, the French show."

"Impressionism? Postimpressionism?"

"I don't know. They had Van Gogh."

"Did they have Cézanne?"

"I don't know. Is he the one with the lily pads?"

"No, that's Monet. Cézanne's not, he's only you might call him precubist, but I thought if you'd seen him . . . these paintings of things on tables. Your eye moves across and every time you reach a piece of fruit or a vase or something there's these little jumps and twists and the line of the table, from left to right, y'know behind everything, is not continuous. Or the focus changes, in and out, the foreground is blurred, or clear, or the background —"

"What's this got to do with . . ."

"Sometimes I'm discontinuous in my affection."

"How discontinuous?"

"Not very." She appeared unconvinced. After a long silence she stood up and led me to the van. "Where we going?" I asked.

"I want to rub your cock and pull on it if I may."

"Well" — take what you can get, bub — "that can be arranged. What about the dog hair?"

"We'll do it in front."

We left Elysian Park for a tree-lined residential street. She undid my fly and reached for my unit. Its stiffness, though I wore no underpants, made extraction difficult, so she opened my belt and peeled down my jeans. She gripped and began stroking, but her position behind the wheel gave her little operating room. We switched places.

Several minutes gone, her pulling was getting us nowhere. "What should I do?" she asked. A practical question.

"Tighter, more towards the tip."

"Like this?" She eyed me with ritual gravity.

"Good." But a far cry from . . . I thought of her smooth thighs, of the time I'd humped her sitting on the toilet. "Play with my balls . . . squeeze them." I thought of her mouth. "It's a little dry. Could you?"

She reached up her skirt and her hand came out wet.

"I'm wet," she said, grinning. She wet me. I thought of someone else's mouth, and another's . . .

"Stronger, really stroke it . . . *yeah*." I came; she kept stroking. "That's enough, whoa." She stopped. I kissed her, thought about car insurance, and noticed a glob of my maleness breast high on her lightly sweaty, but otherwise immaculate, lavender blouse. Whistling, she wiped it, me, and both her hands with a Kleenex from the glove compartment, thus completing our final sex act together in this here life.

WHAT IS THIS THING CALLED NIGHT?

WHAT is most knowable, IS. Plato said that. I dunno most, but how 'bout the converse — what is least knowable, most unknowable, ain't? Dunno that either.

THIS much I do know: darkness isn't dying. (I will not die at night.)

Night sweeps noTHING from the table. "The hand, as dealt," she CALLED to say, "remains unchanged, unshuffled: a three-card flush, a pair of shit in hell.

"NIGHT is paltry life everlasting: everlasting *this* life now."

THE PANTS IN MY CLOSET, THE SOCKS IN MY DRAWER

Let's start with the socks. Gold Toe brand orlon: white, off-white, tan, black, dark gray, light gray, gray-blue, sky blue, navy blue, gaudy golfer's blue like off a '62 Ban-lon shirt, blue-green, green-blue, forest green, red, reddish brown, burgundy. Levi's orlon: white, medium gray, black. From the wonderful folks at Burlington: white, off-white (100% cotton). Top socks one and all.

Back towards the back of the drawer: hose I would rather see die. Oversized orlon, brand unknown, watery ultralight yellow. We all know how much I like yellow — I could not live without yellow — but *light* yellow, g'wan. Padded tennis whoozis in kind of an off-puce with Sears' shoddy ripoff of the Izod gator, a dragon. Only got it to try out my charge card and would appreciate if it wore out enough so I can donate to the Starvation Army, where it'll go unbought — and continue unloved — but at least have a home with like-minded useless cloth *things*. White cotton wonder with red and black stripes, shrunk to one-size-fits-all-dwarfs. Tall gray tube sock earmarked for upper calf use (where male hose ain't *needed*), orange stars at midcalf, hockey player (black outline) down around the arch; please die. Pinkish ski sock — me ski? — worn only during fevers requiring warmth or no socks're left and it's time for a wash.

Which reminds me — socks in the hamper — let me look. Dark brown Levi's, powder blue Gold Toe with the heels going, gone, second pair of golf blues from a sale at May Co. that I've hated myself for buying ever since.

Good socks or bad socks, in five weeks, six or whenever I do the laundry they'll be *clean socks* — and, in moderation, clean can be "neat." Best detergent to launder socks you care about:

1 — powder
2 — liquid
3 — soap.

Never wear shoeless on the sidewalk and remember: NEVER IRON SOX.

Back in the drawer: more socks. In the very back. Hiking socks. Like you see in outdoor catalogues. Woolly & itchy. Orange-brown with a darker brown hint of not exactly a pattern. Off-white with a clearer brown not-pattern, concealing in its rolled-up midst the only key to a file cabinet containing every article I have had published, as of now unlocked so if you steal my sock you can lock me out *but good*. Also: red orlon single sitting by its lonesome, awaiting reunion with its long-lost mate — or matchup with any old nothin' for eleventh-hour duty under a boot.

TROUSERS: 2 pairs Levi's straight leg/blue, 2 pairs ditto/black, pair semi-retired Levi's button-fly/blue, pair laundrytime-only Wranglers flare/maroon;

: pair Levi's corduroy/black, pair ditto/off-white;

: cutoff Lee Riders/blue, cutoff Levi cords/tan;

: polyester with eye, ear, nose and mouth holes (outlined in black marker)/pale phlegmy green;

: leather with tie-up crotch/blue-black.

EXPLANATION, ANALYSIS: jeans, cords, cutoffs: so what;

: polyester with holes: modified to double as wrestling mask during postadolescent crazydays, eye holes cut approx. 2" below groin level, ear holes later sliced to allow for hearing of directorial commands during filming of crawl-out-of-sea sequence for Richard Casey's *I Worship Satan*;

: leather: freaky threads for so straight and postrockroll a cat as yours true, last worn (twice) during salad days of first-generation L.A. Punk, purchased spring '71 at Leather Man (Christopher St., N.Y.), $95 new, belt loops added since, hot in summer, cold in winter, tie-up crotch a drag if you're drinking and have to "go," you can have 'em for 50 bucks, be sure and shake off last drop or will wet inside pantsleg causing dark blue stains to flesh and/or undergarb.

Waist measurement: all items but Wranglers, poly, leather: 33;

: Wranglers, leather: 34;

: poly: 32.

Accompanying holder-uppers: adjustable cloth strap with no holes and brass snap, black; standard hole-punched leather, oxblood, storebought during accidental visit to USC campus.

Neckties: repulsive narrow synthetic with green, red and blue stick-figure unicorns, found in the trash; vintage gold silk with Old English "M" — the family monogram — previously owned and worn by Grandpa Merz; wide white silk with red 8" tongue protruding from the cartoon mouth of JFK — kind of goodlooking.

But not a tad as good a looker as my fabulous BATHROBE, every hue of the spectrum excluding INDIGO, made in Portugal, vertically — and beautifully — striped.

Prettythings come and prettythings go, but the staple of any wardrobe worthy of the name is T-shorts, excuse me, T-shirts. A home without T-shirts . . . do such homes exist? I've got T's, you've got T's, Phoebe Cole of Playa del Rey has got T's. But have you or Ms. Cole got the one, the only PITTSBURGH MAULERS T-shirt with silver and orange printing on [it's raining] vi-o-let? One up for *my* stack-o-shirts. And how about the Melanie Griffith "tee" with a speech balloon wherein she says, quoting Marcus Aurelius, "All is but knowing so" (yellow/black silkscreened on mustard)? You don't got? Well me neither, wish I did and someday who knows, meantime I am quite satisfied with my white Chicago Black Hawks, gray Special Olympics, royal blue Nervous Gender, yellow Rock 'n' Roll High School, white Vinny Golia, red Anthony Braxton, white Everlast Choice of Champions, white Duran vs. Cuevas, black Beethoven Symphony No. 3 in E Flat Major Op. 55, blue Surfing, black New Orleans, white Philadelphia, olive Missoula (Montana), plain black w/ pocket, plain red w/ pocket, plain gray, plain green, plain blue, plain blue-black, plain black, 3 plain white, plain white dyed runny chartreuse, blue & green striped, beige & gray striped, burgundy & tan striped, plain tan, plain red, 2 plain orange, plain yellow-orange, plain blue-green, plain brown, blue & white narrow striped French collar, sea-green w/ red-orange collar, and khaki & black pinstripe T-shirts, all wearable, all worn in sequence in the last six weeks.

As Susan Tyrell said in *Fat City*: "Clothes make the man." Certainly by clothes she meant hats, for no man would be without *several*. Seven isn't several, but at least it's more than six: sailor hat, Mao hat, polka dot novelty rain hat, Mothra novelty baseball cap, Bob & Doug McKenzie novelty toque (= ski hat), Montreal Canadiens toque, brown corduroy "Bob Dylan hat" painted over in yellow acrylic with news photo of "George" in Haight-Ashbury ("Harrison in Hippieland") affixed. And a toy space helmet (*very* good plastic) from 1951 or '52, which makes 8 — so I *am* manly . . . and can prove it!

And for showing off hats to best advantage: shirts w/ buttons. Of which I am loaded. By sleeves: long: 2 plaid wool, 2 plaid flannel, 3 corduroy, 3 plain ordin'ry, 2 workshirts;
: short: Rhode Island Bowling Federation, St. Joseph's Polish Club, cutoff sweatshirt which doesn't really belong as it has a zipper, cutoff jean jacket. Plus a multi-colored Sea Shanty of Malibu uggle found in the gutter, as yet unlaundered, as ugly as Beverly Hills, possibly containing AIDS, but how can you turn down free food, er, shelter, er, clothing?

And when it's free *and* clean, now that is a combo that

cannot be beat, such as birthday gifts (factory sealed). Like the dozen scanties, male, received from Y-----o K----i in seventy-two. She found the undies I'd been wearing a trifle threadbare and gray, heh, and I had to sneak the bundle home past Shelley Kenner 'cause she'd never have bought *me* buying so much of "anything sensible" in a single haul. Decided to hide 'em in the mailbox, too small so I had to jettison half, of which (remaining half) a sole survivor (Fruit of the Loom, 32) still remains. Has holes but I never wear it, I prefer not to squeeze the equipment unless urgently necessary, for inst cold spells, illness, h--------ds acting up, all currently not-so though I do indeed have an arsenal for such contingencies: 3 Munsingwear "kangaroo krotch" (32), 4 Hanes regular crotch (34), 3 Jockey Slim Guy Briefs (36), 1 Equinox Astro-Brief (M). After Y-----o left New York, I wrote her a sweet little note how her thing matched my thing like a globe, make that glove, of which I have also got *some*.

Six, divided by two equals two pairs boxing, one pair winter. Minus one pair boxing (currently a set of sand-filled paperweights) and that's one pair boxing, one pair winter. Minus the winter as last time worn they were *no shield against* frost and chill, and that's one pair boxing. Like I said: some.

THE WIDE WORLD OF SHOES!!! — Pair moccasins, pair Pumas.

Pajamas! None. Just the bottoms from um, I have a bottoms I once used, uh . . . when I had poison ivy. Aprons? Yes I have, an apron. Eyewear: shades, specs. And contacts. Sweatshirts and sweatpants. Sure. Slippers. No way. Wallets: are clothing? Yes yes (are, have). Fourex nonslip lubricated sheep-intestine prophylactic in easy-open capsule. A scarf. Homemade sportcoat — cadmium yellow — with stuffed mouse on lapel which a cat once attacked at a party. Tweed jacket left over from higher ed but still wearable so I do. And various other JACKETS & SWEATERS.

"Fashionable" duds: no-o-o-o-o. Fashion not permitted

on the premises — must be checked at the door. Folks who insist on "dressing up" should consider dressing down. If they wish to be invited — for sandwiches, Parcheesi, "bull" sessions, or tea. Fashion's only function in the human life-o-sphere is if and when: you are fat or ugly. Though a sometime fatso myself, I have learned (as is still merely optional) to live without. Without "protective" coloration . . . or membership in the "club." So kiss my y'know hey *kiss it*. Only kidding! Because *you* can live w/out also, too.

MISUSES OF NIGHT (1)

Hall outside my room, black eleven-year-old, his uncle.

"You always talkin' God. How do you know there's God?"

"Well, let's put it this way. I have *seen* God . . . I have seen God in the lonely night."

Why does such shit anger me?

OLD TRICKS

Oh give me a home/ Where the buffalo roam/ And the deer and the antelope play/ Where seldom is . . . oh, 'scuse me, I was singing. Now I'll do some telling. I'll tell you the story of a girl I once fucked.

Sweet sixteen! Oh she was really a honey. Pam Last-nameitalian. Back in one nine seven and five — or possibly four.

Which would've made it four years — or possibly three — since publication of my v. first book, *The Anemia of Rock*, containing the dedication: "To Cherie Kelner (I wouldn't lie)." Which is funny 'cause by now you've prob'ly got a notion that lie is all I *did* to Ms. Kelner, that or maybe possibly *cheat on* her, a dry and colorless expression for I'd take out my pecker and try and slip it inside gal-holes other'n hers — every chance I got — while sharing an address (and official relationship) with hers truly.

Which for a couple years had generally been pretty easy, y'know mastering use of the residence for getting wet stuff on my thing while she was out at the office fulfilling her art destiny with ill-shapen, poorly proportioned drawings of horses for *Thoroughbred* magazine, but in '74 — or possibly '5 — she was working at home again, which was probably just as well. My antics were beginning to look corny even to me. Tricks of concealment like let's say there'd be a um uh *stain* on the sacred commonlaw-marital sheet, dried combined boy-girl moisture from an afternoon of goodtime-had-by-all, or maybe a goodtime smell.

For stains I'd pretend coffee got spilt. I'd brew an inch of instant, pour it over the driedstuff, rest the cup sideways like an accident occurred. Smells I always hated covering — would really rather have lazed around, basked around nostriling the galscent — but cowardice is cowardice and I'd light up a cigar.

These little import smokes I mostly used for writing would cover airborne cunny really well.

Covering it on *me* was a separate issue. Was a rare day in Umptover when I'd specifically bathe or shower my person for removal of a woman's eau de goosh. Lower person, that is — upper affected parts I could toothbrush and facewash without much pain. My wiener I preferred to leave alone. I still wore undies then, slept in them too, assuming Cherie could not detect a competitor's biz through a layer of garment. Once in a while I'd slip them off as we were lying there in the dark and surprise her with a stiffy, just start poking before there's time to smell it, and in the process mix the gooshes — two in one day! — on my item. Afternoon person's plus Cherie's. (I was quite the poet even then.)

Once in a slightly greater while, traces of an afternooner's full fabulous bouquet would be too pungent and d'licious to waste on poetry, obliging me to save it for the next day's normal scheduled beatoff, during which I could fuel the fervor by smelling my hand, fondly recalling pivotal elements of *plot*. Sometimes even two-three days (it lasted for). Occasionally I'd get nervous and wash things away in the sink, and seven-eight times I dumped beer on my lap to simulate drunk 'n' sloppy, which Cherie flat-out bought because she had me pegged by then for lowlife anyway. Never tested it, but if I'd felt daring enough to wave it in her face she'd've thought, no doubt, *Budweiser peeny.*

We're talking here of like three-plus, four-plus years' penetration, tonguing, the entire so-called adulterous "trip," and by the time of my ejaculation in Pam's vagina I was almost kind of sick of such tricks. Or let's say tired. You'd be tired too from all the stress, strain, evidence on your schlong that 10-12-14 wet, willing newcomers an annum — plus repeats — can produce: the lonely, compulsive pursuit of *fresh moisture* 'cause your mommydaddy didn't really love you. (This was, after all, before I was "saved," before I "knew better.")

Since I wasn't about to pare down the pursuit ("get selective"), not yet anyways, and since juggling evidence *after* the fact was drivin' me batshit, it ultimately seemed prudent to move the whole ongoing adventure-in-clam to a more overt sphere of secondary-dame operations — after, before and during. Full disclosure, honesty as the policy *at least once*, seemed the ticket. Tell Cherie once (what a goodwill gesture!), and afterward she'll believe anything.

So I tell her — this is great — I remind her of her *prior* consent to my insertion in another. Her solemn, only slightly involuntary, vow of '70 that I someday reap, "just once for the record," that most rewarding of writerly extras: fan gash leaping at my printed word. This was for when I got big, y'know, famous, which I sure as shoot wasn't yet, but lez git it over with *now* (she figgers) before I get lucky and score too big. An unknown quantity from Bridgeport — I tactfully withhold the quantity's age — is a relatively unthreatening "once." So I tell her it's lined up, give her two full days' notice, and she tells me, "No chance, forget it — not *here*."

Through which it'd lined up was mail. Got this letter, Connecticut person/female wants to learn writing . . . from me. Photo enclosed: *young*. Sweet face, quite sweet 'n' cute, an authentic goddam yummy of a teenface. Body: not shown (but I can live with surprise). So I write back, tell her some hokum like ignore your teachers, don't read too much, listen to that inner voice, start transcribing blah blah, and she sends me a *box*.

No — no silly puns — a cardboard box filled w/ items. Textbooks, new and used; assorted rockroll trash; Boy Scout snakebite kit; 40-50 marbles; cuddly, flossy dog toy wearing female crotch garment (no stains but oh you kid!), presumably Ms. Lastnameitalian's.

Now these were the days where if I was at a femaleperson's house, a party or something, I would sooner or later, nobody lookin', reach in the hamper and get me a pair, quite often stained. I would sniff, pocket, take home and sniff some more. I know, I know — but I don't *do* these things no more (though it sure is nice to have a past: a past w/ panties).

Panties, mail: combine them and I was a goner. I was Pam's even more than she was mine. She had me by the short-hairs, and I had no choice but to 'vite her in for those short-hairs and write lesson #2. To the Apple, this is an Apple story, you've seen Woody Allen's *Manhattan* — people fuck there. So she rides in to FUCK ME and I meet her — pretty as her pitcher, dark-haired, *small* — at Grand Central Station. Our destination de fuckez-vous: hmm . . . ??

Well, actually there's no hmming at this point, I already know we're headed for Mick's, but b'fore I knew I kind of had to think things out. Thought: Mick is my *pal*, he has *ways* of killing an aft. away from hearth and home, his own missus *works till six*. As generous a pal-o-mine as ever I've known, Mick Tock (rhymes with tick tock) sez: "Sure, buddy, use my fold-a-bed but please [if possible] do the deed on somebody's coat." (This was January — brr!! — overcoats.)

Okay. We're chez Mick's sipping Akvavit, the three of us sipping, smalltalking, giggling 'bout things more or less understood, when Mick checks his Timex, looks a mite stunned, splits for an *urgent engagement*. Alone: she and me at last alone indoors. Outdoors we'd giggled like goonies as youngfolks (aged 15–19) are wont t' do. 'S one of those things they're in fact *good for*; be with one and you will giggle too. Forget conventional b.s. on "dirty old men" — sometimes adultfolks cannot laugh, chortle or titter, y'know freely, and it's simply smart business to hang out w/ those that still can.

OKAY. Before we get to the REAL GOOD SQUISHY STUFF you've been waiting for, an in-depth catalogue of activities barely whispered of in polite nuke-family circles, it would not, I feel, be inappropriate to give paragraph space to my *primary* squeeze of '74 or '5, herself recently a mom by another man (though I'm not complaining): the one and only

Cherie Kelner Robbins — her good points if I can just recall them. Thinking cap on . . . thinking . . . umm . . . . . she was real nice to animals. Real, *real* nice (including squirrels). Cap still on . . . think think . . . oops, recalling her *not* good (should've cast the cap off): *did not let me cuntlap her mushpie, except (minimally) during foreplay, after 1971.*

Which, lapping, the Pam person welcomed, so what can ya do? You go in for a mouf'ful after tenderly assuring her that fine hot fresh menstrue is no skin off yours. "I like my meat rare" is how I most delicately put it; greatest real-time improv of my life. OK: she's no-longer-dressed on my coat on the bed, my knees on rough carpet as I eyeball her young outer bush (soft hairs above — how *remarkable* — none around the lower lips), I wetkiss her pink parts still dry from the nappy, soon they're damp and I'm mouthing and slurping and sucking and licking and 'serting fingers — both c-hole and a-hole — *very* nice up inside each.

And she says — presumably *enjoying*, wishing to *share* — she says, "Why don't you come up here too?" I've a clue what she means so I strip off my undies, my own. Still had 'em on 'cause back then I presumed my doodle (soft) to be *short*. (Days of doodle doubt.) No longer soft, shorts off, the thing's in her mouth, her thing's all over mine. Wriggling, writhing — we wriggle and writhe. Some my-t-good horizontal dancing g-g-golly; quivery minutes pass and slowly, reluctantly, I start angling my pelvis & environs over on top. We'd been foxtrotting sideways till then because guy-on-top had seemed — this time, this organ permutation — *unfair*; I'd of course (not born yesterday) done-it that way but had also along the road learned fairness (goody gum). Finally, fuggit, I'm a vertical slam-machine slamming, whamming the salami into her face, BAM . . . male orgasm (swallowed).

So she sez — just as I'm worried she finds me brutal, cruel, she's such a *tiny* person — "That was BEAUTIFUL."

Like oh boy. Oh . . . *yeah*. So as I'm savoring impression number two of young'uns I have known (gosh are they *eager*: more than hungry they are not yet jaded, not a hint, re matters and manners of the flesh) in walks Mrs. Tock . . . huh whuh?

Take. Double-take. I'm not (that week) as fat as Mick but male flesh at home can be confusing. For a sec I'm playing Mick and she's the irate unfaithfulled spouse, lawfully wedded. Next sec I'm me but her wrath ain't diminished, brunt of which must be borne by two poor romantics in heat. "I'm going down for smokes," growls Mona Tock. "Be *gone* by the time I get back." Like she and Cherie had this nonaggression pact — hands (and cunts) off each other's live-in meatman ('cept for one fondly recalled Halloween "swap") — so maybe that was it. But 's not like they had a deal where you're required to stifle so-and-so's drive for 'tween-a-*stranger's*-legs; Mrs. Tock, I contend to this day, should have kept her pacts on straight.

'Stead of forcing me to rush between Pam's . . . premature to having the goods. Could not get it up instantaneous to need, the need being to actually fug 'er at least once in the primary gal-hole. "Aw, that's okay. Let me suck it again" — an incredible sweety. Sucked it and I stuck it and in 34 seconds I came. A shame as her legs'd been wrapping themselves *nicely* around my back, butt and thighs for let's say the final 29 of those secs, and probably would've continued wrapping — in perfect rhythm/counterpoint to that of her eager little, neat little "pussy" — had I not beat her to the post-performance punch, before she even knew it was post: "That was QUICK." Quick enough so if Mrs. T had come home regular we'd've had time for who knows *how* many male big o's — and a female or twelve for good measure. Divide four hours — 6:00 p.m. minus 2:00 — by :34 and that's a lotta o-ing.

'Stead of wandering through frozen slush, me and this petite honey-sweety with my seed in her womb and esophagus, on a tour of deserted back streets where if it wasn't winter we'd be jazzing in alleys and phonebooths; 'stead of making like Marcello in *La Dolce Vita* as he dials the world for a place where to fucka Anita. Fucking's *important*, see, well sometimes (y'know?), but nobody's home except Cherie and Mona. No more teenaged pudendum today! (And none whatsoev until nineteen seven and eight, or possibly nine.) All that remains but to shiver and die is to buy her some fries at a cold luncheonette, and a tall cup of joe. Likes that joe if memory serves me.

Can't interest her, though, in a warm bookstore, woulda bought her my second monograph, *Vulture!*, aeons better than *Anemia* but what? — *she* read?! — so it's straight to Grand Central, be seeing you Pam, was nice to've been in your hole!

. . . And the skies are not cloudy all day.

PREMONITIONS OF THE NIGHT ALONE

Loneness. Enfolds me like a. Like an army of sandwich ants. There is no mustard on the sandwich. No catsup, no mayo. Margarine: there's margarine. And what's loner than margarine on white with a side of — ants *hate* margarine (will not eat it). Ants are gray and their families are shingles on the walls of hotels in Zurich ("The Gray City"). I'm so lone I could. Croak of loneness and the ants would. They'd. Sleep (perchance to). Actually, loneness enfolds me like Miss G's gummy aperture on my prong.

Here comes the night.

SOME HOT NAMES FOR THE KID I'LL NEVER HAVE

1. Rufus
2. Ruby
3. Brendan
4. Brenda
5. Audrey
6. Amos
7. Bobo
8. Stuffington
9. Stella
10. Gorgo
11. Wini
12. Odessa
13. Rudy
14. Trudy
15. Fucksuckandshit (unisex name)

THUP, THOOM, THEATER OF MEAT

The tree out my window whose branches once held figs now has none. Branches yeah but no figs, no fig leaves. It's a dead fig tree. A good-looking, an *extremely* good-looking dead fig tree. Which I once saw living, I now see dead, but never, ever (as I recall it) saw dying.

Which is something I did see on Venice Boulevard, Mar Vista. At a light awaiting a turn I heard this thup. A literal *thup*, not like comic book onomatopoeia, an audible impact, something on flesh without padding. Not a football sound — equipment, torsos, turf — nor boxing; I had never heard so true a thup before.

So I look 'round and in my side mirror see this pigeon struggling in the opposing fast lane, trying to either get upright or flap away with a bum leg, a bum wing and not much time to spare. A robust-looking bird, bonebroke and in obvious pain, but the feathers are full, fluffy, not one of those raggedy ones you see scrambling through dumpsters, pecking around pigeonshit in parks, alleys . . . and as I'm thinking this the light turns and *thoom*, three cars flatten it. Poor pigeon.

Birds . . . bath water . . . toxin water . . . Venice Beach. Take a drive on a cold, cold night, the Venice Pier, dress warmly and bring along some warmth to spare, some giveaways. You'll wanna give it, all these poor freezy souls a-fishing their supper, families, loners . . . it'll tear your heart out.

Every four-five months the clientele's different — does seapoison off them that quick? And different, well, we're talkin' not only faces but races — a radical ethnic turnover. A year ago most fishers were Mexican, six months back it was Vietnamese, Filipino, and this week it's sorrowful, woebegone whiteys.

Who're out there freezing — you should see this at midnight — cussing, casting, reeling in their grim finny protein 'n' poison. A family of five, brats dozing under gull-stained magazoons, have their hibachi in readiness and, for dessert, a bag of rotten plums. Fog shrouding the lights of shore — the edge of the fucking *world* — there is seaslime and peopleshit on their cozy little catwalk over 12,000 miles of chilly-chilly nightish briny pus juice . . . so leave them a blanket, y'hear? My pal Teenage Steve left a sleeping bag, slightly worn, large enough for three brats and a grownup, casually and at a discreet distance from these proud and courageous brain-damaged piscatorians.

And me, I got to warm a seahag. The Seahag of Venice, she says, "Gimme a quarter, I mean *please* gimme a quarter, I need a bottle so gimme a quarter" — sput, spit — "wouldja please gimme a quarter dearie OK?" So I give her and no sooner have I given than I'm thinking damn, it shoulda been a buck — you should always have a dollar for such an event. A seahag event. Or its ilk.

Did he say elk?

TIME FOR COURTSHIP

No time for courtship, I'm writing a novel. If you want (or need) flowers, specify and you *got 'em*. Earrings, crack, a back rub — anything within reason. Help you with the cross-word, wash your dishes, cups, spoons (but not forks). No Sting or Springsteen . . . even passion has its limits. Maximum court time: 19 minutes. We're at 18 now, this is it, d'you want me? I've got no time for courtship.

DAYS OF BEER AND DAISIES

I haven't been a raving drunk since nineteen . . . eighty. Drunk often yes — but not raving.

Duh *da* da da duh *da* da, duh *da* da like you, duh *da* like you do, duh *da* da duh da. Duh *da* da da duh *da* da — NAME THIS TUNE — duh *da* da your name, duh *da* so ashamed, duh *da* wasn't you, *wasn't you*, and then the chorus, YOU ARE, well it can't be anything but: "You Are Everything" by the Stylistics. You are everything and EVERY-THING IS YOU. I used to sit and *weep* over that one, weep at the chord changes, weep at the sentiment, weep in goddam *awe* at the concept of YOU as essential principle, as *the* essential principle, every bit as basic as Thales' water, Anaximenes' air, Pythagoras's number. I never bought the record or heard it on radio, only way, only *time* I ever caught it was off jukes in bars. I'd be hunched over a drink as it played, ruminating only *occasionally* over a specific you past or present, an actual second-person other, and depending on how much I'd already had, by song's end I'd be either a blubbering, maudlin mess or *sublimely* maudlin . . . you had to be there to see it.

A case of camaraderie. Mike Tonk and I, who for years had been scribbling sentences for the same small handful of youth throwaways, finally met at a luncheon for the British band Grudge. Second thing he said to me, bourbon in hand, was "Let's go somewhere and *drink*." It was one-deep at the bar, the wait couldn't have exceeded a minute, everything was free but okay, *let's*. We found some place on 10th Street where the average age was 80, drank shots and beers till they closed at four, and became great friends, continuing to drink together, greatly. Never drinking buddies in the normal sense, more like colleagues on a fervid inquiry into drink as means and *content* of revelation, we each encouraged/provoked the other to be perpetually drunk (and sometimes write about it). Though the *Village Voice*'s response to a proposed "In Whiskey, Veritas" column was decidedly cold, we contributed essays on liquor by brand (Harper's, Dickel's, Old Crow) to the *New York Squeak* and *Boston Subgum*.

"What is scotch?" — we'd talk like that, get real theoretic. The answer, we decided, was *Scotch is an odd experiment in nu-drink, roughly equivalent to dropping a cigarette in Irish whiskey, as close (in its way) to Drambuie as it is to pure intoxicant.* Purists, we abhorred admixture. Other options open, mixed drinks never passed our lips. Piped Mike when offered one: "Bottled booze is *already* mixed — mixed with water." Tough guys, we were tough. So tough that one night, for the fuck of it, we hit an East Side biker bar with mixed drinks our goal. Beginning with Carstairs & tonics, we moved on to sidecars and bourbon Manhattans, then ordered a single Zeus (vodka, Campari) and a blood & sand (gin, sloe gin, crushed ice). "How's that again?" asked the tortured barman. (Luckily, that day, we'd torn pages from a mix guide at the Strand.) Lacking both essentials, he couldn't make us a 252 (151 rum, Wild Turkey 101), so we improvised a 240 (Seagram's V.O., Christian Brothers brandy, Juan Valdez tequila, 80 each). We didn't even *ask* for a Rasputin (vodka, clam juice, anchovy-stuffed black olive) but were on a collision course for applejack highballs when, at pool, I lost our last fiver to this old guy with one eye sewn shut. Hangovers: no worse than usual.

Four Tuesdays at Lynch's. We're invited, me and Mike, to this taproom in the West 50s, Lynch's Cafe. "You'll love it," says Jim Sibley, an earnest urban fellow, "it's an *Irish* bar." (Ooooh, hey . . . not many of *those* in New York.) Venue for a conclave of "some nice, terrific writers," Jim included, a weekly "literary lunch." Invited, we go: a middle-middleclass bar. You couldn't be more middle. Sanitized, polished, service too genteel, cardboard food. We meet the regulars: hi hi hi hi hi hi hi hi. From *Esquire*, *Women's Wear Daily*, *Newsday*, *Cue*. A freelancer named Jane who's just interviewed Buckminster Fuller for *Vogue*. Jim covers fires for the *Post*. White-collar jackjills whose collars really are WHITE. A round of martinis? Mike and I will have beers. As gents who when we write (dine) (play) get at least *something* on our collars, faces, souls, we rise to the chore of showing 'em how it is done. "This porkchop is *shit*." "Did you ask Bucky if he can still get it up?" "Garçon! — TWO MORE." (Cold stares from Jimbo, from the rest.) Next week, attendance down, we bring a pint of Soul Brothers blended whiskey. Jim, who any stiffer would be uncooked vermicelli, begs us: "*Please* don't let old man Lynch see that." Agreeable to a fault, we keep it bagged, pass it under our seats. Under the table we empty water glasses, piss in them — why interrupt *dialogue* in pursuit of a pot? Third week (more no-shows) we bring meatball heros. Fourth week we're the only ones there.

Solo fright. I used to be SHY with the women. Alcohol has played a role in two-thirds (three?) of my first-date intromissions. Alc. in *me*, probably them too, though you'd have to ask them about them. Even minor doses have made my fool's twaddle smoother, my pawings less awkward, my idiot heart-thump less conspicuously LOUD . . . granted my auto-meatpilot license to extemporize, to *dare*, handed my undiapered hormones the keys to the bank . . . rendered my rawest, crudest o.k.-let's-*fuck* palatable (even "charming"), painted my bottomless hunger wholesome and "natural," helped reveal me as an oft-tender fun guy with a joyous predilection for the BOY-GIRL PLAYPEN — playground — play house. The gift of play: nothing to sneeze at. Play at some point *declined*, howev (and intake continued), what exactly do you do with all the rocket-fueled idiot momentum, idiot frustration, idiot id?

She slammed and locked the bedroom door behind her, permitting me free reign over the balance of her flat. Crooning "Some Enchanted Evening," I found and un-corked her last remaining liter of Sauvignon. With a blue felt-tipped marker I scrawled "KIKE KUNT IS GOOD KUNT" on the inside rear of the fridge, pausing to wack off in a wide-mouth ketchup, and the underside of a faded Eastern rug. Switching to red, I drew swastikas on select pages of *Jonathan Livingston Seagull* and the inner sleeves of Bette Midler, Al Kooper and Carole King LPs. Before departing I slipped a clump of pubic hair in a jar of skin cream and — be my Valen-tine? — dropped the last roll of Charmin in the bowl. Love and wine. Wine, love, truth. Truth and love.

"There are things drunks do that alkies don't," Mike would sometimes, while still lucid, claim. He'd go up and down one of those checklists of al-coholism, "25 warning signs" or some such, taking exquisite care to distinguish the alcoholic from the drunk. "Alkies don't," said this man who was both, "they *usually* don't fugga your mom. But honestly, man, who *gives* a fuck if you 'drink before six' or 'one beer is never enough'? 'Has a cocktail while reading the stocks.' What it all comes down to is either you are or are not someone who drinks all the time. If you're not drunk every day, why bother? You're *wasting your alcoholism,* which is something no real drunk would ever do."

47 . . . 48 . . . where's my drink? 49th floor, overlooking the U.N. Something on the rocks. Where'd . . . then I realize it slipped off the window, the ledge, I *remember* having pushed it with the heel of my hand. Nobody saw me. I believe no one saw. But nothing in its line of descent could still be breathing. A headline overwhelms me: "Party Reveler Beheads Diplomat" — though the impact would also (I hazily surmise) have shattered the glass into frag-ments too small for i.d. At sunset I'd spit over the edge and watched my saliva break up and scatter . . . could *ice cubes* just now 've done likewise, slaying half the Finnish delegation? I look down — too dark to detect signs of life and/or death . . .

but definitely no ambulance.

Another night, another trance. Closing time plus 15 minutes. Tired of ripping wipers off taxis, bending antennas, stuffing dead sparrows in gas tanks — *normal* vandalism — we're strolling down 14th St., me and Mike, when whuddo we see but this huge potted *shrub*. Some kind of budding, flowering object — not a fern, not a rosebush (no thorns) — daisies? A rose in Spanish Harlem, a tulip — petunia? — begonia? — on scummy 14th. Freshly installed, *healthy*, it don't belong here nohow: what to do? "Kill it!" shouts Michael, "KILL IT!" Good idea. With my full weight I dive at the thing, tackle it — no resistance, snap, *take that*. Funny funny. Next thing we know these cops're after us, running up stairwells, a door?, locked, nowhere to hide, gotcha. One cop holds us and I'm panting, thinking *what sentence*, what is the *music* you face for shrub abuse, ten months in Sing Sing, a year? For parole you buy a new shrub, two shrubs, they force you at gunpoint to plant them? Then his partner comes back with the drunk who turned us in — too drunk to recog our faces or clothes. "N . . . no. N . . . no" — lucky us, lucky me. BUT I DON'T EVEN *MIND* GREEN THINGS THAT BUD. (I didn't drink again for a week.)

GREAT CHAPTER

Not in this bk. Coulda been, but I wrote it too soon. To re-write it now would be too big an undertaking, plus it's too good as-is to alter anyway, so let's just 'imagine' it's in this one. Imagine, in fact, that this is *it*. That it *is* this chapt., right here, now. (It instead of this.) "Le Voyage à Cul-de-Cul," pp. 123–128 of *L.A. Is Worse than Lesions of the Eye, Nose and Tongue*, my most recent hardbound delight. I've seen copies at Pic 'n' Save for 19¢, or if they're out you might hafta pay 7-8 bucks at a second-hand emporium. For this single chapter alone $8 is cheap, dirt cheap, and I also recommend: "Night Nites" (p. 203), "A Tale of Two Nipples" (134), and "Seventeen Bucks for a Knock in the Chocks" (163). Many swell pages each, all could be chapters in the present volume, but especially "Voyage." A shame to've already used it. In the service, the dust jacket says, of nonfiction. The dust cover pic is a lulu: buy it. Read it. Tear out the pages and paste 'em to this one. That one. Or fold 'em and staple 'em. Mark 'em:

The protagoniste, rename her Eve Lacy. Change her from western amour #4 to #3. Change the parked Trans-Am she drove her bike into, injuring _____ (injury unchanged) to an Avanti. Basic physical, behavioral features remain the same, but make her a *slightly* bigger lush. Lend cars to a lush and . . . it makes sense nobody's ever lent *me* one. The fictional me would've offered her mine too tho, no diff, and once even did, an outcome of which is I've loaned its successor(s) to no juice fatale since. Nor TVs, nor phone machines, answering machines, nor Carl Perkins 78s, nor $800. Nor $500. Nor my proverbial circulatory organ on too large a platter. Nor my urinary and reproductive . . . wounds . . . scars . . . the winds of time . . . saw her the other day at . . . What am I saying?

Fictional me iced her, murder two, with a badminton racket. (The edge can deal a quite lethal blow.)

ALL THE GODDAM SUMMER SADNESS

Yeah, I've done some mean things to broads in my life, but none meaner — tell me if I'm wrong — than the wrestling gal caper.

There's many I bet who would come and stick forks in my scrote if they knew where I lived — I used a p.o. box.

And sent my likeness to the pen pal column of *Super Wrestling Monthly*, lying about my age, claiming I bowled, liked bad guys (Killer Kowalski my favorite), indicating my preference for "Girls" (as opposed to "Boys" or "Both") for pen pals, thus soliciting bags, bushels, tank cars of letters I had *no intention of answering*. (How else to research human misery?)

All of which I carefully stacked, filed, and I share some now with you in the name of social redeem-ment. Go ahead, have a read — it's redeeming!

Hey Russ,

Whats happening man. Is everything far out and funky. Are you married. Whens your birthday. Mines Jan 1. That means Im capricorn. Do you have sisters or brothers. What do you most, like about a girl. When you get married or if you do, or you are all ready, how big a family do you want, or have all ready. Do you like to give hickies on the sholder or any special place. Why do you like bad guys. Where do you work and what if you do. Send me a picture. Do you believe in love at first sight. I guess I do. Im not a longer writer so this is good-by. Do you believe in making love before marriage.

Wanda Steelbeck
8805 Hastings Ct.
Centre Grove, Wis.
54722

Russell,

Hi. Like most of the others you probably won't write back. But I had nothing else to do so here's my letter. I saw your picture in the Wrestling and because of your face I decided to write. I'm white, I have blue eyes, ass length blond hair that's turning sorta brown. Right now we're living in a dinky little town with six bars, two drug stores and a three million dollar pig station. We've lived here a year and I've hated every minute. The reason we moved was cause my mother wanted to live with her boyfriend. (Billy). He only has half a neck because of an operation two years ago. He has a swollen bulge under his forehead but the doctors wouldn't cut it cause it's too near the brain. Two years ago they gave him three weeks to live but he's still alive and I hate the basturd!!

A few of my hobbies are rifles, jewelry, swimming, nature and "Soul" music. Take care.

(Write soon)

Resa Hovey
Rt 2 Box 21
Priceville, Ms. 39458

Dear Russell,

I would like to know if you receive the letter I send you. The reasons why I wrote is you like wrestling & your favor wrestler is Killer Kowalski. He's my favor too. I like the way he wrestle. I like to know if you have seem him wrestle. How was he? Was he good. The only way I seem him wrestle is on wrestling book & T.V. But, I sure like to see him in person.

First, I'll introduce myself again. Since I wrote to you once, but, probably by now you forgotten who I am. My name is *Bobbie Ring*. I'm nineteen. A senior. Go to the public school. Which is Reservation Valley High. I am an (Navaho) Indian from the northern part of Arizona. Have you heard of this type of Indian? If not, this is your lucky day. Let me say a few things about them. Indian are very friendly people if you get to know them. There are all kinds of Indian in this unknow world of ours. Which you and I don't know about. Lot of chances are taken place between Indian & Whiteman now days.

So don't be scare to write back, feel free to do it. I sure like to know more about "Wrestling" and your place (L.A.) Think it's neat.

What do you like during your spare time? I like to watch wrestling on T.V. And also horse back riding. You don't have horse in Los Angels don't you?

This is over for tonigth, until your response. Could you send me a photo of you? In return, I'll send one. So, we'll know each other, even though we're far off.

Love, Pen Pal
as "Bobbie"

P.S. — Write to me,   my address is: Box #26
      will be waiting,   Sparkle, AZ
      don't regret!   86031

Hello:

First of all I'd like to know what your friends call you . . . Russell, Rusty, Russ, etc? It's easier to relate. Everyone calls me either Leo or Lenore, personally I like Lenore but it doesn't matter that much. It's short for Leonora.

I spent Saturday with my cousin Candy, we considered it and decided to write. We were planning to do a "round robin" but I don't think it'll be too successful. If you do write us separately, do me a favor and write a long letter — on "anything" just so it's lengthy, to Candy. She doesn't have much. They live out in the boondocks and I know it thrills her to hear from anyone. Consider it.

I'd like to take this time to say, I am not a wrestling fan. To sit in front of the TV and watch two people brutely beat on each other, hey, I can go downtown and watch all the muggers at work. You get almost the same savage effects. Perhaps we can find something else that we are both interested in.

You say you like to bowl. I tried it once when I was little — I forgot to release my grip. We both went down the alley — the "ball and I". I never went again.

Me? I'm 18½, 5'1", with brown hair and blue eyes. Nothing special, nothing great — just me.

I'll be frank, I'm lonely. My quest is to reach out to people . . . all people . . . I want to touch them and in turn be touched, be it in words, in feelings or by actual touch. I can't say what I feel because I just can't find the words. People would rather tell me their problems — I've no room to even whisper mine. I've accepted this and reach out to them, though Candy thinks I'm crazy — I have sympathy for the lonely, I want them to be happy.

Enough of that. My interests are endless, almost anything intrigues me. I love music, listen to it constantly, all types. Anything in the area of crafts such as: pottery, ceramics, needlepoint, macrame and just sketching in general. Referring back to music, I play the organ, flute, violin and harmonica. I thought you might be interested.

I love animals and plants — pine trees and ponies, grain fields and baby geese. I love the sea and the mountains — dream places. I love long summer nights and winter days. Just to dream and to live my dreams as reality . . . my only hope. Perhaps if you've the time and care to reach out — enter my dream world. You may find it interesting.

(You will not understand me, yet. I do not expect you to. Just be aware of me. It takes time to truly know me . . . . . time.)

Until . . .
Lenore

Leonora Whitsett
RD1 Manley Rd.
Del Grand, Ohio
45813

(I have a brother named Leo; *if* you write, use my full first name.
Thank you.)

NIGHTLIFE

Why I stopped seeing whatsername. Theories.
(Breakfast. Lack of sleep. Large pimple on her ass. Growth? Not a lipoma.)

FAMOUS LAST WORDS (WE ALL DIE CRUMMY)

You fucking shits! You fucking shits!
> — *Cole Porter*

I only regret that I have but one life.
> — *Ingrid Bergman*

People who refer simply to "God," as opposed, say, to "*my* god," are every bit as puerile, as egocentric, and as knee-slappingly laughable as those dingdugs who speak merely of "Dad" or "Mom," as opposed to, well, "*mine.*"
> — *Jack Dempsey*

Ladies, gentlemen, assembled guests, this tumor of the cooch is more than I can bear. I have just swallowed broken glass and in two hours, oh no, sooner . . .
> — *Mamie Eisenhower*

I've got AIDS, lady. Suck my dick.
> — *John Lennon*

ORPHEUS IN MARYLAND

Do you think I'm funny? I don't think I'm funny. Why do people find me funny? They say, "Mertzner — a funny guy." I think they're nuts and submit as evidence a tale, told, which is not funny at-tall.

Flight to Baltimore. Holiday with "the folks." Smoking or nonsmoking? — why am I using italics? I'd chosen smoking. A poorer than average flight . . .

Super-late departure, arrival. Major turbulence. A hoky-joky pilot. Snotty flight attendants who should just *die*. Talky assflames to the left and right. They even ran out of food. But worst thing of all was the smoke. Miserable, horrible cigareet smoke — no cigar or pipe.

Cigar you know I like, and nobody minds pipes, maybe a couple people. They smell like uncles over 40 and slow-burning logs. But burning *paper* — cig'rettes — how can anyone stand all that oxidized paper? Humorless wretch that I am, it BURNS me how they don't even *permit* pipes, cigars anymore in wing 'n' prayer smokepits. Or bidis, which smolder like leaves, *that* kinda leaf, in northern autumnal America — they don't allow bidis no more either. To blot out, to at least compete with, the stink of paper.

Hey, 's not as if I even felt threatened, especially, by that documented menace: roomborne "C." If I haven't cancerized my innards just by breathing normal air, air *without* the tobacco-combustion leavings of the chumps who ingest it directly — if I'm not 90% there from 30-syllable "food colors" in my current mouthwash, in tater chips I ate when I was 12 — then neither (I trust) will 5-6 hours in a chamber of ingesters up me another hundredth of a percent.

Tubes in his arm . . . ratty, peeling wallpaper . . . the county "c" ward at nightfall . . . noon . . . cloud-obscured dawn. (All times to "d" are as *thuddingly shitty.*) *"Yes, doctor"* — Nurse Peabody *stifles a tear* — *"the gentleman was on . . . jeez, it's sad . . . he sat with the* smokers *on Flight 53."*

But no — whew — that's not the number. The number, once more for the verylast time, is aversion to smell. The *Times* ablaze in the seat to my left; the *Gazette* afire to my right. And in my own lap: *The Sonnets of Shakespeare* — unkindled. I don't smoke.

He don't smoke! He don't smoke! — so what's he doin' in "smoking"?

I sat in smoking, as always, to avoid the company of crying, screaming infants.

Whether smokers or non-, and regardless of their inhalations around the house, owners and borrowers of babes tend to prefer *transporting* the babe in a smoke-free setting. If they've gotta smoke, can't wait, they'll hand the babe to another, walk over back near the toilets, light up, show their lungs a *thrill*. But it don't look good if the babe's in your lap while you're at it. I know — some people 're two-faced. (Fuggaduck.)

Anyway, don't know 'bout you, but I for one would rather be chained to a flaming paper *warehouse* than be forced to endure, gratuitously, a unit sonic discharge of no-quit babypain. Right, I don't own one, would never *wanna* own one, although yes, I have borrowed — that's not gratuitous. But gratuitous or not, it's the telegraphed bloodchill — the grief — the unfathomed trauma. 'S like hearing the Nuremberg Trials in *loud* stereo while brushing your teeth . . . fuggit. I'm just too sensitive, too sympathetic a slob to monitor the woofings & tweetings of infancies I've neither caused nor encouraged, especially in crowded berths high above sea level. Call me a cad, call my ma a whore but hey, it takes all kinds. I'm sure you can empathize.

So anyway: a miserable, horrible, lousy, awful flight. The creep next seat, in addition to smoking a week of *Tribunes*, a couple film scripts, and my Shakespeare while I wasn't looking, would not shut *up* re the "greatness of Cosby" — I assume he meant Bill. Other side, all this guy wants to talk, between choke-tokes of Carlton (low in tar but scarcely in paper), is Jessica Lange — "She can really *act*" — hey, that's great. *They'll have Culture to discourse from adjoining "c" beds.*

But what am I gloating? — meantime my luggage is headed for Mars. While over in nonsmoking . . . well I don't know, not yet, what's shaking in nonsmoking. But over in non — I discover while deplaning — THERE ARE NO BABIES. Not a one, legitimate or il-, on this horrible, miserable, smoky, choky flight.

"Aha," chime the circuits of Pax the Clicker in *Creation of the Humanoids*, "irony! One of the *funniest* forms of humor!"

So fuck *me*.

MORE KID NAMES

1. Oofus
2. Goofus
3. Creosote
4. Turpentine
5. Viola
6. Violet
7. Aphida
8. Dogwood
9. Notwalter
10. Notjohn
11. Notmary
12. Notlulu
13. Deaduglyidiotperson

THE KETTLE BLACK

Over extinguished flame, the still-warm clarinet black handle to a stainless steel whistling teapot, the kind even a bent and twisted bottle brush will not get you sufficiently inside to clean, its decade-evolving incrustations the source of not only increasingly bitter potations but conceivably of headaches and/or worse, bought sufficiently early in the reign of Eva Lake for its purchase to have seemed foolish, at best redundant, seeing as how she already owned its near double, one which we doubtless would be using in common, or in tandem, in the years to come, and the $8.95 might more functionally have been spent on, well, flowers;

tattered, neverwashed dried seaweed black chair cover, formerly a comforter, a gift to Eva from her mother, abandoned by E. before we'd had occasion to make love beneath it when a spider, not especially large or ghastly, crawled on or possibly near it, currently shielding the arms, back and above all cushion of a not uncomfortable easychair found on the street, upon which I once sat, nozzle erect, as Lois Ganz came over and wet it, sat on me, sat on it deep with her ass, facing away;

oversized brick unevenly enameled in oilhoney black which when dusted I can see my distorted reflection in, presently serving as a door stopper, one of several, original function unknown, removed from a house Lois had been trying in vain to sell or rent the afternoon I fucked her in the garden with a winebottle;

mint-condition toothbrush, its black plastic stem as icy and wet as the black blood of dangerous happiness, which I once believed, thought, felt absolutely certain would in, of and by itself entice the "French Girl" to more often stay with me — play with me — to love me all the days of my/her/our life;

low-lustre nosehair black remnant of a ribbon, once a quarter inch in width, possibly eighteen in length, now little more than a stringy adhesion of parallel threads forming a limp bow-knot on the handle of a cheap but sturdy green plaid travel bag obtained in trade with Kelly Charner for a stylusless turntable, the ribbon, when new, to distinguish it from other anonymous grips upon my landing in Los Angeles, this time as a resident, after too, too many years in New York, the last too many under the same roof as Kelly, still on the bag to continue fulfilling such objective in baggage claims of the land and/or world;

scuffed heel black letters in the phrase "10-13 Advise road/weather conditions," one of only three CB codes still legible on a tall once attractive drinking glass, one of a pair acquired for our happy home by Kelly in September (approx.) '75, not nearly as dense or as striking as the garden pebble black x-large panty-girdle worn Election Day next by Marion Safferstein, buttocks like four taut cantaloupes, the first 43-year-old I entered or sought to enter, first woman I entered before kissing or whose genitals I encountered before her breasts, and possessor of the wettest ginch ever to greet me on initial groping, our subsequent frolic destroying its cylindrical partner, at least one shard lodging in the linens where several hours later it would pierce, but not gash, the less abundant buttock of Ms. Charner;

cobweb-obscured fake eyelash, high-chroma burnt cookie black, partially protruding from potted cactus sand gathered in Lancaster or Palmdale, left on the sink beside Yozuki's empty Tampax box the only time we slept, or almost slept, overnight in the same bed, our sole rendezvous of more than three hours without erotic consequence, the first and final time she visited me in L.A.;

single hothouse crayon black pubic hair, no longer redolent of patchouli, mounted on the back side of a lined white index card above the typed ident "JoAnne Sisk," its highlights less redbrown but otherwise the near equal in color and texture of the strands on her head, retrieved from the sheets after she stormed out the time I declined to close the door when I pissed;

flat furrycow black cotton sock suspended by pushpin over the 1" peephole not yet installed in my hallway door the evening a tenant named Jo in blue kimono, nothing under, knocked and requested help with an erratic gas heater, an appeal leading quickly to the singeing of my shirt, the discovery that our bedrooms were coterminous, and her pouring me a Coors Light and herself a Coke, calmly asking, "We could have sex soon or we could have it now — what do you think?," nor in the door at any time while she lived in the building;

three strips of bottom pit blackangel black tape, electrical in lieu of masking or scotch, sealing the top of a three-quarters full box of Cap'n Crunch's Peanut Butter Crunch, now quite stale, procured chiefly if not solely for breakfast with JoAnne, who would not fuck me after 5 a.m. but once did, not in appreciation for the cereal, though, which she deemed an affront in light of the muenster and/or jack omelets she'd already twice served me;

tidewater stove dirt black cassette containing a largely commercial-free Beta version of *The Creeping Terror*, first third of which I screened for a less than grateful JoAnne within moments of her anxious knock on her side of our wall, and of my response on mine, the night she spit cum in my face;

smudged and muddied go-go death car black image of the French Girl's toothbrush as seen in the soapgrimy hand mirror that I tilt in concert with that fronting the medicine chest to trim my not yet graying sideburns while forswearing her luck, her ankles, her syllogisms;

igneous pistolterror black crater, obsidian almost, in the gravy gray carpet, souvenir of my fatuity, hell, my desperation in letting Donnie Irons, a book prick who years before had passed on my work with the comment "Wow. Infuckingcredible. Now write me something I can *publish*," whose cover, when cornered, for a fateful missed appointment had been "Don't tell me time and space *exist*," spend the night on my couch in lieu of his expense-paid, but distant, hotel bed in a whorish attempt to finally sell him something, produced, on evidence, by an awkwardly concealed potsmoke mishap while I slept, behind closed door, a month before he rejected my manuscript anyway, and I crashed — at 200 m.p.h. — into the Goddam Wall:

    black, black, black, black, black, black . . . twelve or thirteen blacks.

COLE SLAW 1900

"She's waiting for me to kick it," whines Sid Mertzler, 70, of _____ Park, MD, "so she can play tennis."

"It's snowing out," scoffs Doreen "Dolly" Mertzler, 69. "How could I play tennis?"

"In the summer."

"In the summer I can play whenever I want."

"You can't wait to play with *men* — mixed doubles."

"Every time I play mixed" — she's talking to me — "he goes crazy."

"I'll kill them!"

"I thought you wanted me to be happy."

"Not *that* happy."

"You need some exercise yourself." To me: "Why don't you take him for a walk?"

"Not now," growls Sid, "I'm doing the puzzle."

"When, then? You need exercise."

"In the morning."

"Don't forget."

"I won't forget."

"You'll forget."

"No, I won't."

"I'm not going to remind you."

"*I won't forget.*"

To me again: "Watch him forget." Naw, *I'll* remind him. After all, we're bunkmates. Me and him in the guest room, *his* room, on rickety modified cots while she's got her own with a queensize.

"How long has this been the setup?" I ask.

"A . . . a while. She no longer enjoys my snoring. It disturbs her serenity."

"You're a typical modern couple."

"I suppose." His snoring, fathomless, primeval, not only keeps me awake but appalls me — this involves oxygen? Is the old man dying?

A freezybreezy suckwhite morning. We pick a salty stretch of concrete for our twostep. "This reminds me of the army," says Sid. "It was cold as the dickens. There was this sergeant, Pat something, Saunders, Sorensen, he said, 'Out of my way, fellows, I'm gonna heave.' We believed him, we got out of his way, and he did." After a cautious 40 yards he ups the tempo, then doubles it, stepping too fast for his cane to take the full brunt of his stride. Listing forward at 60 degrees, he barrels ahead of me.

"You're too macho — slow it." I grab at his coat, too late . . . down.

A woman about 60 lays down her bundle, circles a drift and crosses the road. "Get rid of her," snaps Sid, but she's quickly upon us, help-blood in her eye.

"What's his condition? Is he taking medication?"

"Go 'way, old bag," he snarls. Silently — surprisingly — she does.

For a skinny guy he's heavy — weight in the bone. A major endeavor just getting him upright. Pants ripped, a knee scraped — "Don't tell Dolly." We make it home, sneak past her, I take off his pants and repair the knee. What about the pants? "Throw them out. I hate them."

Enter Dolly, ladle in hand. "That was quick."

"We walked a mile."

"Very good. You changed your pants."

"Yep."

"Any reason?"

"They didn't match my shirt."

"*These* match your shirt?" In his quickest move of the day, he grabs her skirtleg, her thigh, she pulls away, glowers, exits . . . gone.

"They have *something* between their legs," says the old guy, "but do we ever really find out what it is?"

"Dolly, remember when we got permission to be cremated?"

"Permission?"

"In our wills."

"No, it's not, but they all know about it."

"Don't you remember the flak we took from the powers that be?"

"From *what* powers?"

"What have you got to eat?"

A steaming pot of speckled gruel, consisting manifestly of cornstarch and boned chicken lumps, is apportioned for three. With nose and tongue I struggle to discern its deeper essence. "What is this?" I finally ask.

"Kung pao chicken. How do you like it?"

"It's a little on the bland side."

"Well, the chili paste they call for, I find it too hot, and garlic doesn't agree with me, so I substitute diced tomatoes and sesame."

"You got any hot sauce? Tabasco?"

"No. Will mustard do?"

"That's okay."

Finishing his portion, Sid belches softly and wipes his lips. "Where's my cookie?"

From an overhead cupboard Dolly draws a small blue box with willow filigree, shaking from it a single twisted wafer. He cracks it and removes a tiny paper which he examines at arm's length. "I can't read this."

"Put your glasses on."

"Where are they?"

"Where'd you leave them?"

With minimal commotion they are found in his left shirt pocket. "'You are a person of superb taste and refinement.'

That I am. When we had the upholsterer that time, Marilyn said I could —"

"Who's Marilyn?"

"The one from your bridge gang."

"There's a Marian."

"Marian. She and I see eye to eye about fabric design."

"How's that?"

"She said that when you vote, when you go to the polling place, you can vote any way you want, it's totally up to you."

"What's that got to do with fabric design?"

"I forget. Where's my comb?"

"Isn't it in your pants?"

"No."

"Did you leave it in the bathroom?"

"No."

"How do you know you didn't leave it there?"

"I didn't leave it there."

While she investigates, I realize it was prob'ly in the pair he had me trash. "I bet it was in the pants we threw out."

"Don't tell Dolly."

She returns. "I can't find it. Where are the pants you were wearing this morning?"

"You can't find them?"

"I haven't *looked* for them. Why'd you change?"

"I don't remember. I need my comb."

"We'll get you another comb."

"I want *that* one."

"I can probably buy you the *identical* comb. What color was it?"

"Black. And unbreakable. With rounded ends. It was in my pants."

Another search is undertaken. The old boy arises to toy with the dishes, make himself "useful." A domestic-compulsive from way back, he races to effect the task before his mate's return.

"I don't see a sign of . . . no, that doesn't go there."

"Where does it go?"

"It isn't even dry, let me. Do your puzzle."

Pages are flipped in the current month's *Senior World*. "Five letters, '*blank* old flag' " — a pencil moves. "I told her, 'I don't care if you saw the damn thing or not. We took pictures of it.' "

"Huh?"

"Our neighbor Jeri is very opinionated. She insisted when you're in a plane above the Grand Canyon you can't see anything, it's too far away."

"An opinionated vitch, witch, w-i-t-c-h."

"Don't call her, don't call people that. She just happens to be wrong in this case."

"A witch on wheels."

Submitting to a pet compulsion of her own, Dolly swings to the foyer to handwash a cluster of rubber ornamental grapes. I ask Sid, "Do you ever just scream?"

"What about?"

Give me a week, I think, and I'll lay the short list on you. Instead I meekly query, "How's your sister?"

"Emma is fine. She wondered whether I remember Perth Amboy. I told her, 'Mud flats.' We were there in 1925, '26. The cousins and uncles would go on the weekend. We went because her brother Leon —"

"Whose brother Leon?"

"My mother's brother. He had no place to go but Perth Amboy. I said, 'Why is it taking this long for tomorrow to get here?' — it was a long night. She asked me what I knew about, she's trying to prove, she would rather have a party than anything. I would rather look at the historical perspective. Perth Amboy was a small town then. The way the stories had, Emma always kept the archives. A wise man said, 'Don't save things, they'll consume you.' How true. We're swamped now getting rid of all our, prior to moving."

"When was this? You've already moved."

"Before we moved. Emma had barrelsful, she still does. And her husband Jack, who's a horse's rear, found them in the cellar. He had to take . . . not calcium. Not fluorine. Anyhoo, he took it, not a tablet, a white pill. The doctor'd been saying he should . . . not magnesium. I take it too, in the morning, a mineral. Not selenium. Zinc. I take zinc, but the zinc I take is . . . Dolly, what is there to eat?"

Elective activity proceeds apace. When I pall of watching linoleum grow, I count attritions on the head of a pin. Counting done, I poke around for something to steal. Stamps? I can always use stamps. Hankies? Ditto. Rubber grapes? Nuh thanks. Videotape? I got no VCR.

As I 'splain when Dolly catches me snooping, "I wouldn't own one."

"I thought you did."

"It got stolen. Somebody broke in. I'm really glad."

"Oh, I'm *very* pleased to have one. I tape the aerobics and cooking shows. It's especially good for the cooking, they go so fast, you never get it all if you see it only once. And if the host is *engaging*, the hostess, it's that much tougher to follow. Especially, have you ever seen, I can't think of his name, he calls himself the Frugal Gourmet?"

"No, I can't stand those —"

"Wears an apron and a tie and he's entertaining, he's adorable — I replay the shows to see *him*. And sometimes a dish, he shows you how to prepare your own cole slaw, very tasty. I was thinking of making some tomorrow."

"Speaking of which, do we have any plans for tomorrow *night*?" My return's not till the 2nd — will I ever make it?

"I thought we'd just spend a quiet evening."

"How 'bout renting a movie?"

"Rent . . . what do you mean?"

"There are stores that rent cassettes, I saw one on the ride from, all these places that have 'video' on the front."

"Is that what that is?"

"Yeah. You can get, anything that's been out and gone for more than a couple months."

"I never knew."

"By the way, I've looked all over and I can't find, have you got anything to drink?"

"Yes, we do. There's Cherry Heering, I have that for when the girls come over."

"That's all?" I gag at the thought.

"And a little, there might be some orange liqueur left, mandarin orange. Want me to see?"

"No, I'll pass" — I'd rather watch linoleum play bridge. "You want a movie? It's my treat."

"Get something nice, though. Something we'll all enjoy."

No car at my disposal — "We can't let you drive," declares Dolly, "in this weather" — I prowl afoot an hour before scoring a vid joint. Thorough scrutiny of stock leads me to Bertolucci's *1900*, four hours, plus or minus, about Italian fascism . . . they'll love it. In addition to beer I buy vinegar.

Showtime: 8 p.m., to permit us undivided (if unspecified) access to midnight. A sixth of a day is a long time to sit, but Dolly, fit as a fern, who if she doesn't make it to 90 is being cheated, fades only once and is generally riveted. As has been her habit since the '50s, she addresses the screen at key junctures — "You're marrying *her*? You're crazy." Sid, for the most part, snoozes. When his snoring proves distracting, she stirs him: "Wake up, watch the film."

"I've already seen it."

"You have not!"

"Yes, I have."

"Just be quiet." He is. Not a peep until near the end, after Donald Sutherland's been shot and his broad is about to get a haircut:

"What can I eat?"

"You'll have to go yourself." He does. Two minutes later, a thud. Kitchen?

Lying in a puddle of kung pao and cole slaw, Sid jabs about with a sponge. In attempting to clean up before discovery, he instead, it would appear, slipped in the puddle, initial cause not readily apparent. I reach down for his arm — "Don't tell Dolly."

"Don't tell me what? Where's your cane?"

"I don't have my cane."

"You should *always* take your cane. Are you alright?"

"Yes."

"You didn't break anything?"

"No."

"I'm talking about *you*."

"I didn't break, how's the movie going?"

"Who *cares* how the movie's going?"

It's 11:58 and I keep my fucking mouth shut.

I decide I'll steal a grape.

HOW TO USE THIS BOOK

Some guy from the rowboat department of East Florida College (Vero Beach) takes three amazing snaps of the long believed extinct alligator fish. The thing is 25 feet long and can be seen in one shot dwarfing a common reptilian gator. In another, a surfer's leg narrowly escapes ingestion; no *ichthys* ever had sharper chops, or a heartier craving for gam. The majestic alligator fish: extinct no more! (Resembles a barracuda, only thinner, scalier — and a smidge *greener*.)

Brought to the attention of the school's bio department, which hasn't been this stoked since the near capture of a Cunnilimbus shark (radioactive hybrid of the Great White), marine experts take an active interest, as well as the dept. of swimming. Bandwaggers from the school of fishing are told: "Hands off — this is our baby." Which is where I came in. (I was there.)

Volunteering my servitude, I'm outfitted with gear. Scuba 'quipment with numbers and stencils — so I can't abscond — lessons to follow. Underwater camera, film, lenses and lens caps, same deal. I am slightly fearful (of the alligator fish) but not very. More afraid of drownding — am not the best of swimmers — than of being et. And screwing up the photos (am 'fraid of, too). But I'll do alright — and maybe *meet some girls*.

They wear sightly one-pieces at East Florida; the latest styles. At the outdoor snack bar they towel off, remove swim caps and brush their hair. They're as thrilled about alligator fish — about *the* alligator fish — as I. (Is a dream I had.)

HOUSEPETS I'VE IN ALL LIKELIHOOD KILLED OR MAIMED

Cute! Cuddly! Humanly owned/operated livingthings whose lives were brutishly TERMINATED or BECLOUDED through fault of my own: fluffy snuggly!

Bunnies: *possibly*. Slammed one with the headlight of my '49 Packard — reddened hi-beam as clear proof of impact. Question is, did it hop away or bounce away? (A kill or a mere mutilation?) And was it owned, housed, caged and out on recess, a dinner break — or just another hip hop nature-bunny, backroads Long Island '66? Ascertainment of pethood: doubtful. So let's not COUNT IT.

Count my snake, tho. Definitely. My little 7-8-9" ribbon snake or garter snake or whatever in heck the thing was. Drab dark coloration with yellowish stripes. No fangs. Bit me once and left barely an imprint. Wasn't eating worms so I fed it a salamander. Both died. 1959. (It was a *very* dead year.)

It's ALWAYS tragic to step on a snail. Lawn snails . . . street snails (in precincts where applicable) . . . pond snails. *Crunch*, they're done: could Arthur effing Miller be tragicker? Trample yer *own* snail, tho, and you've reached the acme — the ajax! — the *pinnacle* of gastropod illfortune. (Aeschylus could not do you justice.) You . . . me . . . you would have to be dwunk and I was. Couple beers, me and my snail, the diminutive slimer was outside my door in the rain. Streetlamps reflecting off his delicate shell, I lifted cautiously with midfinger and thumb, inviting him in for a Pabst Blue Ribbon. We shared a sudsy glass: he, crawling upside the vessel with shell in tow, bending down at the lip to dip face in froth; I, sipping/slugging in conventional manner. One bottle gone, I stepped lively for another — about face, left turn, falsestep, CRUNCH — a crisp, aurally *pleasing* crunch — you don't get such crunches from Rice Krispies — but a goresuffused crunch nonetheless. O me! o my! o mea culpa! (Have I ever fully recovered?)

Hamsters: none.

Dogs: are too worthless even to kick. Kicking a dog is like beating a rug; killing a dog is like washing one. Dogs are stupid and breathy, rugsmelly, dogloyal: who needs 'em? Stupids? Breathies? Ruggards? Loyalists? So you might kick one to get back at a jerk, for instance Carl Panter. I think I once kicked his. In a halfassed, halfhearted way. His chow chow the size of a pig. Or thought about it.

Thinking of kittendeath. Closeup of a whitewhite babycat. Meow *meow* — zoom in on face — drowned out by sounds of a car engine revving. Cut to gloved hand on stickshift toying with the gears. Swing up to dashboard, windshield, pull focus: red traffic signal from driver's p.o.v. Back to kitten, howling wildly now, wider angle reveals five identical kitcats, each more darling than the next, all inconsolable, their collars lashed to the rear wheel of an orange '65 Mustang. Light turns green, driver lets 'er rip. Wide angle, intercut with closeups, *exquisite* slo-mo of kitty after kitty being mashed to whitered kitpaste by collision with blacktop. — Thinking isn't doing.

And doing isn't . . . okay, I don't care for kittens, for itty bits of purr fur, but grownup cats, sheez . . . I would give my write arm not to have done this. Phoebe Snell's CatMan: not a man, not a bat- (or super-) man, not a hybrid man/cat — a man*like* cat. Cats in gen'ral *tend* to be manlike, not that men are much to write home about, a lot more like 'em than dogs (dogs are closer to goats — or to pumpkins — than to humans), but this cat was quitelike a MAN. A unique male PERSON. With a distinct personality and presence. He'd walk up and start talking like there was no language barrier, no need for cat shorthand, none of this meow/feed me, meow/pet me bullshit. His utterances were strong, complex, and unambiguously specific, and could not've been read as expressing anything other (for inst) than *Another day, huh?* or *Get these damn kids outta here* — he didn't much like children (or their so-called energy), and he didn't like kittens. (Hissed at both.) Clawed the bejeez out of *People* mag (as a decent person would & should) but not *Westways*, not *Car Craft*, just *People*. And like many persons he had pets of his own, *a* pet, Phoebe's ultrane-glected Phobia, in her own neurotic catright a person too: a stunted dumbperson.

His fleas, tho, while his, were not his pets — he didn't want them. Nor I, altho catsitting while Phoebe was in Phoenix I was forced to contend with them. Each day for a month I'd go feed him, him and Phobia, and right off I notice these shiny black specks on my white socks, white T-shirt — anything white — working through the weave to eat me, suck me dry . . . they quiteliked my flavor (apparently). In two-three days I've got 200 bites, 200 bloodscabby itchlumps. I start dressing dark and just to be safe tie a white plastic bag over each shoe and pants leg, bind 'em at the calf and sure 'nough, they're covered with the bastards *instantaneously*. The moment I arrive. The system works, but after a week, ten days, two fresh baggies per visit is beginning to get expensive, and there's always some fleas that go straight for the un-guarded skin on my hands and my neck, y'know, anyway. Time to resort to chemicals and be done with it. So I get one of those flea bombs where you seal all the windows, stick tow-els under the door, newspaper in all the cracks, leave for two hours, come back and everything's dead and you air the place out and start over. I do this, I'm back and I quickly learn two things are notdead. One, the fleas, they're *all over* my socks (which this time are red) — whuh went wrong? The label, the can, I read it and realize the bomb was an egg bomb. Kills flea eggs and fleas that ain't YET, but fleas that are — f'rget it. The monsters tunnel through to my ankles, legs, feet and suck like my flesh has got straws attached.

Two, I hear this catsound, yikes, where's it coming? 'S

faint, I'm thinking one minute more in this deathspice-scented air and I'll faint from the scent — not even the death — I've yet to open a window. Two hours — where? who? Bathroom, no, bedroom, oh no, cowering behind a curtain is CatMan, fuckme, and the look on his face is *Thanks, pal, for saving me.* Me, his near-killer! — what grievous *shit* I was, am, for assuming he'd gone out through the catdoor and sealing it, for not beating the bushes more thoroughly, for not double-triple-beating goddammit, kickme, I nearly killed a cat, this cat!, this cat like a man (among men), Jesus fucking Fuck and I carry him, speed him to the porch and stand helpless as he wobbles down the stairs, sobs and disappears into an alley. To die? Die now? But he soon returns and I offer him food (he declines) and pour water, an entire bowl of which he drinks without pause and cats *never* drink more than a spoonful, spooking me, griefing me into staying the rest of the day — and all night — and his BONES STICK OUT, 12 years old and suddenly 12 catyears OLD, lying there lethargic as lint, this cat who not a month (year?) before had averaged a birdcatch a WEEK and was hearty and bold as a tuna . . . I did it. Me! Or the catclock (or both), and the fleas stab and feast and I scratch and wipe blood with my sleeve and make sure he is breathing. Mid night he gets up and goes to a closet, I follow him in and say, "Don't die, I love you," and only his eyes move, and needy puny Phobia lurks about demanding to be petted, and six weeks later he's catdust.

Catfish: none.

Sea monkeys? None.

THE REVENGE OF "THEM" — I'm still waiting. 19 counts of anticide are bound to catch up with you. 19 ants — an ant farm — one of those $9.98 plastic jobs suitable for graduations and weddings. I was their farmer. I'd sit and watch them dig, move sand around, tho it wasn't actually sand, some kind of white talc-y sand substitute. There is no sub for interest, however, and, burrowing done, these miniworkaholics soon got bored & boring. Meaningful farmwork a thing of the past, they paced like 6-legged seniors on a geezer farm. — *Where's the checkers, Jethro?* — *I'm* tired *of checkers, Zeke.* Weeks came and went as I doled them their dose of sugar-water as required. There must be more to being or owning ants — there MUST — till finally the strain of ownership got the better of me. On an outdoor ant tour I sought and found an off-species nest, one teeming with ants TWICE the length and girth of my own, antennas outstretched like junior TVs, fierce mandibles you couldn't miss from eyeheight away. Conscripting the largest — and fiercest! — I raced home and thrust him on the farm population. Common cause — stave off the invader: it'll give 'em something t' do.

Tougher and fiercer than I'd reckoned, the big fella slew 14 of my boys in the first hour, and by battle's end (VICTORY!) their ranks had shrunk from 22 to 3. The courageous survivors had *at* the marauding sumbitch, tearing him asunder and I do mean asunder, removing his limbs, etc. and HEAD and scattering them as far and wide as farm dimensions allowed. That's showin' him!

Roosters? No.

Roaches? *Not exactly.* In '72 I was living in this okey doke apartment with the lowest cockroach count in New York; you might see a couple a week. There was one we'd see every so often, me and Kallie Sharman, with vivid red highlights you could not have mistaken for anyroach else's. Kallie named her Reddy, and every few days we'd leave her a gob of yogurt, whatever flavor Kallie might be eating, in a nook beside the bathroom sink. "It'll encourage her," said Kallie, "and I'm sure she is a her, to stay out of the kitchen." She was right. Reddy came to know and trust us, never left the bathroom, and would not flee when either of us approached. One day Kallie took a bath. Perhaps she needed it (I'd spread cashew paste on her vulva); she liked her water hot. The tub filled, she was about to jump in when a limp, bloated bugmass caught her eye. Reddy — boiled deady! A rotten way to go. Kallie, for all her animallove, had been quite the executioner, and when roachword got out, the *deluge*: cucarachas in every cupboard and drawer, in our books, wineglasses, bedclothes, licking the glue off envelopes and stamps. It was them or us — let the slaughter begin! — but nonpet roachkills, like fleakills, don't count, and I'm not counting PARROTS.

RAUNCH EPISTEMOLOGY AND THE SYNTHETIC A PRIORI

What if, at the moment a child is about to walk, roller skates are affixed to its feet?

How'll we ever get the hang of night if every time we turn around it's tripped up and oxidized by light?

CRAB CAKES YUM

Q: *And this is when?*

A: Oh, some late month, I was in L.A. a few weeks, a month, still didn't have a phone or a car. I couldn't call her, she knew I, no, she couldn't phone *me*, so I'm outside, about to leave, when she pulls up in some kind of British convertible, an MG or something, couldn't have been the original paint, yellow ochre. She was like this rich person, or the daughter of a rich person.

Q: *How old?*

A: I guess about 27. I'd met her the night before at this terrible party, nobody's talking to me, I'm drinking, eating, she's at the food, looks alright, we start talking. More drinks and food, we ostensibly hit it off, story of my life, story of her life, but she won't go home with me. Tells me she really, *really* wants to get to know me, she has a boat, or her father, she wants to take me out, at the Marina, do I like paddle tennis, she wants to play paddle tennis with me. I figure okay, this is, well, she looks something like Jamie Lee Curtis (who probably didn't exist yet), I can stand her, ostensibly talk to her, I haven't pawed her, no instant hotcha but fine, whatever, maybe I'll call her, she can't really insist I play paddle tennis. I don't have a phone so she takes my address on a business card. She splits and I put my sights on this other one, big tits, bigger than I usually feel comfortable with, works for some music publisher, I talk bands with her for ten minutes and she takes, goes home with me. Hadn't got a smile since my second night in town, and suddenly — feast or famine — one comes home with me and next day another one drives up, "Come on, I'll give you the grand tour." I get in, ride with her and it feels almost giddy, *I* feel giddy, *it* feels silly — like kindergarten or something.

Q: *Where'd she take you?*

A: Well, just to, we got a six-pack of Falstaff Bicentennial, that was the year they, and drove straight to her place, or to —

Q: *Which was where?*

A: Somewhere west, the West Side, I was new in, couldn't really get a bearing on, I dunno, Palms? Culver City? Could even have been Westwood. Anyway, we get there, she puts on I think it was Fleetwood Mac, no, or Billy Joel, fortunately the volume was low, then she takes me on a big tour of *inside*. She shows me all her furniture, some doodads, sculpture, these expensive, we go from room to room and finally I say, "When can I see your clitoris?" "I thought you'd never ask." Drops her pants and while she's still standing I get down there and stick my face in.

Q: *How'd she taste?*

A: Kind of musky-sour, the kind that tastes exactly as it smells, y'know, as it greets you the first time a couple feet off, nice, basic cunt taste that hasn't been washed in the last few hours, cunt and sweat and beer, y'know beer piss, *possibly* a degree tangier than average, with the faintest trace of diaphragm jelly, she already had it in. I had my hands on her ass and I'm eating and eating and she's swaying —

Q: *Did she come?*

A: Well, not at this, it progressed too fast, we were on the floor rolling and lunging, locked in, um, almost immediately. We fucked for *hours*, day into night, and each time was long, it lasted, and I was as hard as I bet I've ever been in my life. These things surprise you when they — why now, how to explain it? 'S a good thing I hadn't come the night before with the music, that woman I was with, we just kind of flopped around drunk and she left, she wouldn't, and I hadn't had time to stroke it that morning so most of my sap was left. Sometimes you get lucky.

Q: *You only did it on the floor?*

A: Just the first. There were three, I came three times, and by the time of, during the second it was already like . . . delirium. It went beyond consciousness, pure physical locomotion but not simply, like being *demented* by meat and exhausted by it, in all senses of — meat exhaustion, meat satiety. It felt almost like *love*.

Q: *How come, if it was so good, this was the only actual time you ever fucked?*

A: Uh, that's part of, let me . . .

Q: *Go ahead.*

A: And the fit wasn't bad, at times it felt like *home*. And I even felt at home with, like here's this person who verbally, the getting-to-know-you stuff, the protocol, I'd probably had enough of already, unless we'd fucked I might not've called her for a while. But things she was saying in bed now, the fuck things, were a lot more interesting, much more expressive and revealing of, y'know, someone I could actually, than anything she'd been saying otherwise.

Q: *Such as?*

A: Well the third time she says, we're doing it dogstyle, she's on her knees with her arms braced against the bedboard, the headboard, perfect position, I can see her ass, her thighs, the percussions are great, they even *sound* great, and she says to me, "It's okay for now, but finish me the other way," y'know, face to face — wow. The other way!

Q: *So did you?*

A: Yeah. And this other, we'd be going a good clip, she'd say, "Do me . . . *do it*," then later, "Fuck me, fuck me, fuck me," always said it three times.

Q: *How'd you respond to that?*

A: Well, "Do me," I got airborne, the lower half of my body, I flung myself and dove at her, without losing contact, maybe just the tip would be in and then boom, as many times as, all the way down until I came. "Fuck me" is what she'd say while this was happening, though I couldn't really accelerate or increase, just took it as encouragement and kept on, try and magnify the acrobatics maybe, the angle of, but just continue full throttle 'til I burst in a heap between her legs.

Q: *Any nonverbal come sounds?*

A: From her? Not really. Heavier breathing but not like, no panting or — that's why I assume she didn't come. So I got up, after the third time I got up, turned on the TV, went to piss . . .

Q: *What was on?*

A: Some Victor Mature movie. I get back, she says, "I'm sore." "*Aw*, I'm sorry," but I wasn't planning, didn't have much left, I say, "Hope you just mean *inside*, 'cause" — I open her legs and proceed to, I wanna make her come and will eat her for as long as, if it takes a week. So I'm tonguing her and kissing her all over, real tired but whatever energy I've still got, and focus, and as geography, geology, it's a *very* nice external pussy, then I notice, suddenly become aware of this chemical taste like hairspray or Lysol or something, which I'm sure isn't her diaphragm, even with all the activity and my goop factored in it's too intense, so I realize it must be the crab medicine.

Q: *Crab medicine??*

A: Yeah, the — a couple years before, three years, I was out in California on, I came to write a piece and brought these crabs back. Which I didn't realize until I'd given them to my New York roommate, which then got hectic. She made me, I had to find actual crablice in her area, I'd shown her mine but she wouldn't accept, *she* couldn't have them, so I picked through her hairs and eventually found one, which completely unhinged her. She insisted on boiling our underwear, it says so on the box, to be thorough you're supposed to not only shampoo it on, the A-200, you have to take out any that might be hid in your clothes. So she buys this enormous pot, aluminum, later we used it, I had to convince her, we made spaghetti, and boiled all our, every possible pair, calculating all the days involved, even stuff we'd already washed. Colors ran, hers, mine, everything came out this kind of orange-gray-green with the elastic stretched out, unwearable. I would never do *that* again, ha, but just as paranoid, as absurd, I'm back in L.A. and I'm thinking this is where you catch, it's where the crabs *are*. So even though nothing, I wasn't in the music woman, all told, for more than, less than five minutes, why take chances, first thing in the morning I apply the A-200. Had a bottle from the last, only other time I'd had sex since I moved, first week out, I did the same thing, it seemed wise, y'know, "worldly." The mature, responsible, so you don't spread 'em, *if* you got 'em — as if I'm gonna, I've gotta do this every time until I get a better sense, somehow, of the distribution of crabs in . . . great moments in world travel.

Q: *So meanwhile you're eating her . . .*

A: Right. Although the taste is like paint remover I plod along, just keep, try to avoid thinking about, then it dawns on me, poison, external use only, but the concentration's too low, I rinsed it off, it's only residue, residue once removed — I'll live. Then I start wondering if it's *mutually* unpleasant, 'cause my beard possibly, hadn't shaved, I hadn't expected, so maybe, but she didn't say, didn't stop, she held my head down and went, "Oh God, oh God," which seemed like approval. She came like a machine gun and I kept up, she came another couple times and then pushes me away. "Oh, *thank* you," and before I know it she has my dick, which by now is hard again — "Let me do *you*." She starts sucking me, wet, deep, with real purpose, real, then she recoils in horror. Crab-knowledge, she's quicker than I was at tasting, identifying — L.A. crab-knowledge! — it's there in her face. If I don't have living parasites where her mouth and cunt just, she knows I *have* had, recently, and who knows what else, and who else — I'm very tainted goods. From something to nothing in . . .

Q: *What was the Victor Mature movie?*

A: I don't remember. Not *Samson and Delilah* or *One Million B.C.*

DECOR FOR PREVIOUS CHAPTER

Dear sir:

Heeding your suggestion, I have used this book to get "off" whenever possible, with your crotchlouse recital providing ample fuel for same. But much as I hopped to the nonpareil fuckstuff [therein], I demand *more* from litrachoor, namely detail and description, both external and in. What of the lady's *walls*, for example, either residential or pudendal? What of her fruitbowls and w.c.? As a writer/fucker it is your duty to provide us nonwriting fans of written fuck with our quota of decor to savor and cherish. Do as we ask, you shit, or I will switch to Raymond Carver — or *War and Peace*.

Wendy Mosley
Studio City

Okay, Wen', I'd hate for you to hafta read either of *those* . . . decor it is.

CARPETING: white. And deeep. Take a step, two steps, your feetprints remain (like walking in fresh layered snow). White — a football coach will tell you — makes matter look *larger*. White same things appear larger than black same things. Don a white jersey, white pants, your opponent thinks: these guys're *big*. White walls: a big looking "space."

For primary space-filling, the filler favors wood, wood direct, or semi-direct, from aboriginal forests. No particle board, no veneer, no wood-pattern formica in let's see, how many rooms she got? Living; kitchen; lavatory; bed; second lav in bedroom; dining. No simulated tree produce *anywhere*. The late Joyce Kilmer would be proud.

Parade of the wooden objects! . . . items! . . . things! Wooden java table ("From Haiti," relates our hostperson); wooden table table ("Hand carved, from Burma"); wooden

Ganesh ("He's the one" — Hindu god w/ elephant's trunk — "whose father suspected him of sleeping with his mother so he cut his head off . . . from the Delhi airport gift shop"); wooden Siva ("Thailand, no, Bali — and it's teak"); wooden platypus ("Let me guess — Australia?" "Tasmania"); wooden limbs on tan leather couch ("An estate sale in Encino"); wood custom frames around wondaful prints/paintings/snaps of MANY LANDS. Woody Guthrie, of whom I'm not really a fan, would be proud.

And in other rooms, well let's begin with *a* room, the lady o' the house's Schlafzimmer — that's deutsch. In this Raum, regardless of linguistic propensity or native origin, you will find: *Objects of menace.* Tiger claw the size of a toothpaste. Tortoise skull large enough, living, to 've snapped off your Arm (Bein) (Kopf) (Fuss). *Objects that could not harm a gnat.* Three-legged camel toy from Kindheit. Handbemalte walnut shell. *Miscellaneous exotica.* Alongside der Bett, ein bowl of papayas. Complete '39 printing of *The Americanized Encyclopaedia Britannica,* whatever *das* ist. You are what you have, somebody said that, and judging from die Dame's havings she ist someone to RECKON WITH.

Reckon with this while we're at it: 24" Zenith capable of receiving both VHF and UHF atop its steamer-trunk perch DOES NOT FACE THE BED, not directly, and thus cannot be VIEWED from same (without mirrors). Likely benefits: distraction-free predawn 'cyclopaeding, maximal walnut watch.

Mattress: FIRM. Bedspread: heather on mauve. Vibrator: not for current exhibition.

No dust! No rust! Richperson homes are always cleanly. Skilled hirelings, toilers with whisk and vac, precede visitation. I search for dust here, there — something I *enjoy* — and find some, finally, in the sofa. Not under. Behind a pillow. Did the maid sweep it there? — I'm too polite to ask. Rust I can't find nowhere. Only rust-colored SPOTS ON THE FLOOR.

Stains you could call 'em. In the Art Deco kitchen. Not

many, but some — these spots are doozies. Ceiling too; rain damage mayhap? Party beverage drip? Is this the TOP floor? Sorry, I forgot to inquire.

Drip, drip . . . hold it. With two fully accoutered washrooms at your disposal, you're never too far from relief. Evacuation, elimination: take your pick. One 'room offers Maori Modern styling; the other, for your seatwarming pleasure, *A Spynster's Tale* (lavishly ill.). Choice not chance on the bountiful West Side!

Moving on to our hostwoman's *personal* premises, I can't believe I labeled the fit "not bad." I meant a *spectacular* fit, or moderately spec, spec enough that even today, a halfscore-plus annums down the line, I find myself composing (only moderately specious) verselets in its BEHALF:

> my dick breathes
> in the lungs of your cunt
> (ex)hale (in)hale
> shallow deep uh
> gasping choking gimme
> breath-of *aiiiiiiir!*

In a word, this fit was *snug*. Not nearly as tight as a hand or an ass, but life-affirmingly windproof from my crown to the root.

If you're asking me, howev, to shed light on the *other* half of the fit, to specify, "detail," catalog & list salient attributes, empirical FEATURES of this outstanding tactile Gestalt — her prod-pleasing intracuntal "ridges," "gorges" and such — I am not *that* good a writer that I would even try (but don't — do not! — read Raymond: your EYES WILL FALL OUT if you do).

Lastly, much as I would love to comply, I'm not at all sure of this "w.c." bizness. If by w.c. you mean wool closet, I did not during my brief stay have occasion to view my companion's woolens — sorry again, Wen', and best of luck in your continuing getoff w/ the volume at hand.

NO-FAULT BITTERNESS

Dear _____,
   No more phone. No reason. Leave me alone. (Thanx.)

                                              Raoul Muzzler

2 PHOTOS, 2 THOUSAND WDS.

I've got poison oak now (first time) and in '69 Wayne
Dana had it on his ass. We were headed south on some freeway, him steering one-handed while rubbing oak ointment or
possibly ivy on his afflicted parts, pants down so he had to rush
'em up when a cop stopped us for backing up a ramp after the
car'd kind of exited itself and Wayne didn't feel like circling all
the way around to get back on again. Our officer, one thor-
oughgoing dunce (I thought then, my first conscious moment
inside L.A. County), sifted through our soda empties hoping
to find a beer, even sniffed at Cokes and Sprites ("Some dirty
sneaks use the cans for cover"), but Wayne had been such a
greasy whale behind the wheel (near-deathed us a couple
dozen times along Big Sur) and such a chud in general (believe
me) that by this stage of the trip I no longer trusted him to
keep our collective ass off flypaper. So I'd stopped stocking the
car with booze — paranoia pays off sometimes.

Us: me, Holly Charwyn, him, his galperson Kris (a/k/a
"Popeye" — she had the arms), their enormous brute Great
(as in Dana), who shared the back seat with me and Holly.
Trip: one of those pathetic late-sixties mistakes (by New York-
ers) (in California). Like Holly had wanted me to take her to
goddam *Europe*, no way I was gonna fall for that one; finally I
got her to settle for a trip to

(250)

"the coast" with the formerly *benign* whale who had introduced us the previous December. Having already been there
(Monterey Pop, the Haight), I couldn't at this point really give
two shits about the place, just wanted to kill the summer taking drugs, watching the Mets — but I hadda take her *some-
place*.

So we hooked up with Dana in Oakland, stayed a week in

this one-bedroom, 18-person crashpad where we started realizing 'something' about the limits of our respective friendships with fatfuck Wayne, also 'bout those of our younglove whatsis with each other — like how we'd been a matched pair of expediently ruffled chipmunks gathering acorns against the stormwindy winter (but here it was SUMMER), how scream-it-from-mountaintops *bored* we were after only seven months. Younglove's sometimes like that.

After bickering daily (me, her; us, the Danas), competing nightly for space on the bathroom (dining room) floor, visiting the zoo *twice* and doing our darndest to ignore the original Moonwalk, which the crashpad majority (Danas included) couldn't be talked out of watching, finally we and the Danas were off to points south — destination Mexico. But since Wayne would let no one else drive, not for an hour, we stopped only where he felt like stopping and — once there — fug us. We lunched and supped on tourist crap in windmill-fucking Solvang; spent motel nights (and bucks) in Anaheim and Torrance 'cause he didn't feel like sleeping under stars along some beach; wasted days pursuing a runaway Great through the streets of Watsonville, Oceanside and

(500)

Camarillo. Worse, we had to endure Popeye (two years after the Summer of U-Know) ranting on about incense and "together cookery," exhorting our driver to drop trou at noon on the highway — "Wayne, be *natural.*" That plus howling-ass crazy Great, who would go insane at the sight of *splashing water,* lying and drooling on our laps (and not theirs). 'Shared adversity,' forcing us momentarily back to acorn winter, is probably what kept us, Holly and me, from breaking up forever in Pacific Daylight Time. Kept us together — kept us *stuck* together — for another seven humdrum, stagnant years. Inertia's often like that.

So by San Diego *this* has happened and *that's* happened, like the night in Del Mar where in a frenzy we dumped amphetamines out the window when Dana turned the wrong way (one way) straight into (looked like, false alarm) cops. This, that, and by San Diego we've opted, sensibly, to go (by twos) our separate ways. Me and Holly get set to fly home and our final night, to salvage the trip, I get tattooed (left shoulder: tombstone with "Mom"). All four of us then catch a triple feature in this old theater with a foot of popcorn on the floor, *Cincinnati Kid, Cheyenne Autumn* and *The Sergeant* for 95¢. Mostly raucous/rowdy young military inside, middle days of 'Nam (which I had that spring 4-F'ed out of — half the reason, the non-Holly reason, for the trip) ('celebration'), but not until the last scene in *The Sergeant* do

(750)

any utter a *peep* of recognition that the flic might have a, uh, homosexual sub- (or not so sub) plot. Finally Rod Steiger kisses John Phillip Law and the place lets out this unison shriek/groan/yowl of *Omigod!!* (In three weeks they'll be maggotfeed in Asia.) We then head for the car, beside which I take an urgent whiz. As I zip up these uniformed goons approach, not cops, not military: we're parked, oh great, next to a *jail*. "Okay, who urinated?" — guns drawn, they mean biz — exacerbated by Wayne's insistence that Great (my designated culprit) could not have caused such a puddle. "Then we'll just have to lock yas *all* up for 72 hours' scrutiny as nonitemized undesirables."

Fuckin' Wayne and two years later I still hadn't forgiven him, but at two-and-a-half, when Holly shot this pic, things got warmer. Here we are at Ulster County (N.Y.) Community College, where he — left, fatter than ever — has somehow become an instructor in history. He's also arranged for me to lecture, $25 to speak on I haven't (at photo time) a clue; been drinking since my bus arrived and by talktime, an hour hence, I'll be incoherent. To our right, Earl Panter, former schoolchum of ours (and manager at the moment of Brackish Light, for whom we've both written lyrics for which we've not been paid) as well as Holly's ride up ("*Anytime*, little lady"), who after I've been urged (dragged?) off stage with only five minutes gone in my

(1000)

The Hermes Record Company Christmas Party, winter before I finally fled New York. Not much of a turnout. Holly's there, me, Mike and Lona Tusk, but only because RCA didn't invite us to *their* Christmas bash. (Nor Warners to theirs.) Present: twelve, possibly fifteen exclusive of staff, and that's including not only us but the sole Hermes act to show — perchance to strut — those fabulozoolous N.J. Gurls. Not much of a crowd to strut for (or at) but strut they do. This is, after all, the Midnight Hour of their big! year! — an image fostered, an LP out on a (nearly) major label, ready to burst out regionally — nationally — interplanetarily. The bartender, meanwhile, could not care less, nor the publicists, secretaries, A/R people, me, Mike, our womanpersons. *Nobody cares.* A heavy dose of 'alienation' — but isn't that what these louts sing about? Isn't it precisely what they *stand for*? Sure, yeah but only in context, that context being: nonironic megastarhood (per se).

As one strut gambit fizzles they call on another. Posture/preen slowdance gives way to a cha-cha, a tango. The first hour passes. A polka? Mama said there'd be nights like . . . nobody's even *talked to them.* Let alone kissed their megastar — ministar — anystar — boots 'n' ass. More baffled than daunted — what *gives?* — they launch into a more furious calisthenic, an arguably less nonrockrollish type of step. Abandoning room center, they degroup and reel about, dervishing into people, recoiling in mock embarrassment to kissy kiss pouty pout. Round and

(250)

round they spin, but random as their motion appears they never come within four yards of me and Mike, stationed at the macaroni salad. Although who knows whether it's the mac (a threat to tummy lines?) or us (a six-month grudge) they're avoiding, they keep away like there's a force field around us. Us the only writers . . . them the only band. A force field with razor blades. "Imagine," blurts Mike, "guys *pretending* to be fruits!"

Which seems hardly the issue. You may not believe it, but this was *before* choreographed, telegraphed insincerity was the name of the rockroll game; before, in any event, it was mandatory. Had there, you might ask, been a prior "people's band" with so *negative* an existential reverb, who had even as shtick been so thinly, merely "about" things rock, who had tendered this aboutness as so lame a claim of novelty and, yes, *integrity*? Hey, c'mon, what *weren't* they full of shit about? (Ersatz androgyny being just too fat, too hand-delivered a target to be suckered into rockthrowing ANYTHING at.) "You think," says Mike, "it gets 'em laid?"

So I'm standing by the mac salad, occasionally dipping my fork, when Davy Joe Gurl yells out, "Save some for meeee!" Oh? So I fling a forkful the twelve feet between us. Aim: good, true but an inch or so short, just missing the lead Gurlboy's red leather britches, which lemme tell you are g-g-gorgeous. Truly, though, leathers are far from absorbent (have worn them myself so

(500)

I know); would not have been stained by the foodstuff. Still he throws a shit fit, a laudable series of jagged, angular, (perhaps) genuinely bemused oh-how-*could*-yous accompanied by arm flails, invective and general harumphing by his cohorts. Twelve feet, maybe less, yet I stand firm, Mike stands firm, no real threat apparent. As perfect a show of rockroll sound-fury/harmless-from-the-getgo as any Phil Collins or Madonna (f'rinstance) would later, via video, bring to the mainstream foreground as *product*.

Eventually we're outside, me, Mike and company on

the north side of 57th Street, Gurls on the south throwing snowballs at us. Again we stand firm, cheek-turners like you wouldn't believe — or at least a pair of "toughies." Our women, meantime, unhip to the bogue marrow of the attack (or dreading our complicity in the whole bum charade), curse us and back their heels to a storefront. Minutes slide, ten, fifteen, as not one frozen *dootz* hurled by these New Age beatboys hits anything but trashcans, lamp posts, passing taxis. Not us — true — and we're not even dodging or ducking. Which can get mighty stale, even tough guys get tired, we're tired, drunk and hoping these turkeys, these duds, who will pull no more ultimate weight than to make the world safe for Mötley Crüe give up soon 'cause we ain't quitting first.

Nuh way, then who shows up but Earl Panter, intent on adding the Gurls to his managerial stable (having evidently struck out with Bonnie Raitt and Foghat at the

(750)

Warners blowout), who by now owes me between five and six thousand dollars (more than I've made all year otherwise) for my share of royalties on "Like Hansel and Gretel," an admittedly retrograde Brackish Light B-side dashed off in nine minutes on a napkin, and who has (if small clues be trusted) been "wooing" Holly at our apartment third Monday of every month (when, conveniently, I attend wrestling matches at Madison Square Garden). At which point Holly emerged to take a series of pics in which this winner was fourth or fifth.

Though her flash has rendered us indistinguishable blurs, I suspect that's me on the left, Mike right. Our homogenized features give no hint of mindset, but our rotation (towards frame right) suggests we're facing the spot where Panter, having paid respects to Holly, has stepped off the curb headed south at 6th Avenue. If in fact I'm smiling (my only nonfrown of the night) it's in response to the wind blowing off his railroad cap, exposing an everenlarging baldpatch, and/or the fate that befalls him as he stoops to retrieve it: snowballs to the ribcage and back thrown by members unknown of a rock-band whose business he craves.

After which I subway home with Holly, certain that we've just witnessed the planet's latest giantstep in Dying. A take she vehemently rejects, thus upgrading it (as I fitfully attempt sleep) to the first official increment of my own march to Dust. "You're no one to talk about

(1000)

MUSIC, DEATH AND BREASTS

A wimoweh, a wimoweh, a wimoweh, a wimoweh, in the jungle, the mighty jungle, the . . . *ah, shut up*.

THE EARL PANDA STORY

WEDNESDAY IS A DAY FOR BALDIES: center of the week like the center of a pineapple ring. From out of a pineapple can. Fierce fibers of pineapple radiating out from . . . from nothing. Cut 90 or more degrees from the ring and you've got yourself a *perfect baldy* — the way they usually "R." Very few have much up front if there's pineapple-magnitude nothing on top. Unless of course they're *Wednesdays by choice* of the Friar Tuck persuasion, and what a choice that would be!

Most WBC's take it *all* off: Telly, Yul, Richard Moll, Kareem Abdul-Jabbald, Marvelous (though what's so marvelous about bald?) Marvin Hagler of the World Boxing Council. World Bullshit Council meantime includes in its ranks EARL PANDA, whose "choice" — get this — is to cover his bald with a ballcap! Well it's not a complete bald, not yet, but under the headgear (who's he foolin'?) he's taking the *fast train to Wednesday*, a ride from which there is no return.

Tick tick tick, it's Tuesday 11 p.m. for not only YOU, Earl, but Sean Connery, Hulk Hogan and a guy you don't know named Dan "Tex" Barton. Tuesday night, better shop early — nightmare of first Wednesday just around the bend. Pharmacies report brisk sales of inositol and choline, and at no additional cost an FWC (First Wednesday Comb). Its teeth, limper than the hairs they groom, will not yank and are made from Wednesday pages of *TV Guide*: Ed Asner reruns at high noon (middle of a Wednesday is as middle as it gets).

There *are* Uncle Tuesdays (there *are*): insecure Wednesdays who shield their affliction be means of a doily de scalp. Hats off to them for their trickery, but not on a winter's day. Wind-chill a dome's thickness north of the cerebrum is no laughing matter. Science tells us: frostbite on one Wednesday too many and you're *Wednesday unto Thursday*, and Thursday's the day for off-the-wall. Hairlessness — miserable, comfortless got-none — in a hairist society will do it every time. "Leak in the Wednesday ceiling" — Earl Panda in how many years?? — equals bats in the belf.

Sometimes on a Thursday you will see baldies in the street with their "spots" uncovered (esp. in summer): it's Indian Wednesday! Tuesday p.m.'ers who have delayed "it" beyond the limit: Indian Tuesday.

Wednesdaes — sundaes with nothing on 'em, just a plain ornery scoop of ice cream — come in fleshtone flavors only: vanilla, chocolate, banana, strawberry; in some states, vanilla fudge. The Baskin-Robbins Wednesdae Deluxe features three scoops, each topped with a pineapple ring. Not surprisingly, reaction has been poor, as orthodox baldies find it redundant, and their calorie-conscious brethren avoid it like the plague. "Hold that ring; center is plenty for me!" (Baldpate plus belly is a fate worse than pasta fazool.)

Favorite celebrations of baldies: Xmas (Yul-tide) and wed.dings. Which explains why: Santa wears a hat (right); bald husbands (over 50) are a common sight. NEXT FAVORITE: Presidents' Day. A little known fact (but baldies all know it): Zachary Taylor and Ted Roosevelt (prez #'s 12 and 26) were *secretly bald*. Earl Panda's favorite, Franklin Pierce (#10), had *receding hair*.

A cure for Wednesday??? There is no known cure. If you don't wanna look like a billiard, better save that "fallout" and stock up on Krazy Glue. Not a proven fact: without mop strands to block them, brain waves can more readily enter and escape for telepathic, telekinetic and telebusiness purposes. (It has not yet been proved.)

NUMBERS NEVER LIE — Since 1945 there have been 230 more Wednesday the 13ths than Friday the 13ths. (Bald statisticians should have a field day with that one.)

Wednesday literary quiz. Circle in blue the tome penned

by a baldy (hint: don't be swayed by titles): *The Earl Panda Story*, *Panda's Progess*, *Earlpanda of Wednesdaybrook Farm*, *Under Earl's Yankee Cap*, *The Earl of Baldy Cristo*, *Earl Panda Owes Me Ten Thousand Bucks*, *Earl Panda Dies Screaming*, *White Whine Winos Go West*. Correct answer: *White Whine Winos* by Booth Tarkenton, his unsuccessful sequel to *Making Martha Cry* (Pulitzer Prize, 1952). He was bald as a beet.

WHAT'S THIS about a Wednesday Conspiracy? According to sources inside bald terrorist org Ash Wednesday, baldies will soon be invading the loo, replacing our Head & Shoulders with Nair! Next thing you know there'll be Neet in our Dry Look, Bikini Bare in our Dep For Men. This could mean war . . .

VFW? *Very* fuzzy Wednesday. Rug, carpet, astroturf, toupee, teepee, wig: all wigged out! Uncle Wednesdays? Sure, we've got 'em: natural thatchers who sport such fuzz to masquerade as fakesters and get on a baldy's good side. If discovered there are no hard feelings, unless that is they are undercover shocktroops of the Anti-Wednesday Squad.

Official translation though is *veterans of foreign Wednesday*, gentlemen who lost it overseas. Peacetime, wartime, what's the diff? When Woden rears his ugly follicles it's goodbye shrubbery, be it on Guadalcanal or in S. Vietnam. *Agent Orange & the Wrath of Woden* — a great title, huh? If a baldy wrote it they'd give him the No-Bald Prize.

Wait! Stop the presses, they've found it! The WODEN PAPYRUS has been unearthed in a suburb of Oslo. Woden was — it says here — a Q-ball himself! Says also that Haircules (while not to *previous* knowledge a Norseman by birth) played a hand in . . . well they haven't deciphered that much yet. Would be premature to speculate, so let's talk about the *hire the Wednesday* campaign. No big thing, hire a baldy: it's only for one day a week!

LIKE HANSEL AND GRETEL

Take a sandwich from the basket
And pass it my way,
I'm as hungry as a child could be.
Though we've lost our direction,
This picnic ain't bad,
The root beer is killer
And you're lookin' so fine.

So don't you think that it's time to boogie,
Shakin' leg on a hyacinth petal?
Good God-a-mighty, we're just like Hansel and Gretel!

Take the boots from your ankles
And lay them aside;
Ain't your pants kinda tight at the hips?
Dad and mom ain't around,
There's no need to be shy;
When you're ripe, babe, you're ripe,
It's a crime to confine it.

Aren't you glad we're a mile from nowhere,
Left the water boilin' home in the kettle?
Good God-a-mighty, we're just like Hansel and Gretel!

Wolves have eaten our breadcrumbs,
There's no more trail,
We're the guests of the buzzards and toads.
But the fire within, girl,
Will warm us tonight
and this picnic bologna
Will fill you 'til dawn.

We got a whole load of backwoods emotion!
Good a-rockin' in some mighty fine fettle!
Good God-a-mighty, we're just like Hansel and Gretel!*

---

*Words and music by Muzz Richards and Floyd Rochambeau. Copyright ©
Shitty Li'l Tunes, Inc. All rights reserved. Used by permission.

I NEVER FUCKED MY SISTER

Wayne went out with my sister. Didn't fuck her. Earl went out with her too. Same result. Can't really knock 'em for trying, I tried once myself in the 9th or 10th grade. Our forebears gone out anniversing, we watched a Bing Crosby movie then a Dan Duryea movie then a Forrest Tucker movie as I inched close, crept close with my brains bounding and my blood pounding and I reached 'round and found/felt her titnotyet, cupped cloth over titnotthere, but I can't lie, I won't lie, I probed not between (nor beneath) (nor behind) for her fawn warm particular, and I ne'er got to sensate her eatmeaty mystery, to know, love and linger in eternalnot sweet daydamp multiradiant napkinwhite monochrome savage dull vacantthrobbing allnight nonight drywild still rivulant irrigant arrogant aberrant errant nappy snappy toasty yeasty thirsty pasty smooth verticalnurturing sour calm sheethot gumthumbed thighhigh rumpplump footloose shoeleathersquidsatin storied moneyed squalid valid varicose bellicose viscous bisquous lifedangering strangering fullservice foolflattering clattering madgladding highwaywidened dreamtime realtime wraparound flaparound socktight assbare whiskeyswilling swineswollen graceboding ambushgoading asymptotic urneurotic peevented shescented mousenested quacktested sheepshorn seatorn thinsweaty readyteddy doorlocked lockbroke luckstruck indeliblestaining squeezeteasy allknown allknowing soleconceiving nevergreenpainted undefileddefiled puddingbeyondknowing beyond imagining.

EIGHT REPUGNANT RASHES

Well, it's not oak, this rash I've got, it isn't responding to storebought oak salve, or even ivy. Rhulicream, Rhuligel — I endorse 'em, they're great — no improvement. Time to move on to storebought cortisone — Cortaid — ½% hydrocortisone (antipruritic). Oh! sore, unresponsive flesh! But what the hoot izzit?

What first appeared two weeks back as a pale pink welt, or group of welts, that *itched*, Jack, itched as only some rare nasty bugbites, heat rashes or plant poisonings can, now seems more like a colony of detentacled sea anemones moored to (and feeding off) my lower right thigh. Shoulda been suspicious when they didn't bleed when scratched, popped or bumped against but emitted this thin discharge, more blistery than pus-y, and that's what they really resemble: blisters. But not burn blisters or sun blisters — I never go near the sun.

Oh! poor, defenseless mortal shell! Defenseless against *what*, though?

Plausible seeds of my ailment: TV soot, cheese mold, sink mildew, window sludge, an atlas from the '30s found in MacArthur Park, newsprint . . . Wait — cheese mold? cheese mold on a *leg*?? But file cabinet microbes could do it, right? Or door-hinge verdigris. It has even been alleged that the stanza

> Any god whose NAME can not even be
> damned can go right out &   Fuck
>   Him
>   Self.

which I submitted to the Santa Monica Poetry on the Buses contest might've been more pivotal than matter in causing my mange, though I've gotta reject this as too long a longshot.

Any divinity pissed about such truck would f'r sure have caused it elsewhere — on the pud, say, or tongue or eyelids — but still, long as I've got it, I will not tempt the cocksucker by touching such parts after handling — treating — it. Nor shall I handle my meat, or anyone else's — for any purpose — before washing — sterilizing! — my hands after contact with windows or curtains or certain dictionaries or telephone grime or lamp dinge or etc.: believe it!

The Riddle of My Forearms: not much of a riddle. But at first I thought, well, something I ate, octopus in cottonseed oil or maybe . . . but I already knew — and didn't wanna know. It was the *sweater*. And sweat: wool and sweat — sweaty wool.

An offseason gift, crew-neck, bulky-knit, tan and black striped; a high school beauty. Maybe it was already April, but why not look kool for the cuteys? On the very first wearing it came, both inside wrists, right where my shirt sleeves, though buttoned, couldn't quite shield me from sweater: what the @#$%?? Looked kinda like burn flesh, but not fresh burn flesh — permanent burn flesh with grafts & stuff. So much for koolness.

Since I couldn't wear just a shirt over the thing — cuff-buttoned longsleeves were and still are for *simps* — and suddenly, implacably, it was shortsleeve season anyway — I hadda continue wearing wool over a longsleeve over paired dressings over efflorescent pulp through the onslaught of serious spring. I could've, I suppose, worn a sweatshirt, but then I'd've really been a simp. Good thing I didn't have gym that term, I had hygiene.

A pair of gauze squares, changed daily, with boric acid ointment — a shot in the dark. In a couple weeks it went from burn flesh to white blotches in reddish pink rotmeat, then unblotched rotmeat, till finally it was chickenskin, then prickly heat, then nuthin' — just veins and wrist skin — gone!

And on my hand I had this pox once, no, twice I thought was cancer. It didn't itch, it didn't spread, not out, around, just up and outward. Round, red, between an index nail and thumb nail in width — a single bulbous bulb like a bloody eyeball. When the nurse saw it she said, without prompting, "Ooh, red eye" — but not bloodshot: a red iris and pupil and a red white part — both red — with rhino skin rimming the base and a scab from when I banged it and it bled like a faucet — a blood faucet — this was some gruesome humdaddy.

So I ask the doc, "Is it cancer?" — thinking if so, what? hand cancer? skin cancer? sun cancer? — like I said, I avoid sun like sin, but who knows, maybe it's not only universal by now but *compulsory* — if I got it this once I will get it again (and again!) just from racing from my door to other doors or the nearest shady overhang — a gallon of sunscreen to go mail a letter — but turns out it's just a HEMANGIOMA.

A wha? "Benign tumor of dilated capillaries." So they cut the muther out, and when it grew back they cut again — keep it.

Almost as red was the variably swollen whelk around a fleabite on my neck which got infected when I scratched it with bacon grease nails: a rocky ruddy atoll. Actually it was less red than purple — purple like a bruise — but viewed head-on it was a perfect circle, as perfect as the Johnson & Johnson Sheer Spot that gave it shape, and whose adhesive gave it life: nice target for an icepick. Treatment with Vaseline Intensive Care — you should always care for your epidermal scuzz — made it a shiny atoll . . . a purple worm . . . a small glazed donut. From then on it was hypo-allergenic for me . . . such a hypersensitive son o'bitch.

Speaking of bandaids: the day, leading up to the night I didn't fuck my sister, that I self-abused it so much that it ended up abused. The entire morning, afternoon and early eve I thought of it, thought about our parents' night out, and couldn't keep it in my pants, and couldn't help but flog it, flogged it six — yes — six! times! — my second highest total for a single day. Abrased, *raw*, in one spot especially, amplified perhaps by the dirty bandaid on my middle finger (nature of affliction forgot).

I say perhaps 'cause what'd *I* know, I was too dumb to even rebandage after odd (or even) flogs. Could it be diseased? I wondered after not-fucking her — though what could it've been, a dose of D.V. (Digit-inflicted Vitals-blight)? — and thought gee how providential that I hadn't spread it to 'er little twat. (Even losers dream ornate.)

The seen and the unseen. — Chronic but so far nonterminal. Bottom half of the back of my head.

A rash, a bite or a pimple? — always in doubt. It itches so I scratch it so it bleeds and pains and inevitably gets infected: scalps are the floormat of the head. Neosporin doesn't always help, not overnight, and every time it doesn't — this has happened 20 times — I think: Is this the one, finally, that *won't* heal, that will only puff out and fester and curdle and creep down my neck and up my brain and . . . dazz all folks? This is where the end begins?

So far Gibraltar has crumbled and Everest tumbled and I'm still standing/sitting/lying here. Maybe next time tho.

Seen & unseen (2). — Pink lace panties. Hally's, but I was wearing. A party in Brooklyn. My own underpairs were all in the hamper. Was winter so I borrowed one. Licking whoever it was's puss in the commode. Afraid if I took my pants off she'd ask questions — the light was on — I kept licking longer than nec. So long that finally Hally banged the door on my head (I'd neglected to lock it). Whatever her name leapt up off of my face.

A week later, just below the lip: crust, excrescence, and dripping, stinging ICHOR. Days passed and the drip, the sting continued. Could I deny the obvious? — I could not. Lip syph: curable, but *still* . . . poor baby. You would think the incubation would be longer, like how 'bout *two* weeks, but what the hey . . .

So I ask the doc, "Is it syphilis?" and he says No but not

what — silence — and my silence — and I slip out before he charges for the visit. . . . Just another nonchronic, nonfatal exanthema!

Then there were the zoots on my balls, or pustules, whatever they were. I often get spots on my nuts, but these were so ripe it was scary. One on my left, two on my right — a week before I was scheduled to leave for Quebec. In those days, wherever I was going, I expected to "get some" on the road. On the fly. At least take it out and flap it. Since you couldn't, in all fairness, blame étrangers for sidestepping scrota with pus-pimps — and the weenies and people that came with them — a drastic solution seemed in order.

Vitamin E, I'd been told, is good to rub on things: scabs, scars, y'know, so why not nut zits? When after two days of oily shorts, oily jeans I noticed no change, I switched to Cruex. Quite effective (and refreshing) on jock itch, over three days of spraying it proved less so on scrod lumps. On to tincture merthiolate — *yow* — day-glo pink, pink-orange walnuts — but it still don't go 'way so with time running shorter I squeeze 'em: pop!: naught but pimples. Or pustules — former pustules. Vive Kaybek!

GAS — FOOD — LODGING — VOMIT

"Lloyd's the name, lovin's the game" — that's how they met. I'd met her myself at a record store a half block from my dentist. When I brought two albums to the register and she rang up but one, I went back, got six more and she rang up the price of a 45. In time I went in not even to buy, and for a while, up to a point, we were like *this*. The day Jim Morrison died we sat around in our underwear (it was hot) listening to sides. Though occasionally we'd kiss and once, maybe twice, she let me nuzzle her tits, we never exchanged fluids, and I only tried once. Close so-called friends. So close that each year for two-three years we commemorated the date of our first meeting, which she'd marked down in her little green book, with bloody marys at the Buffalo Roadhouse. She was the only one I knew who would go with me to *Kiss Me Monster* and *Necromania* on Times Square.

I saw less of her tho after I took her to a Bräke Lite session where Lloyd came over and nudged me, "Who's the bitch?" Bräke Lite — what a shitty name for a shitty group, who after three years of 2nd-unit psychedelia called a meeting one day to consider the question, Can we become a heavy metal group? No, then what about semi-heavy? Sure, why not, let's — and they did. Lloyd played bass.

Once in a while I sent him lyrics which maybe one time in ten he put music to, which you might stretch, I guess, to say we wrote songs together — a functional, if not mutually profitable, arrangement. Beyond that, before the wedding, there was no great surfeit of mutual outpour between us, and but the flimsiest of bases for reciprocal nonaggression (let alone esteem). What he saw in me was I tolerated, didn't outwardly object to, his antisemitism. What I saw in him was he hated Earl Paynter — "I hated Earl before you were born."

I saw less of her 'cause I didn't wanna risk seeing more of Lloyd, see him call her bitch — slut — shrew — to her face, or rip up her crosswords, or punch out her brother over a football bet, altho even before he began pulling that crap I kind of had trouble just sitting with Annie, alone, watching her sew buttons on his shirts. Lloyd's cooties ("aura") had invaded and pervaded our friendship — to play with her was to play with him. For a long time I didn't go near their apartment, and I stopped phoning her, "Don't bring Lloyd" — she'd've brought him anyway, and even if not she'd've brought his cooties — and saw little of either of them. All this changed after Sam the drummer's wedding.

At which I really only did two things, mainly two, two majors, only one of which was truly my doing, my *intent*. First, well, that's the one that wasn't — I walked through a plate glass door. Actually, in fact, it wasn't even through, just as far as — into — it shattered at my feet. Everybody was all concerned, abuzz, until they realized I wasn't injured. I hit it with my head and my knee, this was at night, outside looking in, somebody's house in New Jersey. The door was so clear, so clean, and inside so lit, so festive and inviting, I just started marching and — thungo — my forehead made contact and my knee, still in motion, met and smashed it. A total accident — honest! — which is really too bad, 'cause till then I was in a tolerable mood. Hadn't had more than two or three drinks, but when it became obvious I wasn't hurt, not a scratch to noggin or kneecloth, it was instant fuck you, you drunk, pay for it. Gimme a break.

And two, the second, well maybe 2a and 2b — an hour later — was do the grind with the groom's mom. A slow dance, tight, my hands roaming, occasionally groping significant anatomy. A kiss initiated, returned, fondles accelerated, unresisted (at least not noticeably resented). I reached down her leg to lift gown and slip — that she resisted. Another kiss, closed-mouthed but real, a two-way squeeze — then Harrie poured a highball over both our heads. (Assist to Harrie.)

106

After which nobody would speak to me but Lloyd. The only guy in the band, and not only speaking but digging — "You wrecked the wedding — you were great!" The last one, all things being equal, I would wanna speak to, and he starts calling me once, twice a week, let's do stuff. A sucker for acceptance of my hellionhood, wholly merited or un-, I complied. I could probably rationalize it in terms of how he'd prob'ly now write the music for *two* of my lyrics in ten, a task which at this point nobody else in the band was gonna touch, but the self-interest animating this routine was cheekier and cheesier than that. Male bonding: a sick joke then as today.

Two-three times a month I made the rounds with him: arguing baseball, breaking lightbulbs in elevators, releasing live roaches in the 8th Street Nathan's. Usually we met outside, so I still saw little of Annie. One time at their place — she was out — he showed me remnants of a Moroccan hash pipe he'd smashed with a shoe when he found her smoking it. "I don't want her doing that shit." "Hash? What's the big fucking —" "Don't make me talk about it. It gets her goofy. She cuts her hair, does her eyes, comes out like a freaking social worker." "So?" "A dyke social worker." "Yeah, so?" "*You* go live with a dyke social worker." I withdrew from the bond for a while.

Then one night he calls and it isn't to do stuff; Annie has left him. "You're an asshole — why shouldn't she leave you?" "What's that gotta do with anything?" "You sound funny." There was this hollow, echo-y sound. "She took the furniture. I was rehearsing, I come back — the bitch cunt whore took everything." Moved in with a coke dealer. Lloyd hated coke, had always "forbidden" her to use it. "It's a bitch to find a place," I blithely assert. "She couldn't just move without moving *in*."

So I went up there, 18th and 9th, and not solely, or even especially, to commiserate. With my own relational charade at critical mass or close, it seemed a signal occasion to prewitness the wallop of long-delayed inavertible breakup — breakdown — the heartbreak of heartbreak — repudiation, remorse, reprisal; all such shuck; to preview some parameters for my own merry coupling's impending implosion of love/hate/tedium/acrimony/etcetera. Relational end (nonhipsters would call it divorce): to make it, somehow, to the transcendentally inconceivable — too conceivable — *other side* and be done with it, even if far from done with being done; like watching the dying, having died, be dead, it looks easy but still, howdy do it? Curious and no less apprehensive — with Lloyd/Annie now done, the demise of me & Harrie, in this sequence at least, no longer loomed or lay as simply imminent but *next* — I dreaded it, welcomed it, but who, pray tell, could *I* move in with?? — which of us, Harrie or me, would even be the one to have to walk? — I took a tug of Lloyd's mezcal and surveyed the not-empty room.

Dusty black hardwood, no rug, no chairs, ten or eleven crushed beercans, fragments of vinyl and torn empty album covers, a kneehigh dune of papers, mags and clothing, some crumpled rock posters — "The cleanest it's ever been," I tell him; he belches loudly — a black phone, no clock that I could see, no stereo, TV or band equipment — "It's a good thing I left my amp at the studio."

But she hadn't taken the bed, seven feet tall with a ladder, eight feet — a table used to be under it. Too massive to mess with. She took the bedding tho. "You actually used to fuck up there?" "Fuck?" — he grunts, hands me the mezcal bottle — no glasses — "Y'mean *fight*. The bitch monster once kicked me, pushed me outta there." "Oh, you threw out her *New York Post*?" "Not that time — fucking commie rag. I told her she was ugly." "What a lovable guy. Who's the broad?"

I gesture at a thumbtacked glossy of a majestic blonde, the only item on a black, black wall. "My wife. I couldn't hang it while Annie was —"

"Your *wife*?" "Yeah." "How'd that happen?" "Oh, she came to see us play Stockholm. Gary's a minister in what's that, you send them a fin and anybody can, you know, so I got him to take out his card and recite these — we're not *really* married but *she* thinks so." "How could she be so dumb?" "Maybe she doesn't believe it, but she doesn't let on." "And she never called you here?" "I told her not to." "So you never fucked *her* in the bed." "I only fucked her in Sweden and Denmark and Amsterdam. And Paris." Pause. "Gonna call her tomorrow from Atlantic." "Tomorrow's Sunday." He thinks of something, jumps for the phone.

The Bed recalled. An afternoon three years before. Lloyd was out on tour. I brought beverages. At some point, apropos of nothing, and everything — the way of afternoon flesh — I eyed the ladder and the bed and I looked her in the eye and said: "I bet you often do it on the floor." "Oh no you're not." "Why not?" "*No*." "Annie . . ." "Keep dreaming." — Let the mummery begin . . .

Then I realized he was dialing the hotline. When he'd phoned me before with his big tale o' woe he'd been threatening it — to call this number from an ad for turning in dope dealers, y'know anonymously, and direct them at Annie's new beau — and I thought I'd dissuaded him. "Yes, my name is Howard Cosell. I'd like to report —" I grabbed the receiver, or tried to, at least got it far enough away from his face. He glared at me — why was I betraying him? — and shoved me off hard enough to also lose both halves of the phone, causing me to stagger backward into the dune, the waste heap of Lloyd/Annie detritus. Retrieving the receiver and finding connection lost, he yelled: "You shitfucker!" "Hey, fuck *you*. You're doin' it to show off for *me*. You wanna get drunk and smash windshields, let's get drunk and smash windshields. I'll buy another bottle." "The fuck ya got there?"

It was an old comic book, dislodged from the heap in my tumble. A beat back issue of I forget, *Metal Men*, *Metamorpho* — some defunct second-line D.C. Comic. Annie really loved comix, saved 'em — so why'd she abandon it?

Lloyd read the date, October or somesuch '66 — "This could be worth something." "Not in condition like that." Wrinkled and puffy like somebody once spilled something on it, its cover rang a faint, distant bell. Then we turned some pages and the reason, the reasons, well one reason, one for both — the beat, the bell — became evident, though by no means (in toto) to both of us.

"The bitch slut!" He got half of it anyway; how could he know that it wasn't, not strictly, a used one? Long dry it indubitably was: a pale leathery dried 6" salt cod with saffron highlights. The blue rubber ring round the unclosed end was the tipoff: it was clearly a Fourex. And the rusty staple — oh yes, I remembered — I'd stapled it there.

Yeah, right after she laughed off my shabby attempt if you c'n even call it that, when in the hoky heat of things, in pre-premature anticipation, I'd taken out the blue plastic container and bit the cap off, to which she actually did laugh — ha ha — it was probably funny. When she went and took a piss I found a comic and a stapler and I stapled it somewhere — even un-come-in lube bags are wet — cruelty to paper — and she never later mentioned it.

"The slut bitch!" He threw *Metamorpho* or *Metal Men* across the room, kicked a beercan, rocked in place clenching and unclenching fists and hyperventilating. To avoid provoking him further, I kept still as a stick till he muttered, "Let's go." "Where we going?"

We got a pint of Early Times and rode a cab to some number on East 35th. "You sure ya don't wanna just destroy some property?" I asked. That I coulda handled. "Let the air out of tires?" Silence. I passed him the bag; he declined. Outside Annie's new address he tore open and ransacked a dark green Glad bag, then another, in futile search of a suitably intimidating object. "Gimme your shoe." I gave him. He pressed upper-floor buttons at random until somebody buzzed. Refusing to participate in this phase o' the folly, I sat on the stoop sipping, gulping drearily, listening to banging inside and shouting — "Let me in, you pigs!" — must've been the first or second floor. Three minutes of this, maybe less, he comes out, tosses me the shoe, "They're not home. I need some smack."

Another cab, this time to the Lower East Side, where Lloyd harangued me while a tired middleaged white woman in a white bathrobe, her husband a.w.o.l., couldn't wait for us to finish snorting with a rolled up single off her pitted kitchen table and fucking *leave*. "This is what you should write about." "This?" "Smack. Doojy." "You think so?" Across from us she sat gloomily and fidgeted, at times almost twitching. "'S the only thing leaves every customer satisfied — no complaints." "You think?" "Well, whudda *you* know that . . ." When we left she prob'ly shot herself in the spleen.

Back at the shack, Lloyd had more left than I did, cert'ly more on-off, more nightspark. My entire goddam body felt like stone, craggy, no, smooth stone, with no moss tho possibly some insects. "You shouldn've drunk so much," he snickered. "Heroin and whiskey don't mix." We split the dregs of the former and I soon nodded off on a clump of clothing, but not befo' the following exchange:

"Y'ever bang a Swedish broad?" "Japanese, I think one was German or — no Swedes." "You dunno what you're missing." "You gonna fly her in here?" No answer. "Gonna fly her in here?" "The fuck do *I* know?" He says no more. I say no more. The next thing I know I'm in a pile of socks, face down, dirty socks and shirts. With great effort, I make it up to an elbow and see sun — or something — streaming into the far end of an otherwise darkish room. Though my vision be mud, I noticed Lloyd (or someone Lloydlike) at the window or portal through which or from which the beam appeared to gush.

From tip to toe every cell of me seemed dead. Getting up to piss was like hoisting a corpse, someone else's corpse, which hoisted with corpse energy was like carrying a truck. Pissing was like turning a stuck faucet with your nose, opening a hydrant with your teeth. The only sensation I felt one to one with was the fire in my eyes, twin pyres glowing *hot* in the wells of my face. Aflame and defective, they were not much use as eyes. I couldn't see dickshit, well, most wakeups I don't see much, but oh fuck — this 'splained it — my contacts were still in, my lenses; I hadn't had the sense to pop them out before retiring. Now they were all pasty, like mucilage or mushroom soup. I wrapped each in a fold of paper and slipped one in my left pocket, one in my right. Hadn't brought a lens case or glasses, didn't expect to spend the night. No specs, but it wouldn't have mattered anyway: the focal length of my biologic eyes had been severely altered. Happens and it happened — for a day or the remainder of (y'never know) a life. To match 'em with man-made lenses that actually made a diff could take a week.

Squinting my way to Lloyd, I caught him doodling in the margins of *Metal Men* (*Metamorpho*?) with a red ballpoint. "I've been writing her a song." "The Swede?" "No, Annie. Got the riff worked out and some words." "Words?" "An *awesome* first line." "Yeah?" He turned the comic sideways and read, "'When you love a whore.' Wanna help me write it?" "Not now, man." "We could rhyme 'whore' with 'more.'" "I gotta go." "Or 'door.' I'll share credit with you." "Gotta go-o-o-o-o." "We can title it, whudda you think of 'Lady of Pain'?"

No, I couldn't see beans, but there's one thing I saw clear as cake: the one who gets away at least *gets away*. Annie got away — away! — and I, too, would like to be the one to get away. Away from Lloyd but home (sweet home) to Harrie . . . *gotta* be the one that gets away. Pounding ill-seen streets, I quartered the distance, halved it, when the first pang of nausea gripped my parts. Another block and I lost it, massively vomming on the curb in front of — where was this? — a church. Splashes of bright, cheery color — oh, didn't I mention it was Easter? — April something, year of our Lord nineteen hundert sev'ny six. Little old ladies — and big — in the thrall of paschal bliss, and me urping regally down the front of my shirt — what a show.

Blind, smelly and homeward to Harrie: today is not the day to get away.

THE MODE

There's the mean, the median, the mode. The mean —
the average — would be, who knows, I don't see how it's aver-
ageable. The median — midpoint — is, well, give me an
hour . . . probably around Lynn Rausch or Muriel Skinner.
The mode, by comparison, is a snap. In the Full Index of
women I'f ucked, one name occurs more frequently than any

of the key. I rolled over, bit a piece off the nearest mortadella, con-

other: Della. Della Flett, Della Wintz or Mintz, Della
Schwartzcohn, and Della Veronico.

Della Flett, second infidelity of the Haddie Sherman
Era, first besides an "unplanned" falldown with a certain
N.L.F. — Name Lost Forev — had only one complete hand.
A finger had been lost (or misplaced) somewhere — I never
axed her how. A part-time receptionist, her undypants were
weather-beat and faded — the kind leery mothers warn you
not to wear. She made me pea soup and we bounced and
farted and laughed and she cried because I didn't love her.
True love, any love or no, our lovemeats seemed to *belong together* — young adultery's like that — and though I scurried
promptly home I would slink back for more on two (or possibly three) further occasions.

On the last roundup, post-bounce, she coveted my Spiro
Agnew T-shirt, which I told her I'd give her but not this time,
I needed to wear something home. She proposed a trade but
her own T's were too small, she moaned so I told her *really*,
nex'time (and meant it) but there wasn't a nex'time — All she
was good for, swore grim history and my penis, was to serve as
a fully formed falldown, a worthy vanguard entry on a roster
of backstreet falldowns, and having accomplished as much —
poor Della! — 'specially with new ones, *hot ones*, lining up on

backstreets nearer home: not interesting or mysterious or ultimately appealing enough so g'bye. . .

The perimeter of Della Wintz or Mintz — I can't 'member which — was immense, and so was her hollow. I filled it as best I could while filling in for John Swock from 3 AM to 6 — KKFP's "Reet Time" — though where I earned her fleeting gratitude, I would sooner compute, was out in her outer zone, with lips, tongue and related muscles. Spinning John's discs, engineering myself, at 3:30 I got up and wandered. Lights on in an edit booth — a colossal back, headphones, ponytail, tent

sumed the rest of it, and got up to survey the remaining slices. The

dress — fat chance. At 4 she came in, "Good show — is John sick? Stop by if y'got time." In ten minutes my lower face was down there, working — "Ooh honey — you really know *where*" — with swampland so vast I suppose it might be easy to miss things.

Incursions by my sausage, howev, even with exact coordinates plotted, were eventful but in no manner efficient. In all the vastness, as stiff and hot to pop as I was, once it was in there bumpin' and pumpin' I couldn't keep it *in* for a minute. Standing, one leg on the rung of a stool; from behind, slouched over the tape console; on her back, ass propped on a phone book — whatever the position, it kept flopping out although solid as a broomstub. Every so often I'd get up and rush pantless to the control room to change a record, cue an entire side of Sun Ra or Pharoah Sanders — was one person listening? — pulling my shirt down over my rod should anyone be prowling the corridor, and each time I got back she'd be in a new position awaiting another shot at it. Finally this one time she's standing there, dress up to her navel, she beckons me onto the stool. I sit, she mounts me — a solution — no slipping out with *her* beef cascading over me — and we rocked and heaved and I came and she went back to her editing.

Keepsakes of the x-perience: assorted chafed bodyparts

(from fiberglass on the rug); an uncommonly fragrant after-taste — as spicy as Thai food. Fat women're often like that — it's the extra sweat or something, the metabolism — but you shouldn't make fun of fatties — or at least do so sparingly.

Della Schwartzcohn of Della's Donuts — three South Bay locations — invited me home with her after a reading at the Either/Or Bookstore, Hermosa Beach. Following prelimi-nary necking she announced: "You can't fuck me, but I'll show you my behind." Just inside the crease, to the left, was a lick-on tattoo, slightly smeared, of a sad-eyed clown. She spread to

one closest to a full circle I saved, saved 'til it was liver-colored and

show me — "Don't touch" — revealing also an attractive set of rectal hairs. I told her so. "Well, what do you think of *this*?" — she turned and flashed, then covered, an unevenly shaved slit. Twenty minutes later she playfully (but actually) bit my dinger, and an hour after that we were fucking, sort of, in her primal-scream box.

Inside, but the door was open. The lining was bluish naugahyde, all four — all six — walls, counting the door. But-tons like on couches. A satin sheet thrown over it. No pillows. One of those long fucks whose duration is mainly illusion, which if it has any real energy or life to it might eventually find its legs but not this time — dozy, hovering between sen-sation and not, half the time stroking just to keep (or allege) the continuity or chuck it. Was she two-thirds awake? Still as pâté with her knees at a weird angle which no bodily encour-agement, gentle or athletic, could induce her to change, she got very animated towards the end, biting my ear and jabbing a nail in my neck, but respiring not a sound.

My earlobe was bleeding. Her eyes met mine sternly. "I came, but I didn't orgasm" — oh? "You'll have to go — I need an enema." "I'll help you with the nozzle." "Leave — *right now* — I don't know you."

Outside the whitecaps were saying . . . well they weren't

saying much. My ear was still bleeding, or let's just say bloody. I swore off random-person fumblings for a month.

"A Man Needs a Maid," that old Neil Young thing, I used to think a man needs a waitress — anyway it's what I told Ms. Della Veronico. I told her lots of things. Told her her job, my job — in many ways similar. She wore a uniform and I didn't, or if I did it was one changed five-six times a week, but anyway check it: WAITER . . . . WRITER. WAITER minus I equals WATER — that's cool. WRITER minus I equals WRTER — inotherwords bullshit. (There ain't no writing

rigid, more opaque than translucent, the size of a beer coaster, at

without the I.) But the single thing common to both waiting and writing: y'always give more than you get.

Waiters get tips, though, so why the deuce not writers? If diners can lay perks on people who risk blisters & backache dishing 'em stick-sizzly platters of flapwings in futt sauce (treacherous work but someone has t' do it), why not readers on ahtists who as vessels for ill-tempered muses are yanked pillar to post in the service of feeding & nourishing mankind — womankind — humankind — *non*alimentarily speaking? Give me, send me, a tip: I who enrich the world; who from the typer spout, gush, slobber love, far more love (yes: "that" kind of love!) than I'm ever on the rebound receiving — hey, maybe I don't love you a lot, but I do love you *some* — it's time you considered evening the score.

Hate to score it, but all I stand to make on this fucker after agent's fees, before taxes, unless half of Delaware buys it pre-remaindered, is 6400 bucks. Not asking you to house and suckle me, soothe and salve my worntorn prow from all this traffic with dawg-damn hostile *words* — sheesh — but at the very veryleast y'oughta send me — *any* writer you have scanned, skimmed, et alive this many chapters of — send them, send me, *something*. Since the most I can possibly realize from your purchase (or theft) is a percent of a percentage of a percentage, why not send me my percentage direct — 15% of cover price (unknown at time of writing)? That would buy my love (or make a feasible down payment) — cash of course preferable, but checks, bonds, stocks, food stamps and money orders OK . . . and if y'don't, I can't be worth a ding dang duck dick. C/o: Little, Brown & Co., 1271 Ave. of the Americas, New York, NY 10020. — Just a thought.

Anyway, Della. The Della I in fact spent the most time and sperm with: my 6th or 7th L.A. sweet, um, sweetperson — okay, you can call her my girlfriend. She was mine, she was

which point I flipped it, flung it, like a coaster out the window: the

mine! — 'til her boyfriend returned from Alaska. "He'll be back, don't forget" — in three months, but I bailed out after two. I just couldn't take the synthetic.

Her firm roundness was quitenice, and for a time quite sufficient. She wore stockings with the uniform, which made it nicer, when she could have got away with basic pantyhose. Within limits, I could have sat for a full nurturing puss banquet (menu changed daily). Expansive bedthink was strongly encouraged. But it had to be *in* bed — never outdoors or on the kitchen table. And it had to fit the Program, see, which made it all feel play-acted, forced, like hardly the fruit of nascent desire, of unfeigned young gal snatch itch. The ease seemed synthetic, the unease, whichever. While Chuck was up working the Pipeline (or was it the pipe shop?) she was keen on becoming a "complete woman" for him — a "woman of the world," a (this is a good'un) "real hot tartlet." My role, it dawned on me, was to help streamline her action for Chucky. She was ten years younger than I was.

When fucktime was nigh, she methodically asked: "Can we do it side-entry, but frontal, this time?" She would come real loud, and each time try and come louder. "Care for a little mouth-fuck? Ladies like to give it, you know." "On a scale of 1 to 10, how would you rate that?" Then I tried to eat her while she peed, and she closed her legs on me — "You're such a poozle hound!" (Chuck would never do a sickthing like that.)

A week after giving me a quaalude for my cold — "Try it, it works" — she took her top off at a party and to practice being "loose" — her theme that night — had me lick guacamole off one of her nips, then bean dip off the other. Looseness can tire you, and after subsequent servings of chocolate icing and onion dip (both declined) she departed for my place, our normal terminus — she lived with her parents — to sack

farewell fling of a pinch-hit poozle hound.

out for the breakfast shift at Du-Par's. I stayed another hour and on the way home stopped at 7-Eleven for a package of mortadella. Stealing in silent as a half-sotted ghost, I unwrapped the parcel and warmed it to room temp, then raised the covers and arrayed slices on the sleeping Della's belly, thighs and chest. Petting her muffin opened her legs reflexively, and I slipped her my dipstick with circles of greasemeat between us.

In the morning (had I heard her shower? dress?) she left without kissing me conscious. Beside the phone was her copy

NOCHE DE LA NUIT

Okay, let's ride — you wanna ride? Into the cold clear aromatic night. We'll drive leisurely to, well, let's make it Gardena this time, no . . . Long Beach. And as we're making speed you'll relive just like me the time in the boy scouts we hadda go out one at a time with this deluxe compass searching for landmarks each at so many paces, so many degrees east, south, whatev, and first stop inside the woods I put the thing down to look around and find whatever in hell I'm supposed to be looking for but I can't, my short-legged steps are way off the average only I'm too dumb to know that, and when I turn back around the compass isn't there, every stump looks the same, it's supposed to take five minutes and I'm gone thirty (and still no compass), what a four-eyed little scug . . . my yearly guilt, regret, remorse over the fucking *junk* I used to get coerced into buying my grandma, the one that looked like Martin Van Buren, for her birthday — powder puffs from Rexall for 35¢, plastic mirrors, rancid soap — why couldn't I just give her nothing? how could I let the bastards make me buy her such miserable rot? . . . the stone cold panic that swept and almost snuffed me the night the Melanie album I'd borrowed from C. only because she forced me got stuck on the turntable of B., who I was playing it for just to impress her that I a carnivore could actually be listening to such yech, and after side one we couldn't get it off and hours went by with me working harder and longer at loosening the record than her pantsuit — rotating it on the spindle, bending it 'til it almost broke — until finally it was time for me to scram home to A., for which I hadn't even preplanned an alibi, an exit, and B. didn't understand, didn't understand . . . and all variety of bad *baaad* horror terror shit. Sit back and n-joy it.

But first let's go to Sears for a half dozen snotrags. One

on Santa Monica Boulevard, west of Western. Now that the front entrance is sealed you gotta go in past actual bull shit: steer manure in the Garden Shop, great big stacks of it (bagged). Inside as always they're giving away digitals, or else it could be chains. In exchange for you sign up, apply for a charge card. Digital wristwatch, digital pen watch, gold-plate chain for your ostentatious neck à go-go. (— Choice of one, while supplies last. —)

It could be tomorrow, it could be tonight, it could be yesterday. It could be many days 'cause *most days* lately it's Russians applying. By the busload, run in from one of those "multipurpose" centers to cop some free — no strings — to full extent of law will allow. Same faces tonight, last night, maybe even some twice, three times per, keep the penmanship small (lines narrow), your name, your bank, and if you wanna make it look *really* good: your address, theirs, some income figures (real or contrived), mailing address (if diff.) you want your card rejection sent to.

Allow four to six weeks for etc., and doncha think it's really *jake* that immigrants are still getting melted, y'know into the Pot? *A round of claps* for their gumption, 'cause by now they have prob'ly got: chains for their children, digital for their dog, digital and/or chain for their shoe, sock, cock, clock and wok! Let's ride.

To the odor of oil rigs down La Brea — "the tar." Lights cake the dinge of our windshield like a colorized Utrillo. Girl Talk, a bar: pink lips on white, four of 'em. On the second tier of a lost & lonely minimall, U.S. Home Land Real Estate. Algiers Motel: nothing Algiersian about it. Dapper black guy dragging a bike with one hand pushes a late '70s Buick to a gas station . . . blue 76 on a red-orange pumpkin. Southern sky . . . drifting silver clouds. Railroad track at Exposition. Billboard for Toshiba, bus stop poster for Kirin Dry, what an e-z one: Yazuki wet . . . dry . . . *out to dry.* A relatively innocuous self-loathing.

Shoot, let me count the things I've felt or feel worse about than having "discarded" her, if that's what I did — cutting our amatory interludes from every week to every second or third after she'd elected to stay in New York to "be with me" — and what guilt there was/is was always halved, divvied out to both ends — me-me as much as me-her — not having the courage or audacity or mettle to allow myself a new full-time sweety, or a greater part-time one, though by then her once-imperative gully was feeling less so . . . and that horrible spray on her hair. Was it even guilt? Well — accountability. The self-conscious want of admissible alibis. A short-term squirm and even there we're not talking catastrophic, the kind that transcends mere culpability like, okay, my run-in with the Giant . . . college computer dance where F. and I figured the only way we could fix it to get each other would be to put ourselves both down as 6'7", both physics majors, Presbyterians, "totally uninterested" in sex, only instead I got this giraffe who must've been 6'5" with pale pained eyes that said *Oh fudge, and I was hoping real bad for some boy-height* and I felt such distress f'r her I couldn't talk and F. had to get me out of it by telling her I was *hers*, see, but hey she could still have F.'s computer match, this anemic scarecrow of 6'3" or 6'2", and afterwards I vowed to never ever be blithe again with defense-less anthropogeny, never again treat it "abstract." Which Kazuki wasn't, not defenseless, nor abstract: a semi-attractive MA in what was it, African studies? semiology? — and that Eagles show she made me go to, and all the fucking Zen she was making me read . . . the disfavor was more than generic . . . or maybe I choose to forget. In any case, painless. Comparatively.

Window open . . . strong scent of thistles and musty brush . . . souring weeds . . . Baldwin Hills the double spoiler — pamperer, putrifier — and double spoiled . . . as stagnant as if the whole soggy stretch had been enclosed. Roar of distant airplanes . . . sexual guilt, anger, grief — but whuddabout

"pleasure"? . . . fetor of plantdeath coalescing at last with —
here we go — well it's been stronger. Weak night for petro-
leum. Hilltop derricks, not derricks — those rigs with heads
like mantises, crickets, bobbing unlit against the sky. The
combined vapor suggesting, of all things, a New York subway
ride . . . incipient headache and choke of confinement . . .
boxed in by dark hills, a tunnel . . . except there's no crowds.
Just me 'n' — you still with me?

Smell of donuts we won't be stopping for. Smell of
chicken. You might be stopping but I won't. Nor following arrows to Hollywood Park or the Forum. Two streets named
Nutwood and Kelso. World Won For Christ Ministry. Mara-
Lu Nail Art. Marciano-Louis. Rocky versus Joe. Face beet-red
in high school fooldom. Some kid asks was Rocky any good, I
say yeah, he knocked out Louis. This guy overhears, butts in
like I'm a dummy that Louis by then was all washed up, and
Rocky's real (and only) distinction was his 49-0 record. Red
foolhood. Later I knew better. Prob'ly I knew then but not
better. Memorized datums ain't knowledge. Pugilist knowledge is power. Boxing guilt, grief, shame and anger. It was
months though not years before wins, kayos, draws at-
tained . . . pertinence. What I knew was I knew I'd know better. Was this the jump start of the better? Chump foolness.
You expect a reward for such foolness? Reward for such foolness is a bean pie and coffee at Inglewood Stop-Quik.

Ingredients: butter, pure vegetable shortening, eggs,
navy beans, sugar, cinnamon, nutmeg, certified color. Probably won't kill us. Not tonight. Shriek of a low-flying visible
whatzit, an L-1011? Working right to left on the north wall of
a Tune-Up Masters, workmen with a steam thing, a solvent
under pressure, purge the final letter from a spray-painted
phrase which without it reads, I CAN KILL YOU IF I
WANT TO AND I WIL . . . couldn't it wait until morning?
Imagine: a town — a city! — that can't love its own graffiti —
if that don't beat all . . .

Wait — hey — where's our keys? Furious slapping of jacket . . . pants, a rigorous probing of pockets — *gone*. Winds of panic blow fireicestorm blear icy knifeneck. 'D we leave them at, how'll we, how will *I* get in the, how c'n I drive — NO! they're in the ignition. (What a fucking wuss.)

The night is a there not a where, *there*: the Cockatoo Inn. There therefore no where where some where there all where . . . bad joke. So many many, so many many: lights. Taillight for sore eyes, headlight for your eyes, green the reddened greens of Eve Lach, yellow her neverworn squankflaunter briefs, red for the teaspoons of warm wine I once fed a baby, a tot. Hippie party, watch your step, toddlers underfoot. How could I do it but I did. Half a spoon, two halves — testing a hypothesis. Controlled trauma: give them a neutral (and harmless!) ad hoc jolt and their systems will momentarily overload, enough so even hefty draughts of Parental Squalor cannot in the short run filter through — the earlier you occasionally do this the better — besides, wine provides prime topical relief from the directed mayhem of Normal Parenting. "Child abuse"? Call it motherhood, fatherhood — child *rearing*. You don't agree? Then ride separate, dammit, I could use the space. Keep a car length away from me.

. . . so I give this impressionable lump of I dunno, 18 months, two years a lick of this cheap jug wine::yum that's good, gimme more. More, nobody cares, nobody's watching::giggles and gurgles and then the kid cries, cries — Bwah!! — where's Mommy? A hypothesis, by the by, I've long since abandoned, though if certain folks ever knew my name or my face they would probably by now've ripped the skin off my bones. Make it two lengths apart.

BUNK BEDS $169 — block letters tall as a car — DINETTE SET $89. Straight, straight — like driving through Jersey '63 — no building tall as a phone line. A mile and then another. And then another. One building tall as a phone line. A dull road but wide — the walls are not closing in. Two buildings taller than phone lines. Walls're not closing yet, and there's always the skylight, the ceiling. Can't evade the Void — night: There! — vertical infinity.

Several tall ugly buildings. Numerous tall ugly buildings. Low ugly buildings are like ugly friends (why is that?), but tall ugly? Raise high the Uncity. Hawthorne Plaza: *continuous* tall and ugly. Ugly grief & anger, no guilt save the guilt of still living here. Time was, time once, infinite vistas stretched horizontally as well — on a clear, unblighted day you could see 30 miles. Never too many clears, and 30 miles of so-what, but distance itself can be seductive. Now tall blocks the blocker, the blight — smog — and implies urbanization. The architectural cognate of smog, ha, only twice as pernicious and 46 times more invasive. Lawndale Medical Plaza . . . Lawndale Business Center . . . pink, green . . . four tiers . . . nautical pipe railing. Walls closing now — *fast* — quit yer honking — and what the poot's this? — a geyser, a flood. Truck leapt the curb and took out a hydrant. Lanes bogged to a slog — Let's get some ass on the freeway.

And hurry, shake it — before they gentrify Long Beach. 55 . . . 60 . . . 70'll do it. Postcards of distant ununcity. The usual empty magnificent. Tonight is no windhowling five-star eternity. Inscrutable rain-in-the yeh yeah it isn't. Nightcards of Jersey '63 '37 — the Blimp! the Blimp! — moored. Noshit. Goodyear Airship Operations. The goodword from Ben Kaiser Ford: Be compassionate with the Aged. I yam. I have. Henry the Hat. *Get you lain.* He wore one, always. In '72: hat. '73: hat. 73-yr-old Henry the Hat of O'Connelly's.

Mistake was in the giving living upstairs *isn't he a doll* Henry bent and spitting. Above O'Connelly's. "We're broken and ragged people" voice of shirts of beers I hope he included me. Gave him a T-shirt promo Stones the one with the red tongue traded gave him right off my back for the flannel grungy one sleeve half ripped away. Pals we became then the giving more wrote then I gave him "The Wide World of Rye."

Wrote it for a mag. Title he reads it "Rye! . . . rye!" and I'm stuck with him pals ragged "I'll get you lain!" Says but I don't think about it would you 'til a torn '50 *Popular Science*. Then and "That's Amore" 78 can't accept insists I take it let's all sing it backslappin' palsy walsy. Then beers then beer tomorrow upstairs pretzels pickled eggs "Be right back" winks I look around alone w/ spandex lipstick woman of 60 or 60 in black slacks red lips brunette hairy bulge on nostril. Smiles. "You like Henry?" "Sure." "Isn't he a doll?" Think oh so this is get the is this get me lain ol' Henry's plan to get the gift is hers herself she says there's more. More? Beers in the kitch or am *I* the gift she gets up pours me fresh did I see *Love Story* it's beautyful. Lust smells of grandmama's toilet wasser '55 I make no move she makes none. No knee language no eyes tatta tat time out. Henry's cornucopia. Good line his repeat it "right back" works I'm gone so sorry really. Look him in the can't generous Henry. Time to switch pubs. Even his hat decades dust. Not your greatest pal I.

And friends today? No time for it. No time for I., J., M., N. . . . ad infinitum. No time for laughs, no time for tears, beers, talk, listen, to or w/ them. No time to spell out why. No time for anything but neglect. You're lucky I've got this much time for YOU.

. . . you you you, me me me me — what say we park it and scope out some THEM? On damp sidewalk outside Freedom Bail Bonds, a shoeless feller in paint-speckled wool socks and hunting vest sleeps deeply, clutching to his chest, his heart, a mostly empty King Cobra Malt Liquor. Scabby, unwashed, beard like a nest of butter-fed centipedes, he appears not uncomfy and at relative "peace." Relative, that is, to the Old Testament stringbean who two corners south quavers, "And the MOTTO of 104th AIRborne is 'AssHOLE, your money OR YOUR wife.'" I give him — no, you give him — a dollar. Outside the Long Beach Greyhound station, a cabbie accosts us: "I'm here to pick up a fare named Ulf."

"I'm not Ulf."

"I *know* you're not Ulf" — glares. Um — no hard feelings. Down a few doors to the Stage Coach Tavern. "Your Very Favorite Mixed Drinks." Nine drinkers, nine Buds. We'll have shots. Framed prints of racehorses, sailboats, but no wagon wheels, no steer heads — nothing western. TV, volume high, exotic species of lizard snagging bugs with their tongue. Vintage varathane bartop. Backlit "Bud Light Salutes the Raiders" icon. A silent juke. Very pregnant woman downs a Bud beneath the "Pregnancy & Alcohol do not mix" sign. Bartender slices limes (just in case).

Down the bar to our left, a goateed rolypole jaws with a young jarhead headed back to Camp Pendleton:

"But none tastier than catfish."

"Oboy do I love catfish."

"In Pennsylvania we called them bullheads. Caught 'em by the sack."

"Sack?"

"Easy to skin, no scales. They got one center, the spine, the meat just falls off."

"I *love* catfish."

"You ever eat raccoon?"

"No."

"Ain't bad, got some meat on it."

"Lizard?" — cocks a brow towards the screen.

"Never ate lizard. Grasshopper."

"Grasshopper?"

"In Rangoon" — the continent-hopping gourmet.

"How 'bout bees?"

"Yes."

"Wasps?"

"No, never had . . ."

". . ."

". . . but the . . ."

"Scorpions?"

"..."

"..."

While over to our right a dude in a frayed plaid trench coat makes lively small with a nimble buxom fortyish platinum blonde:

"Driving this morning was a *bitch*."

"Watch your language, there are bitches present." He lights her Lark.

"I'll tell you one thing, at my age it's better to pull over and screw the car."

"And how old is that?"

"Fifty-eight in May."

"Well, you're getting there. In ten years you'll be up at the speed of sex."

"What's that?"

"Sixty-eight. At sixty-nine you have to turn around."

"I'll take sixty-eight — 'Thanks, I owe you one.'"

"Or seventy-seven. That's *eight more*."

"Depends on who gets eight."

"You sure one lazy s.o.b."

"Ain't it the truth."

"Hey, where do I leak it?"

Barkeep directs her accordingly. The channel is changed. Twenty minutes later, again. "How come it's on?" I ask.

"Background noise." *Oh.* Bar sets used to be on only for the World Series or something. Title fights. "Events." But pro beach volleyball *interviews*? Reruns of *Quincy*? Bar folks when they talk can seem so *wise*. So how come they vote for scum like Bush? Ans.: television. Little dives like this were once an *antidote* to TV heart-mind-soul control. (The world is coming to WHAT, my friend?) I gesture inquiringly at the juke. "You want it lower?" I nod.

Without preselecting, I empty a pocket and insert. "Groovy Kind of Love" by Phil (Dim Brit) Collins . . . "So Rare" by Jimmy (Long Gone) Dorsey . . . "Snowbird" by Anne

(She's Canadian) Murray . . . hmmm, why don't *you* pick 'em? Smack of disinfectant wafts up from the mat below the machine.

Back at the bar, ms. with-child signals for another Bud. The bartender stalls, comes over bottleless, addressing her with a look, a tone, half avuncular, half Karl Malden-nosed pitiless priest: "Don't you care about the baby?"

"After the second trimester it don't matter if . . ."

"I don't know squat about school, lady, but common sense says . . ."

"It ain't really none o' your . . ."

"Look — I can't legally refuse you, but . . ."

Leave her alone, leave her alone! though lemme think it 'fore I spray it — I would hate to embarrass you. She's oppressed enough already, you can read it in her eyes. Why would she, why would anybody waste ten minutes in a dump like this unless   calamity   the burdens of   some point about   another helpless wight trapped in   I take back what I said concerning   . . . lost it. Got it. Chicken! . . . egg! . . . all the bale and travail in the world! If the body is the temple of the soul, and a pregnant body is the temple of two souls, and a gin mill is the temple of solace — that's a lot of ifs and temples to hafta contend with — No wonder Samson tore the . . . OK, *why* did Samson tear the temple down? *Because it was there.* I could be wrong, but I know I'm right. I'm sure I'm right, although what's the big deal — in 45 years I'll be dead.

THE SHY GUY AND THE SOLIPSIST:

~~Winner of the 1958 Pulitzer Prize in Fiction, Ridge Muleser has worked as a writer, a writer, a writer, a writer, and a biter. His first book, *The Hydrocephalus of Rock*, currently in its 400th printing, was awarded the Canadian Society of Authors & Whatnot Medal of Achievement for 1971. Shortly after publication of his next effort, *Glug Ulch Yuh*, for which he received the 1973 National Book Award, he suffered a relapse of ulnar meningitis and lay flat on his back for the next~~ how many years, he don't know. ~~Finally returning to the writing wars, he found prose "too~~ much ~~to hoe" and turned his attention to poetry, copping an '84 Ezra Pound Fellowship (the "Poundy") for the deeply evocative *Vermin in My Heart Say "Marlene"* (Really). In short order he regained his touch for multi-page bulk, pumping out the first two volumes of a projected seven-part autobiography, *Early Worthless Oof* and *Scalding Frozen Malfunction*, '86 winners of the prestigious Hohoppenploptop and Pluggaduck Awards, respectively. In between these outings he found time to compose *Soilure Here: Ridge Muleser's Guide to the* Common *Dung of Los Angeles*, for which he was handed a second Pulitzer, this time in Music.~~

~~Presently serving 8 to 10 for manslaughter at the Chino (California) correctional facility, Muleser (rhymes with *ulcer*) is busily at work (or is it play??) on an encyclopedia of facial tics, for which he will probably be knighted.~~

LOVER MA'AM

Ready or not, it's Eva Lace Week. Wheel out the ki-
nescopes, roll the tapes — migod I haven't seen these things in
years . . .

Saturday, 4 PM. Is she sleeping? Is she dead? Relationing
Eva Lace can present prob-lems. When she won't answer the
phone, when she will not respond to a ding-dong-ding at the
door, a peep through the bedroom blinds is often required.
Respiring? Expiring? Should peepsight fall short, and break-in
prove recurrently essential, this capsule course in window repair is strongly advised. *This Old House*, PBS.

MACHO, MACHO MAN — Norman Mailer is in fine
spirit as host of *Le National Macho Awards* (Wednesday, 9 PM,
ABC). Presenting me le statuette for Verbal Macho, he lauds
and applauds my nearly forgotten parting line to Ms. Lace,
"Even infinite love has its limits." Concedes the widely famed
author of *The Deer Park*: "I am one tough blustery hairyape,
but [verbally speaking] Ric Smeltser has me beat." Thanks,
Norm!

This could be the start of somethin' . . . She (the image and
likeness of Eva): "Number one, on the first date, after having
made love THREE TIMES and finding your spent & satisfied
partner drifting towards sleep, what would you say to interest
her in another 'go'?" He (mistakable for my mother's son):
"The only thing *to* say, 'Can I stick it in again?'" She: "That's
not very romantic!" He: "But I bet it'd work." She: "Well . . .
perhaps." (*The New Dating Game*, channel 9, Tuesday at 8.)

When the swallows DON'T come back to Capistrano,
that's when there'll be a decent Squirt commercial, but the
one starring Eva Lace is NOT TERRIBLE. Says E., ravishing
if puffy-eyed in a green sari, hair awry, glass in, whoops, it *was*
in hand, now it has fell, broke and a sliver has sliced her

person: "Squirt and — *hic* — Squirt — *hic* — and — *hic* — Alma —" — pauses to lap blood from ball of foot, falls on ass, sari flying loose (great jugs!), then gawks up at lens — "Squirt and Almaden chablis is my *flavorite* drink." I *knew* the hiccups were fake . . .

Great realism!! — Voices in the dark: "Then how'd the bed get wet?" "I *don't* know." "You been drinking again?" "What ever gave you *that* idea?" "You could at least have let me know *when*." "You sicken me." "I'd've enjoyed the sensation on my leg." "You're *too, too* vulgar for my taste." (Dialogue by R. Smeltser, E. Lace.) *McMillan and Wife*, NBC, Sunday, 9 p.m.

The suck and the puck of it — Interesting locales have been the byword on "Z" Channel's *Suck-a-Dick Film Fest*, which this Friday will air a pair of suckoffs to completion by Eva Lace of Brentwood. In the first, I am blown by Eva in the parking lot of the Hollywood unemployment office, where I have graciously driven her, while she waits in vain for a spurious claim to be processed. "Plenty of time — want some head?" I appear to be enjoying myself, but too much teeth, only sporadic use of the tongue, and too wide a "grip" to effect adequate suction make for an only marginally coherent b.j. Far better is her playing of my skin-flute in deserted section 46 of the Forum during period three of the L.A. Kings-Washington Caps game of 2/1/78. Even without sound, even with two lengthy (unedited) beer stoppages, this blowjob *sizzles* . . .

PERSISTENCE COUNTS — Dramatic full frontal shot of an imploding Sony Trinitron will be seen Sat'day on *Science Wants to Know!* (ch. 58, 10:15 AM). Ably assisted by Miss Lace, host Don Herbert was able to pull off this beauty in only three attempts, all shown. After her Adidas misses (wide left) and her antabuse bottle lands right on but bounces, Eva's phone receiver makes serious contact: fa-TOOM! (In stereo where available.)

SHE'S FAAAANTASTIC! — Spotlight on Eva, at aisle-seat ringside during round 3 of Alberto "Superfly" Sandoval vs. Eliseo Cosme, bantamweights, Olympic Auditorium, Feb. 2, 1978. Asleep since the first prelim (too much 2 dwink??), she awakes with a question, "What are all these MEXICANS doing here?" after which she hoists high her dress, removes a tampon from her darling snapper, and replaces it with another as the ethnically slurred GO BERZERK. (On *Hubert Humphrey's World of Boxing*, ESPN, time and day to be announced.)

If you're deaf but not blind you indeed 're in luck, for not one but TWO Lace-related offerings are in the closed-captioned offing in the days ahead. At 3 a.m. Thursday be sure & check out the underrated econo-budget *I Worship Satan* (with Dick Miller and Irene Forrest), first, and sole, feature cast by Eva Lace, casting director (ch. 56). Same channel, 21 hours later: 200th rerun of "Stuck Up Shirley," the episode of *Laverne & Shirley* E. thought she was watching, pre-syndication, at 8:30 in the morning (blinds drawn) when actually it was 8:30 at night.

Tuesday, 7 AM. As 2,000,000 broil under a petulant Lisbon sun, as 9,000,000 Calcuttans sip after-dinner liqueurs, as 8,700,000 Moscovites gobble chicken 'Kiev' and 150,000 Aucklanders dream of kiwis and sheep, you can, may and by all means SHOULD tune in *Barbecue with James M. Cain*, featuring this wk. a rare voice-over by James M. himself. Croaks the late Jim while sultry Eva, with sexsuburban smirk, twists on a skewer a penile *membrum*, stalk crackling like a Lou'siana link, its seared head a miniaturized likeness of the kisser of don't-call-me-Ishmael: "Is to be under another's absolute spell *categorically* objectionable? Isn't the act of *falling* in what we call love, the fact and state of *being* in love, a declaration of hopeless, lethal, ineluctable susceptibility?" (Orange County Public Access.)

HOSE THE MAN DOWN — Video for Arthur Brown's "Fire" (*Fri Nite Vid Yo*, ch. 13, 11:40) has a cameo appearance by ME, fully clothed, being "cooked" by my own Lacetime INTENSITY. It's wild . . .

Free at last! Great godamighty I'm . . . Following a week's incarceration at the Sybil Brand Inst. for Women (DUI), the Lace person accompanies her liberator & principal hugbunny on a picnic jaunt to Will Rogers State Park. Blanket spread in a none-too-secluded glade, a quick repast and then . . . madness. Position: missionary. Dress: Levis (cock through fly), skirt (intromission via tear in leotard). Requesting ev'ry inch o' my love she tugs at my belt and pockets, pulling my pelvis hard upon hers as the fornication thunders to conclusion: a multiple-orgaz wet-humperoo with Cub Scouts perusing from horseback. "Fine fun" — *L.A. Herald Examiner*. (*The American Horseman*, CBS, noon, Sunday.)

NO ES RECOMENDA — "The Roll-ons in Eva Lace's Cabinet," on *Cinema Pluralist Playhouse* (HBO, Monday, 9:30). A literal rendering of the time I went and used the key I'd never returned to recover a hammer I didn't really need and possibly acquire a souvenir, lots of zesty garments to cull from but I didn't wanna chance their containing the drippings or droppings of my replacement, Eva's new sap Seth, the lawyer she'd met at AA whose traveling set of Kiku and Aramis deodorant, cologne and aftershave products were now in the med chest alongside her cold cream and henna. Superb atmosphere, superb lighting, but without Smellorama to really bring it home it is *not recommended*.

It is no mean act of courage for channel 20 (Riverside) to rerun the controversial "anal blooper" installment of *The Flintstones*, the one where Wilma's voice track contained wds. spoke by Miss Lace following her surprise appearance at my door bearing bagels and coffee three weeks to the day after an all-expenses-paid D & C: "I *might* be fertile, I don't, or maybe the — is anal okay?" Last time on, it scored a lowly 2.6 ratings share that had station execs wagging their ties. In my totally subjective opinion, this program is "entertaining" enough for prime-time consumption, and hopefully viewers will wise up and prove me correct. (Saturday, 8:30.)

Speaking of tracks, you will kick yourself if you donot see *Erratic Behavior — A Cure This Century?* (Health Channel, Wednesday, 5 p.m.). Propounds host Joyce Brothers: "Few things are more startling in those with EB than utterance swings during coition." Audio tape of E. Lace at two stages of a single sexact is played for corroboration: "Ohhhh, your nixon says the *sweetest things*" . . . "Get done — I've taken quite enough of your *monotonous thrusting*." As Dr. Brothers then explains, "The cause can be brain cells, improper attitude, or chronic circulation, but *not* junk food, and not 'nutsness' — that outmoded catchall has got to go." Indeed . . .

WHY D'YOU THINK THEY FINISH LAST? — Fox pilot for *Mr. Nice Guy* (Monday, 10:30), starring Molly Ringwald as Eva, Howie Mandel as me. Striving to please his thankless truelove, haggard 'cause he hasn't had a solid drink in weeks — settin' an 'example' — Howie eschews judgment, pays for this, that, rises with the sun to fix her a decaf, take her to the burn clinic or in for a Pap smear, find her a lawyer, chauffeur her to court, but best is when he gifts her to gold-sequined crotchless panties — "How disgusting." "But you ought to have it *framed*, it's that good." "You make me ill." As with all dramedies, there is no laff track.

Time change: SmutChannel USA's *Resilient Cunt Special* has been moved from Wednesday 1 p.m. to Tuesday 2:45. Should work or a manicure appointment present a conflict, I suggest setting the timer of your VCR, as this highly enlightening broadcast is worth a watch. Yes, I cannot more highly endorse the program that takes you INTO the living vagina of Eva Lee Lace, and not simply because the fingers on tape are my own . . . two fit fine, three fit fine, FOUR adultmale fingers enter (with ease!) Eva's orifice, "stretch out" flat like a judo/karate chop, four fingers PLUS PALM to the base of the thumb, then "scrunch up" to tick-tickle her innards as thumb lovemakes her beloved clitty (the famous "G" spot was but a *theory* when these tapes were made), flat/scrunch, do-it!/to-it! . . . orifice then "snaps back" sufficiently to pleasure the spud of a dwarf. WAIT, hold it, 's now on Thursday 6:15: catch it w/ din-din — a mealtime, familytime treat!

Some news is "good" news (aesthetically speaking): KTLA's coverage of the Intensive Care crisis. RN in white bra & nurse hat, knees wide, maincourse displayed, pink vibrator in left fist: "We used to have *no competition*. Since she checked in" — close-up of the world-class fanny of E*v*a L*a*c*e, IV in left cheek as it and its partner jackhammer down/up, down/up on the supine form of a hirsute biped w/ stethoscope . . . pan to Eva's mangled Schwinn, to the lineup of docs and interns stretching to hallway & beyond from bedside right — "we haven't had *caduceus* up ours." Back on camera, reacting to a sudden increase in the tempo & amplitude of girl-boy meat-thrall, she turns her head, scowls, spreads knees wider and inserts the buzzing plasdfghjkl;'

Didja Know Dept. — As high as 13 per 100,000 pop. have never been properly taught the principles of thirst & its quenching. So claims *60 Minutes*, with excellent footage (of Evy and myself in Death Valley) to back it up: "I have *such a sore throat*." "You're just thirsty. Take a long, cool belt of this flask of tapwater." "That's revolting." "But it's all we —" "No *thank* you." Well, that's 1 out of 4,000,000,000. (Sunday following Colts vs. Rams, CBS.)

Quench alert, part 2: *Moisture Denial Telethon* — 'for those who've been denied the goods for more than a month.' MC Bob Newhart tells it like it is: "A little moisture can go a long way in helping the deprived through the long, lonesome night." Towards this end, a rather instructive short will screen hourly, based on the latest research but illustrating principles IDENTICAL to those I employed with the dormant E.L. Lace: how to get fingers wet from behind while j.o.'ing in the sheets *w/out* waking her . . . it *can* be done (but do it correct). Ch. 18, Sat. 9 PM-Sunday noon.

SIBLING SERENADE. "So He Sexed Her Sis," a student film by Kent Beyda, premieres next Friday on *Love Finds a Way* (TBS, 3:30). A moving glimpse of life in the pain lane, its theme should appeal to audiences of all persuasions: Angry over a certain birthday article, Eva declines my company, so I grab a shot of scotch, call upon her sister in Van Nuys, weep out my heartache, and get to pork her *royally* — one of only three recreant saddlings during E's tenure and, all told, the best. (*Very* nice mammary stubble.)

The Face of Lace . . . *Beyond Saran Wrap: Contraception for the Nineteen Seventies* makes fine fullscreen use of the preburned mouth, nose and chin of birth control enthusiast Eva "The Fever" Lace, i.e., from just before the mishap with the deepfat fryer and the fifth of Stoli. Intercut with post-burn stills from Hiroshima and Nagasaki, this segment is so visually stunning that the *message* of the message — Eva's terse but trenchant statement to her nation and her Time — is lost in the shuffle: "I *intend* to be fitted for a DUI, a, no, an IUD some day soon, when I finish being this manic." . . . And well she should! (NBC, Monday, 7:30.)

BUT CAN SHE SELL THE BROOKLYN BRIDGE? — Miss Eva on how to convince 'him,' following cataclysmic inebriate conduct including mirror-busting, refrigerator-busting, a fistfight with your boss's wife, and (later the same night) saltwater fishtank-busting, that you've turned a bran'new leaf and are thus entitled to unsupervised use of his motor vehicle though admittedly a 'risk': "A three-day juice fast, preferably carrot, should persuade *anyone* you've changed your ways. Invite him to join you — to 'cleanse his system.' The precious car? Continued 'moral support.' Who but a heartless *brute* could say no?" Sounds plausible! (*For Wimmen Only*, Saturday at 2, ABC.)

"Have a haphappy writing day and I'll be seeing you" sez the guy on *Let's Write* (ch. 50). Entire screen is taken up by the writing of letters by a right hand and wrist (he's a "righty"). He is writing them from memory (photographic); there is no chart, diagram or cracker box from which to copy. "The G glides into two beautiful O's, a lovely tandem of ellipses." Before y'know it he is done; the letters have formed a word; the word is GOODBYE. The camera moves up six inches — no more — and the subtle undercurves of breasts are seen. Why, I'll be dipped! — the wd. has been written on Eva Lee's belly! Jus' like *I* wrote it (in lipstick, not felt-tip pen as the gent has been using) the time I got her home, undressed her and got her into bed when they called me from her office 'cuz she took the seconal! Ain't life funny? (Art Pepper's recital of "Goodbye" soars over end credits tho at times — poor audio — it sounds like the Sonny Rollins Village Gate "Doxy.") I forget what day it is on.

ADD

PBS'S FINEST HR? . . . *My Auburn Crack*, the pulp paragon that helped me through an excruciating interval of cooze withdrawal following E's adiós, has finally been adapted for the cathode screen. On *Masterpiece Theatre* Tuesday at 10, this rousing production stars natural redhead Marsha Mason in her hottest role yet. Scene where she humps the cobbler (Andre Gregory) is tooooo much! When she 'cukeholes' Aunt Lettie (Susan Strasberg): like w-wow! Stovetop self-grat scene: oo-hoo-wee! Proof that videotheatric pornography *delivers*. As opposed to jean-commercial pornography, or sitcom pornography, or anchorperson pornography, which just make you squirm, itch, ain't got, got t'have — the need equation exploiting YOU! the viewer — write your U.S. congressperson NOW.

CAST OF

FAITS ACCOMPLIS THAT WERE NOT

There's beating it after and there's beating before and there's not beating it. A "sure thing" looms, but how soon — and how sure?

I met her at Barney's Beanery I think, or some other such crowded, dark — or not so dark — by the pool table. In a trio of gals she stood out, or maybe not so much *out*, to the eye, but the heat — woo — I felt this surge of nu-sex like a car battery feeding my accessories and leaking acid simultaneously. Could it've been the sweat-drenched mascara star on each cheek? Three wild inches of thigh between skirt and kneesock? Completely submerged in an xtra-large teeshirt, paraboloids? ellipsoids? hyperboloids? Wanting-her, wanting-her, all I could spit out was "Dexter." Gordon. The Herman Leonard pic with all the backlit smoke and stuff. On her shirt — white on black — which she'd probably got at the Heaven on Melrose or Beverly Center. "Whuh?"

"Dexter Gordon." I point. Almost touching.

"What — no, isn't it Don Coltrane?"

"*John* Coltrane. But it isn't him, it's Dexter." And that's how it started, and stayed, but I got her number.

And went home and beat it — twice — and twice the next day — envisioning far-flung sexfeast strategies and *possible* outcomes. A saucy babe, a saucy babe — I will eat her 'fore I poke her — natch — and poke 'er, oh, three times at least, that's not too much t'expect — on the couch first (or floor) more likely than bed — from at least a couple angles. Ain't done it seated in a while — okay — but save it for second roll — nu-thigh straddling me like All Thigh, all World-accessible world-wobbly Flesh . . . ass? Prob'ly not the first date. If I *lick* it, sure, she will likely, for sure she'll lick mine —

saucy — but poking's dubious. I've always had trouble keeping it up fantasizing *im*possible — unlikely — sexual occurrences. (Why waste good beating on absurdities?) But meating her on the veranda if she's got one if her place it is, that I can picture — on the stairs, the garage, the beach, no blanket, sand in her boogie — watch out! — in the shower, tub or broomcloset. Back seat of a nightbus? alright . . . a latenight and a day of such practical speculation, then stop to let the sap replenish.

One day, two days, then call her. If she wants me right away, the well needs some depth to it. Two days of sap restoral — in and out of various modes of erection. Continuous sexthink to the point of derangement. Escalating tension, stress — sexthink without beating as an option. The chore of deciding what wash to do — which shirt I need clean for her — the black permapress? — and at the laundromat seeing bras, panties spinning, just what I need: triggers: heat, I'm in heat . . . STOP!, really stop — before it gets boring or, worse, *old*. And the call! the call! calls for substantial preparation: determining the most propitious hour (9:20), selecting appropriate lighting (a 60-watt lamp), playing *Dexter Blows Hot and Cool* (side 2) to get psyched, brush teeth to simulate real conversation at intimate range (even had to brush 'em to WRITE this) (brushing while reading it? optional), develop a headache from enough beers to render me fluent. Suddenly, Jesus, it's 10:30 — t'night or never — so I dial, it rings, some Asian voice: wrong number.

But sometimes a right one. Bookstore in North Hollywood I worked three months of nights at for four bucks an hour. This dame came in once a week, twice a week, designer clothes, sort of a dazed expression. Bought paperbacks, hardcovers, lotsa stuff — always asked me what to get. Knew I was a writer and we talked it — kind of — she worked at Universal — if I'd had anything in print then I coulda sold her easy. At first the daze put me off, she seemed so distracted, but she's in the store as much as anyone — could it be because of me?

Then one week, a pen in her mouth, point out, as she removes her check, lips done messy like without a mirror (in a hurry to see me?), something CLICKS. I breathe in her face like a smoke and think *hey, I can look at this face, this person; can and could look at it and her both during any (position permitting) physical act* and — eye contact — I assume for that moment she is thinking reciprocally same.

She pays, leaves, her scent lingers awhile, then is gone. Urinating in back, my own pallid fart murmurs star systems of lovebreath even at their merest an infusion of Primal Ah into thin sexualized air, oh . . . got t' see her or go mad — off at eleven. I find some sherry stowed in back for "special events"; it doesn't calm me. Customers look at me like they mus' know, they mus' know — an open stroke book. More sherry, get the number off her check, wait till everybody's in the far racks, then (heart racing, skull-flesh seared and popping) dial. At first she don't know me. "Oh, the writer." "Yeah, I was wondering if we might *get together later*." "I don't go out with employees." Um — "I wasn't thinking of out — I thought we could just fuck or something" — *click*. Woman at the counter with a cookbook, wants to know if it's available in paperback. (I go in back and come in seven strokes.)

Then a right one where I call and she says: "Sure. Tomorrow. Your place" — she wants me in my trappings. Photog I met at soandso's who hands me a card, she'd love to shoot me some time — do a "study" — I have such provocative features. A sandy-haired narrow-hipped shorty — her quince will be tight — I phone the minute I get home. Lightheaded, tightbellied, bubblefaced — if she's *that* hungry to see me she must be HUNGRY: back in the small-person saddle!

So I go through this frenzy of prearrangements — let's see do I need condoms, what wine to get, is there time enough to get a white and chill it, some kinda snack, maybe oughta dust select spots, semi-clean the toilet — but no vacuum — can't cook, don't want the reek of food in the house, is barefoot more rugged than socks, black jeans and which sleeveless teeshirt, make the bed, no, but throw a cover over — then the waiting: late, later, really late she is. I finish half a can of almonds and a third of the wine. Auditioning candidates for side to be spinning when she shows (changed every five minutes) — "Congo Blues" — "West End Blues" — "Lonely Woman"? When she arrives *New York Eye and Ear Control* is twelve minutes gone. She shakes my hand but even after wine won't let me kiss her. After minimal consternation it turns out she's gay — "I'm gay." That's cool — "So how 'bout if I eat your pussy?" "How 'bout I just take your picture?"

I can adjust. And sometimes a private triumph. Like it's all private, right? — conspicuous but to myself — the tenor and intensity of anticipation, of my hyperinvolvement in the merely possible, of my ensuing (not unpredictable) disappointment. Only I stand in witness to the unfolding plot, and consider for a sec all the bodyheat required to *keep* it that way — to conceal it from a prescient (laughing!) world at large while rushing it, coddling it, to not-impossible witless fruition. Turndown is but the tip — the end tip — of the obsessional iceberg. And the longer SHE hasn't been cued to her role in the obsession perhaps the better. And better sometimes still when obsession finds its cutoff forward of schedule — end hallucination — end of spell. More than once, more than twice, a machine has done the trick. Readiness anxieties in overdrive, I sit still finally for the fatal connection which will not only clue me to things real or realer than the hyped-up Plausibilities I've been livingbreathing for days which weigh like weeks, but which will make it official that it wasn't *already* a pipedream (hey I called — coloring it REAL — and establishing as real my spit & spunk for enduring the goddam fixation). *I* can cut it — have no fear — but what happens, I get an answer machine. What're you supposed to say — "Hi. Remember me? Have I got a hardon 4-U"? So I don't, I call back in an hour, again the machine. Another day and try again? Same shit. Which sort of says it wasn't too real anyway — fuh — but ah! the relief, the *peace*, when at this

point my fuse blows — K-BING — stupefaction cut short (w/
privacy maintained) — short will do. (Don't begrudge minor
triumph.)

IN ORDER OF APPEARANCE

OK, I'm a writeperson. The perils of text — on page, in
the street — have mangled & branded my tuber sure as still-
born love down the pipes: surer. (Y'know, *that* kind of writeperson.) The early presumption of an editorial score will
guide me over falls, into walls, into dank rusty bins where after
certainty evaporates hope freezes and I shiver like a fucking
teenager.

I wrote for this slick once, an early rival of *Playgirl*, they
were throwing money around — "You wanna do a sports column? Five hunnerd bucks." Boy boy boy boy: this was the
'70s. I hadn't made that kinda — 'bout time, I says — sure, I'll
do it. Did it. And three columns, four columns, four issues
later, as I'm jollily awaiting my first paycheck, the fucker folds
still owing me.

Not that even checks always signify payoff. Publishers or
their lackeys often "forget" to sign 'em — hey it happened
once. Or like checks for anything they'll bounce — big deal. A
100 times? 20? I wouldn't wanna estimate all my unwanted
stacks, reams, mtns. writ on spec.

Worse than unpaid, tho, muchworse than unpaid/unpub-
lished, is paid in the wake of butchered copy. Editors *love* to
fuck with people's writing. Left to their own device they will
lovingly pass it through a Roto-Rooter, pick out the chunks,
and slap choicer ones together with flour paste or, as a favor to
YOU, your own now glutinous sweat — sometimes blood. Or
like the piece I did for this ed who tells me 4000 words, I give
him 4000 words, almost on the dime, every comma in place —
I'd never in my life been both so hot and so *precise* — break my
ass, beat his deadline by a day, give him time to — thanks,
you're welcome. Then the art department tells him no space,

144

the illustration, um, type size they want . . . tells him cut it by a third — this is ripe — so he cuts every third sentence. Or they'll surgically remove every negative, change key adjectives, rewrite your punchline, turning a pan of some shitty record into a rave — gotta sell ads, right? Y'can't win. Editors got jobs t' keep, they make more than you (and operate from a more middleclass hand-as-dealt than you'll ever have); they're pawns and stooges of the rabidest kind . . . cafeteria monitors . . . crowd controllers . . . and the last thing they'd ever cop to being: billyclubbing pension-happy eternal rookie COPS.

So to gain some leverage on these beasts, well maybe not your everyday paper & mag beasts, mainly those at book companies, I decided at one point to get me a highpower agent. Or even low, somebody who would at least return my phone calls, *occasionally* get the point — recognize my immense writepersonal charm and appeal — unlike the stiff who was casually, too casually, then representing me. So I call up this new one — well I don't exactly call, I look in *Writer's Market*, which Ike Tork had just used to find a live one for him self . . . I go for the same one as him. Found this guy handles various swells, a name agency, tough motherfucker, editors beware, all such bullcrap. All you need, all he asks, is a current book deal — y'need a title in the works, not yet out but under contract. Ike had one, I had one — howeasy, howeasy — why'd'n't I go for this sooner?

I write him the particulars — a 'stream of consciousness' sports book, pub date in three months on an old, respected midsize press. In my enthusiasm, I type the name all in caps and for goodmeasure throw in my previous titles — the muhfuh's gonna love me (love me!) — and he writes back — quick — set for life! — tear open envelope — only to tell me, "Small presses, small change — you don't have much of a track record, do you? Our client list having grown to near capacity, it is critical that we limit its growth to those with less spotty résumés than your own. Thank you for thinking of us, however, and all best wishes." Wahhh! Where if all I'd mentioned, like fucking Ike, was the current title (and the midsize) . . . Longago, longago — and still it hurts.

(The wages of expectation.) Then my editor gets canned (even cops need track records) and his projects scrapped. So much for contracts. And by the time they release my manuscript it's too dated, says my agent of record, to peddle it anywhere else. Stream of sports consciousness, he gibbers, is still sports, which is topical, which is . . . fuck you. While meantime Ike's bk. — a treatise on light rum — never came out either — and he's still with mr. highpower, reaping etc., alltheseyears later.

Books is mis'ry. Writ or unwrit, to have one set then lose it is to have soft carpet jerked from under — no — have it napalmed. Multiple books: multiple mis'ry. Once upon a dream (upon a joke!) I had a two-book deal with an edit guy, thought I had one, and maybe did, until faux pas — plural — undid everything. Both books unwrit, each with but a word-of-mouth proposal — sounds like courtship, eh? (though who was courting who?) — our first dance danced, he waxed avid at my asininest utterance. He'd flaunt me to confreres — "Repeat that for Peter — phenomenal" — whatever horseshit. Convinced he'd sit for anything I said, I 'took liberties.' To beat my drum — *beat it!* — seemed a sound idea. First taste of discord was my voicing the opinion that returning POWs ("They'll have *lots* to tell us," he fancied) were war criminals like any others. Next was my loud repetitive use of the G-word (*grabber*, meaning pussy) in his favorite Greek restaurant. Then I was too loud in his favorite Indian restaurant. Final straw (it hardly took much): not even coming on to his wife — I swear — not remotely, or spilling a drink on her, or putting out my Tiparillo in her curry — just kissing her little hand goodbye, dryly, upon which he remarked: "Writing isn't living. Don't you know the difference?" and afterwards I felt I'd bungled *everything* — total devastation, total loss.

ONE-HORSE UNIVERSE

Why izthis? How can the violation, rebuff, betrayal of paginated wordspew — of not-yet-existent paginated word-spew — constitute so deeper a stab wound than that inflicted, for comparison sake, by no new ginch on my bo-log? By the prospect of no ginch ever on my bo-log? Maybe no-book isn't always more dire than no-love, but unfulfilled once-*objecti-fied* book — chapter — page — certainly bloodies worse — bloodier — than unfulfilled objectified love. Does this write-boy, anyway. Why, how?

Some thoughts.

There may perhaps be such a thing as impersonal sex — I'll grant it's possible — even nonnameless sex can in principle be 'anonymous' — "unauthored" — but there is not, has not ever been such a thing as Anonymous Writing — no such pel-ican! Even pseudonymous writing is onymous. Even pur-loined ('acquired') preexistent text, lifted whole cloth, is nonimpersonal — some person lifted it. Even never-credited *lost* texts are . . . you get the pixture.

Subject: object. While the face, the name, of unrequited love may shortly fade, my most wayworn and weary of retro-spects still include names and faces from the long march of uniformed edit creeps — one of each, one for each. Even face-less, nameless readerships have vivid two-eyed mugs. (I can see YOURS clear right now, Ace.)

The Dual Dance? It works like this. Seen as indicated 'gimmes' — or once-onlys — or one-nighters — or much more, women I've hotdang desired (but still not tasted) I've pretasted in the stewpot of desire for *them* — their sex-organ Being is centered, and center-of-gravitied, in the same place They are. With publication blazing in your sights — desider-ata-in-print — there are *two* foci to contend with, the gulf be-tween them distinct and often immense: editor at a door, barring entry; and the sweet anguish of future typesettings, presupposedly, Beyond the door. Two tangibly discrete others, two disparate emotional packages — one unpleasant (the equivalent of having to deal with, dance with, gals' mothers in order to get at, slowdance Them — chaperoned — like jr. high or something), the other maddening. And the stretch — the stretch! — between these opposing fandangos: few pairs-o-legs (and fewer groins) can hack it. This dancer's can't — a Clydesdale roped to each could be no more sundering. Nope, there's never any "fun," none on a par with even that (qua sexual 'play') of a forecasted fuckact which ultimately isn't, but so what, in the enervating psychodrama surrounding this dual-approach twist. Interruptions in which — at either locus of which (single *equals* dual interruptus) — can only mean, well, any decrease in displeasure occasioned by cessation of the one (struttin' with mister ed) is never enough to stem the rude increase produced by termination of the other (the Publication-hope Hop) — even with crotch relief from no-more-stretch thrown in. (Imagine filming *this* paragraph.)

Fuck me; read me; come and git it: I can, when so driven, be a twenty-course showoff of a guy. Without an audience, full meals (with full Shows) lie fallow. But where sexmeals uneaten may draw flies — roaches — maggots — eventually they dry up and (for all their vaunted protein) become powdery shrivels on cracked ancient plates. Writemeals untouched will draw suckbugs FOREVER. There's always something left on the china — an undiminished residuum — "Here, loud!, is the pith and substance of my ritual loneness" — self-spotlit evidence of loneness writ larger than ever — *documentation* of it — beaming loudly at the audience to the near side of my nose. Minus a more than imaginary *external* audience: the lonest and alonest of solipsisms, the silentest and loneliest.

Even the withness of the setup is no bargain. Generated *in* private, *from* privacy, with fewer experiential resistances, at sucessive stations of outpour, to its ultimacy of expression, the directed intimacy of writing is if anything more all-pervasive, leaving its originator more all-vulnerable, than that of loving.

The reader *gets it all*, is in any case *given* it all — no stumbling, *no secrets* — meaning fuller meat on the block to be chopped, bigger doggy bags to be stuck holding. Pants terminally further down, heart even more an open manhole: on this killing floor, a given work's "need" for readership can far outlive all authorial "desire" for it. Author as caretaker of the need, minister to the addiction, protector of flammable paper: only publication will free it from his keeping, and with it him from the dusty unheated unpadded firetrap dungeon of the preprinted page. Even I — Mr. Black Hole of Self — lack the solipsistic means to throw parties on that page.

Look, I don' need (or want) the illusion of an automatic mass (or even multiple) Thou out there, and certainly not a passive one — I'm no wimp with youse guys, doncha be one with me. I need an audience willing to do what I can't: complete the work, kill it, use it up like a squeezepacket of mustard, a bottle of dish soap, make it ephemeral as foolish nookie . . . finito. Finite. (If it ain't finite it's infinite.) So much of this 'postmodern' bulltucky is let's-pretend-we-can-kill-it-ourselves: can't! DIVISION OF LABOR: okay, we'll divvy things up. You can deconstruct my 'authorship' (go 'head, viscerate it), my 'work' isn't precious (piss on it) — but no way I'm gonna disown (or let you undercut/repudiate) my bloody *labor* at having done it, humored it, designed & maintained entire strange possible worlds for it to feel comfortably at home in. Thankyouverymuch.

Talk about worlds: chew on this one. A one-horse universe in which it is actually anyone's plight — as happens to be mine — to be strung out on THIS aberrant hogwash — literature!! —; to have IT as obsession and lifework while being synchronously Wise to it (couldn't be Wiser!). Literary panic — it'll wake you screaming: as preposterous and painful an epiphany as lying dying at age 10 — it all leads to THIS?? — why meeee? Sexual obsession, *any* sexual obsessions, high-yield, low-yield, even many/most high-delusion 'career' bents, are all more or less "understandable" — there's something at least intelligible about the incentives — but even in a *wooden*-horse universe writing is not, i.e., it doesn't lead even inconsistently to explicable joys, it doesn't even *micro*experientially feel altogether real, and only the stone maya of 'success' — a score, a sale, a review — can remove or assuage the onus of engaging in bizness so patently *un*real. The real problem being I do, indeed, desire this hogwallow more — wantneed it more, I daresay, than the hotwet cuntessential cavity — and Desire is what eats me alive . . . or have I simply had limited experience with *requited* literary desire?

And what of my one-ass saddle sores? Since an erection can generally be counted on to renew & refortify one's insulation from reason, increments of abrasion from the unit sexobject event gone awry are rarely factored in, before the fact, next time out — I ride full-tilt as ever. Not so for writeobject detrition, which invariably carries over to the next write occasion . . . and the next. After hitting enough walls, no brakes, at 100 mph you learn to slow down — or are somewhat compelled to consider it. Mapless navigation and meter-blind velocity become less automatic, thus jeopardizing the mileage and spectrum of text, neuroticizing driver-seat solitude, eroding operational confidence. At least I believe — know! — my dick will work tomorrow, and sleep soundly in the knowledge that it is "mine"; I have no such assurances regarding "my" ability to write. To be gripped, as does in fact happen, by the imperative to write "it all" — that which I somehow already have — all again: I could sooner — sayeth my being — outrebound Wilt Chamberlain.

Smashing into sex walls at 400 mph may smart, but afterward there's always masturbation. With writing there is no conceivable release-in-kind, momentary or otherwise, from the gravity of crackup — the notion of writing *as* masturbation is farcical. Stroking can erase, make you unknow knotty (or unwieldy) yearnings, but how can writing unknow *its* muggy origins? And what *release* is there in using your best licks, applying all your licks, on paper, towards *someday* wrapping up? The tension is never depleted, not in the short run or medium — the time frame's too great — you've gotta *be* wrapped. (Imagine a jerkoff that took two weeks.)

A sexual mirage is fair grist for jerkoff; an editorial mirage is NOTHING.

MEET DONNY

A telegram, eh? Two telegrams. "Do not despair" — now what the hell did that mean? "You will never be unpublished again." Which I already wasn't, and should've realized wasn't meant for me but for your-name-goes-here (I didn't know!) — sometimes even 'concrete' signs are pisswater fancy. And to think that when the damn thing fell through I took it as a rain check, a promissory note — just a matter of time — what a frigging innocent. My anthology, Donny — that one! — remember? And the next one and the years — the years — you pecker. You and your face like a sea horse.

And your office, the one we met at with the Leonard Bernstein poster and the map of Dickens' London and the potted plant — objects you later disavowed — it was "somebody else's" office — you were never *that* big a square.

And that Szechuan place you took me — "Study your soup . . . I mean spiritually" — this was after you got Kozmic — "You should *commune* with food before consuming it." Then we went to your pad, oh joy, to listen to entire sides of Beatle albums — it was already what, '73? '74? — and I tried to change cuts but you insisted — "Get into their heads as *auteurs*, man" — bully for you, you'd read Andrew Sarris. And the Macy's parade I like a turnip let you talk me into — "You'll flip" . . . all the balderdash I put up with — without wincing — Christ what a little whore I was.

Even after you lost my, how many was it, 200 poems? 300? in the subway . . . true, they were mostly groggy discards written way before on drugs, your only excuse for reading 'em in the first place, but what the puck. And my hardback Heraclitus, and my *Surfin' Bird* LP — why'd I ever lend you that? And the three different, four different companies you burned me at, although that's prob'ly too strong a word — my wretched innocence again: the anthologies, *your* anthologies, and finally *the* anthology. *See End Dub L. Ewe* — you were quick with the puns — writings on country-western music. *No Success Like Failure: Great Tales of Modern Ruin. Short Shots* — stories one sentence and longer. *Best of Short*, the sequel. I'd write for these, our goodpal Ike would write, lots of people, and you'd flip us a pittance — $25 per usable submission. Meanwhile you're getting royalties (on top of four-figure, five-figure editor's advances), adding rooms and lawnchairs to your home (w/ land) in Massachusetts.

When Ike and I squalked, or anyway balked, at 25 a throw, you pitched us a hotte one. Peace, love and equity — you could live with it. For one project anyway — next on your drawing board — *Late Grate: Eulogies for the Dead and Obnoxious*. A collaborative prank, a "goof" — we'd divide the thing three ways — me, you and Ike writing the whole thing (under 20–30 pseudonyms), splitting the pittance pool between us. You did the calculations, gave us a page count; in a couple months we delivered. Turns out — well you know what you did — that based on your count me and Ike had each written half, not a third, while you wrote nothing, made out like a bandit, not only wangling your editor's cut but cutting into our piece of the pittance.

And the afternoon you sprung that dingaling on us — "You boys are into the sixties, right?" — who either had or hadn't done a book on Janis Joplin. Friend of hers. "I bet you could show her the town." We walk her to the docks, she pats her belly — "There's a yellow fetus inside me. The father is a Chinaman," then: "Janis is *lonely* where she is" — this was five years after she died. We hit the Bowery, that doesn't shake her, she wants to read our Tarot for a sawbuck each. Instead we catch a cheap movie where our women who join us stare dag-

gers and grumble — where'd we *find* this one? She asks for
our number, any of our numbers — "You guys are a *groove*."
Up close she smells like buttered masonite, or buttered copper
(it wasn't the popcorn) — I mourn for all the world's pennies.
And gulp hard and (as no other is forthcoming) give her mine
as Addie stomps my foot — I was only wearing sneakers —
fuck YOU, Donny. Donny Aarons. (Bane of my existence.)

PARENTALS

M	F
male	female
mother	father
mother	female
male	father

(the em-eff principle)
whut gives?

M	P
ma	pa
martial	partial
mutant	parent
marriage	porridge

? ? ? ? ? ?

THE FIRST MISSUS PAMPER

Waiting. Watching. Legs. Not recently shaven. In
Hampton beach house she takes a slow, languid b.m. Naked
from the waist she irons the pants of one I call enemy (tho not

always to his ears). Caramel nipples thru the loose blue weave of her cardigan. Pink puckered asshole like candy. Husband should be gored by a narwhal. Once brushed an arm and she rubbed it against me. Entire body an erogenous zone? Slip her a note, "I would love to fuck and eat you some day." *Serious* relations for an hour. Thick as a brick? "A rich inner life." Anything odd in the line of her lip? Six warm words about armpit hair. Could she be mine for a night (or a day)? Wood she? I didn't want her *that* much.

AN ENTIRE FRIENDSHIP

Notmany (Each) months (encouraged). Agents (me) provocateurs (to): a (piss) couple (the). The (other) young (off.) man (So), tootoo (each,) provokable (in), was (turn,). Make (could) him (be) be (there) the (as) badboy (ally), by (to) turns (his/her), to ('wronged') each (partner.), the (She,) other (for).

Generous (example,) with (would) their (get) expense (me) accounts (to), but (talk) in (sex) strict (in) accordance (front) with (of) a (him,) system (to), they (go) took (onandon) him (about) for (my) meals (women —) and (he'd) drinks (had), to (so) the (few —) San (eat) Gabriel (yer) Mountains (heart) to (out,) see (sport.) snow (Sport,) in (meantime,) April (preferred). Too (inciting) goody (me) two-toed (to) to (get) winedine (her) each (goat) other (with) on (trivial) their (acts) employers' (of) combined (public) tabs (mischief:) by (loudness,) making (lewdness,) up (defacements) new (and) phony (the) client (like.) names (Unaware) every (of) time (the) out (ruse,), they (as) roped (they) him (may) into (well) the (have) uneasy (been) role (themselves,) of (I) prop (found), and (it) three-four (hard) times (to) a (avoid) week (the) it (bait.) was (Being) he (alternately) who (spurred) served (and) as (berated) questionable (by) client (either).

It (party) all (was) fell (a) apart (drag), and (to) not (say) a (the) moment (least.) too (But) soon (when), when (they) the (sicced) badboy (the), without (bouncer) instigation (on), seized (me) a (for) stack (taking) of (some) import (Heineken) beer (coasters,) coasters (that) from (did) a (it:) favored (done.) bistro (Between). So (wife) teed-off (and) was (some) she (half) that (starving) hubby (putz) took (he) her (chose) side (wife —) f'r (fine.) keeps (I'll): neveragain (live.).

CORPSES IN MY ROLODEX

Three friends, no lovers, one editor, two publishers.

THE STORY SO FAR

The twin Life impulses, cunnilingus and urination, versus the twin Death impulses, vaginal intercourse and writing — a neverending battle — which will win?

Slated to appear on a radio talk show at 7, our principal cuts his thumb shaving, arrives at 8:15, and is told, "You're late — We don't know you — Get out of our sight." Taken aback, he runs to his bud Johnny, who sublets him a bare, beat studio behind an old grocery 9 feet from the sea. The building has wooden pipes that need replacement by winter, and the wily grocer, who for St. Patrick's Day is growing grass in his hair, offers him a choice: "Walnut or oak?" "Oak, no, walnut" — a decision he will soon regret. Skies blacken, the seas rise to within a foot of his window, and a power tool outage forces him to move to the Shad-Mar Hotel.

There he meets Pinky, an amputee with a taste for 'plugmeat' (= podo) — and a secret as big as your barn. "Why don't we just drive . . . somewhere?" she might say — "The night has a thousand lies." Late one day while she's bathing her stump, he pores through her chest and finds $12,000 in carbon tetrachloride — Cuban issue. Tall weeds whistle and owls howl, flies buzz or at least *one* buzzes, loud, and a trainwhistle screams, and night falls *hard*, and weeds whistle and owls howl as he phones Mrs. Dunphy with the skinny: "What would y'say, May, if I told you I knew where to *get some* — t'night?"

Just then Pinky, all venom and virtue, stumpwet and sassy, blazes wet — wet! — gazula crying *Stuff me, you big smelly hog*. I slam the receiver. In walks Joe Monkey. Pinky drops her trowel.

BASIC QUESTIONS

Where is what I'm looking for? What is what I'm looking for? Is it too late to look for whatever it was? Where might it, what might it be? What might I be?

KNEEWEAK

A cone; no, a narrow isosceles triangle, rotated so its vertex is pointed at 196 . . . 5. It's pointed at '65 and possibly '64 but pointed *from* (and *in*) '66, where it. I. She. Whom I may later specify — first or second love — it doesn't matter. Stick-figure knee bent.

Down. From standing you're sitting. Kneeling. Knees buckle under me. The violence of the shock, the shock of the admission, have canceled my underpinning. She is "seeing" her dance teacher — "taken up" with — it doesn't matter. Bottom. Fall down all Downfall.

Seventeen years until kneepeat. 'Til the next kneetime. Jolts-to-come and jolts come, many shapes & sizes, but no bends, measurable and involuntary, 'til the first aftershock to the first earthquake big enough, I don't remember how big, numerically — not a big one — I had the hap to experience in vivo; intense enough to make the wood not only creak but *smell*, the beams, the foundation being rattled, battled, everything held up by old failing timber — a toothpick in the wind. And ever since.

But then. The quake itself I was in bed. Woke me. No time to get up under, whatever they tell you, a doorjamb. Car alarms off in the street. The teevee moved two inches. Paint chips on the floor. Particles settling in the walls. An hour later, another one. My knees shook — slackened — what they held shook; I hadda sit down. I'd been on boats before, I'd lurched, rocked — this was totally different. The sea supports you — they call it "buoyancy" — but not (I now knew) land: solid was no longer solid, and terra firma something less than firm.

And every time since. For weeks after a quake every tremor, every little baby rumble — every time a truck goes by — I feel in my hinges this is It Again. The bigger It tho, it for Real: this time it's *all coming down*. On these hinges hang the limits of my courage on earth — this slaying planet — nothing not kill'd by it — but it's not death fear we're talking, or dying fear, or rather: nothing is *added* in the process to my rocksteady awe of annihilation, to an already metastatic dread of lousy endings.

'Cause if you want death fear, I could show you some death fears — A-bombs, polio — how about tetanus? — and all they've ever done is freeze the hinges. The flaps. Immobilized, I couldn't stand even as a prelude to falling. Rigored without the mortis. This seismic baloney leaves room for collapse — flaps oiled — fold — like a ton of potatoes. But greater than potatoes or meat is the weight of a troublesome image, and I ain't talking beams on my skull in the bath, a cantilever or two thru my thorax.

Which occurs to me, yeah, you bet, and yeah it's unnerving, but the vivider aftermath, from where *I* stand-and-fall, is not me in rubble but — there's a lotta buts in this chapter — all my goddam contingent *things*; not my own death or dismemberment but the tenuous safety of my records, my papers, my *collections*. My precious junk with no roof or walls to protect it. The awful burden of property come home to roost.

Fear of having none of this — *is* it fear of having none of this? No: but of having to grovel and snivel to keep on having most or much or any of it. Total junk loss I could handle — not well but I could (in principle) outride it (as mere idea it doesn't normally give me the willies) — but obligatory do-something with wounded "belongings" — Quick! save the Stuff! (pick up & Move!): now *that* prospect gives me the shakes. What a bourgeois mahoney.

I'm a fidgeting fussbo. Inanimates worry me, I can't leave 'em precarious. That flimso-plastic Space Soldier helmet (why do I keep this shit?), can't leave without adjusting its placement lest a temblor while I'm gone topple it to flimso oblivion. Better push the typewriter back from the edge. Shouldn't the aftershave go in the cabinet before an earthshuffle eighty miles offshore knocks it off the sink and I can't walk around barefoot? My Sonny Liston "bobbing head" doll, on its back on a shelf, has fallen over twice now, and it's probably best to leave it fallen.

(I walk on eggs.)

And the shuffles keep shuffling, and the buses and garbage trucks keep passing, and even when they don't: reminders. Vibrations you can't even feel have an impact. Like the bubble-over of a geologic unconscious, this hooey loosens bulbs in their sockets — they begin to flicker, you inspect the fixtures, the wiring, finally you just tighten 'em. If only I could tighten the 40-watt bulb which illumines my life: a bag of sand ripe to run gut-open thru the cracks in the floor.

What rickety muck to have built a metropolis on; an insidious transient endeavor. This isn't a town I want to "be in it together" with — when my bag of sand joins all the other bags of sand and they pick us up (in order of wealth) with a spoon . . . what a drab mass calamity.

FOUR DULL DREAMS

The Earl of the Pampas wore a long (long) greenish-tan and black striped scarf around his neck as his plane swooped down on Lake Ronkonkoma. It was wrapped around his neck and bald and nose, which was pointed like a cartoon witch — but it wasnt pointed yet and he had white-rimmed child's glasses on. He got shot in the palm and blood gurgled out like A-1 steak sauce down his wrist but he ignored it cause he had to keep on flying but he couldnt fly for long with it bleeding that badly down his arms.

When he crashed he didnt bounce far and he was placed in the clear inverted plastic dome provided that had ridges and was transparent like those plastic things they pack meat in so you can see the bottom of the meat through it. He was hard red plastic by then and the stripes on his scarf werent painted in yet (and the room was dirty gray linoleum).

One dream. I owe you three.

VENGE PARTY

¶I hadn't moved yet and I hadn't left Adi or New York and I hadn't yet emptied what meager grace remained for me in local accounts. And Vivien Pampa hadn't gone to bed with me and I hadn't pissed out Danny Ahrens' window or danced across the keys of his acoustic piano. Nor had Ike Torf thrown me a party or decided to throw one only to find the going rough when no one he asked was more willing than he to donate his/her apartment for such use. He hadn't yet spoken to Danny, with whom he was still on more affable terms than was I, and learning of his planned week in the Berkshires used the loss of his own digs to painters, a canard, to shake from the dickhead the keys to his loft. ¶And I hadn't served Errol Pampa a Windy Mary (a bloody mary with Windex) or tried to pick his pocket. And I hadn't spread dip on Danny's mural of Jesus, Buddha and Marshall McLuhan nor had I graced it in ketchup with the legend The Medium Is the Sausage. And I hadn't interrupted my stream out the window to save some for Danny's drawerful of tie-dyeds. Nor, discovering in a closet a five-year-old manuscript with the notation Return to Meltsner, had I run outside to get shit on a pair of Danny's sneakers with the aim of grinding it into the keyboard of his second-hand Baldwin upright. ¶And Adi, in direct but delayed response to my having carried on brazenly if to minimal avail with a number of women, which I hadn't done yet, hadn't ripped the buttons off my shirt, prompting me to remove it and (soon) the rest of what I was wearing, inanely hoping to induce others to do likewise or close. And I also hadn't blared, What kind of party is this? There's no decorations, and gone and unraveled several of Danny's cassettes and strung them around the room like streamers, at a later stage of which Adi hadn't stung my uncovered ass with the flame of a Bic. ¶I had bought my ticket and made a reservation but I hadn't packed. And Garry Maulk's wife Joyce hadn't told me, You can dish it out but you can't take it, and I hadn't said, Oh no? and smeared gobs of party cake in my hair and ears. And I hadn't grabbed a knife and told Adi, Get off my back or I'll cut off my cock, and she hadn't said, Go right ahead, and I hadn't instead slammed it into what was left of the coconut cake. ¶And Errol, whom I hadn't invited and never would have invited and Adi hadn't yet but inevitably would invite, hadn't arrived late in his velvet suit and leather cowboy hat — You dumb ugly fop, I hadn't told him — and I hadn't offered Vivien cake on my stalk and I don't like coconut, she hadn't said. And sick of my shenanigans Adi hadn't hit on Errol and Vivien seeing this hadn't responded by telling me, I think I will have some cake. And I hadn't pushed the bed tight against the door and we hadn't fucked and emerged both naked to find Adi and Errol gone and presumed 'together' for surely not the first time (or even the fourth) and shreds of my manuscript all over the floor. And Ike hadn't slipped me $23, a generous half of the sum found in Errol's money clip, which he hadn't as yet lifted. ¶None of the foregoing had I done or they done; then I had and they had. Farewell but not fond.

THE THREE OF US

I'm glad I'm not me.
I'm glad I'm neither of me.
I'm okay, they're okay?
Don't tell me we're okay.

AN ACTUAL PIECE OF *GUERNICA*

Hi, howya, come in, lemme show ya something. From a tan glueless envelope, 1½" square, the kind used for storing stamps, coins and various other miniature collectibles, he removes a speck of hard white paint no larger than a fennel seed. *I peeled this off of* Guernica, *you know the Picasso painting, the big one? Museum of Modern Art, New York, they had it for a while. I waited till the guard was turned away, then I went up and — that? The gold record? 'S for some old, some junk I wrote in another life, dunno why it's still hang — lookit this. Robert Rauschenberg, y'-know his assemb, those construction things? It's from the one with the stuffed goat and the tire, nobody guards art-things like that, not well, a clump of goathair, I just pulled it off. An' lookit this art-thing . . .*

MEANING: look LOOK [I wanna be in your pants . . . live in your pants . . . eat, drink, sleep, fuck and *shit* in your pants; meanwhile] lookit this art-thing. It's how I start them off — gals who were born to love me — an hors d'oeuvre before the *main* showandtell, one that never fails to show th'm what a uniquely intriguing sonofagun I am, after which they're *mine*. After the boxing.

. . . *a Marisol, one of those huge doll-things she did with the, this was a ribbon on one of her doll-things.* End art. Begin boxing. *Benny "Kid" Paret, first man ever to step in a ring champion and leave dead, actually it was a week later but he really — see these holes? — even the poster has stigmata. It was nailed to a wall outside the Garden, the* old *Garden when it was at 49th and 8th, you been to New York? West Side. Midtown. Sixty-two, March 24, March is a big death month* [Charlie Parker, d. March 12/55, but that's another show and tell], *I was in high school. I even have his blood on a program somewhere.* With nervous, hasty effort he dislodges boxes, crates from an overstuffed closet: the "stash."

Here. I was all the way up, the rafters, when the stretcher guys, they carried him out and I ran down, on the press table, some reporter left it, right under Benny's corner. Just this one dried spot, a dainty *little circle* [gimme gimme good LOVIN'], *the splash marks are like sunrays or something. And here* [baby], Ring Magazine [BABY!], *August '49, Jake LaMotta wins the middleweight,* you saw Raging Bull? *"Title Regained by U.S.," that's as far as, Jake wasn't too popular with, he's not even on the cover.*

From a box within a box, from which all Mike Tyson-related items have been banished (bad for showtell: a beater and raper), a whole array of dandy little cutesos, the kind women love, are then drawn. Thumb-sized gloves, complete with padding and laces, from the nineteen twenties. Buttons. Abe Attell. *Featherweight champ, later he was bag-man for what's his, fixed the 1919 World Series.* Tami Mauriello. *Knocked out by Joe Louis, one round, I wonder if it's from before or after.* Boxing cards from 1910, 1½" x 3", edges slightly worn but images unmarked, bright, chroma higher than in inks in similar use today. Honey Mellody. *Welterweight, they spelled him wrong, should be two L's* [take my load, take it!], *a real pretty card.* Pale green arena backdrop with spotlights fuzzy/furry like a Monet cathedral. Knockout Brown. *He was cross-eyed, says bantamweight here but he was bigger, a lightweight, never a champ, doesn't he look saintly?* Young Nitchie. *Never heard of him.* Cards from the early fifties. Eugene Hairston. *A marginal contender, middleweight, "Drives a special make of car for deaf mutes," nice to know* [are you wet yet?]. Matchbook, stirrer and promotional sugar cube from Jack Dempsey's (1619 Broadway, CO 5-7875). Wrapper from a d-Con roach trap with the image of Muhammad Ali shaking a fist. *My all-time culture hero, last of the fighter-saints . . .*

This part always gets them.

. . . like before TV all fighters were holy, they without reservation put their brains and their looks on the line, and their eyes, both kindsa looks. But Ali was so supreme, so beyond physical vulner-

ability, that he had to, in order to complete his boxing cycle and enter the pantheon, y'know, his *way, he had to end up* more *brutalized than Louis or Sam Langford or — he had to, after his reflexes started going in his mid thirties, after the third Frazier fight* [I love you!], *had to risk going brain-dead like any clubfight bum played by Maxie Rosenbloom. 'Cause he didn't need the money, he wasn't broke, or any additional boxing-*historical *accomplishments, all that was left was to go punchy himself and I think it was willful, on a more than deathwish level — especially the Holmes fight — an extremely spiritual (boxing* qua *boxing) type of . . .* And if that doesn't work I go with my capsule history of the heavyweight division.

Of which there are two versions — long and short. Usually I do the short. *John L. Sullivan, "The Great John L.," was the last of a long line of bareknuckle champs. The Queensberry rules came in — gloves, three-minute rounds, ten count — and after winning* that *title he pretty much ignored it, fought a little without gloves, including a 75-rounder there 're actually photos of, but mostly he just drank and didn't train and in 1892 he lost,* with gloves, *to Jim Corbett, "Gentleman Jim," Errol Flynn played him, William Frawley was his manager. It's hard to know beyond the myth if he in fact was any good, a prototype maybe of a more mobile sort of boxer (as opposed to just a puncher) than the times were used to, anyway in* his *second defense he got beat by an overgrown middleweight, not even overgrown, in the 160's, Bob Fitzsimmons, who knocked him out with a solar plexus punch.* And I check *her* plexus (and want it) and her belly and her knees and her feet and I'm swaying as I'm talking and my talk momentum and my sexurge momentum are just going going and the sex adrenalin and the talk adrenalin and the wine adrenalin conspire and compel me to CONTINUE.

Jim Jeffries. Marvin Hart. Tommy Burns. Jack Johnson. Jess Willard. Jack Dempsey. Gene Tunney. Max Schmeling. Jack Sharkey. Primo Carnera. Max Baer. And for some reason, I don't know why, I occasionally get stalled at Jimmy Braddock.

That Irish fighter. Unemployed longshoreman. North Bergen, New Jersey. And while I'm stalled I let her get a word in edgewise. *How's work? Seen any movies?* (Fine. Great.) I resume. I finish. And if that fails there's always my jazz show & tell.

LOSING HAND

The whirl turns (and turns) and I haven't fucked the woman I currently love in . . . a while. Entered, yes, but not come in, or cared to come in. (A losing hand.) Ten minutes and it falls out, I'm too busy thinkin' about . . . not thinking. Can't feature how long I'll luck out neglecting her needs, although why inflict this tomfoolery on someone you love? Intimacy endures, has legs, but when the hunger and the mystery are both gone, why bother? "We need more passion," she decides — but how long can a left hand express passion for a right? Lust, I avoid mentioning (for I am chickenshit), is a time-coded operation.

Hunger and mystery? At least half the fucking I've done in my life has been by day. Nearly all my final-draft writing has occurred at night. Day is hunger. Night is mystery. Or is it?

MYSTERY

No, the solution is: night date means a night's writetime lost, hangover to follow. A day date has its hangover, if any, in the night slot of day #1. (And night hangovers of day dates are *writable*.)

WHAT THEY DRANK AND ET

Burger King at Vermont and 2nd. Next booth, two women talking *singers*. And fat: singers and fat — relation between. Fat singers sing better *when* fat (seems to be the gist). Figures on the ladies: neither thin *nor* fat. Y'know, average.

Lady: "Since Pavarotti started losing weight his voice has declined considerably."

Other lady: "That's true, that's really true. And they're saying the same thing about Aretha — with *some* justification."

L: "I know. And they used to say it about Ella."

OL: "Right. Also Mama Cass."

L: "Mama Cass?"

OL: "She was losing weight before she died. And her voice wasn't as good."

L: "I didn't know that."

OL: "And Kate Smith too."

L: "That's fascinating."

Age: 35. Meal: two salad bars. Beverage: none.

THE MAN WITH FIFTY TEETH

Though I'm told there are dentists (and others) who pursue, poke, and occasionally even marry one, I've never had much of a "thing" for dental hygienists.

Dentists themselves it's difficult visualizing as sex matter for anyone, and Maxine Henner's May '29 recording of "Dentist Chair Papa" — "I got a deep-tooling dentist to set my mind at ease/ He puts my feet in the stirrups and fills my cavities" — can hardly be deemed more than a pre-Crash novelty of the most bathetic sort. Nor, unless we're Jack Nicholson (Bill Murray) in *Little Shop of Horrors*, need we take Dinah Washington's "Long John Blues" — "You thrill me when you drill me" (he's a dentist, dig) — with anything but a grain of that salty stuff which, diet permitting, we sprinkle on eggs.

A rich source of double entendre perhaps, but if they stopped drilling — let's say they *hammered* — they'd cease being good for even that. They'd be good for nothing, and yet . . .

And yet the metaphor, the poem, the composite . . . sex/dental pain . . . pain/dental sex . . . ("painless dentistry"/ youch yank ouch) . . . does kind of persist with a certain je ne sais potency. One that isn't wholly comic.

I was in for a cleaning. New dentist. I'm more fickle with these clowns than the Fickleson Sisters. A new one, and so long since my last cheery "visit" that dental facewear had changed drastically. And handwear. Masks and gloves where previously there were none.

Yes, apparently, the blightful scourge of AIDS has altered another lifestyle. The *dental* lifestyle. The noisome workspace of drillers, yankers and their breed has forever been transformed, a new poetic resonance subjoining itself to their sour, grimy task-at-hand. Th' hell with sex and pain; sex and *death* has become the couplet wherever molars seek service and succor.

Tristan and Isolde meet Steve Martin in the *Little Shop* remake . . . Romeo and Juliet rub teeth with Walter Matthau in *Cactus Flower* . . . a grander theme enters the frame.

But of course it's *extra*-dentalchair whoopee which has drawn the Reaper to the dental sanctum. Basic sack sex, arse sex, or even just . . . blood contact. Blood and spittle — let's not forget spit — a little spitty mouth blood has struck FEAR in their dark dental hearts.

Heck, dentists have never minded draining *my* blood. Three yankers ago I lost between a pint and a quart when the fugger nicked an artery during "routine" wisdom extraction. Four pullers — and another wisdom — back I lost a pint from just a vein.

So it was my-t-great to see, well, maybe not a dentist but his hygienist lackey flinch, *cringe*, every time her tool struck capillary paydirt. And it wasn't from the mere sight-o-blood — that old routine. It was the *meaning* of blood. Blood and pestilence. Blood *as* death. My blood and saliva spiraling down the sink, I gazed at her panicky blues as *they* gazed — at the spiral. Blood, spit and panic: look who's squeamish now!

And the lamb turns tables on the butcher.

Speaking of which, butchers, what are *actual* butchers gonna do — and how far off can this be? — when the first lucky heifer with HIV up her privates starts spreading it to the steer, i.e., beef population? Slaughterhouses, butcher shops, little stalls at the Farmer's Market — all this *possibly* tainted blood flying 'round, landing in meatpeople's eyes, nostrils, fresh razor cuts; soaking their socks, entering their system through breaks in their athlete's foot. What're they gonna do, dress like astronauts?

And what happens when we the beef-buying public no-tice the weird togs and ask blunt questions requiring frank an-swers? *Thorough cooking kills the virus, see. Well-done is safest.*

Medium, a slight risk. Rare, how 'bout some life insurance? Rumors of illicit cow-poking at the Double R Bar Ranch will be *vicious*. It should be interesting . . .

Back to dental love: gloves. You could bite through 'em easy. As she slips digits gumward, take a whiff. Yes! The swell smell of old-fashioned rubbers, the nonlube genus that're still fun to play with on your peter (but are barely functional for sophisticated penetration). You could bite through 'em in your sleep, but the bite threat has always been there. Always — yet it's never made a dent in dental arrogance . . . insolence . . . indomitability. The butchers have persisted, they've persisted in spades.

Now's the time to put our teeth IN it. The eternal quid pro quo, the trade-off we've for too long declined — take it! Cuspid through rubber, incisor through glove. Slap some bloodcurdly *terror* — not this trendy *cautionary* biz — on their pastel trout-fishing face.

And tell 'em Seltzer sent ya.

PROFILES IN CARTILAGE

Mirrors can be helpful. Left side of my face is Kerouac, that classic shot of him on East 7th Street, New York '53 — his right profile. *My* right is, I dunno, Sam Elliott, Bradford Dillman — someone innocuously 'handsome.'

Which, in the proper lighting, will get the broads? (Which will intimidate them less?)

Head on I'm Peter Falk, De Niro. (No choice there.)

A CLOSER WALK WITH ME

I'm a city boy. I was well beyond my teens before I realized, *knew*, that direct sunlight, as opposed to daylight, is a heat source in winter, so it goes without saying the physics of moonlight has likewise eluded me. Yet without gaping starward I'm aware tonight is moonless: I would bet so. Lumenless swart above streetlamplow streets — this is daytown. Suntown. At this hour they're all inside, 've got no use for outside — no joggers or cyclists, no dogs — or are they? I see no active insides, no fixture- or tablelight streaming or leaking through blinds, shades or curtains. Dark impermeable property qua property. At street center I lean back, rotate 360, detect no clouds, few stars, no moon — or has it simply not risen? Dark on dark in a County of Death. No windows to peep in. But even a *mid*-case scenario seems oke.

A warmcool, coolwarm nevercold night, mostly cool. Would or might be cold if there were wind but no wind, no breeze. No teevee sound or stereo, nor carradio talkvoicemusicsports. No doppler, seamed or seamless, of vehicular comegostopgogone. Birds, by sight or sound: none, and no cats, dogs, squirrels, snails or slugs. No dew, no humidity. No cricketchirp. Pavement, though, lots of it, and masses of stucco or adobe and contiguous shingle and snatches of overgroomed plantlife, or not-life, or what-life — no spotlight (or flashlight) on iceplant or ivy or fern. No skateboards or joggers: behold. Suburbia without night jog. No parked or silentcruising 'neighborhood patrol' scum; no helicopters.

Early, as always I'm early. An hour to burn, I can do three miles, no, three 'll wear me out — make it two. No motel or hotel like some people get, so it's move and keep moving or sit in the car. In a county of death but not murder, it isn't easy killing even Time: hours. Somehow I've killed three at a sports bar then a mall. Enough screaming not-life for one O.C. trip: now to wander an outback where deadliving deadthings scream nothing more dreadful or deadful than valueless Value. Value less in gold or in beauty or comfort than in safety-in-distance from mexesafrasians less real and living (while less in-fact distant: Ethiops in Fullerton; Khmers in Garden Grove) than hypothetical. A good stiff miletwo's encroachment upon which should cue me, set me, *on*: readycued to roar and spill *This writing shit   Never saw, never really ever Not by   It just fell in my*   Bad. Start again. *I'm the great unsung*   In an hour I can roar it at a sales rep.

Dim streetlamps cast dim shadows. Me: mine. Easy to ignore it. Fencemetal and hedge: boundary left. Right, a carpet of sunbaked sod maybe two meters wide, the type Southern Californians (and perhaps others) call a parkway. Between them, a footfall-echoing ribbon, uniform and rigid, without tilt, fissure or ripple, impervious (apparently) to rootthrusts by cypress? mimosa? — I can't name this shit. A parched palm, fronds drooping: dryworld? Kemptworld: no dandelions or dogdrop, no trash. No nightdiscernible rust or feelable splinters to guardrails iron or wooden. When everything nightseen is dayshown, and the only thing dayshown is Surface, and surface roles are all played in *place*, for anything stray assume effusion from the Bowels (or escape from Hell). Recentfallen six-inch leaf: a lizard?

Ten minutes gone, no coral snakes, eels or BMWs encountered, arms aswing but not whistlingsinging, just trudging, rehearsing *The labyrinth   After fifteen years I can actually, well, alm   No, actually*, I trudge like a drudge: heel toe clickclack. Heavy heel, small foot, half a size smaller than they seem to produce in the states anymore. In Mexico, howev — something to remember — they got smaller average persons, and Mexican shoe stores, even stateside, stock 6½'s, even 6's, though the numbering system is different. At Cañada in Pacoima they sell male adult shoes in kid sizes practically, or literally, shoes that fit perfect though the only ones I could stand to look at were a low-slung zipper boot, western stitching, OK, which by virtue of boothood also had heels.

An inch and a half o' height — not shopping for but I'll take it. Unbroke in, though, height hurts — been in 'em now since noon — is this how a woman feels? In her highheeled sneakers. Bootleather on concrete . . . why am I doing this? At a property line, the parkway mutates green and seductive as a putting green. A switch to grass — thanx — and my heels sink down to the sole. Wet, I get it: Water is Life. Tapwater. If it ain't wet, it's dead (or soon will be).

Yet for all the grass, wet or dry, there's no appreciable grass smell. Nor much of anything floral. Nor car fumes or chimney or foodsmell. Some smell, wutz, well certainly: eau de moi. My own dampsweet essence; such a *sweaty* old dawg. I'll have to clean the jacket before I return it. *In San Francisco once* No, don't tell that one. Shoulda brought a change of shirt — well, next time. At least I can go back, change the shoes. In the trunk. Track shoes I drove down in.

Done. And at the back gate: peek in. As long as I'm here, a preview. From a safe distance. From the darkness. Half a block closer than where I parked. Beyond the attention of earlyscurrying valets. An earlyarriving bookco. person — I know her — must avoid — I've bent her ear enough already. Four hours at the AAB Convention — Amer. Assoc. of Books — I was asked to attend. Got a piece in this collection due out on a mid-major N.Y. imprint — we've all had one once — me and 40 others, some old pages tossed off before the 'dada' coin flip which effectively delivered me out Here. "You live there," it was said, and true enough, though the irony of my living in *either* there, my own (where books are ignored) or this hour-distant spookhouse (where they're burned), was not lost on me. Me and 3 others who Live Here — all invited, and only I show. Bathos and vanity: did I say I don't crave attention? So they stand me on point should a roving reviewer (or retail store geek) seek intercourse with a contributor to this vital hunk o' fluff. Polemic, poetics, my favorite color — I'm prepared to field questions. But no questions, no questioners. A washout.

And the room, sheez — how many soccer fields of books? From stall to company stall, a great gray pacificat-lantarctic of 'em — unburned for now — as many maybe as O.C., county of murder, has ever allowed in one discrete place. Altho books, shit, who am I to talk? I've written a few, I will probably write a few more, but never have I felt what you might call a "general reverence" for books. When I worked nights at the bookstore I would wait until the boss was gone and turn spines to the wall, make it impossible to find certain stuff, argue customers out of purchases — books I didn't wanna sell I wouldn't sell. Other people's books — books I'm not *stuck* with the grimgray bookish being of: keep 'em. (Sugar Ray Robinson never went to other people's fights.) And the aggregate *human* face of such quantum bookmongery: THESE are the traders in literacy? A vast grisly ocean of booklife, and the hours roll by and I'm thinking: while still afloat in so pestilent a sea, swim for shore.

Swum. The second the bookco. dame deemed it pointless to stick. Fled: having talked no poetics, having jabbered with no one but her, having no room at the Hilton to hang out at 'til the party. For some jerko mealticket — millions in print — I never heard of: so many authors. At which I will meet — she swears — a small horde of sales reps . . . what the hey.

Gone, but not before running into, almost tripping over, Danny Arena. What you don't expect you can't avoid — our first material contact in a decade. His face now more seabass than seahorse. Fortunately uninvited to the party. Gonna be up in L.A. tho, "Why don't we, I'd still love to publish you" — working for the Blue Maroon Press — I give him my phone number. As we talk I feel him staring — judging — the beige linen sportcoat has him stumped. A strange turnabout, 'cuz before that I'd marveled, or not-marveled, at the item's effectiveness: the fact that on this, the first (and next to last) occasion of my wearing it for anyone (not my college tweeds w/ the sleeves too short) — an experiment in ??? — it was "working," "doing its job," verywell (I think) (yes: verywell): nobody looked at me funny. Then *this* bag-o-shit, this black turtleneck turd, comes along, the fucking conscience of casual? Why'd I give him my number?

ABSOLUTE NIGHT. Night from which the gratuities of night have been removed. Nightless night. Night is not the womb. To-night isn't. Night with the same worthless inertia as day. There is nothing Gothic about this night, nor British landscape, nor dark impastoed Corot (nor Ad Reinhardt). Night as neither cloak nor mask nor shield, nor warrant for amok, nor legitimate clockphase of daily Nature (which only by inference locally Exists).

. . . Walkin' talkin'. Lopin' hopin' . . . actually I'm hopping. A frog in track shoes, one leg at a time, bend sharply, pump 'em, snap 'em — jaunt not speed. Sounds of water. *If I'd known it would take me half this long to get it right, to finally, I would never   I would sooner have become a plumber*   Behind a chain link fence with strips of tennis-green plastic, water on water — *running* water: a pool? No talk, no light, no swim or fun sounds . . . dunno. Water in the gutter, no sparkle or shimmer, but a modest stream of it, flowing. Tail it upstream, one block, two blocks, no drain on every corner — these folks mus' not like taxes — sharp left to a lawn being sprinkled. A dog behind a short row of hedge catches wind of me (what wind?) and barks, keeps barking. Although braced for this all night, I lunk back and stiffen, embarrassed.

Benighted night (alone). As alone as at the typewrite. Alone and not a comfort (as alone can often be). Of the forty-eight things alone is good for, only one feels in play: freedom from the petty shame of observed behavior.

So where have I been all your life?   In the trenches   For the last fifteen   Eighteen   Back it up. *There's a ring in every nose*

No. Earlier. *It was easy   If it hadn't been, at first, I'd have quit in a week   Writing wasn't something that in any way appealed to me From the outside looking in, y'know, as a way to spend my time   I would never have* chosen *it, sought it out, as a "means of expression"   But filling pages was great fun   Fill one quick, you feel like filling more   Once I did forty in a day, day and a night, forty good ones   Always one draft   I never proofread   And certainly never* read, *not for pleasure, and not for cues, tips, how other people do it — only things I had to review, or like factual research   It was a point of pride with me that I wrote more than I read   It was easy, too easy, and also portable*

If I'd been a painter   Scratch that. *'Cause I fancied myself as a painter, a sculptor*   Ha. For maybe ten minutes. *Made all this cumbersome crap, filled entire rooms with   And when it was done, when I — what to do with it?   So in writing I found   Small piece of   Eight and a half by eleven, you fold, in your pocket   Or the mail   It travels   I got hooked before I knew*   Dull. I'll need some drinks to jazz it up.

And, but mis   A neophyte's sense of mischief kept me going Keeps   Wrong tense? *I'm the guy who introduced "ain't," "gonna," "wanna," deliberate misspellings, run-on, mixed metaphor, and most of that shit to rock crit, pop crit, and beyond   Plus regular use of all the cusswords   That was* my *doing (true)   (Give me a medal)   Not to mention, dot dot dot*

Raw   Unpasteurized   (You should actually read me)   The great unsung master of Anglo-American letters   Lay it on. *Unprocessed   Even now that I proof   At some point I started   And reading myself got me reading others, and reading other people got my critical overkill working, going — if I could be tough on* their *act, I can be tough on* mine *— I aim high*   So cut my throat, please. *Now even my mischief aims high   There's a ring through Unhung*

Famefortune has eluded me   Fine   Fine? *Living in this shithole I'm invisible   I'm amazed how I've still, that I've actually made a marginal living doing   Never a middleclass, or anywhere near it, but   From not just what I write, that kind, for all these*

crummy little — but from writing at all   Most writers, real writ-
ers, 're always chasing other work — they're cab drivers or they're
mailmen or selling socks — that "enables 'em to write," it's the nor-
mal   While sapping them   Or a teaching gig, if you can get, or
keep — and writing can't be "taught" — correcting papers of   The
drain on your juices — the daily/weekly time loss — it works both
But when writing *is your primary job — 's all I've basically* done
Hammer and anvil   Fire   The pitfalls of that   Can it!

    Street smart   Bullshit. Meat smart   If not for some rotten
luck   No. Even the hardships have helped me "mature"   Bought
me time, forced it on me, to catch up with my wild inspirations
So?

    I'm this well-kept SECRET   The undersung bla bla of la la
Since I left New York it's rarely even got me laid   Undersung,
slung, now before I get hoarse I wanna SING MY SONG, strut the
bloat-belly grandeur that is/was me

    For sales reps? Blinking strangers? I told you I was one
stupid fuck. Or didn' I? Everything has led me to this. This
discomfort; this freedom; this ecstasy. This solitary path. So
clearly, so surely, that it even feels written. I didn't write it. If I
had, I wouldn've on so pale a page where every bleeping
thump looms in boldface/all caps. The impulse, the hunger
are too strong (reduce 'em). *In miniature   Listen   This ring*

    Out of nowhere, a divided roadway. Grass up the middle,
two lanes each way, still no cars. I hang a right and follow
three blocks to what by day might pass for a commercial dis-
trict: strip malls of three-four businesses each, longer strips
with fewer active units, and a handful of semi-detached single-
unit enterprises. Some light, not much, less (qua advertise-
ment; qua self-assertion) than would probably be shed at more
trafficked forks in kindred woods at this hour. From biz to biz,
an amazing load of wood — is it wood? I rub and smell:
yup — prematurely, calculatedly weathered. Seems like they
oughta have swinging doors and wooden nameplates that

hang. Western saloon moderne? Hitching posts for horses, and troughs. Ghost town moderne.

At Southcoast Leisure Advisement I read aloud: "Silent alarm, ASAP Systems" — permit code, 24-hr. emergency number — "an O.C.B.F.A.A. community service" — Orange County Burglar & Fire Alarm Association? Nose to window, I peep in at two desks with potted cacti, four leather-upholstered chairs. In back I find a small, short dumpster, open the lid, remove my jacket and reach deep. A cardboard mailing cylinder from Thermo-Style, Inc., Pompano Beach, Florida. A flattened styrofoam cup. Some filtered butts: Benson & Hedges . . . True . . . Doral. Is that a 'woman's smoke'? 'Cause if one's a woman — hey — and I can tellmytale to a *female* sales rep — whoo HOOOO! (One *very* stupid fuck). But be sure not to kiss her tho, not even her cheek (knuckles) (stroke her leg). Not unless.

Ghost town at ghost time. HIGH NOON OR NOTHING. No moon at no noon. No noonmoon at moonnoon. Nearby, a lone cricket chirps. I spit my gum in the dumpster.

In everybody's nose, firmly in place, 's already there, chained to master control, somethingorother central, you know   Something basic, antediluvian, forever; something recent and nasty   And my job, my duty, is to take the ring, the chain, and yank on it hard, harder, 'til they almost bleed — so they realize it's there   Then, and only then, can, will they take it out   A service I'm only too pleased to perform

Oh watch me do-it

THAT GIRL FROM DACHAU

A single book's sea. Waiters dressed as seamen — fishers or pirates, Long John Silver, nuh, more like Tugboat Arnie in galoshes — and fliers with leather goggle-hats and fleur-de-lis. French fliers? There's copies of the book around — L.G. Van Ett's . . . *and Boats . . . and Planes* (too bad it wasn't butts and planes) — but I'd never ask for one — I'll never know. The vittles: onion soup, crêpes, nine types, pastries, presumably French, a dozen types, and over on the fisher side: mussels, shrimp, salmon, fish & chips, deepfried squid with some kind of sour sauce. A meal on the mealticket.

When you're earlier than sales reps you can eat before you drink or drink before you eat, no rush. I ate before I drank.

Two, three, four. (Hrs.) Reps in the fatting crowd. Probably. (Repping.)

When from out of the sorry night comes this severe-looking creature of indeterminate age, severe but also soft, or not quite hard-edged — she wouldn't cut or bruise you over *too* wide a swath — or maybe it's just that she's totally in brown. Her pantsuit is brown, shoes brown, hair brown, eyes (different sizes, no, different *intensities* — or is she crosseyed? no, the discord isn't ocular) brown: the universal softener. From 10–12 feet I see her seeing me, already moving my way, moving at my eyes, my face — more than my body. I can't duck her, do I even want to?, too fatigued to bother. "Dance with me," says not so much she as her being (harder & darker than brown marble).

But I'm shot. is my plea & I spill it. Dance with me. no request this time, a command. How 'bout we sit and have. is my substitute offer, take or leave it. *Dance* with me. she lays down the law like a lawman. Alright, let's.

Then sit. Chat. Writer, meet bookseller. Stores in three states.

"What sort of writer are you?"

"I'm this secret treasure. The unacknowledged genius of American prose."

"Never mind — look at this." Ferrets through her purse. "Oh, it's not here. I'll be right back" — grabs my wrist. "If you're not here when I get back, your book is dead meat in Kentucky."

"I don't have a book."

"Yes you do."

Returns and hands me — oh my. On a hand-painted bookmark, an Edvard Munch type screams beneath a six-pointed star on a background of flames. "What d'you think?"

"It's . . . *yeah*. Is that you?"

"Why, does it look like me?"

"Not exactly."

"I've never shown it before."

"Why me?"

"'Cause you're Jewish."

"How do you know?"

"I can tell. I spent my last life in a concentration camp."

"The whole thing?"

"No, only the end."

"Which camp?"

"I don't know yet."

I try and estimate her age — 29? 50? Is she even young enough to've been there, died, and been reborn? "But what makes you think — like I could be Italian. Jews and Italians both look . . ."

"You're not Italian."

"Well they're both Mediterranean. I wouldn't guess you're from Kentucky."

"I'm not. I was born in Ohio. I've also lived in Spain."

"You ever live in Detroit?"

"That's a stupid question."

"I mean in a past life."

"Don't make fun. I don't believe in past lives."

"You just said . . ."

"No, I said my *last* life. It happens that I've lived before. Not everybody has."

I try to contemplate sex with her — will it be required? Try to get up, get another beer. "I don't want you to go" — she grabs both wrists. "Not until we've discussed *persecution*."

Okay, writer, write me out of this one!

GUILT MOISTENS THE TUB

Well I've come up with a new version, a new *speed* version, and I'm glad. Never again will I tackle my

    1 — face & beard
    2 — ears, back of neck
    3 — hair & beard (shampoo)
    4 — back
    5 — pits, arms, shoulders, chest, belly
    6 — crotch & ass
    7 — left leg & foot, right leg to ankle
    8 — right foot

in that exact (and exacting) sequence. Never again will I waste so much *time*. In my biggest breakthrough since eliminating step 9 (shaving), I've honed the bastard down to a streamlined 5-stepper:

    (1) — 1 and 2, as above (but continuous)
    (2) — 5 through 7, ditto
    (3) — 8, as above (unchanged)
    (4) — 4, ditto
    (5) — 3, ditto.

By continuous I of course mean one rinsing, once under the spigot at the finish of a given scrub cycle. (Suds on, suds off.) Anything else is patently absurd, *has* been absurd, and finally after thousands of repetitions I've learned — no more superfluous rinse-offs! — never again.

From now on the only fits and starts'll be if I gotta stop 'n' rinse midway through (2) 'cause my h--------ds're active and soapsuds sting 'em, or the eyes get shampoo-stung in the course of (5). Neither of which was the case during my first trial run — done! clean! — and I don't foresee problems since switching to Johnson's Babe Shampoo. "No more tears" — I use it *in* my eyes.

Yup, to fend off the dread BLEPHARITIS ("crusty lids"), for which docs prescribe "one drop Johnson's to 5-6 drops water. Dip swab in solution and scrub eyelids, avoiding . . ." *Drop dip* — didn't Dion sing that? — but I'll *never* sing in showers, only scrub.

Scrub-a-dub, scrub-a-doo, not a care in the world except . . . well, no *new* cares — showers don't add 'em — but warts remain worrisome. Not one, not two but THREE on my little right piggy-stayed-home. And where do they come from? *Science doesn't know.* Viruses? *That's right.* (But not much is known.) Could be I have got AIDS and am therefore susceptible to sundry invading what-thems — but that ain't the stuff to lose sleep over while in the tub.

No, not with the clear and present danger of living wart viruses virusing about menacingly in the unprotected waters about your feet. Soap is protection — well, *maybe* — but who's to protect the soap???

You, I mean me, I've gotta admit how ingenious it was to REMOVE SOAP FROM HANDS following step 7, old system, and now (2). Well there *is* soap in hands, actually *on*, but no handheld bar to directly engage killer warts. If suds can't do it, what hope (I ask) has a bar? So we give the ol' bar a well-deserved rest, but not before lathering the fingers for a wart-foot blitz offensive — suds on, zoooom, suds off. 'Stead of risking an infected bar and, in turn, tomorrow's face or, by our new #'s, today's aching back. (And if hands, perish the thought, should in spite of all precautions turn to toadskin, better hands than back, face — or possibly even pork.)

Backs . . . fronts. But what about sides? (Ribcage.) Sides're touched on during both (2) and (4). If all goes well, if both these scrubbings are strategic, adroit and above all conscientious, the "touches" will intersect and, with any luck at all, they will *overlap*. (Side dirt gone!). And why *add* a step, a time-consuming side step, having already mollified shower-time's claim to our precious LIFE time? (Why do you suppose they call them shower *stalls*?)

"What ever shall I do with all the time I will save?" A good question.

And the greatest savings have to be those in the twin realms of WAITING (for the tub to drain) and CLEANUP (shorter drain time means reduced accumulations of gunk and scum) made possible by the shrewd move of delaying the shampoo phase from 3 to (5), i.e., from early to late in the game. Late hair = reduced clog time. I congratulate myself on the move, and have thus earned the right to not only a beard but the otherwise extraneous steps ($1a_2$) and ($5b$) (and, retroactively, $1b/3b$) as well. Well done!

With the time saved I can take up skydiving . . . shop for a treehouse . . . lobby the state legislature in behalf of cripples and gimps . . . visit Indiana . . . lose 30 pounds . . . gain 80 pounds . . . copy *The Red and the Black* one word at a time on the back of my stamp collection . . . no limit to the nu-things I can do!

TO THE WIFE OF THIS GUY I DON'T MUCH LIKE WHO PLAYS THE STEREO TOO LOUD DOWNSTAIRS FROM ME

Lady. It best you dont know my name. I bang you old man. He a shit. I hope you punish him good. ~~Marla~~

STATE TERRORISM

Of all the wrong, sick things you can DO WITH LOVE, the sickest, the wrongest, of course, would be to submit it for sanction by the gleeless legions of civil intrusion/coercion. To in fact CELEBRATE love by registering it, voluntarily, with the STATE — who could be so nuts?

Like if let's say you ever wanna rob a bank, lam out on a car payment — or blow up the Washington Monument — fart in the post office — they'll just get out the ledger and know where to find you, where to begin. How many hours — minutes — before they put the jackboot to SOMEONE YOU LOVE? It just makes it too easy for 'em . . . widens their net . . . gives 'em exponentially more havoc to wreak. Talk about things that *aren't* mandatory — as ridiculous as sending 'em a list of all the drugs you take, or going to confession *without* perpetual damnation as the whip. What the hell business is it of THEIRS? Am I right or am I right? Willfully supplying your partner's i.d. (and in some states, the health of their blood) is as sick a surrender of privacy, not to mention secrecy, as welcoming them over to drill holes in the wall and WATCH YOU FUCK.

It was bad enough being enlisted — twice! — as best man at other people's wedlocks — I deserve a nail in the head for having done it. 'S not very smart to encourage such things.

The only imaginable happenstance which could ever impel ME to submit to this tyranny — to register *my* love — "marry" — would be if a primary love object's coerciveness became itself so great as to EXCEED, DWARF, and ultimately SUPERSEDE any personal concerns about, the state's: fear of loss c'n do it. Not justify it — 's never justifiable — but effect and "explain" it. That or the blinding blindness of "poetic inspiration" (love love love: you write lovelets on the wall, in the air, in the sky — so registration "seems" like but another hot new poem on a NEW & UNUSED SLATE), though such 'spiration usually wavers after the FIRST TEN MINUTES, two weeks, whatever. Leaving you, for undivided inducement, with the sleazy disquiets of the lone lonely nite.

Should my current p.l.o. force me to the wall, for ex., especially at a time when the thought of dissolution leaves me clinging to a wad of toilet paper in a flood — in The Flood — no quick sink down any drain (or o'er the Edge), just rage swept forever AWAY . . . if . . . then . . . then I *might* let them register us.

I grow gray, I grow wearied . . . but even in dog surrender I would demand the dignity of a personal wedlock address, a conjugal vow in and of my own penmanship. If compelled to deliver one TOMORROW, I'd be ready, oh I would! — it would go like this:

"Okay. First off, from the top, let's get this degrading business out of the way. I commit this vile act because all prior evidences and gestures of my undying Love have proven insufficient on their own to convey to you its towering import, and indeed would amount elsewhere to pigpiss in a pot. I thee wed, with profound and unavoidable exasperation, for one reason only: because you insist.

"I accede to the deed, therefore, not as definitive demo of love/devotion/affiliation, which knowing you I must regard as finitely undemonstrable, but to make it tougher for you to get rid of me with malice and haste; submit to a farce politically reprehensible in let-me-count-the-ways, not the least of which *this*: I cower before (behind) (beneath) (astride) the thought of losing you, and if this be the glue that bind you to me for even one extra day, that forestall for that duration your casting my walnuts to the dung beetles and crows, if, if . . . fuggit, lady, give me a break (I wish. I wish)."

A gong sounds. "You. Me. Before infinity sucks the bark

from our bones. Here's the pitch. Your mess is my mess, but mine — you don't hafta. Wait, no, you asked for this: hafta.

"Lie with me, die with me — oh, you've heard this before? — in the shit, the pit, the spit, the cum, the sum, the suck, the slick, the dick, the beef entrails. Melt into and become me, leave me the fuck alone, cease and never be born, bear and repair me, share me, grab me by the ankles and dangle me over Krakatoa — if you drop me I can't dangle you — lick my toes, pick the hairs from my nose, how's it goin'?, without you I'm, stay go, dear me, fear me, reduce me to dry heaves and sobs, swallow my metaphors whole, put my tongue in a box and toss it down the steps, damn me, scam me, live with me live with me two days a week — at your place — I *won't* give up my office — till we hang on the dead sidewall of x-cetera, two lichen-covered gargoyles, to the last lost syllable of imported time — Anything short of that you can fucking KEEP. But no honeymoon this week because Roscoe Mitchell is playing, but I'll stalk up if you'd like (let me know)."

Then the question-answer part: Are you naturally platinum? Your favorite Mexican vampire movie? Did you ever fuck a cop? What's the capital of Cleveland? (a trick question). Name five trumpeters who have recorded with Duke Ellington. What's the value of pi to five decimal places?

And her vow is completely up to her — we can flip for who goes first — and her questions. Neither should know what the other has come up with beforehand, and obviously perfect symmetry is neither a goal nor an especially desirable outcome. (It's a life!)

A HUNDRED YEARS OF YEAST

(fiction)

I finally did something I'm not ashamed of. Which is not quite the same as I'm proud of but *you* know. I went to this thing out in Malibu, this unpleasant ... thing. With Georges my French friend, who didn't really have to twist my arm. Guru Maharaj Ji — Georges was curious. And I was curious about his curious, so we drove out to this weekly meet where suckers in seersucker sit around and listen to these guys. A guy and a gal, one of each, softselling (while standing) the litany of their pudgy imported savior. Maharaj Ji, who fifteen years ago was "The Kid." Now he's just a rich prick who hasn't named a town for himself (so they don't deport him). Another yuppie role model by-the-sea. Georges, consumer-shopping transcendence, has recently done meridian plant therapy ("It weel save thee world") and this shit is possibly next. So these guys start grocery-

(nonfiction)

On the morning eye was born, March — , 19 — , my palsied pop, a beeswax chandler and dealer in second-rate china, promised my ma: "Never will *our* son watch golf on television." 6'4" naked with my heels on the floor, eye played center-forward for the Seton Hall JV, averaging 14.8 points, 7.3 rebounds a semester, receiving a baccalaureate in Welsh Studies; graduate work at the University of Cardiff. Taught Spanish as a Second Language, eight years, Tucson, Denver, Boca Raton. Unofficial mayor of Plainfield, New Jersey, 1968. Eye get two days from a pair of socks, four days from a drinking cup, three point five weeks from a meaningful relationship.

Slogan: "The fallacy is in thinking that if it plays three *quarters* of a night, it can play all *night*." Hobbies: paint-by-numbers, duck f--king.

(art criticism)

I can no longer get a handle on the objects of my own nostalgia — have I simply used them up? I don't *care* about Elvis, gore films, now-defunct candies and cereals, football autumns circa '62. Dunno what I "miss" — do I even miss "missing"? Call me MAMMAL — I need to have those mammal things stirred.

(food)

"A can of snapper soup will make you happy." I have never been unhappier. I've been unhappier, but never with quite so little overt *cause*. Causes:

1.	2.	3.	4.	5.	6.
7.	8.	9.	10.	I	can't

think of one.

Okay . . . Snapper Time! Contents include: thick brown slop, good 'n' chewy turtle bits, modified food starch, rehydrated parsley, wheat flour, margarine, turtle broth. As you cook it the brown gets browner — plop, slop, bubble — it's thick! Mm *mmm* — a rare canned potage that requires no additional seasoning. (WARNING: Snapper meat resembles tiny, disgusting bits of *liver* — so don't look.)

(sports & recreation)

I wanna put a bullet in the head of the . . . of the WHAT???

listing the available bliss. The male sways slightly, he's like nine feet tall, 100 pounds, he's wearing cashmere and he says, says, keeps on saying: "It's really so-o-o simple. When hungry, eat . . . when thirsty, drink . . . when tired, sleep. So-o-o simple." The female, hip new age jumpsuit, thinly veiled fuck-me-or-I'll-die-1965 look, speaks with but a hint of embarrassment re before she was saved: "I had *everything*. I owned not only a beautiful car and a terrific home but my own skis. I'd be on top of this fantastic slope — the sky was radiant, the view was *breathtaking*. And I thought to myself, 'Gee, y'know, I'd rather be water-skiing.'" Never satisfied, never satisfied! — the Malibuers (chuckling lightly) can dig it. Finally, any-questions time. Georges, curiosity unsated, his product hunger in a holding pattern as urgent as waiting to shit, wants to know: "What, specifically [French accent], is the *system*

(film treatment)

There's this zooship, see, twice as huge as the spacecraft in *Alien*, all full up with these *animals*. Live ones, grisly and ferocious: slavering tigers, killer wolverines, bubonic Alsatians, rabid porcupines, anacondas which have not eaten childmeat in more than a month. Earth beasts in simulated habitat, spare no expense — these critters should have it so good back in Nature. Destination: "Space Suburbia." Space suburbanites, it seems, are more than glad to exchange hard-earned space gelt for viewings, rentals and (highly illegal but money talks) purchases of fearsome animules. Short on kicks, these jaded jackjoes have periodic need to recharge their beast-fear: something — anything! — more intense than programing (and endlessly *re*programing) the digital flush-bowl.

(guest lecture)

"Seems like everyone's becoming a mom. People of penis are motherizing gals at alarming rates, and the gals're saying: 'Thanx boys for fertilizing our gal eggs.' I would never do such a thing. Nor would I conjoin with a mom. When you join a mom, anyone's mom, the world becomes a hostile parade of mafuckers. You've no doubt seen the calling card: 'I have given up being Macho but am still the one for plugging your wife-mom.'"

(fiction, cont'd)

you employ?" The tall goon gets coy — "Be patient . . . Malibu wasn't built in a day." Five minutes' evasion goes by, a woman in Topanga tie-dye asks, "Is it anything like meditation?" Ha — time for some ha's as the guy relates how he's been asked if it has much in common with *breathing*. "'Gee,' I said, 'I would certainly hope so'" — haw *ha* — "but if any of you are genuinely *interested*, I'll give you my card, we'll set up a personal, private session [and please bring your purse or your wallet]." At which point I blow my cool, my top, and stand like a stick to be counted: "Look, sir, we are busy people. We have been lectured by snake oil salesmen up the old wazoo. We are not rubes. Before we reach for the deed to our Mercedes, what, may I ask, is the nature of the oil *your* firm offers?" "Um, tee

(book review)

High upon a shelf at Wilshire Books, 3018 Wilshire Blvd., Santa Monica, scribbled on p. 50 of an overpriced second-hand copy of *We Loved Supreme*, Susan Sontag's tumid account of her brief (but steamy!) affair with John Coltrane: *This book is dogshit. Don't be a fool. Read Jackie Suzann. (The Original Owner)*.

(health notes)

There are things I'm a monist about, but theism isn't one of them. "In God we trust" should be replaced *toot sweet* by "In god(s) we (may at our discretion) trust (provisionally)." And if the Cincinnati Reds, who during the Red Scare fifties were dubbed the Redlegs, are once more merely the Reds, then how's about we purge another keepsake of that sorry decade — "one nation *under God*" — from the Pledge of Allegiance?

(travel)

I am always the disturbance in everybody's life (including my own), the anti-catalyst at every gathering of however many, the key ingredient that makes it all add up to *not adding up*.

(fiction, cont'd)

hee . . . "— then prolonged awkward silence and *polite* bullshit queries from the seated. Christ I hate this stuff, and sometimes (by extension) myself as well. I've always let Jehovah's Witnesses off too easy when they've wakened me at 9 with a *Watchtower* and a knock — "Thanks but no thanks" (the expedient response) and back to bed. But fuck, here I am all the hell out in goddam Malibu, I'm seething and teething and I'd better get some *mileage* from the ordeal. "Hey!" — listen, dammit — "how come you talk about 'hunger,' 'thirst,' but nary a word, not a whisper, on *sexual* appetite? You've scrupulously avoided the only imagery that might conceivably have made you jerks seem *human*. You're just a pair of G-rated windup dolls." Adam's ap bobs in the guy's storky throat — "Oh, we could've mentioned *orgasms*, ha, but we thought it might *affront* . . ." — but it's hopeless. The throng departs, meeting's adjourned and I'm not ashamed. Compassion for poor Georges (who now must shop elsewhere) or I'd feel *proud*.

(investment tips)

If you mix tea and coffee in the same cup, you die. If you mix
ink and aspirin, you disintegrate.

(true crime)

Twelve-thirteen years ago I was visiting friends in upstate
New York. We're sitting around drinking, goofing, and this
exceptionally dull ten-year-old, no glint in his eyes like in
some of his age mates', keeps hitting on us for dimes. It's June,
he's been left back for the second time, and he doesn't think
his folks'll be giving him pocket money. I get drunk (and
drunker) and finally I give him some paper, a one. Which
scares him — that much the weasels will assume he stole. So
we find this spot, there's a baseball field behind the house, I
tell him hide it under home plate and eventually he'll figure
what to do. Fine, awright; for the first time since we met he
isn't a basket case. An hour later, still drinking while he's having dinner, I creep back and slip a five under the one. Later
still, a ten. Finally it's like two a.m., I look in my wallet and all
I've got left is a ticket back home and a twenty. So I go add the
twenty.

(gift suggestion)

I now realize — I hope it's not too late — I take a large, not a
medium, T-shirt.

(serving suggestion)

Ladle your snapper on a bed of brown rice sprinkled with
whole cumin seed, diced pickling cucumber, scallion and
endive.

(whimsy & eyewash)

I will root for this country to win Olympic gold the day (or night) a box of cornflakes opens the Playboy Jazz Festival on tenor sax.

DAY PROVES THE NIGHT IS RIGHT

More often than not lately — and not simply during hangovers — when I spot an object in frame that I haven't previously noticed, been aware of, I take for granted its having *moved* to have entered context, to have suddenly impacted upon an already more or less max-focused visual consciousness. From unnoticed to noticed, unseen to seen — the auto-response is to postulate (hallucinate?) motion.

On the printed page, on the other hand, when whole sentences, paragraphs change on me as new swarms of letters emerge willy-nilly from typefont ether, *that* I don't perceive as motion 'cause it isn't basic *behavior* for letters to move. Not like with *things*.

Rates, speeds, accelerations vary. Occasionally an item will just pop into focus — instant arrival, elsewhere to here — zero to infinity in *nothin'*. Other times it's like, oh, three whoozits in four seconds. (Independent of size or surprise.)

Departures from frame, by definition, y'don't notice. From awareness to not. This is just eye stuff. (Love, for instance, scrutinized or not, you'll notice *gone*. Or going.) The eye, as sensor, can *at times* be just as sighted as the heart or lovepulp.

Oh, I get it. At eye-midnight, when (in frame) even bowels don't move, arrival and departure are functionally equalized. How egalitarian. (Is that it?)

MISUSES OF NIGHT (2)

your life
cycle is here-
by re-

THE AUTHOR AT 40 (A PREVIEW)

". . . and it gets to where" — this is what he tells them, friends, 'colleagues,' when they merely inquire how he's been — "there are like these *demons* sitting on my lap. Or some call them daemons. Y'know?" He asks if they know because, really, it's not the sort of thing you tend to know. Not unless you've been there, completely, totally *there*, and he hadn't either. Not till his 70th-plus day — none off — of eight-ten-twelve hours a-writing. Or some number like that.

"And it's not just the toil" — is he saying it's not from the toil? "Like I've had deadlines, gallows deadlines, 5-6 AM, I need three thousand words by 8, I've got deadlines like that all the time. Certainly, yuh, they take a lot out of you. And I always go longer than they want, or expect, anyway, more than I need to satisfy *them*. They say four pages, I go nineteen. That's given. I've always been a pump it out, nose to the grindstone type guy, and it always leaves me thoroughly, uh, mega-exhausted. Like I just ran two marathons. But it's not the work, I'm sure it's not the work, even though I haven't got half the stamina I did at 30, or even 38. It's not the workload, it's the no respite, the, er, consecutive."

Days? "Days. Weeks. 'Cause I'm already *thinking* the stuff, living it, anything I'm in the midst of writing, all day every day, every flucking day until I'm done. So I'm familiar with, I was *already* familiar with, with that whole setup *within* the unit day, the nerve-racking, um, it's back-breaking even when you're not actually doing it, typing it, from sun to sun to whenever. You know: sweating tears, crying blood — all that nonsense — but big shit, that's the life, the gig. A debilitating *job*, disabling *preoccupation*, unbearable dedication to, y'know, but so what? What's different, though, this time is never before was it so many days, full days, uninterrupted, of exactly that, and not just the thinking, the rehearsal, but the act itself, in a hardback chair under a hot light at this clickety-clack, y'know, runaway railroad of a keyboard. That's when it goes from normal one-dimensional unbearable — overwork, ouch — writing *is* physical labor! — to the brink of . . ."

Fun and games? Laughter? "No, come on. It's nice of you to be taking this down for, instead of me, thanks, but don't you think you oughta get things right? It was like a quantum leap, this last siege of it threw me, dumped me, I'm assuming I'm past it, at the doorway to fucking dementia. Like these corny stories you read about artists going craaaazy. Artaud, what's his, Van Gogh, that shit, *A Bucket of Blood*. A cliché and a half but there *are* such things. And it had nothing to do with drinking.

"'Cause I didn't, I don't think I had a six-pack, total, the whole time out. I used to do four beers, minimum, every time I sat down at a typewriter. It was never, it wasn't really about sparking, firing my invention or any of, um, like Ray Milland tells the bartender in *Lost Weekend*, that silliness, nah. It's more like it just makes certain operational decisions easier, makes them terminably *possible* — word choice, sequence, drop this, change that — and writing as a *chore* is such tedium you gotta have something to bring it down to scale, to *humanize* it as an activity. So I'd have these beers, or sometimes shots, anyway this time I didn't. And the result was, well two things happened. First, without my usual assist to cut it short, keep moving to the next crossroad, without the chemical *license* to just say yes, this'll do — 'cause in the end I'll be settling for it anyway, or something basically the same — it took me longer to do everything. Maybe two-thirds longer, that many additional rewrites, that many further occasions to . . ."

Have to get up and piss? Not have to . . . "No! You're as bad as . . . just be quiet, I'll let you know when it's your turn. One of the *rewards* of writing, and there really aren't many, not of the *work*, is just being finished — even a page. A sentence. And so by not drinking I'm robbed of those, some, probably a lot, the small goals met on a regular basis. The writing itself, the, it always feels good looking over what I've got, what's done, short, long, *when* it's done — and this was, no joke, the most satisfying bunch of pages I may ever 've filled — but the moments of elation were too isolated to do me any good. Although, looking back on it now, it really wasn't much more than an amplification, or contraction, whatever, of my standard, um . . . it was simply more — or less — of same. Of certain aspects of the trip, but only a *quantitative* modification. They must've contributed, the additional time, the fewer functional perks, but the bigger factor, as far as not drinking, as far as the madness, was number two: loss of discontinuity.

"Like if I drink while I'm writing I'll forget stuff, obviously, in the day-to-day process of hacking it out, at various stages of getting the fucker done. I don't mean in a data sense, content, all this info I need to be transmitting sooner or later (so I'd better not lose it), any of that. It's more, uh, it's something positive, utilitarian, erasing the emotional, the hard edges: glaring, jangly pieces of my life seeping through. And not from the writing, erasing from *me*. Symptomatic relief for all the torture and shit which are kind of inevitable byproducts of all this 'sandpapering your soul.' Without periodic relief all you've got is a direct confrontation with *stuff*, with subject matter, with yourself, no letup between you and it, and you and you — nonstop till you wanna howl. It's bad enough at the one-*week* point, do it long enough and you're sandpapering with a Black & Decker. And souls, psyches weren't built to handle that kind of sanding.

"Keep at it and eventually it's a *drill* you're using, your worst fears realized — writing as *literally* a trip to the dentist! — a shovel. Dig deep enough and you start hitting pockets of, living toxic *motherlodes* that gush out, rush out and engulf you, and no skin's left to hold anything back, to hold it *in*, there's no bone, not enough muscle to fight the shit off once it's out circling the room, invading your dreams, etching patterns on . . . It's like those S. Clay Wilson 'nose demons,' 'tongue demons,' cartoon thingies streaming out of wound holes in some guy's, his stabbed and bullet-ridden body parts. Every under-repressed personal monster, and some not so personal, your basic hideous Universe biz, 'the nature of being,' whatever. Like there must've been times before when I'd go on multi-week binges and get *somewhere* near there, that neck of the woods, *from* drinking — or the physical aftermath — but never, what a shock, from *avoiding* the whole thing.

"By doing something rash, being 'nice' to myself, to my body, I cut myself off from a principal means, one of 'em, of *limiting* these thingies, their frigging run. Of course I could stop writing, ha, but when you're on a *mission* — some chance. Finally I'm on the trail of some hot lit, right, so I stay on the trail, *got* to — and it's never gonna hurt any less. Not if it's any good, and not without the booze, the beers, but I made this big health, this life decision, and life has never made art exactly easy. So instead of what you can and sometimes do pull off — writing as *cathartic*, you triumph, you prevail, small-time demons get the bum's rush, g'bye — this time the demons just got stronger. Way before the end they already had the advantage, the leverage, and for the last couple weeks I felt, I tacked this card on the wall with an inscription, 'I have to think there's a better hell somewhere.' Good line, actually, but that's how it felt. Every bit as fucked as my worst rejections by women, or of my work by editors, y'know, publishers."

Only *as* fucked? "No, you're right, it's not your turn but true: *worse*. I've never felt more bruised and contused, minute in, minute, no, that's too art-romantic, too melodramatic, I'm not, but speaking of rejection, no, it's more from the other end: compromise. The notion of 'compromising my work' has always driven me bananas. Okay, so anyway there's *that* torture, forcing myself, which I'm finding pathologically harder and harder to do — dentist chair again, writing chair — agreeing to write, for survival reasons, or a favor to some jerk, what essentially I *don't wanna write*, to somebody's rigid specifications, *their* style sheet, their field and yard-marker. All the extra effort of not only coming up with copy I don't really care about, or if I do at first, slightly, I won't for long, but of playing this imbecile game where I try and actually *envision* it as something I don't mind doing — I'm a *lousy* method actor. I can never finesse the motivation. I cringe, I grimace, I flay myself for taking the assignment, for wasting my chops, my 'talent,' I punch walls and pace around cursing everybody's guts including my own, but finally I jump in, or fall in, and endure the, for however long, and it's over.

"Whereas when I write *exactly what I want*, like this last batch of, with nobody looking over my shoulder but me, it's eternal hell, the now of it is eternal and it's hellish. The horror of living inside your own vision, even if *it's* not a vision of horror, y'know, terror, but to have to continuously monitor, follow it to its logical, ultimate what, whatever, or even just peek in, take *notes* and get out — you'll get blisters either way — for that to be your sole calling besides eating, sleeping, shitting and having the flu, just that for two-plus months: fuggo. Or you could say hey, two months, big deal, but let 'em hook fishhooks in your face for two months on PCP: whoopee hey!! And by inside the vision I don't even mean tight, uh, like the compromise number, *that's* claustrophobic. This is fat and wide as the goddam galaxy, and nine times as merciless."

Wait, excuse me, this time I must interrupt. "..." Are you actually claiming this as something *new* to your experience? You who in recent years have rarely let a week lapse without wheeling out some fatuous artist-in-torment tommyrot? I wonder, have you even got a different *story line* anymore, that and whatever's handy in your imitation leather Life Stinks briefcase? And what *was* it you were writing this time that drove you, if let's say it even did, to this higher level of impalement? (Please elaborate.)

"Well okay, sure, *yeah*. Of course I've had eyefuls, extended, uh, glimpses of, but never so *immediate*, personally immediate, intense. It's like I was just a voyeur before, a passenger. I can't be more specific, don't, sorry, my prerogative — maybe I'll show you sometime. Let's just say the subject, well, whatever it was, subjects, plural, forced me deeper than I'd, but *enough* of that — anyway, the repercussions are still . . . repercussing. 'Cause not only have I finally found the time, the opportunity, to do these projects that couldn't be closer to what I *prefer* to be doing, but I'm doing them at 80-90-95% capacity, uh, I'm that close, at times, to satisfying myself. Which, since nobody's rougher on me than me, a sterner judge, is no mean feat. And just as I finally get so lucky, about what I'm writing, what I can probably get *published*, and at the same time I'm finally 'good enough' to almost spit it all out in words, accurately, and rhythms, that actually don't make me sick, just when I make the breakthrough, when I'm confident, creationwise, I could write my way out of *relevant* wet paper bags, I realize — simultaneously — that the wear and tear of all of this is so *immense* I'd never wanna do it again."

. . . . . "So I'm thinking I'd better pin something on the wall to warn myself, next time I consider, in case I forget *how* bad . . . 'Cause aside from the question of who wants writing — who *wants* the little eyesore, black type, white page, this maze, this cell? — is who wants to *write it* . . . at such a cost? Like I really can't see sitting down, mining the depths — realistically; bracket the crankiness — more than once or twice, not even three times a year. 40 pages, 50 pages, max. More'n that, where's my straitjacket? — y'think I'm kidding? So in terms of 'the mission' — what, *abandon* it? — now *you're* kidding — I've got this dilemma. If I write from the bottomless shaft of my own yuh yuh, heart and soulville, exposed ganglia, open veins, I'm a goner. So that's out. I write the light stuff, 'humor,' I do that instead, I'm a third-rate standup. Which is not to say I've 'lost my sense of humor' — shit, no — it's I wouldn't know, not to save my life, how to be funny *lightly*. Or light serious, same deal, without the world (or my fucking psyche) depending on it. And if I knew I wouldn't *do* — light equals light*weight* — a fucking dilemma."

But, hey, isn't there some simple *tactical* solution, say, like a brief vacation? Time off from the rigors of . . . "What, two weeks in Oxnard's gonna change things? You think I won't bring *along* my obsession, huh, profession — possession! — compression, CONFESSION: I'm so inarticulate sometimes I could *cry*."

You're right, pops — no solution. But you've got your health. This hot milk — say goodnight — it's yours; and a salt-free tortilla chip. Sleep well, veteran of NINETEEN YEARS' service at 'alternative' sheets like *East Village Itch* and the *Berkeley Backside*, the literal LAST MAN, WOMAN OR CHILD who wrote for 'em then — at the literal *dawn* — and writes for 'em now (and is bitter). Who still daydreams of submitting features to *Argosy* — does it still exist? — *Antaeus, The Ring* and *Family Circle*. Whose 'problems' have something, but not a whole damn lot, to do with 'art' — he was just as forlorn at 30, when he thought of himself as a hack. He's . . . confused. Needs a nightdream of frogs and sushi (or 'the french girl') to set him straight. Needs, well, just drink your milk and we'll take it from there.

A TOWEL FOR ROCK MAZDA

Dripping wet, back to the translucent curtains which by day tint the room an eerie blue when closed, I slide right the left of two plastic metal-frame doors and reach for one of at most three oversize bath towels which hang from the wooden rack on wall left: patternless red; patternless white; white/blue/black "zodiac" pattern, found abandoned at the La Brea Tar Pits. With varying degrees of diligence I wipe hair, beard, shoulders, back, arms, chest and gut. Continuing downward with little pause, I step from the tub to a beach towel which has not since the seventies dried more than the soles of my feet, and whose bouquet becomes gamy when wet, and wipe dry my crotch, ass, left leg and foot, right leg to within an inch of my wart-toe.

Returning my towel to its spot on the rack, I grab and slip into the terricloth robe which swings from a nail above the inside knob of the bathroom door. With a hand towel from either of two hooks to its immediate right I blot further moisture from my hair while preliminarily "shaping" it to the needs or whims of the hours ahead. To facilitate my use of the mirror, I lean over the tub, draw aside the curtains and raise the window a notch. Its frame rotting, it will not remain open on its own, and a three-inch by four-inch plywood rectangle is brought into play. Except in winters crueler than most, I normally exploit the four-inch opening. Did I say gamy? I meant piquant. Like thyme or turmeric or stale ale.

SIX HITS OF DIAPARENE VS. NONE — There is dry and there's *dry*. Cornstarch exceeds the chafe protection of talc. In the thigh and groin region I am one crotchedy monkey. Diaparene Corn Starch: the best. No date looming, I loosen my robe and lift my left foot to the rim of the tub, resting the ball on the metal runners of the shower door. With my right hand I invert the container and shake it directly over my upper inside thigh, then the palm of my other hand, which in turn applies powder to the rear inside thigh. Exchanging feet — left down, right up — I shake four more hits to the same palm and apply them to my balls (but not lovestub), right inside thigh (front and rear), inner cheeks and butthole. Under the sink tap I rinse starch traces from my hand, from both hands. Then dry them on the hand towel of my choosing.

Date looming — agreeable to nosebuds, starch is less so to tonguebuds (and gals're entitled to the true taste of *me*) — I abstain. Nogal will lick it, even kiss it, with talc or starch runoff from neighboring fleshposts. A good policy: no-starch when a galmouth is remotely feasible. Risk of chafing or worse: worth it with galmouth on the line.

"A Q-Tip or two makes do . . . a dry ear is second to none." The 2-Tip system gets my vote: Tip in each hand, beginning with right, cursorily swab furrows and gutters of outer ear; plunge boldly into auditory canal and wiggle 'round, fearlessly risking permanent hearing loss; repeat with unused tip of each Tip. As in double-blade shaving (goes the theory), what the first twin tip misses its partner won't. Systematically I swab and wiggle, staring stoically at the framed glossy of Up With People o'er the crapper w/ swastikas scratched in their smiles and some eyes blotted out, thinking 'Deadthings, oyster scissors,' then fling ear-soiled Tips in the trashbag alongside the pot.

To the bedroom for pants, outer not under-, cutoff or wholeleg depending on season; remove and return robe to its nail. To each of my armpits: a splash of English Sterling light musk cologne, a "sweet" as opposed to "tart" ("astringent") smellum, but only when critical I not stink. To conclusively establish whether my left pit sweats less than my right — it seems so — is something *wrong* with me? — it is crucial not to interfere in any way, any *possible* way, with normal perspiration. Besides, why throw money 'way — and a vital resource?

Unless someone is gonna breathe you deeply, intimately —
not bank clerks, checkouts, the mailman — why deplete the
planet's scent reserves?

Should upper garb de jour be a tightnecked T-shirt, and
donning disturb hair shape as already dealt, rewipe with a dry
hand towel and deal again. Selections include: "bangs" . . .
"spiky" . . . "full." If shirt is loosenecked or button-front,
rewipe only if initial design and/or execution have proven
faulty. What a comfort not having to shave, although groom
and trim later — shit — maybe I should just shave the sucker,
scrape it clean, then every third day I can, anyway, *now*, nothing undone but to slide right the shower doors, pluck hairs
from the drain, follow the rush of bathwater to its final reward, think (or recite) a sentence with 'babies' in it. *Finis.*

Pisces, burbles my sopping bath towel, is "lovable."
Virgo says "Have a nice day."

TALES OF THE EYE CLINIC

When I belch and it occurs to me, usually I form the word *But*, I never append anything. I say *But* and that's it. Actually, when I'm bored sometimes I belch *Bah*. Without the *t* to cap it, it comes out real big. And I have tried to extend *but* to *butter*, but generally it comes out *budder*, the *t* gets dissipated in stretching it out.

WORTHLESS PEEPERS: OUR SIGHTLESS COAST POETS

For many, seeing is a way of life; for others, screw 'em but it ain't. But for All, let there be *sight*. Which as fate would have it is a far tougher toss than just lifting lids: you hafta earn it. And there lies the irony.

For while among the surest of earners, poets, even those with flawless 20-20s, barely use these organs when composing verse; it is their "mind's eye" (and in some instances: "heart's eye") that attunes them to a world of truth and beauty beyond spectrums and light. Actual retinas are not necessary. Even with both lamps shot, an accomplished verser can "see" earth & heaven in pic-perfect clarity, sometimes (you guessed it) a smitch clearer than those luckyducks of poetry with both orbs intact. 'Cause let's face it, *suffering* is what makes good art good, and great art great, be it painting or pomes, and it's an honest fact that no one loves a blindo. If anyone suffers more than blindos I would like to know who. They can't find their way to the latrine and must wear diapers (sometimes but not always).

So when it comes to pomes, blind is an advantage bar none. Only further edge would be to live out West, specifically the Coast (southern part), as that is your well-documented "place" where people live and are free and in touch with the latest and profoundest of human feelings and emissions (it said so in *Newsweek*) — and pathos is one of them. Blind, the West and poetry were made for each other, and the world is a better (if profounder) place for it. Two rich and fertile examples of this exciting new scene immediately follow.

meetcha
for a pizza

if it is not good we can
go out and
fuck
in
the
car

Above the stove of Rubert Metzl's sunbright Hollywood flat is a placard which reads: "My nights are darker than yours." *It* reads, yes, but he cannot, as Metzl is sightless, a condition which has been his since 1980, when a laboratory accident caused caustic solution to eat out his eyeballs one hundred percent. Los Angel State's top ranked lab major at the time, he was shunted to liberal arts by callous instructors who nixed his crusade to mix blindness and test tubes — to his distress and chagrin.

If not for the intervention of a sympathetic prof, the strict but venerable Podio Botsnard, Rubert would've been up shit's creek. Botsnard, an author with several pomes to his credit, advanced the "write route" for coping with the post-eye blues. In no time flat, poesy was letting Rube expound his upsetness in an immediate, direct and coherent manner (the "three manners" which all aspiring poets must someday embrace). The rest is history. Professor B. contends his former pupil is "perhaps the farthest out of contempo Coast metered poets. His deficiency has if anything aided his search for the ideal poetic time, as there are no clocks in the endless night. It would have been nice to see him bag a Nobel in science, sure, but one in pomes is nothing to sneeze at."

Underplaying his leadership role in Coast Poetry's New Blind, Metzl (rhymes with "pretzel") humbly states: "If men and women without eyes could attain their rightful esteem, and if a string of lines with dopy punctuation could be the means, this empty-socket smuck would be more than gratified." Standing steadfast in his mind-eye vision of a blind culture completely self-sufficient by the year 2000, he has coined the movement's rallying cry, "Let the *blind* lead the blind." Could Homer or Milton have put it better?

> my hands are as sticky (& possibly CLAMMY)
> as my feet and my neck is TIGHT
> like a clammy STOOL
> and i feel like a clammy CLOG
> & i'm gonna go to one of those
> good places & get some . . . . GOODNESS
> and if it's clammy i'm gonna
> kick something (really)
> i'm gonna break a lot of shit!

Since his tumultuous '85 appearance at McCabe's, Red Matzo has come on like a one-man Angry Young Blind. Contrary to prevailing scoff that his legend exceeds reality, a peek at the Matzo bio tells us diff'rent; if any young poet has grounds for anger, Red is it. Unsighted at birth, he was orphaned at 6 when, en route to acquire a seeing eye dog, his parents' van collided with a bus. Blamed by a vengeful uncle for the elder Matzos' passing, the friendly pup was "put away" on the ginger lad's next birthday. Foster homes followed. Unwanted, uncared-for, he was given a Braille stylus by a vacuum salesman with blind kids of his own. In the darkness of his life he began pecking pomes when no one was lookin'. His third foster mom, howev, saw no poetry in the holes Red poked in her shopping lists. Calling the moody child a "no-eyed misfit," she spiked his eye medicine with lighter fluid and abused him to near hysteria.

A stay at the Center for the Blind & Disturbed in Downey was hardly a merry one. From his second-floor ward, he could hear the taunts of local eye-bigots gathered at the gate shouting, "No see shit! No see shit!" One holiday, an anonymous donor left him a teddy bear — with corneas blackened and the message, "This is you, zero eyes." The scars remain deep. Yet there was a happy sidelight to this rather dismal period of his life. One shiny day he awoke to find his optics working! Just like that! Ain't life funny! Deciding on the spot that he would be "copping out" if he failed to devote his life to a poetry exlusively for the unseeing, he drew up papers that day to make Blind As A Bat, Inc. (its motto: "A tin cup up *yours*, eye-man!") a publishing reality.

BAAB's first venture, due to hit the stands in June, will be ish number one of *Blindfold — The Journal of No-See-Dick*, an all-Braille quarterly. Says Matzo in the no-holds-barred dedication: "If the seeing-is-believing brigade wants to sample our powerful poetics, they will have to learn Braille, because dat's de only way we gonna run it. It will cost them time and effort, but the fruits will be worth it. In swift order they'll be swept by the power, acknowledge the work it takes to be blind, their fingers will do the believing and then, who knows . . . may they never mock, maltreat or razz a goose-egg eyes again."

Who knows indeed! And a hip hip hurrah to all the many others of Blind Los Angelez' golden age of poetry!

DON'T GET AROUND MUCH ANYM

But I do get out, and today I saw this hepcat, this blade, the greatest thing I ever saw in my life. His underwear was sticking out over a classy apricot button-down, out from under silver beltless polyester slacks an inch too tight. The shorts were loose at the band and stuck out *two* inches. 'S enough to make me wanna get out tomorrow!

MY POEM OR YOURS?

Wear your sponge to readings:
a poet may want to take you home.
Or (if you prefer)
a trip to your place
will broaden his horizons.
Visits to new lands & cultures
will help him map out
which way is up.
His nails are clipped
so in his explorations of your
fjords and crannies
you will not be lacerated:
poets respect your being
(they will not bite
what isn't food).
Nurture: poets need nurture.
It's the gravest of sins
— at least a callous oversight —
to let one starve.

I, a poet,
a so-called macho poet,
have not left a reading
with an actual broad
in more than four years.
I'm an old fuck,
I jack off a lot
and rely on memory and speculation
(in a word, poetry)
to fuel even that.
A poet is a poet's best friend:

won't you please befriend me?
Be my second best and
listen to my every word,
to the virile heart
that beats behind it,
pumping blood and poems,
new poems,
hot, never-to-be-transcribed poems
you will be the first
and last to hear.
Generous to a fault
with my blood and poetry,
I have bled and poemed
for your ma and your pa
on one-way streets of the soul
from here to Kalamazoo.

In my spare time (when
not writing poems)
I'm an all-round neat guy,
a passable stick man —
and let's not discount
the tongue.
I know three-quarters of everything
worth knowing
and am an animal when and
where it counts.
You've probably made bigger mistakes
in the last hour
than you could possibly make
coming home with me,
a more accessible poet
than anyone else on the bill.
More macho and more starving,
I'll sing for my supper.

I'll play "Willow Weep for Me"
on my rented baritone sax;
I'll show you some *fun*.
Hey (time permitting),
I'll write you a poem!
I'll even let you title it yourself.

THE WAY WE WE'RE

    After me
there is nothing for you
but confusion
and death

and Duz.

LOVE STALKS LIFE UNTIL DEATH

What, another piss story? I'm a real pisser. If you want you can skip ahead, but it's a good'un. A pre-AIDS tale about not only bladders but lust, higher learning, friendship, price of liquor in the ghetto, porn films, flexible afternoons in the big city, the right angle in architecture. The year I moved to L.A. Spring? Indian spring? Whenever.

Errol Pander calls, tells me he's got this friend teaches psychology. Jill somebody, says I know her; I don't. At CCNY, City College of New York, where my mother once went (and I'm glad I didn't). Psych instructor with thus and such a midweek undergraduate course. He's invited, expected, supposed to go help her do something, which he now wants out of — could I maybe go in his place? Immediately I smell rat. A rat in an alley.

Ali Sherwin, who I'm still living with, he mus' figure he can swoop down while I'm out — it's an afternoon class. What he don't know is she's working full shift at an office again. Art director for *AM/PM Reporter* — a scandal weekly. I'll bet she hasn't told him. "Tomorrow?" "That's right." I would *love* to foil this scumbo so I tell him sure. He wants to speak to Ali.

"She's out, but I'll tell her you said hi."

Take a train uptown to discover I've been roped into a *test*. A class on it; Jill Schuyler, Ms. not Dr. — no doctorate — is gonna test me. Some sort of low-intensity intelligence whuzzit, not even an oral rorschach or an occupational screening thing, just standard IQ-type crap. Arithmetic, meanings of words, no multiple choice. She'll read off a page and I'll respond, aloud, students taking notes or whatev. We're supposed to've met at a dinner somewhere, but I can't cognize her from adam.

First the math, fundamental fare like five plus seven

equals twelve, problems with apples but not apples and oranges. Can't believe she's wasting an actual class on this, they could be cadging it off bookpages at home, maybe she likes "presentations." Keep 'em *attentive* might be the gameplan — persons (live) beat books (dead) — but my eyes dart at their eyes and 'tain't much glimmer, of attentiveness or anything. And couldn't she have used one of *them* for the demo? Which suggests the whole idea was Errol's to begin with. For me to be this mere warm body, sitting still for math when I could be home critiquing owlshit for some rockmag.

Every time I answer correct, which is always, she says, "Good," once in a while *"Good!"* and finally math is done. Break before the word part and I'm feeling itchy, gotta leave the room (reminds me of 4th grade), the building (same), the goddam campus. The whole drear gray dry environs, which don't remind me of college 'cause where I went was mostly mud. I invite her but she can't leave, so it's me alone in Harlem thinking buy some scotch.

In those days whiskey still usually meant bourbon — or irish — but I never minded enlarging my sphere of experience. I'd given up on Cutty Sark as a viable alternative to Jim Beam, but the first thing caught my eye in this neighborhood package store was a green-red pint of J&B, flashing me to the tango scene in *Last Tango.* (Brando gets drunk and moons the squares.) You'd hear all these stories then how ghettos pay more for everything, and whuddaya know if a pint wasn't 75 cents more than I coulda conceived of paying, tops, down in the Village.

You learn things some days, and soon I was back on official learning turf, bottle-lip protruding from bag, several slugs to the wind and wayside. Students're amused, teacher less so (but not exactly protesting). It's definition time, and she feeds me *moribund . . . importune . . . nugatory . . .* nothing I can't shake from the academic memory box if not from routine personal usage. Teachperson herself, who I'm beginning to in fact *notice* — thin, dark hair, approximately "pretty," not too far from my current facial "type," medium chested — is giving me curt *okays* instead of gushing *good!s*, but a couple inches down the scotch I'm thinking hey: I can, I believe, choreograph a number vis-à-vis *her*.

Y'know: wide, wonderful world of affection and vaginas and stuff, like after class we can talk Jung and Karen Horney après (or avant) licktheclitoris. Like, reasons the drunken halfwit in me, the professional in her has gotta be digging my transformation of a pedestrian exercise into something cogently, radically special. This is after all a psych class, and what's more germane than out-there behavior? So I take some word like *travesty* and tugging intermittently at the acrid liquid work up a three-minute oration complete with references to Watergate (or something) which even weasly notetakers chuckle at — unless it's my hiccups — at which point I figure ONE MORE, just one more semi-radical act is all it should take to earn, buy, guarantee me access to her redolent rosebud (by nightfall).

Then it comes to me: freedom from inhibition can't help but be the key. So I walk over, take it out and whiz a *gusher* in the knee-high corner wastebasket. (Ah, them sweet ecstatic mysteries of courtship & exhibition!!)

The period has meanwhile ended; by midstream students have begun gathering their books; by the time I'm finished they're gone, and I've thus lost the chance to bask in their joy at having just witnessed the Genuine (psych book) Article. Too bad — I enjoy feedback — but I know my priorities, and I still have a date to wrap up.

Everything from that point south is a blur. Teacher and me on a fast-moving train is all I can discern through the haze. Can't recall words, smells, knees touching, a face beside mine, stray intended gropes or *anything*. Only the fact that I'd somehow hoaxed her into a liaison, not that night but *soon*, and a vague recollection, no it's stronger than that, of unzipping in a dark, dank corner of the Christopher Street station and — as she stood elsewhere — splashing loud & proud against the wall. Musta been a *total* loon to keep pushing the whipout-is-romance button but such is life: a life in which not only was she gonna see me, not only did we share a home subway stop, but I wouldn't even need an instant alibi for Ali. I could work on one for the better part of a week.

Week goes by and the way it plays is Ali will no longer buy out-with-Barry. Barry's just been married, and I've gone to that well too often anyway. Ike's no good 'cause she knows (or thinks she knows) (or would like to think she knows) he's a "repro" and a scoundrel — a nugatory character witness. This is justincase my clandestineness overlaps when Ali gets home from work, like by a couple hours or something. Best *alone* fabrication I come up with has me spend late afternoon/early night at a porn theater. *That* she'll believe — attendance-wise — but beyond that who knows, she might insist on hearing storylines.

So for research I catch the prenoon show at this three-for-five-dollar dive on 14th Street. The first two are people meet, they fuck, no plot — nothing to use as an alibi for chess-playing. Then in one called *Stack Sluts* a chunky librarian leads a guy to a book on fire engines, he goggles at the pictures, she examines his crotch — "I'm gonna ride his log till he shoots like a firehose." She rides, he shoots, she then trips into legs on a ladder in the 'women with women' segment — rear shot of puss 'n' buttcleft — "Come on down so I can finger your fabulous wet cunt." Good film, good throb, superior dialogue. Could I have scripted it myself? Mebbe, mebbe not, but for once I keep the thing zipped. It won't sit still but I reassure it *real woman* awaits. With not only wetcunt but a masters degree.

I'm out by two, gonna meet her at three; carefully I head for a bar. And by careful I mean *careful*: stopping in shoe stores, ducking in doorways, peering around streetcorners in case (by some outrageous chance) Ali should emerge from any of three possible subway exits, half a day early from work. I'm in one place half an hour, working on a beer, when I get antsy and bolt for another. One closer to prime train stop number one (but also ms. teacher's pad), forcing me to tread flat against buildings, sideways, crablike, squinting at distant moving female clothing — this is some dizzy shit.

One more beer and I make my penultimate street move, sloppy but by now time's a-wasting, to the liquor store nearest her place. Wine for what's uh — read the card in my pocket: Jill — savings no object: a six-buck French red. Which I never woulda bought for myself, which would prob'ly run $14–15 today, and which, coupled with the fin for the movies, and the beers, hadda be my steepest outlay yet for bald naked carnal prepossession. Emotional disbursement I was used to (never spent less than my whole sweaty wad) but financial, well, I was making four figures then, a *low* four figures — so this tryst was momentous indeed. Indeed: while not my first mattress date w/ someone I'd not yet coherently conversed with, or whose face and voice I had no clear sense record of, it was clearly my first with anyone I'd *met through an act of urination*, through nascent naked infantile effusion as enunciation of self.

Hence my caution. Here at last was somebody willing to fuck the two-year-old in me, to remove Pampers and make a mattress a playpen per se. Should Ali suddenly materialize, and I not de-materialize — *Fancy meeting* you *in Sheridan Square* — scratch the mattress, the Pampers, the playtime.

I step *briskly* for whatser's address, head down, collar raised, shoulders hunched — made it. Elevator up, heart hammering like a nine-ton Selectric; gotta stop, wipe my brow, let my breathing subside before ringing the bell. Which all I get from doing is a fucking dog. Barks.

My first assessment is she (herself) is possibly pissing, or showering, even douching — preoccupying herself needlessly (considering *my* unprotestant tastes) lest her natural flowing essence "offend." I wait a full twenty seconds and ring again; she'll be glad to hear she needn't have bothered, and next time (gladder still) she *won't*. After ten minutes of ring and bark I skulk back down, repairing to bar number two, source of a phone even more than the drink I need. Tangled, tottering, fresh anxieties heaped on the same shrieking old ones, I reach it, deposit coins and dial.

And again. Then consult direct'ry assistance and recommence dialing. 'Til maybe 5:15, by which time I'm tapped, bleary, ready for stinging retreat. Burned, apparently, for *not* being hung up and strung up! For being a dashing flashing (spouting!) dicksman-and-a-half! Do things right and look whatcha get! No justice righteous etcetera shit!

Motivic sexboy dander: irrational, rational?, any & all other states.

Regret as only the truly impassioned can know.

Acknowledgment of blithering idiothood, make that *curbsucking fucksucking dogshit on the pavement* idiothood.

But still plenty time to make it home before Ali, only she'll never believe the wine so heave it in the trash, okay?

Hey, I *like* this story.

FRIENDS & NEIGHBORS

A rare dreamless night and the band on the watch by my bed is bent upward like the legs of a woman in love so I'm thinkin' I killed somebody. I'm a fat ugly fuck and maybe I killed somebody. Like I once caused a geezer in a pickup to swerve around me — crushed steel, broken glass — then I just drove on, I was late for karate class. Didn't look (or sound) like death but maybe this time I killed somebody. Salli Harwyn killed Gandhi with a chair in a dream once and I buried him with sheepdogs snooping 'round and carpenters eyeing me funny but *I* didn't kill him, cross my heart — I didn't but maybe I killed somebody. Or drank someone's Guinness, ate all their sardines and pawed their wife through pantyhose or tried or wanted to and in the privacy of their john a droplet of mine might've splattered off the seat onto their bath mat. Got out alive if that's what it was but I'm not sure I killed nobody. I get the shivers, the shakes, people blare at me from eighty directions like air horns at a hockey game but I don't think I've killed a single manwoman in recent months although I don' know — did I kill somebody? Tell me if I did 'cause I just don' know.

FIVE VERSIONS

Of "Night Has a Thousand Eyes." Coltrane's I'm sure you know. The pulse gets clogged occasionally, and he misses all these fat chances to really just *take it out*, but it's still really only just a notch — or less — short of *major greatness*. You probably haven't heard Lee Konitz with Michel Petrucciani, that shorty, no, actually it's, who is it, Harold Danko. He turns it into kind of a gauzy nursery, um, what do you call it, not lullabye, nothing really of or about the night, unless maybe it's night as afternoon — which is fine for a take — clouds on the late horizon, not especially dark, or nightfall as this ultra-dark huge future-tense dam beyond which . . . not even mystery. It's okay for a few listens. There's a new one by James Moody where he soars out the gate like Booker Ervin or somebody, which is sort of akin to him purposely doing a young, more ferocious paraphrase of himself, but he can't keep it up, it's 10 minutes long. If you think about it, there really are no bad versions of the tune — careening, lurching, searching, all that shit — though the Sonny Rollins-Jim Hall record comes close. For a guy who when it was cut was still master of the literalism-irony continuum, Sonny, here he's, well, it's neither scripturally faithful nor, what's the word, sarcastic? satiric? — just uninspired deadpan. Actually, there's one by Horace Silver, on that Epic LP, *Silver's Blue*, that *is* bad: Donald Byrd kills it. It would be alright if Mobley soloed sooner, or figured more prominently in the head, but by the time he gets his turn — a perfect tune for him, even more than Coltrane — it's too late, Byrd has already tee-tee'd it through the floor. There's supposedly a Harold Land version older than any of, or not older than Horace's but anyway seminal, a paradigm. I've never heard it.

HOME RULE FOR SCOTLAND

A sortie to CONSIDER for the holiday season is take 'em to Wettler's. Wettler's Pies & Lunch (18401 E. Whittier Blvd., 818-535-3106). Take 'em for a tasty ham & swiss with lettuce and Heinz mild mustard. TAKE 'EM ALSO for creamy clam chowder (Fridays only), lemon cream pie that is not too tart yet crusty as GONORRHEA, and all the ice tea they can ingurge. Remember: it's better to "give" than receive. Give 'em Wettler's.

But even the BEST of food is not the best of gifts. Eat it, it's gone. Only thing quicker is a wheeze or a sneeze, and who'd ever give one o' those? Iodine is better but don't give me, I already got. I've also got a shoehorn, an eight-dollar chair and 109 issues of *Sumo Digest*. My needs are simple. All I need is a battery for my Datsun and/or A WORLD WITH-OUT YOGA. Either one will do.

But we're not here to talk about me, we're here to talk about you. Your gifts given and got. How would you like to give (or get!) the GARBAGE TAKEN OUT FOR A WEEK? I'd be all too willing to execute this dirtywork. Cost to you, $350. I'LL MOW YOUR LAWN IF YOU BUY ME GAR-DEN GLOVES. For: an even $600. WILL DRAFT A SHORT BUT INSPIRATIONAL ACCOUNT OF YOUR GRANDFATHER'S WAR WOUND: 7000 clams. Complete saga, handwrit and legible, of the time I got off the schoolbus and this guy at the grocery as I walk by sez do I wanna make some money delivering a package to a lady and I say no so he sez c'mon she'll tip you and I still say no and finally he strong-arms me or insults me and I do it but since I can't carry both the package and my books (I'm such a pipsqueak) I leave the books on the hood of a car and the lady gives me 35 cents and when I get back the books're still there — story bound with your choice of paper clip or staples: $456.

NECK RUB & CUNTILINGUS: 1000 smackers. ME AS THIRD PARTY FOR YOUR FEMALE PLEASURE DUO: two forty-nine fifty. TUBE OF ARTIFICIAL IN-SEMINATION JIZ FOR YOUR WIFE, DAUGHTER, MOTHER OR SIS: $169.98.*

Own a VCR but too lazy to bother? I will tape the show or movie of your bidding for $317/hr. Anything starring Van Johnson: you pay double. Triple: *Name of the Game* episodes with Gene Barry. (Specify VHS or Beta.)

Can't find that Giuseppi Logan elpee you have got to hear RIGHT NOW? Can't remember WHAT the hell you did with *Kink Kontroversy*? I will A

L
P
H
A
B
E
T
I
Z

E your albs for the low low price of a buck forty a disc (minimum 200 discs). Let me STREAMLINE YOUR MUSIC LIBRARY by removing unlistenable blap like everything by Philip Glass and selling it for goodbux — my fee is 80% plus 300 up front for listening to the junk.

I WOULD LOVE TO EDIT YOUR MASS-MARKET GLOSSY or that of a relative or friend (one issue) in exchange for COMPLETE CONTROL AND 18,000 BIG ONES.

For hippies only: I HATE YOUR ASS FOR LOUSING UP U-ROY AT THE ROXY (1981) BY SMOKING ALL

---

*Price for novelty use only. Purchaser and inseminee must sign notarized agreement that no actual conception shall occur. Otherwise: $169,980.

THAT WEED AND METHOD-ACT "ENTHUSING" LIKE IT WAS THE GODDAM GRATEFUL DEAD but I'll sew patches on your jeans for $1165 a patch.

Spice up your seasonal gathering with the GIFT OF GAB — I will rant (and rant!) on appropriate subjects for the reasonable rate of $9000 and a liter of Laphroaig. Stale or bland appetizers: I collect $500 more.

Bargains!! Oil change, $89.90. Scissor that works O.K.: ten and a quarter. Bulbs changed in your basement or den: $21/pair. Bat bought in '80 for a game against a team of actor swine led by Joe Santos of *Rockford* and never used again (Dave Kingman model): $13. 1979 *Information Please Almanac* (slightly moth-et): $11.70. "Home Rule for Scotland" poster: $2.05. Grab bag (BIG surprises!!!): one percent of your annual income.

FREE (but you pay postage): empty Kiwi shoe polish tin. One color: neutral. (I won't throw it out if you let me know by week three of Dec.)

Last but noway least: I play Santa for your kids — *ABSOLUTELY FREE!* (But I get to steal half their presents.)

STILL LIFE WITH POLAROID SPREAD SHOT

And my favorite gift/received is this oil painting, heavy on the linseed, dating it no earlier than the 14th century, which makes a bit of sense since the shot itself was taken in 1978. One of the v/best black-and-whites I ever took: Shirley Harwitz squatting behind a tree at the L.A. Zoo. Nineteen months after our final split, her skirt upraised, knees uncoupled wide, the crotch of her panties is drawn to one side by two fingers, unveiling a portion of alluring black thatch and medium-gray galmeat. In a dark pixyish hairstyle we haven't seen on her before, she projects a vague sense of what, distaste? displeasure? — she's not delighted — not quite disgusted — but *not* not smiling — humiliation with a touch of pride? — in reaction less to my having urged her to bare labia for my prurient amusement than to the fact that with her cousin Cele, with whom and whose husband she is staying in Covina, also present I am endeavoring to record the event with a Polaroid Swinger, a model for which it was difficult to still obtain film, on its final legs. And *her* legs: 'shapelier'? 'comelier'? (anywise less nondescript) than I would otherwise, without visual aid, be driven to remember.

The cousin's you don't get to see, just pantslegs — black denim, three-quarter frontal — as, declining my request, she has passed on posing likewise, tut-tutting away from both lens and Shirley out the right edge of our shot — taken at this point, pre-further request, for fear S. would soon change her mind, let me browbeat her no more, let her skirt fall etc. — and then we'd have nothing. Where in fact there was a later shot, with Cuz turning to look — more prurient, n'est-ce pas? — only Cuz (or was it Shirl?) tore it up. Close your eyes and pretend, no, all the 'tending in the world will not bring it back.

Nor the make of the tree Shirley's behind, well, one knee is — no defining leaves visible. Live oak? eucalyptus? — or is that the San Francisco Zoo? A bark expert might help us but it's not that important, and I wouldn't mention it, except the artist (or someone) has cast an odd, seemingly undeserved judgment upon it, scratching the word "DULL" into the paint, almost down to the canvas, and an arrow aimed directly at its not unhandsome trunk.

A dull tree — oh, so that's it: adultery. First time, believe it or not, Shirley and I were technically adulterous — "extrarelational" — with *each other*, or at least I was with her, having bedded down the afternoon before (as we would again a day later) behind the comatose back of Eve Lane, whom I was just beginning to experience 'doubts' about. Doubts, concerns, comas irksome and substantial enough f'r me to not only diddle an old used-to-be, and take her to the zoo, but to actually WELCOME — briefly — her reappearance in my life: the Right Time for a visit (if ever there could be one).

You've heard of time frames, well here's a space frame: places. Right in the frame itself, additional scratches, the guy's a real scratcher. "PHILLY" ... "FORT WORTH" ... "TORONTO" ... "CHICAGO." Each x'ed out with an even deeper cut, alluding surely to cities I'd thought of, and sequentially unthought of, relocating to; places I'd wet my oiseau as a rockwriter/magwriter on the road, a traveling fool, all of which dried up, the trips, the minute I moved: to escape Shirley, editors, bedfellows, playfellows, rippers of the clothes off my back, newyawkculture, everything. He (or, sorry, possibly she) left out St. Louis. On the table in front of the shot: a U.S. quarter like the one flipped — Chicago vs. L.A., two out of three — to finally settle it, its perspective too foreshortened to make out the date, but that hardly matters.

Oh and here's one not crossed out, scratched only half as big, "NEW YORK??" — there's a question there: an allusion, one surmises, to Shirley's proposal to move wherever *I* want, either coast or elsewhere; her expressed willingness, in spite of my having harassed and embarrassed her at not just the zoo, in spite of the loud replay of old hateful tapes including that of our acrimonious parting, to get back with me if I'll have her. She still has our old apartment, and dwellings that size (at that price) are hard to come by. Or my place, where I brought her to fuck her, she can stomach. A generous overture. She's in town for a week; I have the rest of the week to deliberate.

Ruminate. Four days of brooding and mulling over facets of the deal — at a time, a nexus, where I've yet to forsake the illusion of Alternate Mates — throughout which the offer hovers and wavers, never without a certain modest appeal (Like it's not half bad seeing her again, really — in spite of ev'ry old lingering badtaste in our mouth///The apt. might be tempting if I wanna retrogress to New York; it would rebuild (repaint) at least a leg o' *that* bridge — one I'd probably as soon keep on wrecking///Return to place, no, all place is mistake, it's where mistake *is* — so what c'd be gained, or regained, the illusion of what, 'normalcy'?///Or maybe I'm just lone-lee, and even a recycled Shirley seems choicer than a full-o-tricks but oft unreachable Lady Eve///Yet the gesture of re-ordering her life to suit me is kind of touching, or is it simply a prologue to future recriminations?///Backlighting it all: the leer of impending disaster — but whose & which one?). But there's just no defying the historic bottom line, the event beside which all else is secondary, an act intimated by the object the spread shot leans against: an unopened roll of Scott one-ply.

"On your *first night with her*?!" she asks, disbelieving.

"In the morning."

"You sure know how to pick 'em." Let her twit but yeah, *I* thought so — or thought I thought so — in the weeks (months) following the dawn morn Eve sucked me while I took my morning dump. *All's well that starts well* — that starts *that* well — and I told this all to Shirley though not to taunt her, no, but 'cause things like that embolden you — you can't shut up, you gotta tell the world. I tell her but I don't 'splain her — I can't be that mean — that baring beaver at the zoo is one thing, and all credit to her, but suck-it on the bowl is quite another — and I don't relate my doubts. That Eve will ever equal that performance, or one a tenth as sensational — or be sober or nonindifferent enough to again dial a phone.

But that's the gamble and worth it, iznit? — I mean if you still got some hours left of blazing witless juniority. Libidinal adventure — misadventure — get me an option. Which is not to imply that sex with Shirley was without its subtle fireworks, although what're these buttons, huh, pinned to the suede jacket bunched up at table left? Joan Baez, Yma Sumac — now it comes back to me: fireworks (or something) exactly twice:

— the "folksinger" fuck of '73 where her movements and soundings suddenly struck me as those of a free-ramblin' folk slut — guitar packed, rarin' to go (but where in heck'd she get 'em???) (I didn' ask);

— night the Yma flic at 2 made it weird and otherworldly, lending our in-and-out a surfeit of colorless intensity and strange alternate codings w/out cipher or heading.

The jacket itself is *familiar*, reminding me now — as I needed no reminders then — that if *non*adventure sex with S. had its plus side, 'twas that it was always that as well: familiar. As familiar (and dependable) as my hand — for both of us I'm sure — only wetter.

But the jacket *is* familiar. Dark greenish gray, you could call it olive drab, paint stains on the cuff: I'll go out on a limb. I am sure (pretty sure) it's the one I wore the day we had "our moment." First briskness of fall, some early year together, it was chilly so I gave it to her, off my back to hers. Nice breeze, blew us down 12th or 13th St. A very dry day. And on it, all our non-wet-coded couple stuff — "love," "companionship," "shared experience" — came to not-naught, thank phuck; it's where it all crystallized, and in memory shines crystalline — once — forever . . . in other wds. our lifetogether was barely a boil on the nates of a newt.

WITHOUT A SONG — Not even a bad song. The painting sez *no song*. For me & my gal Shirl. Just a yellowed blank empty 45 sleeve to table right. For me and her prime predecessor, meanwhile, the Early One (still nameless) who ran off with the dance man, there's the full-color picture sleeve from "The Last Time" (b/w "Play with Fire"). *Our* song. Mine and Shirley's, well, we never had one. Whatever, if anything, we did have in common felt by zoo week quite as ancient as the Early One herself, and less memorable. Even in her own time, Miss Harwitz was a distant number two. 'Cause let's face it — I will if you will — she was never much more than a "presence in the room" — a warm passive spirit — an allowance to be silent. Never a great love, only long love, which could not on its hottest run beat out relative new love, even tarnished new love with a fuckaloony juicer. (So ciao, Shirl, and give my regards to Broadway.)

Dimensions of artwork: 48" X 63". Additional objects rendered: spool of turquoise thread; broken whiskey bottle (we'll see now, won't we?); stuffed parrot.

In the final analysis, a trite old-fangled work. Can't really say I fancy it after all, but I'll keep it (if there's room) in a closet.

BIG DICKS WALK

Voice of Mike Fort: "It was Super Bowl Sunday, January of I think '77, the Oakland Raiders and some team, whatever apartment I was then living with my so-called wife Lorna. My younger brother was in town, and my wife's brother or somebody, so I say, 'Let's all get together and watch the Super Bowl.' Your erstwhile slumber pal Sheryl was still peripherally hanging out with Lorna, so it was like Sheryl, I don't know if she had an interest in football, not that I did especially either, but it was like 'Can we join the party?' — let's all continue being pals or some bullshit. Anyway, she shows up with this, this jerk — I don't know, some guy who was like . . . blank. And the TV we had at the time it was almost impossible to get reception and it had aluminum foil on the antenna, so it was a big production getting it tuned in. The game starts and it's tuned in its own very precarious way.

"We're sitting around watching and this guy Sheryl's with, who's either Joe or Bob, some name like that, lightish hair and sort of real just un — the man without a face — and like beer is in the kitchen, which isn't, the whole place isn't too big, so the guy gets up for a beer and what does he do, he smashes into the antenna — so there goes two hours of fighting for reception. The whole room, it's like 'Who the fuck is *this* guy?' And Sheryl is defending him with her eyes, y'know, and this guy Louie who plays the trumpet, 'Oh my God, there goes the game,' y'know and everything.

"So anyway it's like, without me even asking her, 'Where did you find this jackass?' she says, 'He's a very nice guy, and he has a really big dick.' I don't know whether either of these things were true or not, she told me this beyond hearing range of everybody, and hearing range of the guy himself, and that was the first and last I ever saw or heard of him. The guy didn't have any special bulge in his pants, it was not what he ran into the antenna with, I can tell you that.

"I don't remember what my response was when she said it, but I might've like laughed at that point, and it threw her off, like what's *funny*? And I don't know if she told Lorna at the same time or before, and maybe Lorna told her she deserved it, y'know like broad talk, but even on the level of broad talk it seemed desperate, y'know what I'm sayin'? It was like Sheryl was grasping for something beyond broad-dom or something, y'know?

"But to get back to the dick, which is the center of everything, leaving aside whether the guy had an abnormal dingdong or what, was it like that was what she equated, the first thing that came to mind as like a saving grace for somebody? Who nobody seemed to like or . . . that's the puzzle, you should ask *her*. Although maybe she don't remember, it's the only day she ever saw him. She seemed lost — fucking lost. And plenty resentful, y'know, from being left behind. And also very artificial on a certain level. I was trying to avoid her to some extent. *I* didn't fuck her, not at that point, if that's what you're wondering."

SUMMER OF MY DAYS

Okay, kiss me, I'm 41, which means I just got finished being 40. A whole year of it, as whole years go, was, I confess, not intolerable. There wasn't a moment I thought *sheesh, I'm over the hill, man, washed up, washed out, old olde, ole mold, lost it, past it.* That stuff I thought, and got out of my system, when I was 28.

Two score and zero was, and is, so damn benign. I'd comb my hair, assay a pimple, eye pertinent reflected details and note with pleasure that everything was fundamentally . . . fine. Not much gray, teeth tartary but mine, the weight's down, my blood pressure, I'd survived six years longer than Wardell Gray, sixteen longer than Stanley Ketchel, and was no more thoroughly miserable than *usual.* I'd occasionally know despair, sure, but it was seldom age-coded. I felt no closer to the grave than at 36, 32 or 24, and even 20 years at a shitty trade, the *same* shitty trade — making beans add up to bean salad — did not appear to have terminally enfeebled me.

So I'd greet my image, when appropriate grin, and toast it, quite aloud, *hey, bud, you made it.* Two-plus decades of hard living, hard loving, had neither slain me outright nor particularly overwhelmed me; lucky fucking me, clap clap. *Congrats,* I'd continue, slightly giddy, *for making it this far etcetc., and double 'grats for having still not (far as may be known) donated molecularly to the fount of all Neurosis, i.e., become a father.*

Like there's all these persons, female, on the cusp of 40 — that seems the cutoff — stampeding, at their final blush of somatic "opportunity," to exactly what they *avoided* (because they knew better!) through 40-minus circumsolar caravans. What a waste, a negation, of laudable momentum to one day announce *I must spread 'em rightnow, during ovulation, as my still functional uterus is advising, nay, ordering* . . . the male version of which I suppose would be *I must make full, immediate use of my underuti-lized shoulders by piloting 18-wheelers on the nation's hi-ways . . .* stoopid, stoopit (so STOPPIT!). I ain't driving no trucks, at 41 nor at 40, and I hope to hell I have not made no babies.

"Biological clock" — now that's a good one. Unless I've totally lost my mind, hoke that baroque is more about bogue sociology, cultural perfidy, than personal (or collective) body poetry. Ovarian vogue dressed as ovarian destiny: a prime-time digital countdown with breaks for commercials. And lest I risk sounding (ulp) sexist, an equal knee to the nuts of *male* sociology . . . sperm-side complicity . . . the spectre of grown men urging innocent dollops of dough to say *poo-poo, dad-dy* . . . haven't they learnt in 40 years of breath to say *shit*? And you want biology, okay, how are mommydads THEIR AGE gonna deal, just as a teaser, with the permanent loss of SLEEP? What're they gonna do, how they gonna BEGIN dealing with preadolescent energy, with preadolescent needs and DEMANDS, at age 50? (Babying as a "solution" to per-sonal ills — shortfalls — longings — is like throwing gasoline on a fire the size of the sun.)

So, well, yes, age-peer behavior frequently aggrieves me. I will sit for no more bee-ess re the undying wonderfulness of "my" generation, or must I say "our"? Mine/ours has dumped more self-awareness down the chute than any prior coeval horde (far as may be knowed) ever had to begin with. Like se-cret 20-year alarums (speaking of clockwork) finally ajangle, even diehard horde peers have sprung twitchy of late to some formidable dumping, brushing from their vests every boulder or crumb of ur-recognition that by dint of cosmic contingence ever there landed, in the dumbsick name of "getting on" with the "bizness of life," i.e., the sundry stations of abject bour-geois submission . . . but that's another rant, 'nother hoot, an-other fusillade to the melonhead of friend, stranger . . . LATER. Rightnow I would rather be a HERMIT.

I sit home, read Abelard, listen to "South" by Bennie

Moten (1928). Leave the homestead? For what? In the last year, two years, I've all but officially scotched, eliminated, stopped factoring in, whole subsets of "outside activity," incitements to excursion, that I'd probably used up by 35 anyway. Rock clubs — and rock bands — you could send to sea with no oars, no steering, no boat, and an anchor. (And then burn the sea.) Bowling? Enough a'ready. Fine dining? *You* do it. Parties: I *loathe* parties — and I used to SURGE in underlit rooms jammed with cohorts, antagonists, bothneither. Burnt some *great bridges* at parties in my day — great flames and kicks, great ashes — my craving for which seems to have dwindled along with available bridge fodder. Ditto for britch fodder (as monomania, "hobby"). Sex as hobby — collect 'em! follow th' dots! add water & stir! — it crosses my mind, is *possibly* as ludicrous as sex for procreation. I still, of course, jerk off once-twice daily (and gladly accept what falls in my lap).

It occurs to me, though, that I haven't yet used up my youth — alas — give me time. Infancy (0-17) was no easy haul but I made it. A cicada's lifespan of erupting in *non*disposable diapers. Childhood is mid infancy; adolescence, advanced. Don't know your story, but precocious I wasn't. (No less a babe at 16.8 than at 1.2.) 17–42, a quarter century, should do it for anyone: youth. Fresh laundered diapers worn as armbands, as headbands — much weight to bear. Got a year left, the dregs. (I will not fucking miss it.) 42 to the dregs of the whole hot show: adulthood. I'll soon be grown. Time off for good behavior, for points accumulated eating pussy, and we'll call it even. Used up my youth and I'm proud!

I have not, however, used up the Contempo World. There *is* no Contempo World. All we've got is a meticulously calibrated, perpetually self-adjusting recapitulation of the pre-rock whitebread 'fifties, and Worse is yet to come. Today's kidcreeps, who in spite of etc. have AT LEAST the means of my own former kid peers to know better, to fucking *unplug* for crying out loud, are blinder and blander than what walked the boards in 1953, as unhip as these hotsos you read about who would fake their i.d. to join the Marines at 15. The most soullessly materialistic pack of yulps in my lifetime, yours (and possibly any): give 'em their yuppie-bucks, five years, and keys to the calibration, and they'll take us back to the literal berrypie 'forties. "Future shock"? Don't pull my wango.

Bitterness? Ain't used that up either. And I still get a thrill out of cobwebs, rusty rivets, day-old french fries, lemon the color, abandoned women's underwear (outdoors), the sound of full soda bottles breaking, and burnt out one-, two- and three-story homes with the roof caved in. And I reread Anaxagoras and make bookends filling tea tins with street-metal and plaster and practice "Chi Chi" from the *Charlie Parker Omnibook* until somebody somewhere yells out, "You're not getting any better," and I'm fine, dandy, don't need Ovaltine to get to sleep, I take alfalfa for arthritis and am pleased to report it *works*, the old 'r---ds haven't bothered me in . . . whoa, hey, just tryin' to REMIND you that four-oh's benign, accessible, ANYONE can get there, only way you could miss it would be something like a deficiency, y'know, immune, C., Lou Gehrig's Disease, prescription codeine overdose, a deranged relative shoots you, struck by lightning, a falling safe, or smashed by a milk truck. So cross at the green: you owe it to YOURSELF to reach this mythic late-youth milestone — the summer of your years (not, as myth would have it, autumn!) — only a puckface or killjoy would call it "middle age."

SOMETHING FOR MY HEART THAT ISN'T LOVE, SOMETHING FOR MY MIND THAT ISN'T SCHOOL

But I hate summer, always have. All it's good for is you get school off. And after school has run its course, ha, it ain't good nohow. If I had air-conditioning maybe, but all I've got is a 22-inch floor fan which even at medium blows everything around, all my unweighted papers and such, until finally I get up and rescue 'em, weight 'em, and eventually stash 'em.

And stashing some letters I found one, stored in a folder labeled "Writ/Unmailed," in a torn, addressed envelope with the stamp peeled off. No postmark, undated, but I'd estimate somewhere around '80.

Occasion: ??? (Just another drunk loveless nite of exacerbated self-visitation.)

Loveless enough to beg for it from those least likely to give it, an old habit, and later on plead with them to fly out and stay with me.

Which — the latter — is mainly why come morning, having unsealed and read it, I breathed a deep, long miracle sigh over not having put on my shoes and dragged myself to a mailbox. The thought of being stuck with them, their sight and smell, put all my cells on edge, though the bulk of the missive I could probably, with only moderate stress, have lived with them seeing:

> My Dear ancestors — WHAT'S IT ALL ABOUT? I mean I love you guys (for what it's worth) and all these years I've been shouting who the hell knows what, makin all kindsa noise and who knows what the hell it's all meant for godsake. Lotta tension & agner on my side of the fence but I've never really felt like it was just my own,

really (really) when you get down to it it's OURS, I mean your standpoint & mine ain;t that disparate or any of that shit if you get my drift . . . Look, here I am all these yrs of age and funny (very) funny from this letter of yours it seems you guys want me to believe that NO LONGER AM I THE BLACK SHEEP OF THE FAMILY or some kinda scapegoat for family idiosyncrasy (trophy would now go to Marty) which to me is sure a surprise cause for chrissake I was born to bust barriers & &tc. and now that you're almost ready to dignify what I'm doin as finally after all this time *respectable* (at leas not *unpardonable*) all I can say is from the time I was 4–5 years old I was never doin anythung but, like what I am now is the same goddam what I wa sthen cause it's true (true), period. And what I'm doin on my plain is what YOU'RE DOIN ON YOURS and if maybe I'm interjecting a little (ha!) more flamboyance it's only cause I can't help overflowin: but really when y'get down to it *my* approach is *your* approach — *our* appraoch — despite whatever disagreements over content might occur. It wou;d help tho (wouldm't hurt!) if you masqueraded harder at getting what I'm doin, like this tattoo horsshit — c'mon. Ain't sure why it still bothers you, okay I do see (the tombstone). You talk like we never had it out: now's the time. Can't you take a fucking joke? Don't you get the "statement" (the "absurdity")? Mom, I ain't killing you off! Stick around! (Please.) But myabe it isn't clear, do I make myself clear? Dunno if I do or I don't, all I kmnow's you people are the ones who — whether you feel like admitting or nor — made mewhat I am, don't mean I'm blaming you or any o' that, I'm actually *thanking* you and you should know I'm *doing it for you too*, going out on some fine limbs YOU programed me to and I;m taking you both wiuth me whether you're WITH ME or not, I mean it's all implicit so whuddya gonna do? Come along with me on my LIFE OF CRIME: I'm the criminal in the family (every family needs one), my crime is I write. The tattoo, that was writing, but my *writing* writing is where I really break on thru. My latest innovation — I think I was 1st — is intentional *bad* writing (this is not an example!) and I don't mean "bad boy" writing, I mean like the movie "Mesa of Lost Women" — have either pf you seen that? Probably not but no sweat cause it stinks, what I *like* about it is it stinks (it's on here a lot, maybe there too, you should take a look): it's not easy to be that bad (and that good!) but well that's not intentional. If you did it intetionally just think how bad you could probably get. Look, one of you useta read archaeology and the other could do cube roots and both of you KNOW that there are systems for ANYTHING. And sometimes teh systems are *yours*, sometimes they're within your *grasp* and sometimes you *ain't got a clue*. WHATEVER THE DEAL IS neither of you is a godddam PUNK (I mean you can *dig* it, right?). Anyway you might be wondering what my so-called personal life is all aboutt these days: "Cunt is whut I wunt" — that's it in a nutshell. Finding outlets for my dingo is a factor that concerns me, like if I had one (or two) regular sweeties I can depend on to deliver the goods on a regular (semi-weekly) basis I'd be pretty much set in the metnal and physical health dept, but not to worry. The point is here I am older then YOU dad when you finally threw in the towel & tied the knot and I'm *still a bachelop*, still gotta think about who's gonna suck my cock and share my run-around and all that shit, point is I can *deal with it*, I don't care particulary who as long as it's somebody (my main criterion in a woman is *availability*), as long as she doesn't get mad or act suprised when I take off her blouse, that sorta thing. And as long of course as she has half a brain (tho I prefer 3/4): CONVERSATION has to accompany vaginal excitement and by conversation I mean a little *sharing of oompah* if you now what I mean. I THINK YOU KNOW WHAT I'M TALKING ABOUT. And you MOM, I got all these dreams about you, I would say I've probably fucked you more times in dreams than Betty, possibly more in the last two years than any single other dame (dreams and real combined). Sometimes you're easy, sometimes you're hard to get, it's always a special dream — as *wet* as any I've had — great hot dream-cunt! Don't know what it "means" but the Freud reading might be you got this image of Mother and subsequent dames're the result of that, well I may have been built backwards but I get dreams about you that seem to say that maybe I;m just built backwards cause you're often a stand-in for some woman that I know who I either fucked or wanna fuck altho occasionally it's just you playing you, the point is I reach up your leg sometiems and you close em on me before I get to the gold so what you represent to me dream-wise is (probably) that 1000-to-1 shot, the one you really gotta work on, one well worth the effort but you still gotta work work to get at. (You used to close em, now less often.) I hope this cunt-talk doesn;'t offend you (as you mighta guessed I'm DRUNK so what the fuck) but I think we're basically on the same common wavelength, I mean it's all in *our* DNA or life-o-plasm or something, y'know this long-repressed search & fumble for who the f knows what. If you can't think of a birthday sometime (insteada the same usual $20 check) you might wanna send me a pair of your panties (but wear em a few days first). Red or black preferred. And dad (if it still gets hard enoug), fuck her for me, okay? (You ever eat her? — you SHOULD EAT HER.) On second thought don't — she's mine (only KIDDING). On the issue of AN-OTHER use of the male fluid, Betty's impending brat, you shoulda told me sooner so I could tell her sooner — or have you tell her. Since I don't talk to her no more — not dirrect — I wish you would tell her: the gift of life is not a gift (is that a truism or what?), at best it's a high-interest loan. Too high. Tell her: born-to-die is a piss-poor setup. And: you're born alone, you die alone, it's not fair to inflict BOTH ends of that one on anyone . . . it's *mean*! (And for those 10 minutes or so you're not alone you're NEVER ALONE and nobody else is: once there was no room at the inn, now there's no room AT THE MANGER.) Somebody should tell her so you do it, okwy? (If I can think of any more I'll let you know.) Actually I should thank her cause now you'll finally have a grandbrat of your very own, meaning *I'm* off the hook and speaking of hooks: hook my whanger to the wall if you get wind of me even thinking about causing a bratperson — these wimmen can turn your head, to keep em you'll do *plenty* — come out here infact and cut it off. Blood BLOOD: waht's it mean? Blood as hot blood and cold blood, that I can see, but blood like in MY son, MY daughter, MY cromosomes — how nazi! I hope it ain't blood that connects US. (If you'd shown me your cuntblood (mom) maybe I'd feel different.) What I'm askin is I wish you would try and *drop the blood* and FINALLY AFTER ALL THIS TIME acknowledge your son — me — independent of sonhood — as being in the same cosmos as you (just a wd. will do) cause I ain't no rebl, I ain't no malcontent, I'm just one still-hopping soonyboy who's gonna still be hopping for a long fuggin *time*, Jim. What I'd really like to know is WHAT DO EITHER OF YOU EVER *THINK* ABOUT BESIDES WHEN YOU GOTTA PAINT THE DISH CABINET OR WHAT YOU'RE GONNA GET 9TH-COUSIN BEULAH FOR HER GRADUATION THAT YOU GOT INVITED TO BY ACCIDENT TO BEGIN WITH (I mean the real "occasion" is taking place *somewhere else*), I'd like to know what you've got in mind this year besides voting Democrat and paying tax or what new gadget you just bought to trim the hedges . . . Tell me: am I too imposing, do I ask too much??? I remember all too well you (mom) singing "My Blue Heaven" for my goddam afternoon nap (do you still remember yourself?) and feeling REAL GOOD to hear it every day (brings fucking *tears* to my eyes to think of it, no fooling) and you (dad) singing some throwaway song from World War I or something, can't think of the name but you useta sing it (not "Smile the While," that's the one you useta pick around on teh keys of Nora's piano in the fucking Bronx, there was another one you useta *sing*), anyway I know that you people are people of PASSION even if the passion is narrowly defiend (don't mean to sound nasty, it's just that you ain't exactly Ralph & Alice Kramden, right?), would just like to know if you ever think of ME in a genuinely fond way, just *wonder* from time to time . . . Okay, what the hell, I'm gonna seal this in an envelope and mail it right now and maybe I'll feel stupid in the morning (clocl reads: 3:15 AM), *so what?* The point is if you ever feel like visiting this part of thr world I'll sleep on the floor and give you my bed (big enough for two: a fact I've substantiated often), sorry if once upon a time I made it seem like I didn't really want you nosing arpund here, come out any time you want (any!) and I'll be your willing host, no lie. Stay as long as you want so I can monitor your decline down the abyss — a foretaste of my own death — you don't mind if I peek, do you? (Just joking!) ANSWER ME WHAT-EVER WAY YOU WANT but lemme know what YOU think it's all about, okay? If you don't what I'm getting at *please ask me* to explain cause I ain't trying to be elusive, just trying to reaffirm EVERYTHING WE AS A FAM-ILY HOLD DEAR WHETHER WE (YOU) KNOW IT OR NOT, I mean I ain't no hero, I ain't no fucking martyr or messaih or any of that, I'm just a guy who knows that 2 and 2 is 2-&-2 (which equals ?) who hopefully in the not-too-distant future (i.e. while both of uou're still kicking) will PUT IT TOGETHER, I'll conquer space & time and you-name-it and yabba yabba yub . . . LUCK IS ON *OUR* SIDE (because we're *not* assholes!). (Like I said: *love* you both, really do, you're as full of shit as parents all the time are but I can take it, I'll be alive for another 10 years at least so feel free to speak to me in any way you consider appropriate tween now & then, lookin at me is like lookin at you if you wanna really face it so

GIVE HONESTY A CHANCE and tell me I'm not an asshole — if you ain't then I ain't — okau?

"There is not enoufg love on the entire planet to fil the heart of ONE lonely man"!!

Your loving son,
Reg

THE WAY YOU LOOK TONIGHT (ALONE)

11 PM. I sit with you as you read this — I'm reading over your shoulder. At 11:03, as a courtesy to me, you begin to read aloud. Occasionally you misread a word or supply unintended emphasis but I don't object. You hesitate at phonetic misspellings — how bizarre. At 11:07 you sneeze on the page — willfully if not "deliberately." You put on a sweater. At 11:11 you turn to me, say nothing, pack it in. Bleak are both our lives and the capital of Idaho is Boise.

FLAG DAY WITH THE MIZZAS

Ah! those brightish balmy days of presolstice yeah yeah oh yeah! the bar-b-q bratwurst! muskmelon & honey dew! marshmallows en casserole! corn niblets w/ butter sub! cool wet mugs of sarsaparilla! gooseberry muffin tarts! smoked skate and pickled carp! a pig! a hawg! plucked of bristles and roasted, a pear in its maw, its gizzard and pancreas braised in raisins and cel'ry, Beer Nuts and secret ingredes! iced decaf and kiwi fruit sherbet! pistachios and pale ale! a feed! a feast! on tables and lounge chairs of late vernal festivacity and etc!

Yes, it's that time again, June 14th, as we Mizzas gather *en famille* — as we do every year — to pay tribute to the flags of not merely our own but of all — most — many lands (hey, we're lib'ral). Hate to seem like Sea World, but once again there's a "theme" to our flagging. Last time it was flags with five- or six-pointed stars but no white or orange. This year, by popular vote — a tie — the honor falls to (1) flags which closely approximate other flags when rotated 90 or 180 degrees; (2) flags exactly the same upside down.

From here, from there, from everywhere they come: Mizzas (rhymes with "pizzas"). My half-brother Unc from Syracuse. Sister Woona (a crackerjack plumber) from Tarp, PA. Offspring E.Z., Fuffy, Zane and Pluz from Omaha, Dubuque, Tijuana and Huspo, NY — the fabled Pus Bowl! — with spouses Mo'reen, Ju-Boy, Osco and Teets. Grandchildren Ulf, Ssess, Vulvo, Johann, Porcelain and Groucha (garsh, she's tall!). Niecenephews Giordano, Salada (the family "hoor"), Uha, Digby and Pants. Cousins Bib, Beph, Shlomo, Theck, Beluga, Toetoe, Peony and Thubb. Plus assorted in-laws and shit.

And for the first time as a member in full standing — from out of the shadows! — now that my dear wife Eleanor has gone to her, ahem, reward: my longtime mistress Janique

DuPree — the French Girl. (Had to sneak her in — as upstairs "maid" — until this year.)

Not present: grandson Upto, whose dad last month strangled my least favorite daughter, Eff, along with siblings Wug, Seabase, Buzzbo and Floonce. Upto, off at med college (the U. of Canada), is to be excused for "avoiding kin" this F-Day, but he did send his best: "Hoist one for me, Gramps." We will, Upto, we will.

And me?, oh, hi, I'm Rex Mizza, bearing the tricolor of Botswana — at your service.

"Mizza," by the way, is Middle Rumanian for *hoister or bearer of colored or patterned rectangle symbolizing nation-state or maritime alphabet code* — we didn't ask for it, none of us did. It is simply our Heritage, however these things happen, and precedes us, so to speak. (Make way for the Mizzas — the clan that knows "how"!)

Okay: presentation of the Categories. To be followed by Activity and, where applicable, Research and Report. We Mizzas don't just raise our flags — we live 'em. (To the best of our 'bilities.) Zane, Ju-Boy and Thubb of this year's Categories Committee — they've been at this for weeks — have got the list for us. Okay, fellas, present 'em.

Presented:

1. Flags for watching sports. We get this every year, it's tiresome. At least this time Ulf has brought his cache of Freddie Blassie tapes. "His famous mid-eighties 'I support *winners*' speech — when McMahon accused him of consorting with Iranians and Commies." Groovy. So grab the flags of Laos, Poland and Monaco, take Ssess and Johann out to the tool shed. (TV does not belong in a house.)

2. Flags for lining shoes with. A natural, but they'd hafta be thin ones, I trust . . . any takers? Porcelain (formerly married to Kenneth Cole)? Uha (enrolled at the Footwear Inst. of Pascagoula)? Great, good . . . here's Ivory Coast, Luxem‸ burg and a carton of brogans . . . see what youse two can fig out.

3. Flags for stamp collecting. It's a nasty habit, stamps, but if you must collect, why not paste 'em on flags of the countries . . . sounds acceptable. Peony, take Indonesia, some glue and a bag of Sukarno magentas — see what shakes.

4. Flags for dueling. I dunno, seems more dangerous than last year's flag tug-o-war, but all right, let's try it. Teets (Jamaica) versus Shlomo (Japan) — en garde! Lunge . . . thrust . . . oops, I knew it . . . there goes Shlomo's vitreous humor. Somebody get a mop. When're they gonna blunt the ends of those fuggers?

5. Flags for driving. Y'mean up on the antenna? Hmm, I 'spect it could work as a makeshift staff . . . no, the breeze, too close to waving — something a Mizza don't *do* . . . bad Category. Although wait, Beph, why doncha sit in the 'Vette with the flag of Peruvia, feel it out . . . nope, no keys . . . best to keep it stationary.

6. Flags for reading. A nice bright flag will help you concentrate. "Me me me!" shout Woona and Vulvo, who retreat to the den with *Forever Amber*, *Bondage Trash* and the banners of Thailand and Libya.

7. Flags for writing. Anyone for prose? Poetry? Bumper stickers? Pants swaggers forward, brandishing the standard of Switzerland, pauses a moment, tosses off a gem of uncommon wit and concision:

It goes against my religion — none.

8. Flags for Family Fun. Whatever in tarnation *that* is. Hey, I'm only the patriarch here. Nobody wants to tackle this? Good — let's drop it.

9. Flags for ideas. I'll take that myself. Mali in my left hand, Ireland in my right and I'm set . . . here 'tis. The solution to all the world's ills, the first emormous step anyhow, is to limit network adverts to a thousand dollars total production expense — strictly enforced. So nobody can sell you nothing you don't want, don't need, and "consumption" would not seem in and of itself so compelling. Nothing, not Cadillac, not

Nike, not Diet Coke, would look any better than local dogpiss at 3 AM — "Buy or rent an all-purpose folding ladder" — or the Home Shopping Network. A thousand bucks including actors, script, camera work, transportation, everything. It's a felony if you go over (9 yrs. in federal pen).

10. **Flags for flag sake**. A.k.a. flags for hoisting. Perhaps the most important of Categories. So important that we've again enlisted Unc — former president of Staten Island — to deliver the ceremonial "Ready . . . hoist!" command.

Wait — do I see Bangladesh? DNQ! DNQ! — does not qualify. No, Johann, the circle is slightly left of center. Believe me — it would not be the same upside down. Here, spray it over with this — the black flag of Anarchy. That's a Q. Ready, Unc?

Oh, and remember now — no waving. Well, it's okay to wag 'em a little. Nothing wrong with a little wagging. But careful around the pool, don't get them wet, because afterwards we burn 'em.

LET'S KILL JOY

Hi, it's Roy. Returning your . . . Oh hi, I'm having another rock trivia game tomorrow night and I was hoping you could . . . *Where'd, who gave you my service number?* Mark. Is that okay? *Well, there's not much I can . . .* I was hoping, 'cause the questions are so lame, the songs they use, I'm making my own tape, and Mark's gonna make one — could you make a tape? *I don't think there's time, uh, why's it have to be rock trivia? It's the game that's lame.* What would you rather play, poker? *No, poker's about money and what's rock trivia, "honor"? I don't really give a hoot about either of those this week.* I've never played poker, you have to memorize all the red cards and black cards and the counting. You probably win all the time. *Well, no, I've never actually won an entire, never come out ahead. I haven't played in a long, got no money.*

And the other thing I was calling, you'd be the one to, what's a good McCoy Tyner album? *In his own name?* Yeah. *There aren't any.* I heard his latest and it sounded . . . *He's just awful. He was always a symptom of Coltrane's latent conservatism — can't do without a piano, can't shake, no matter how far his music, blow the top off the Milky Way and he still needs to have, not only, not even just as a metronome, a compass — 1, 2, 3, 4, give me the changes — but to have somebody there tickling, y'know,* being all these by-then *superfluous cornball things your average competent player still generally tended to be. In terms of sound, his basic attack, to me McCoy Tyner is like a florid cocktail player with some hardbop pretensions who learned how to maintain, y'know, this trance pattern Coltrane gave him, this sort of pre-New Music repetition module or . . .* What about "My Favorite Things?" *Well, okay, at his* best, *and he played his assigned role perfectly, but it was, in and of, it was so* not *a big deal that you can hear, by '62 you get the same monotonous line done to death, in totally conventional circum-*

stances, by Cedar Walton with Art Blakey. I really like his arpeggios on the *Ballads* album.

Well that's Coltrane's worst. His worst on Impulse anyway.
Oh, I really . . . *That was the one he did after, Bob Thiele must've, like the Ellington album wasn't somehow evidence enough that he could play mainstream for the, he had to do these tinkle-tinklers like "Too Young to Go Steady" and "Nancy with the Laughing Face."* I really like those. *Well, you want ballads, he'd already, well the one after that with Johnny Hartman . . .* I don't know that one. *Oh, it's great, it takes that theme so far it comes out the* other *end of squaresville, but even before he'd already done "Out of This World" on the* Coltrane *album, the one just called* Coltrane — I don't know that one either. *— on Impulse, the blue cover, not the one on Prestige — which is a really nice over-the-edge, 14 minutes long, not one of these easy-digestible bite-size things like on* Ballads, *it's like the hogwild stuff on* Live at the Village Vanguard *and* Impressions . . . Those I have. They *are* good. . . . *where he's over the edge of, whatever metaphor you wanna, and McCoy Tyner, even there, still hasn't, he's this incredible rhythmic/harmonic drudge, he's still playing "My Favorite Things" while Coltrane's already a full, whole stage or two beyond* that.

He's like telephone wires stretched out tight, extra tight, with Coltrane flying over them, and he's flying so high you've gotta distort the perspective just to see them, and you still wouldn't see 'em unless they enlarged 'em, the wires, a couple hundred times — how many kinds of unreal sync do you need? I mean why Coltrane after a certain point felt he needed any *piano for what he was doing is really, the proof he didn't* really *mean business on* Ascension . . . Got that. But I don't play it. . . . *is he brings in all these guys, like Archie Shepp solos, John Tchicai and Marion Brown take amazing solos, all these people blowing, blowing — and this is when blowing your brains out was practically an end in, a priority, that's the con*text — *and he lets McCoy, the straight man of the session, half a step up from Ahmad Jamal, solo too!*
You can't recommend . . .

Okay, if you, let me, um, there's one on Milestone called Echoes of a Friend, *buncha Coltrane songs, at least it's a familiar reprise of, I'm sure it's out of print.* You're talking solo records, trios? Yeah, or larger. *Well, his, I dunno, quintet albums, sextet, I can't sit for that shit. His idea of hornplayers — okay, Coltrane fires him, replaces him with someone even worse, his wife, then* he's gotta replace — his *replacements for Coltrane, he's had some really godawful, Hubert Laws, Gary Bartz, who's he got now, John Blake? The only violinist worse than John Blake, well, okay, trios. The first album he did in his own name,* Inception, *I bought it, it was no great shakes but it's from that same, when he was still with Coltrane. There's a CD out, I'm not sure, it's two Impulse LP's combined, one is probably* Inception, *I'm guessing,* Nights of Ballads and Blues, *if that's the other it wasn't horrendous.*

Speaking of CD's, I just got a Doors CD you might be interest . . . *I can't stand rock CD reissues, haven't heard one yet that, whenever I play one side by side with the vinyl the CD always sounds like a* blueprint for, uh, like no more than a diagram for what, from the vinyl, I know the true sound to be. Well this doesn't, it's pretty close . . . *I dunno, Elektra, you ever, the only Elektra CD I've heard is* Forever Changes, *which I used to love and I can't even . . . it's so absurdly* clear *you get details audible that were in the realm of total conjecture, total, wild guesswork on your part, listening to the original.* Well that should be good then. Wasn't, that was an album where details were the best part. *Well I'm not, well, details, there was also lots of good murk, the sloppy, murky mix was what the record auditorily* was. *As far as, what you in fact* heard, *every detail, real or illusive, plugged into, or you extracted it from, this viable dense mess. It wasn't foreground in some brittle diorama with arrows pointing and outlines drawn around everything. Maybe mess is the wrong — but also vinyl is just so much* warmer, *no CD I've heard, even jazz, is as warm-sounding as vinyl.* This Doors thing isn't very different.

Is it remixed? Remastered. *They didn't add bass or bring up the drums or anything?* Not so I could tell. It's really okay.

There's this other one I got that I *know* you would like, an unissued Byrds, I forget the title . . . *That thing on Re-Flyte.* Is that . . . Never Before. Yeah, that's it. Isn't it . . . *I hate that album, I have, somebody sent me the vinyl. It just — how much more sleazy can you get than falsifying, it's like Jane Fonda doing her, revising the sixties.* Whuddo you mean? *Those mixes are from six months ago.* You sure? "Eight Miles High" is completely different. The guitar parts are different, the . . . *Well that's an actual alternate take, they say, although, uh, I mean that lunacy about "true stereo for the first time" — didn't you read the notes?*

What, they went back to the original four-track and . . . *I dunno, some might be the, I didn't read all, most seem to be brand new mixes. Jim Dickson, he was once what, their manager, I don't think he ever produced their, not on Columbia, him and some other guy remixed it.* It sounds great, though, "Mr. Tambourine Man," the stereo is . . . *See, I consider it a travesty to do anything to the original sound. It's a hallowed document, you don't fuck with it, who cares if you've only heard something in mono, or fake stereo, whatever? It ain't fake if that's how you heard it, and how they released it, for whatever motives or expediencies or . . . If it doesn't reflect the actual push-pull, the sociology of a band, working as a band — McGuinn wants this part up, Crosby wants, the A&R flunky's fidgeting, Hillman's asleep — what's the point? And anyway, just to toy with, to scare up another nuance, even if you could, now, this far after the fact, is nuts. It's like traveling back in time so Mister Bluster can wear different shoes on an episode of* Howdy Doody.

What about the previously unissued cuts? *What, "Triad," you gotta hear Crosby do it himself? The lyric isn't, Grace Slick wasn't silly enough? "Never Before," nothing special, you can see why they never, "Thoughts and Words" meets "Don't Make Waves," and even if it isn't why release it now?* Why release unissued jazz then? How . . . *Well, jazz is more about ongoing, its whole history is the unit — everything is simultaneous — and the* rock unit is maybe a moment if even, a micromoment, a succession of barely connected micromoments. *What's past is dead-dog past, and if it hasn't played the first time, meaning if* you *haven't internalized it, since* you're *half of — if it didn't impact on your consciousness then, and your sub, during its brief, allotted uh, it didn't exist. And since it didn't exist, it doesn't exist — there's no rock and roll outside that tearaway, throwaway type of time. You can't put it, shove it back into time if it wasn't there to begin with. I may be one contrary cretin, but there aren't* ten *rock songs from before I started listening that I later heard that meant anything to me, some Carl Perkins on Sun maybe, a Little Richard or two, but . . .*

I see we disagree.

I guess. Well, when you come over you can tell me what Coltrane albums I should get. *Should I bring beer?* No, I've got beer. If you want, if you don't like, is Corona okay? *Yeah, fine. How 'bout we just sit around and play records?* I don't think you'd wanna listen to my import Troggs collection . . . *Probably not. I guess we should play.* I can't get you to make a tape? *There's not really time.* Okay, well I'll see you. *Yeah.* 'Bye. *Goodbye.*

WINDOWS THEY COULD HIT ME THROUGH EASY

I've said it before and I'll say it again: this isn't my home, it's my office. Of course there's also a stove, a bathtub, a bed, three dozen $500-fine-for-possession plastic/metal milk cartons jammed with records, books and other amenities of actual residence, but that doesn't alter the dominant thread of the occupancy. Officelike things occur here with predictable frequency: at 8 AM I'm working, at noon I'm working, at 4:37 and at 9:49 I'm working. Fewer people die in offices than in homes or hospitals, so statistically I'm probably all right — but ponder *these* stats:

3 singles, 2 doubles: 5 windows. Or depending on how you count, 7. 14 windowpanes. Through which may be seen 8, 1, 3, 3, 4: 19 rooftops. Who knows how many hundred windows and vents. Semi-concealed street positions. Trees. Tens if not hundreds of thousands of sight lines, down, up, right, left, head on. All the hours I'm here, so many opportunities.

Likeliest: kitchen (east end), the *office* part of my office, where the desk is wedged in, facing out, always a lamp on. The blinds are drawn so just aim low — a miss to my face gets my neck or torso. Next: bathroom. The horizontal cross-frame is flush with my eyes when I'm showering. (My bedroom could be somebody else's, the bathroom is *probably* mine, but the write-room — window nearest corner — could be no one else's.)

A 12-unit building, security door, my name and apartment are right there on the buzzer, any dumbo could suss out the location: second floor, rear, north, they could climb a ladder and be level with my teeth (furious sounds of writing would easily cover it).

Do you hear the shot and the glass and then you're dead, or is it instantaneous?

SCREAMS IN THE NIGHT

From my living room window, from out there some-where, another window: "Harder, please. I'm gonna come." How nice — do I know you?

. . . From nightsonicnothing to cunt!alive!some!thing — sounds about 30. Signing on . . . signing off.

Usually I have no patience for other people's pleasure, their *manifestation* of pleasures of which I am nowise a part. Friends' exclusive pleasures are bothersome enough, but strangers'?

Well, honey, I have patience for yours.

(A Tuesday at 10.) (And never again.)

Holy *Christ* am I hard.

LULLABYE OF BROCCOLI

Woke up, there was this green stuff, warm and wet. I don't puke in bed much, so at first I fought the notion that that's what it was. But the hangover, almost as severe as my guilt over having had no-fun getting it, was beyond debate, so I couldn't really fight it too zealously. After 20 minutes of lying there cussing myself — I hadn't gotten laid, hadn't insulted anyone in a loud or novel manner, hadn't . . . and sheez, all this *slime* on my pillows and face — I admitted it was puke, but why green?

It didn't smell like bile, or is bile brown? Tequila? I hadn't drunk tequila. Seaweed? It was seaweed-colored. Then I remembered the broccoli.

And worse, ugh — the poet pups.

These spongy undercooked cookies shaped like *dogs*. Cookie dogs! — shepherds, chihuahuas, collies — with little jolly tags on 'em, ribbons. Paper tags with eensy scripted names, no, not of breeds: with *names of poets*. A scotty w/ "Pound" — I ain't making this up — a dachshund w/ "Byron." I et several, many breeds, and one tag — "Jeffers" — to go with my leafy green vegetable.

Which, had I wished, I could easily have stretched into vegetables, plural — there were also jicama, zucchini, red and green pepper — a genuine plus when all you've really come for is all-you-can-drink and the chance to be publicly obnoxious. Yes, I'd been invited. The publication party for *Smiling at Matter*, Valerie Pasadena's eighth (twelfth?) sampling-o-verse, an artist-catered "function" at the Plusminustimesdivided Gallery. This was not her first function, but her first trial feedbag of poet pups.

"Freshly baked!" she half cooed, half sighed each time a new invitee stepped up to inspect the booty. "You remove the collar and nametag — ooh, *Auden* —" — she demonstrates — "and dip your pup in the luscious, creamy *poet paste*" — again, she made this up, not me — "consisting of creamy, delicious whipped cream and I won't even *tell you* what else." I forwent the paste after pup number two, sticking, glopwise, to dill dip and cuke dip for my veggie.

The pup platter dwindled, lights dimmed, and Valerie Pasadena recited her stuff. Titles included: "White Corduroy," "The Glans and I" — who says women don't write genitalia filth? — "Endearing Ceramic," and the interminable (I had to pee twice during it) "After You've Taken Your Trilobite Fossil Set." I won't quote lines, this is *my* book, let's just say they're the sort that gives pottery, pardon me, poetry a bad name, that makes sensitive look like shit. (As a poet and a sensitive I take such shuck *personally*.)

Actually I'd quote but my copy was discarded — it was there in the brocchuck — along with the pillows and 'cases. Bedpuke you don't keep, except on a blanket. Which I sent to the laundry; now good as new. Visit me, you can smell it.

Valerie herself smelled kind of floral — the kind you get in certain aerosols — as, buoyed by five white wines (they never have red at these things), I tiptoed over to proffer my critique. "Atlanta," I told her, "you can be a *superstar* in Atlanta. They have these afternoon movies, opposite reruns of *Maude*, you come on during intermission. It opens with you watering the plants. You look up, 'Oh, hi, how you doing?' — you sound *so* sincere — then you read them a poem. Two-three of those I-talk-to-objects whatsems in that breathy voice of yours" — maybe I meant breathless — "and they're *yours*. The housewives of Atlanta, Birmingham — fuggit, *Pittsburgh*. Nine days a week they tune in *not* for Ma and Pa Kettle, not for some stupid Eve Arden film, but for *you*. Shuffle in a little of that wreckage-of-my-life, I mean the love stuff, like do 'em 'Sainted Sump,' and in six months you'll be mayor. At least the city council." (And I meant every word.)

" 'Soap,' " she corrects me, not exactly gnarling (gnarling ain't her style), "'Sainted *Soap.*' And it's not a love poem, it's concerned with the bittersweet ironies, the dichotomy —" and, clearly, I won't be snuggling *her* sweetmeat tonight, probably not tomorrow night either. But nah, that's not what I attended for, not with her anyway, though I would certainly have acquiesced had her dampness been tendered. Would've licked and/or dicked her though not fond of her writing — geez what a cad I can be — nor in fact fond of *her*, then vomited on her mons . . . or a sacred ceramic.

So it's prob'ly just as well, although, really, the principal vom components weren't ingested till after she took off. Well, components, yeah — though maybe such yug won't get spit up *40* times out of 40 — I probably mean *catalysts*: the final five or eight of my ten-twelve drinks, which by the time they closed the joint had me talking to, and smiling at, objects, too many of them female and animate.

That and the Jeffers tag I chewed — and swallowed — to impress a short one after Valerie bolted with some doofus (gold chains, nonathletic shoes) of apparent preselected vintage. (So I couldn't've copped — Pasadenawise — anyway.)

There was ink on that tag — gold ink. Which could've been the thing to tilt the bedpuke balance.

TODAY IS THE LAST DAY OF THE REST OF YOUR LIFE

At least I've never awakened with a fresh tattoo of unknown origin. My second and last pigmented scarification — skull with a crow, right forearm — I fully remember getting, and why. "Bird rises above death" — got it the day Greeny died, well, possibly not died — the day that I killed him, sealed his doom.

Greeny — what a nowhere name for the only feathered actual friend I've ever had. Cheryl was the namer, and she probably felt entitled, it was near her birthday. A long story, always a long story, but after this we're almost outa here.

I get a call from this woman I vaguely know, typesets at the *Soho Sentinel*. "You're sort of an oddish type guy, I've got an oddlike proposition for you." What's she wanna do, rip pages out of phone books with me? Scotch tape cooch hairs to subway posters? "How'd you like a parrot? I have to get rid of it. You seem like . . ."

"How big?"

"Small, parakeet size. My old man can't stand, he's threatening to . . ."

It's easy being odd sometimes. "Okay."

She brings it over, big brass cage with a velvet cover, and quickly dashes any hopes I'd entertained that ditching a parrot wasn't all she was after. Handshake, cage, remove cover, g'bye parrot, handshake, g'bye. Nice little guy: emerald green with some sky blue and white, a touch of yellow, maybe six inches from tip to claws on his perch. A barren cage — no bird toys, no mirror — and a many-pound bag of seeds. Sunflower.

I let him out and he flies around the apartment, landing on one thing then another, settling on top of the venetian blinds, where he drops a load, and eventually on a wall mirror, gnawing at its wooden frame. When Cheryl gets home he flies down to her head, climbs down her hair to her shoulder. Within a couple days he was regularly sitting on my shoulder while I wrote, flying alongside us when we took down the garbage.

In a gumball machine we found him a plastic monster and some miniature NFL helmets which he'd grab in his beak and toss along the floor. When we left the house we put on records and tapes for him. I built him a feeder above the kitchen doorway where he sat looking intelligent — smarter than a dog — holding food up in front of his face, examining it. (Parrots have that handy two-and-two claw fingeration; parakeets, with one-and-three, can't hold anything, gotta settle for birdseed on a stem.)

A month goes by and the *Soho* woman calls again, wants to know when she can come by, pick her bird up. Fuh — "I thought your boyfriend . . "

"I'm back working as a hairdresser now, and he'd be great for the store."

"What, with all the chemicals and hairspray and shit?"

"Hey, there's nothing wrong with —"

"We don't even cage him. He's not an object. He hasn't been in it in —"

"Look, I want my parrot back."

"That's too bad, we're attached to him. And he's attached to us. You couldn't wait to get rid of him."

"Don't hassle me, I'm coming over."

"Bullshit you are." And she don't.

In her place comes this beefy ex-cop with a windowshade pole. "Where's the cage?" Cheryl had taken it out. The bird's up on the blinds, won't come down. "Get the fucker down." "Fuck off." He cocks the pole, I grab a broom, two-hand it like a crosscheck, he swings and splinters it. Greeny frantically circles the room. "I'll be back." He never comes back. A year passes.

Peacefully enough, especially at bedtime. After the first few nights of tricking him into the cage we'd decided to let Greeny spend the night as he'd spent the day, wherever he wanted, which not unforeseeably turned out to be right near us. We shut off every light except a bedside lamp and he whooshed in from his mirror to the headboard above the bed, closer to Cheryl's side, and stayed there for the night. Which felt kinda cozy, y'know, and next night and every night after he did it again. Almost nestlike for Cheryl and me . . . and Greeny makes three — a not unbearable illusion. Some nights he'd tire of waiting and fly in ahead of us — by then he knew the route in the dark. In the morning before we fully got up he'd custom-carve the board and occasionally hop down to play with us, sing to us, *kiss us*. Beak on lip, a touch not a bite — scoff if you wish (I'll live).

The wood chips we didn't mind, nor did we particu'ly mind his shitting. Just as he did elsewhere, he dumped copiously from his bedboard roost. Tail feathers to the wall: birdshit on headboard, wall and floor. After one attempt to clean the stuff, one cleanup — when birdshit dries, if you get it under a nail it's like being spiked with a caraway seed, ouch (plus the peril of infection) — it seemed advisable to minimize future cleanings. We put sheets of newspaper directly underneath and masking-taped others to the headboard and the wall down along the floorboards. The coverage seemed total — a job well done, might need to change papers once a month — and then not the first night but soon we start hearing this commotion. A scratching sound, not limited to any single spot and commencing shortly after lightsout, which we assume to be our normal dispersion of bugs, just louder, 'til by the third or fourth night it's so blatant we're thinking mice, *many* mice, hadn't had 'em yet but y'never — so with some trepidation we turn on the light, have a look.

You ever see ten roaches together, same area, a food bin, box of cereal, you ever see a hundred? Well, this was *hundreds*.

At least three hundred, on the newspaper, under the newspaper, all sizes and temperaments, eggcase-bearing mamas and newborns, teenagers and full-growns — all feasting on Greeny's guano. I whacked at as many as I could with a rolled-up *Art News*, I mashed them under newssheets — that was fun — I stomped 'em barefoot. Greeny paced along the headboard, Cheryl stayed under the covers, but I wasn't gonna miss the chance to massacre as many as poss before the light totally scattered them. Got around fifty as the rest, energized by the snack, legged it to safety hundreds of roach-steps ahead of me. I ripped out and garbaged the newspaper. If there were gonna be shiteaters in the bedroom, and obviously there would be, at least they wouldn't be shiteaters on newsprint soundstages.

Shit wasn't all they ate. Leavings of Greeny's cashews — Cheryl got 'em raw at the healthfood store — were all over the place. Entire pieces would be roach-et down to thin slivers by morning. You'd see it in progress on the way to the bathroom. But none of this actually bothered us, we coulda lived with it, continued living with it — what bothered us was birdnoise. Not a chirp or a caw, or a hoot or a squawk, more a honk or the bird equivalent of barking, an iron more than a tin sound: SKRWONKWONK. But it didn't start happening for a year.

Our friend began announcing sunup like a rooster, though for a while I had some influence on it, or thought I did. One morning I yelled the word *spogfire* at him and like magic it worked, and kept working. Precision of delivery counted of course — "*Spoggggfire*, Greeny" (less a yell than a throaty grumble) — though sometimes that didn't shut him up either, and ultimately nothing did. SKREEOWRONK-WONK: through any and all chapters of daylight and nightlight — at least the dark quieted him — until finally even nightnight — 2 to 5 AM — became a fixture on his daily squall agenda.

Causes? Dunno. Maybe an appearance by Wayne Dean's dog or the loss of his favorite armchair. Like most everything in the apartment, everything furniturial, the chair had come from the streets, and after the stuffing fell out to the streets it returned. When he wasn't on my shoulder during writing or perched on the mirror, Greeny was often on that chair, on the headrest. Sufficient to trigger? To turn a sweet life sour? Who's to fucking say?

We try to placate him, pamper him, find him another chair, serve him his favorite treat more often: rice cracker with fresh-ground peanut butter. He eats it, then back to the noise that kills. At the pet store they try to sell us something called Quiet Pet, half a tablet in milk for a cat or a dog; how many fractions down for a sawed-off parrot? (Cancel *that* longshot.) In anger we discover that putting him in his cage and covering it does quiet him. But's too, too cruel so just that once, no more.

There were stretches of relative silence — an afternoon, an hour — but one day finally I'm writing, or trying to write, some deadline review when up on the mirror he erupts at the top of his wee little birdlungs and I JUST CANNOT TAKE IT. Can not. Stifling the urge to throw something at him, I beckon him down, lure him in the cage with his New York Jets helmet and cover it, feeling like pig-pus, and this time he whimpers a sad, sad metallic whimper, loud, and I let him out and he's louder than ever and I cover my ears and he bends down off the mirror and roars right at me: what the fucking fuck DOES HE WANT? What's he need, crave, what's he demanding? (At least with a goddam kid — past a certain age — you could ask.) Too, too much two-way trauma — from the illusion of interspecies rapport to THIS. Too much too, too much much. What to fucking *do* already?

Options discussed: give him to a full-time practicing birdlover; give him to anyone willing; give him to the zoo. Advantage with lovers is they don't *always* cage those they love. Fine, so who do we know that might in fact thus love him? Cousin of a friend (loosely defined) in Brooklyn Heights. Has 200 birds — feathers're his passion — entire rooms winging free. We flip for it, I gotta call him. ". . . a beautiful parrot . . ."

"Why do you have to, why do you *want* to?"

"They put in this no-pet clause, and some tenants who had to give away their cat complained."

"How do they know you have one?"

"They heard through the wall."

"What kind of parrot is it?"

"He's a delightful little conure."

"Well, I can see why they complained. Conures are the noisiest, most temperamental birds I've ever handled. For their size they're — I have one and one is enough."

"You don't want another to keep it company?"

"*No* thank you." Well fuck you with feathers. And so on down the options . . . they run out quick.

Around this time there was an article in *Sports Illustrated* on birds and whatnot adjusting to unlikely habitats. In New York (it said) there were hawks f'r inst living in the ducts of apartment buildings. If hawks, why not parrots? It was summer, he'd have at least until winter . . . might it be in the cards for him to "adapt"?

On a hot Sunday night we take photos of him with his toys, with each of us, then cage and cover him one final time. In the morning I hop a cab to Central Park West, the jostles sparking whimpers — "What you got there — birdy?" Me and birdy decab at 70th St. and head for underbrush. I place the cage beside a sycamore, raise the cover enough to open the door, whisper, without looking, "Goodbye, Greeny," and about face outa there. Emerging with a flourish, Greeny has other ideas, landing on my head, stopping me in my tracks. YONK YONK — the acoustics are different out of doors. Down to my shoulder, YONK YAWNK, as if to say: Okay, what now? To have to improvise at a time like this, shit, so I get him on my hand and fling him, gently, a few feet wing-ward, but he only returns to the front of my hair, dumps a load down my cheek where a tear would soon be. Without wiping I offer my hand and this time heave him with enough force to send him ten feet before he flies back — PHONK CLONK — a note of triumph — he likes this game.

I wipe, gather my strength, cock up and gun him like a softball pitcher, run like a batter to first. I don't go five strides before he catches up again. No more Mr. Nice: okay, take *this*: swat him off with a backhand, more a push, low intensity, medium malice — I wanna see how he plays it. Plays it the same — oh woe o ow — I give up. But I won't leave him there in the cage.

Could an outsider fare better? I hand Greeny, cage him, depark and call Mike Font. He arrives, I brief him, take him to the spot and split. At 72nd and Broadway I enter the subway and ride. End of the line, 241st St./White Plains Rd. The Westchester border, Mount Vernon. Within three blocks lie three tattoo parlors. Banned in N.Y.C. proper since the sixties, health-coded out of existence (hepatitis — policing needles — made it too expensive, let's just ban it), these joints are a healthy mix of suburban antiseptic and border-town urgent. Several needy persons in each. Persons need tattoos.

I case the wall designs, the tats they have stencils for — no freehand f'r me — and see no parrots but some eagles, swallows, cardinals — nah — then finally some crows. Crow on a cocktail glass, crow peering out of a human skull, crow above a skull (wings spread wide and laughing). Suddenly I'm struck with the horrible thought, What will he eat in Central Park? Hadn't thought it before. I go with the last of the three, get stenciled, drilled, bandaged, then return, distorted with self-hate and sorrow, to my grimly quiet address via 7th Avenue sweatcar.

That was a Monday and Friday we go to the movies,

Mean Streets. It's been a louselousy week and the movie, hnnnnh, I'm in foggy anguish. Johnny Boy is this insufferable make-your-life-shit and yet Harvey Keitel can take it. If Harvey can take it, Harvey who don't exactly even *love* Johnny Boy — not exactly — then what's a little SKREE SKWONK SKRWEEEEETWONNK from someone you love? How could I, how . . . and a third of the way into the pic — it's a long pic — I'm thinking what should I do, what should I do, I'm watching and not watching and never not thinking what should — I can't shake it for a second. Thinking what I'm gonna do and what I'm gonna say I'm gonna do: what *exactly* I will say to Cheryl. How I will tell her what.

So deep in whatthought and howthought that when Johnny Boy gets it in the neck, or is it the face — I haven't been focused on *his* problems, *his* miseries, just how they might affect (or complicate) Harvey's — that it takes me a minute to scope out the ramifications of his getting it: his getting it frees Harvey; his getting it leaves Harvey without a viable ongoing penance; his getting it changes nothing. Takes a minute, okay, and in that minute I lose the thread of my, of what I've measured and rehearsed for two-thirds the picture. But quick — say something.

"Listen, I've been thinking about Greeny."

"I was too."

"If he could stand Johnny Boy, if he could put up with . . . then I can't believe we abandoned Greeny just for making noise."

"But we . . ."

"Let me say it." Wipe eyes and nose. "I'm going back to the park to try to find him."

"But the cage won't still be — what would we keep him in?"

"Since when have we kept him in a cage?"

"This is *not* a good idea."

We walk home and I'm painnumbed, I'm numbpained,

I'm unfit for living. Then from out of the blue she blurts this astounding line: "Sometimes you even have to give up those you love." The first wise-sounding, comforting thing she's ever said. What'll she do for an encore? And why wait so long to get wise?

I'M THE ONE WITHOUT

shitist heo new ithf li esoni t
shit tist heo new ith f li e son i t   '
                    e o
                         w t
                              h f   n i
                                        i t
shi tist he o ne w i th f li e so n i t
shiti st he one wit hfli eso nit
sh it is t he one wit hf lie s on it
sh i tisth eon e withfl ie sonit
s h i t i s t h e o n e w i t h f l i e s o n i t
s h i t i s t h e o n e w i t h f l i e s o n i t
s h i t i s t h e o n e w i t h f l i e s o n i t
s h i t i s t h e o n e w i t h f l i e s o n i t
s h i t i s t h e o n e w i t h f l i e s o n i t
s h i t i s t h e o n e w i t h f l i e s o n i t
s h i t i s t h e o n e w i t h f l i e s o n i t
s h i t i s t h e o n e w i t h f l i e s o n i t
s h i t i s t h e o n e w i t h f l i e s o n i t
s h i t i s t h e o n e w i t h f l i e s o n i t
s h i t i s t h e o n e w i t h f l i e s o n i t
s h i t i s t h e o n e w i t h f l i e s o n
i t

MAD TERRY'Z 'NCLE

Some oke (but not great) anagrams for Rod McLtzer, he of the dixploits and loneness, he I me of the plain pain and theorized folly: M.R.'Z OLD CERT (= Monty Rock's stale breath candy); T.C.'Z MODEL R.R. (Ted Curson's Lionel); E-Z CLOT DR. RM. (not the difficult clot drama room); L CD TREMORZ (50 — count 'em! — compact disc quivers); DL-OZ. MERC TR (the fuel-guzzling 550-ounce Mercury TR); RE: MORT'Z L.C.D. (concerning Sahl's low com. denom.); M. ORDERZ C.L.T. (Meg requests codfish, lettuce and tomato sandwich); R.D.L.R.C.Z. TO ME (*really* dirty, lousy, rotten, crummy, zinky to me); R.R.'Z ODE T' MCL. (Rocket Richard's stirring tribute to Rick MacLeish).

If my surname instead was McEtzler, we could squeeze out even more: LORD'Z MERE C.T. (God's basic tease); CORDZ LET ME R. (pants let me ratify); LET'Z RECORD M. (Mendelssohn! Mantovani! Metallica!); RECORD MELTZ (in the broiler, yes); CDR.'Z R. OMELET (commander's yolk & radish); D.C. MOTELZ ERR (room service flawed in our nation's cap); R.R. MELO-D'Z, ETC. (Ricky Ricardo arrangements and *then some*); ZERO-L.R. TED M.C. (the no-legroom teddyboy motor club); MEL, T.D. ZCORER (8 touchdowns vs. Duluth); D.M.Z. TEL. OR REC. (your call: telethon or rectitude in the Demilitarized Zone); OL' TERMZ CER'D (former conditions rosed, no, *cerised*); LEM ET ROZ, D.R.C. (tongued 'er but she wouldn't come — discreetly resists climax); ELMER'Z ROD, CT. (80 miles from Hartford); ELMO CRED'Z R. (T.) (Zumwalt credits Rasputin — *true*); RED CRELZ O' MT. (the fin-tastic red mouth crel, Montana's leading sportfish).

If on the other hand I was *Randy* McEtzler — and I sure wish I was — there'd be a whole *heap* o' fine 'grams ripe for

the picking: ARMY LEZ TREND "C" (still top-secret); MY
RECTAL ZEN RD. (route I avow w/ Sphinctral Buddhism);
CLYTEMNEZ'RA DR. (just up from Agamemnon Ln.);
LADY TREEZ MR. C.N. (scares Conrad Nagel up an elm);
MERRY DENTAL C.Z. (a cavity-free Canal Zone); ALT.
MERCY END, R-Z (euthanasic alternatives, from razor wine
to zipgun in the snout); CRAZY T.M. LENDER (loans her
transcendental meditation to seals!); MR. ED'Z CRY: "EAT
N.L." (bolt and digest the National League); ARTY L.C.
MERDE/N.Z. (pretentious lowercase shit, N. Zealand style);
R.T. DAMNZ CELERY (Russ Tamblyn prefers chard); D.L.
ART'Z R.C. ENEMY (dicklick art's greatest foe: the pope of
Rome); MY TENDER CZAR L. (Lufus III, "soft oppressor
of Sverdlovsk"); RCLD. N.M. RAT'Z EYE (recycled New
Mexico rodent lens); R.R.'Z CANDY 'ELMET (Rex Reed's
white chocolate headpiece); "CRA-Z M.D. REEL" — N.Y.T.
(whacko doctor film sez *New York Times*); REALTY, CEM.
'ND ZR. (land, cement, zirconium — the Three Pillars of
sound investment); DERRY LAMENTZ C. (Londonderry
mourns the death of Custer); NERD MEAT LYR'CZ (to the
hit tune "Abraham, Mutton and John"); TRY CLAM-EN-
DERZ (and never jump & squirm for clam again!); TRENDY
M.-L. CRAZE (the ever-banal Martin-Lewis revival tour);
'ARDLY RECENT M.Z. (mythic zoonosis of several years
back); L.D.'Z 'CENERY MART (where Lee Dorsey vends
scenes); RED'Z MET'L CAN'RY (foremost purveyor of tita-
nium canes); RY NEEDZ MTL. CAR (Cooder seeks Montreal 4-door); MANTLER'Z RYE C.D. (Michael's
whole-grain corn dog); CRY DEM ANTLERZ (weep 'em!);
CARMEL R.N.'Z DYE T (Calif. nurses take their Earl Grey
blue); LET'Z R'MANCE *DRY* (or'f y'want we c'n do it wet);
MERL TY DANCERZ (as seen in the Merl Ty production
of *A Chorus Line*); TYLER M., N.C. 'RE D.A.Z. (Mary T.
Moore, Natalie Cole are Daughters of the American Zygote);
NARC'Z REMEDY: L.T. (controversial drug treatment: lute-

string through testicles); RENY'Z C.L.T. DREAM (a codfish, lettuce and tomato nightmare); RET. MEN'Z C.R.L. DAY (Retired Men's Christian Rumplove Day, April 30); RENTA'Z DEM. CRLY. ("Theft is property": renter's democratic corollary); CREATED N.Y.'Z M.L.R. (literally *invented* the Manhattan-style mucus, lettuce & raffia sandwich); N-E MARRY'D CELTZ? (wedded Welsh? — I believe there are); N.R. MY-T Z. EEL CARD (nonreturnable winning ticket in the Zambian eel lottery); M-T R'D ENC. LAYERZ (empty refried enchilada strata); ZYLDA REREC MTN. (tallest peak in the Central Ukraine).

And if somehow I got born again as Rafael McUrxznobateauty—call me Rafe — we'd be lookin' at:

RAZMATAX COUNTY LABE FUR-E

I should be so lucky!

SEX D'AMOUR ON THE CÔTE D'AZUR

This place. That place. Places. In Albany, bored stung, I grab the white pages, the yellow, open to "Massage," notice Ooh La Lay Outcall, an excellent name. I dial. "It'll cost you fifty dollars." I ask for a redhead.

In twenty minutes, a knock. At the door, a blonde, pink lips, hefty in a manner neither unappealing nor appealing, lightly scented. "Hi, I'm Arlene."

"Ray." She extends a wide hand. I take it.

"If you pay me, we can get started." The exact sum, pre-folded, I draw from my wallet. She sheds a paisley jumpsuit, nonmatching bra and bikini briefs. I remove T-shirt and cut-offs and am motioned onto my stomach. Crosslegged to my left, she jabs knuckles at my kidneys, neither pleasurably nor painfully; at my spine. She stops. "Would you be interested in any optional services?"

Rolling over, I study her shaved pits, stout bosom and hedgeclipped bush. I discern no life aroma coequal with the cosmetic. Sexual woman at her least teeming, most mere? "I just might."

"Good. First I have to ask you, are you a member of the Albany PD or of any other municipal, county or state peacekeeping force?"

"No, but couldn't I be lying?"

"Not if you're a cop. I'm required to ask. A straight lay will cost you a three-digit number beginning with one and ending with zero."

"What's the middle number?"

"The middle number is zero. Go-down is a two-digit number beginning with seven and ending with zero."

"Any discount if I also go down on *you*?"

"No. It wouldn't be more expensive, but it wouldn't be

cheaper. Half-and-half is a two-digit number beginning with eight and ending with five."

"There's a dollar sign in front of all of these?"

"That's right."

"Have you got anything a little less . . ."

"The cheapest thing I do is a two-digit number beginning with five and ending with zero. That's a local."

"A local what?"

"Some guys call it a handjob."

"How 'bout if I eat you while you give me one?"

"That would be extra."

"Why?"

"That's the price list. I didn't write it."

"How much extra?"

"A two-digit number beginning with one and ending with five."

"What if I just eat you?"

"That's not on the list, but I could let you have it for the price of a local."

"For how long?"

"Three minutes."

"You don't have anybody's stuff in you?"

"No, I'm clean. Everybody wears a safe."

"How much if I stick my hand up your pussy and snuffle it?"

"I don't do that. Get your hand away."

"Well, what if you give me a few tugs, get it going, then I finish on my own?"

"That's the same as if *I* finish you."

"Or let's say I beat it myself and come on your tits or —"

"That's two digits beginning with six and ending with five. And you can't come on my face." I notice, under makeup, a cheek pimple and a chin pimple. "Look, I'm in a hurry. Make up your mind."

"What's the rush, you got another stop?"

"I'm going swimming?"

"In a pool?"

"Uh huh. Gotta go now. You might wanna give the lady a tip."

"How many digits should it be?"

"That's up to you."

"Well, next time, thanks."

"You're *very* welcome. Sure hope you liked the massage."

"Sure did." But not as much as the 'rithmetic.

THE MATH WE DO FOR LOVE

eighty-eight
nighty-night

N.e. connection?

PRIDE OF OWNERSHIP

on the good ship. on. can't recall why I removed it. t' show it? tell it? writeabout it? must've. and it must've been me, I'd've let no others near it, and I can't remember putting up a fight.

when.

what I used to cut it. the cut is quite clean. nothing jagged or snaggly. a keen blade, a heavy blade, I'm sure. not a steak knife. perhaps a cleaver. cleaved.

a thick-stemmed mushroom — finely veined — wider than thick. a veal skinned, blue veined beauty: I am *fond* of this one. flexible, resilient: you could bend it, shake it, play ping pong with the thing. bang nails with it, or tacks in cork or balsa. fat pink fat carrot. proud it is mine.

(an eagle saved. an eagle round. my bulb in a basket. sliced but sound.)

but will, if bounced, it bounce? if dropped? don't chance it: dance it. prance it. write it?

dare I?

may I? shall we? or have we exceeded the bulbcopy quota, *anatomical* bulbcopy? pages, para. to be counted. better check.

one. three. good count. only nine lines so far about my wong. writeaway. writeabout: *a punis in tunis*
                              is a penis betweenis. but the slash is now scabby. the scabs and the there where. the how to connect it? tubes go with tubes and the veins are. arteries in . . . ? tubes that. everything with. rive point exact where. balls still attached but. thick wide neat scab on. squeeze scrape draw flow blood reconnect correct. line direct pressure. pin needles thread.

                    now here's the hard part:
                    routing the root

off the floor
for a stitch

it was there
'hind the hinges
then it limped
into a ditch

it's yours
and you love it
but it's sing'g
along w/ Mitch

y'know:
Me & My Shadow
Just A-Walkin' in the Rain
and Under My Thumb

gotch. now what.

choice of twine, yarn, mucilage, shoelace, tomato paste. choice of wire: plaid, copper, zinc. don't want a doc, don' need a doc, just saw the doc, no doc for a dong. thermometer: mercury. hands that have been. wash. procedure. water no water the dish soap. wisely wipe fingers on sox slacks. no slacks. clean grab grips flap crisis. bottom flesh flapping like taffy. peach pear vanilla with strawb sauce. quick the peroxide. oh no fizz. no time to lose call the store closed. temperature none. get the tube kit.

fleshtop is mush in a mushbag. a marshmallow golfbag, a two-wood. a towheaded twoheaded line up the red tube. the green tube is shattered, the white tube. the pump tube balloon tube the bone tube. in for repairs at the one out of six is no-good call a doc wake it up, Jack. we better now better we wake or. awake is the wake it you listening? wake us it wake out of this one wake wake i —

tankyou.

thanks.

FORGIVING THE VIET VET

When dreams don't write it, and they sure ain't writing *this* page, let alone speeding completion of our goddam so-called 'novel,' and the seven years the mess has thus far taken feel like twenty off my life, and 'great book,' even 'good,' have been scrapped and buried as even counterfeit goals and all I wanna do is have the fucking thing be done, and I can't imagine ever being done (at best, perhaps, like death, it will someday creep up on me), and dust piles high on unfinished paragraphs, and mold forms on untrashed coffee grinds, and fatigue ever deepens in the bone, and the longer this goes on the surer I am that I have no-o-o facility for this game, no 'language skills' — hey, who would want them? — only now I need them: when I have to beat myself with a club to find the right synonym, any synonym, for "beat," and it takes me three days of beating and eleven trips around the block to come up with "no doc for a dong" — you think a dream actually wrote it? the very WORDS? — and I lack the arrogance of nuance to even *impersonate* a writer, and the part of me who doesn't write is coveting the life of virtually anyone who *really* doesn't, and doing his darndest to wrench control from the part of me that does and get us both down off this bloody highwire NOW and 'prematurely' call it quits, and every morning I pound imaginary spikes in my chest — though is it he-who-writes doing it to he-who-don't or vice versa? — and every chapter is a long-long tunnel (you know *that* one) not only coal-black but sloped either up or down with sharp unpredictable turns, never a light 'til I'm actually out (then immediately into the next one), and few remain left, true, but at this point few is many, and the only valid diversion, the only one that won't mire me deeeeeep in self-lacerating guilt, is a good full once-a-day, twice-a-day shit, then it's time, by George, to rethink a thing or two.

I got this friend, not George, let's call him Fred, who's always whining how guilty he feels that people he knew went to Vietnam — couldn't get out of it, didn't bother to get out of it, in any case didn't get out of it, went over and died or came back irrevocably affected, if not afflicted — their lives dry leaves in a wind tunnel — and he didn't go, saw a shrink, got him out of it. Feels now it was dead wrong for his 'privilege and education' to have given him that edge, the 'cultural' head of steam to do it, and there but for etc. it could've been him — and since it could've it should've — what right did he have to exclude himself from the cattle car to nihility?

To which I tell him hey, I'm willing to compare my guilt with anyone's, never shirk it, but there's something every bit as cultural (for ex.: macho as surrender to shithead fate — tough guys don't resist — obedience as dance step and rite of passage, the stigma of being branded a peacecreep or sissy, mindless discipline as badge of virility) and in the end run as crudely purposive about getting in (or not not getting in) the cattle car. If anybody's guilty, *they're* guilty — those that went — of crimes against self and MEGAMULTIPLE OTHERS.

Fuckit: the imperative was for *everybody* to get out of it, see a $10 shrink, fake deafness, cut off a finger, or just tell 'em you're a fag — whatever it takes — 'community' scorn be damned. On a crass 'survival' level, you either went that extra yard to save your skin — *pre* having to napalm rice paddies to do it — or you didn't. There's culpability even in the docile accedence to pawnhood, and if you're already a pawn the topical deathstink — and I ain't talking just yours — has still gotta make some bells go off, and if somehow it doesn't, or if Merle Haggard, LBJ and your gonads have deafened you for life, it damnsure truly is sad SAD — and all such — so let's cry for the suckers, cry an ocean — but *guilt?* Shit, man. We're talking guys of course who went but didn't *mean* to napalm rice paddies — those who meant it on top of being pawns, as a key flavor of their pawnhood, no pity for *their skin*.

To this day, every time there's a ballot initiative, should or shouldn't we float a bond issue, give veterans interest-free home loans, or roll back their property tax, whatever, I vote NO, A THOUSAND TIMES NO, me and a few hundred others, and everybody else — even people who vote no on everything — votes yeah, sure, whynot, and it passes by millions. If it was only retroactive to past wars it would be bad enough, although theoretically I could live with it — throw some crumbs to the maimed and whatnot, the suckers — but no encouragement should be given to young-hormone bozos, current and future, to think lifetime payback will come of 'serving their country' — they sign up for a sick two-year job, it doesn't mean they're entitled to a medal, a pension or a bungalow to take out loans on — it's not like they're coalminers or something. Especially officers. (Officers, for their service, deserve at least the loss of a toe.) And if you wanna settle CLASS MATTERS let's redistribute wealth before the fact — don't need wars to make the ghetto eligible for its crummy ration of crumbs — give 'em the keys to Bel-Air. Anyone who accepted the draft to eat should be fed, natch (and better to mug bankers than enlist), and everybody in coalmines or jail should of course be given a generous stipend.

(They also oughta reinstute the draft — it's not from compassion that Carter and congress got rid of it. With no draft there's no draft resistance, no mass opposition to much of anything. Fear of deceasement gets all the balls rolling, as much as they roll. Bring it back.)

This is always my line. But now I'm thinking: I'm as big a sucker as anyone who went. I who have submitted unforcedly to what now amounts to trench warfare with shit, rats and tarantulas in my pants, and probably need it to 'be a man' to boot: if I can get in that soup, stay in that soup and not only refuse to quit but possibly forgive myself, which I will (or may) if I ever finish — and promise never to Do It Again — swear! — or maybe not so much forgive as condone, anyway cease to beat up and bully myself, well I gotta keep bullying, now, or I'll NEVER be done, but anyway: then amnesty for vets would seem equally in order. *Maybe.*

But the Gulf War vet? — the folks who blew up Iraq — our all-mercenary military — there's no forgiving *those* pig-fuckers . . . NO.

ADJUST

In "Pride of Ownership," change "wake it up, Jack" to "wake it up, Mack."

In "The Story So Far," change "bare, beat studio" to "bare, dilapidated studio."

In "Pixtures, Please!," add the 310 area code to the Rhino Records phone number.

In "Lover Ma'am," change the film title *I Worship Satan* to *I Worship Stan*.

In "Kneeweak," change "Seventeen years" to "Twenty-one years," but only if you dare.

Change "scum like Bush" to "slime like Bush" in "Noche de la Nuit." In the next paragraph, change " 'Groovy Kind of Love' by Phil (Dim Brit) Collins" to, I dunno, an insipid '80s/'90s pop remake of your recollection, and give its singer a comparably demeaning parenthetical sobriquet.

Change the spelling of "gray," wherever it appears as adjective, noun or verb in either simple or compound form (with the exception of Wardell Gray in "Summer of My Days"), to "grey."

Add Sun Ra to the last tier of the jazz roster in "Woeful Blind Sap" — #16, between Sidney Bechet and Jelly Roll Morton — and replace him with Frank Lowe in "The Mode." Delete Al Cohn from "Woeful" (he wasn't dead yet).

There's too much Coltrane throughout the book — cut his appearances by a half (your choice) — and too much McCoy Tyner, so delete the entire "Let's Kill Joy" — no, on second thought I need it.

A CLEAN, NIGHT WELL-LIGHTED

a a A about acts all any anything, are bared. be been beseech blow blunting both brackish but can't center clock; combined. coming constrict Could days' do doing?" down east Easy eye falling find floor for for forethought forgot, forty-four forty-three) forty-two free-fall fucking fucking gelid glum good handkerchief have head he-who-doesn't hold honor I I I I I'd I'm in incontrovertible is isn't it it know late Learning live living lost lung moment, my my myself. necessary? neither Night No, nor nose nostrils not. Not of olding on on on (or out. over pants. parade passes Post-life pouring pray pulp reverse risks." roll, rolling rough, save scabrous secret seemed self slashing sliding slipped soundless "Spontaneous spurn St. staining such taking talk tawdry that the the the this thou thy Time timeless to tumid unstoppable Walking was, wasn't wayless what, "What whether with with with with without witnesses. wonder Would wounded wounding years. yesterday. you your

GREAT MOMENTS IN ALONE

Now that I'm bedrid' with cancer of the dick (a *terrible* form of the illness let me apprise you), I do durn near all my trekkin', my truckin', my step step step steppin' OUT, between the ears, behind the eyes (which are useless anyway). Without my wondraful mem'ries I donut know what I would do, but got them I do — up the yi-ho — so stick around, all R welcome! Do not go 'way as I "free associate" — I do this every morning — to select the day's itinery:

Cancer . . . candor . . . cinder . . . Ella . . . Feller . . . fastball . . . curve . . . ellipse . . . eclipse . . . moon . . . balloon . . . a loon . . . alone — that's it: my most favored times spent alone lone *lone*, those absolutest of moments passed without accompaniment. Limit this week is seven mem'ries daily — dr.'s orders. (The "road to recovery" is slow lane only.) (NOTE: If the journey at times seems a bit "pedestrian," bear in mind that even before my mal de pene I was no fancy stepper.) Okay, let's "step"!

1. Companionless in Ottawa, miles from anything I'm acquainted with, hours late for the concert which is my sole excuse for being here, no money for a cab — my wallet fell off a bridge — I follow a street map and walk straight into an airconditioner, head high, jutting from a hotel facade: bang: oof: bruise 'n' bleed. Airconditioning? In Canada? It gets hot like evywhere else.

2. Daybreak on mescaline. Wake up to bugdrone. They *said* mescaline; it feels more like acid. Psilocybin. Something that won't give an inch. Crickets and 'squitoes and flies — that's all the world is. Up and explore — rural — no one around. Sun refracts bugsound to birdsound — more bite, less drone. Sparrows, jays, grackles? (I'm no birdwatcher). With stones I chase them from the nearest tree to the next nearest.

The din resumes. Chase them to the next one, the next. When they're enough trees up the road that I can scarcely hear 'em — fuck nature — I hop back in bed. (Slowly they return.)

3. Skin and sky '62. Inside view of my left elbow. Drenched in suntan oil — I burn easily. From a distant blanket, "Point of No Return" by Gene McDaniels. Suddenly, closer, "Raindrops" by Dee Clark, closer, plus the too-familiar inflections of uh-oh: "in" crowd. Just what I hiked to this off-beach to avoid. The lies, the name drop, the phony gaiety — twenty feet away. Must lie rock-still till they go in the water. Waiting, waiting . . . no sea for me today. In an hour they swim, I scoot; not *too* bad a burn.

4. Alone in dreamland: mound of Trojans at the end of the world. Was I twelve when I dreamt it? Unwrapped, the lily white tubesteak balloons form a hillock ten feet high, thirty across — the last mound on earth?? Bareassed and barefoot, I romp on it, climb it, admire my good luck. All I need is a *pretty girl* — like Barbara Nichols, say — we can fuck all we want!

5. Don't ask how I got to be at an Up With People event. I'm at an Up With People event. Don't know no-body. Not even to say, "Is this shit or what?" I am for all intents and purps *alone in a crowd*. So alone that when the music's over I don't turn out the light — I try and hit on an Up With People chick. Black tights, decked out as a "beatnik" — it's a tribute to beats (or the '50s — I wasn't paying attention). "Well, what do you think of Allen Ginsberg?" "Who's Allen Ginsberg?" "Can I get you a drink?" "We don't drink." "Want an oyster?" — at the oyster bar. "No thanks." So I take one, drop it sopping wet in my pocket.

Home, me and my shellfish, I put on a record. None of my knives're sturdy enough to pry it open. Try a screwdriver, a soup spoon. Finally: a scissors. Works. One skimpy mollusk. Lemon. And when "When the Music's Over" is over I turn out the light.

6. Add turkey to the list. (*Oh* it hurts to rem'ber this one.)

Dinner at Teenage Dave's, who wasn't. Many diners, including "an old friend of yours." "Who?" "You'll see." A gin & tonic, a gin & tonic, a gin & tonic, a gin & tonic, then who shows but Eve Laker, spiffed up from AA and a 40-thou-a-year ticket broker job; rimless spectacles. No longer wedlocked, technically — in "breakup counseling" — oh kiss my ass. Six-seven years since my last sight of, ah, but the old hanker, the old ache. Kiss kiss the nape of her neck (slaver) — reach up her dress: repulsed, repulsed; again. Rude joke of at last I'm kra-z sloshed/disordered, she's not.

Rude awaken later, alone & dehydrated. Matter in hand, our final coupling recalled kinesthetically. Time after her abortion — stroke stroke — what's that smell? Hand to nose; kind of like, almost like, Jesus, could it be? Did we do it in Dave's cloakroom? Hard to believe I could black *that* out. Scarier thought, will this be the start of something re-newed? (Do I have the heartstrength for it??)

Continue stroking, scratch my lip — other hand — sniff: identical. Well, whud ya know — hands, not pecker — food, not Laker! Main course: Dave's turkey. I'm a 2-fist barehand feeder. The hygiene of a hog, apparently — but why wash AFTER eating? So many things smell *something* like cunny. A fresh-opened jar of Quinn's calcium/magnesium (did you know?) smells like cunny. To that list now add Turkey à la Dave plus trimmings.

7. Absolute social zero! Without an ally 'cept my secretary Eunice, who comes by once a day to open the mail, scrub the bowl, read me Rilke, and administer my dick medicine. I said great moments, I didn't say good, but it's certainly good to have a present-tense contribution.

Now, Eunice, pleeeze!

I'm a fat purblind ugly fuck with cancer of the dick and maybe I killed somebody.

THE WISDOM OF EUROPE

Born alone, you die alone, and sometimes not-alone you're not-dying.

On the cracked macadam of a hot, winding street at twilight cool as spring water, cool as butterscotch pudding, lies a boy on macadam at twilight, surrounded by neighbors, gardeners, nannies with strollers: park and watch. "I don't want this," he moans, referring, it would seem, to the neck brace, the cast on his foot, the hank of hair missing from his scalp, only now being dressed, or to the largest crowd ever assembled on this street. "Don't anybody touch me," he remonstrates, neither paralyzed nor dying, as attendants prepare to load him into the emergency vehicle — "Get out of my life." Or was that *light*?

Alone, not-alone, alone, not-alone . . . sunset over Los Feliz . . . gather round!

CRISWELL HAD THIS DREAM BEFORE HE DIED

Dear Mrs. Onassis: We the gourmets of America would like to make USE of your pudding and fundament. Would it be too much to ask if we replaced your derrière meat with cheese? Your tush is already the spittin' image of 2 round cheddars from Wisconsin, softer tho 'cause it sure does *move around* under those tight miniskirts presidential widows're so fond of wearing — like liquid marshmallows in individual plastic cheese sleeves. Marshmallows're horrible f'r teeth tho so CHEESE IT IS. Which can easily be AGED IN THE BUTT 'stead of cask or the vat and all that bouncy buttock movement will keep it *ripening right*. BOWEL MOVEMENT however is a whole 'nother story as feces can contaminate prize-winning ched till it's bargain-basement colby or BRICK; care must be taken to insulate it from the colon so it may mellow unbrown to tangy, delectable maturity. Mature cheddar could then be removed a PIECA ASS at a time. Cheese knife is *no good for removal* (n.g. for r.), that real swell outer skin we're sure you have got should only be punctured by cuspids. Take a good chomp: you don't want no puny slices at the WINE & CHEESE BASH OF THE CENTURY!

What goes best with 14-yr-old cheddar is Chassagnet-Montrachet (Fr., white, dry, full flavored), Pouilly-Fumé (Fr., white, semi-dry), Grignolino (Ital., red, dry, medium body), Crackling Rosé (Port., slight sparkle and sweetness), Muscatel (mellow sweet w/ pronounced muscat grape flavor) and/or Steinwein (Ger., white, full body, dry to medium sweet). No domestic swill for this party; crackers available. Sesame rounds're FINE and so is your HIND. Following initial excavation chances are ched chunks will still be lodged in the alcoves of your caboose but 'tain't no problem for us. We'll simply yell "Open Sesame!" — your signal to part them cheeks on the crack-er of the v. same name. For refilling your wide open glute space a rich gorgonzola is recommended, and if th'original ass-skin hasn't been cast in the garbidge by invited guests it may of course be reused again and AGAIN the good Lord willing, i.e., provided you live so long (and we figger you'd surely WANNA so your great-grandchilds c'n feast off your seat and in turn have somethin' great to tell *their* great-grands about).

Should this request for some reason not meet with your approval, please lend an ear to FABULOUS SUGGESTION #2: spades and trowels in the bowels — a plentiful ass-garden just past your sphincter. Nicknamed Chocolate Park, it would supplement your allowance from Ari thru the sale of admissions, not to mention charter memberships, as horticulturists from far & wide flock to your stunning array of assflowers and assweeds. BUTTercup, GerANIum, CrabgrASS, Carnassion, Lily of the (Ass) Valley, Gladiolass, Doodysuckle, Asster, Chrysassthemum, Morning Doody, Poopy, Forget-My-Ass-Not, Cornholeflower, Bungnolia, Brown-Eyed Susan, American Deauty Rose, Rhododungdren . . . and let's not forget corn & limas for an incredible-edible succotassh, possibly even some fartsley . . . a regular botanical doolite! The vegetation will grow big as a beanstalk as it'd be just plain dumb to bring in the mowers what with your hemorrhoids — one false move with the revolving blades and we've got ourselves an ASS HEMORRHAGE that surely would flood the fleurs. FIRST RULE OF GARDENING: Don't overwater.

Sounds swell I know but mayhaps you'd like another pick before you decide. To wit, fantastic PROPOSAL #3, covering your epicurean's dream of a vaginal goosh: the meat use of your privates for a burger break. No one on earth has yet offered a cost-effective solution to the sorrowful dearth of porkburgers and vealburgers 'round the globe. That they oughta be available — commercially — is a foregone conclusion. Ditto for sheepburgers and goatburgers. But it would be *mucho más bueno* if they made 'em outa CUNTPULP. Raw, unground: MAMMAL SUSHI like G-d intended. Or char-broiled, on whole wheat bun. Hot sauce or ketchup. Pickle chips NOT compulsory. You can pickle peppers, you can pickle cukes, you can . . . *pickled puss relish 13¢ x-tra*. Might your goulash be availed of for such purpose, or that of your sister Lee? We await confirmation by return mail. Yours, we who hunger.

IN THE MEZZ

But I still haven't told you 'bout a pencil I neither love nor loathe and either use or peruse that is either mine or someone else's; a ride I'm either taking or giving to a place I'm unsure either I or my driver or passenger is all that committed to going or being; distant cause, recent cause, current condition: reverse sequence and bearing; a relentless finality, end without end.

THE LEGEND OF "NIGHT"

If you're somewhere that's grey you go somewhere that's green. (The green is cardboard.)

Love's future crashing to love's past settling to compost for seduction. La jeune fille française, gone! — jus' like that — parlayed into sticky new soma rubbing mine. Details of Redondo, verbatim. Over happy-hour margaritas Lisa listened. The day at the pier the sun had gone down and we'd watched it, the j.f. and I, melt bit by bit into the Pacific. A sea lion dove, quarter-hours passed, sailboats passed as we followed it down to the last orange dot. Lost in pleasant converse, in retinal accord, we missed its final extinction, an oversight bordering on tragedy — boo hoo — as it could never/would never hap again. Lisa Gant of Home Dynamics, Inc. ("Where sales begin") listened and spread for me — both entrance and exit.

"I prefer women my own age." "Which is . . . ?" "Thirty-four to forty-five" — and we went home and I ate her. A finger in her ass, two in her socket, I played a hunch and reversed it — two and one — and her object signs of excitement rose markedly. She came and I fucked her, frontside. And a little later, backside. An alternation which with slight (and notable) exception would hold up for the couple years I continued seeing her, sometimes as often as every 6-8 weeks, a two-chord sequence so clearly and utterly the norm that every deep juncture, each organ pairing, doubled as a foretaste of its other, a pattern neither of us ever raised serious objection to: front, back, front, back — union after union after union. Occasionally, by mutual consent, a bottleneck (or carrot) would be substituted.

But we never discussed it (after our first meet we weren't very verbal). About the only thing of pressing concern she actually said, except in the throes of an act, was "I didn't like it last time, all we did was fuck." Which struck me as comical, y'know, 'cause by then there were meets where I would just as soon 've *not* fucked: the way of all attrition. My heat for her had ebbed to where, the previous outing, *I* had been no sub for a crisp raw vegetable. It kept wiggling out (when we even got it in), and I hadn't once entered her rectum. So this time I made sure to — early — right after eating her. First lusty load of the night. (While fingering her clit.)

She slept sound that night, rose late, missed a sale, a big sale, and just pulled my cock to her. For tomorrow was another day — or so someone had told her.

I wanna be in your ass
        I wanna be up your ass
                she came to my
house in the
        morning and I
           fucked her in the
                ass or
                    consid-
ered calling
        's a good thing I didn't
              call her
                (my name my
number
     my heart
        my phone
           my cock up you' ass
           & we both need a piss)

    Hi I'm Ryszard, make that Ramon
    and you can't have my current unlisted #
    but you can always have
        my cock

if you peed right now
you would still have
     my cock
if you yellow the sheets
you will still have
     my cock
if you weewee'd the mattress
you'd still have it

(hey and I *hate* mornings I've got the aches and haven't even
    had a drink

    and my heart is a beached
         whale
on Zuma Mazuma Beach
with spears running through it
but my cock still works some-
       times)

MYSTERIES

One remains.

Why is water at foot level so cold to the touch just after I've begun showering? Possible answers: (1) The bulk of what originally was tested from the faucet, i.e., before it heated up, has not yet drained. (2) Temperature of the tub enamel itself is still relatively cold.

Does that exhaust it?

KISS

This was written without a word processor. (Kiss my wild Irish ass.)